EIGHT

HEBREW
SHORT
NOVELS

EIGHT GREAT HEBREW SHORT NOVELS

Edited by

ALAN LELCHUK AND
GERSHON SHAKED

With an Introduction by
ALAN LELCHUK

A MERIDIAN BOOK
NEW AMERICAN LIBRARY
TIMES MIRROR
NEW YORK AND SCARBOROUGH, ONTARIO

SIDEWAYS, by Uri Nisan Gnessin. First published in Hebrew in *ha-Z'man*, 1905. English translation by Hillel Halkin, copyright © 1983 by The Institute for The Translation of Hebrew Literature.

NERVES, by Yosef Chaim Brenner. First published in Hebrew in *Shalekhet*, Revivim, 1910-11. English translation by Hillel Halkin, copyright © 1983 by The Institute for the Translation of Hebrew Literature.

THE VENGEANCE OF THE FATHERS, by Yitzhak Shami. First published in Hebrew by Mitzpe, 1928. English translation by Richard Flantz, copyright © 1983 by The Institute for the Translation of Hebrew Literature.

IN THE PRIME OF HER LIFE, by S. Y. Agnon. First published in Hebrew in *ha-Tekufah*, 1922. Translated from the Hebrew by permission of Shocken Publishing House, Ltd. English translation by Gabriel Levin, copyright © 1983 by The Institute for the Translation of Hebrew Literature.

FACING THE SEA, by David Fogel. First published in Hebrew in *Mitzpe: A Yearbook*, ed. F. Lachover, 1933, and reprinted in *Siman Kriah*, 1974. Reprinted by permission of *Siman Kriah*, English translation by Daniel Silverstone, copyright © 1983 by Daniel Silverstone.

THE HILL OF EVIL COUNSEL, by Amos Oz, copyright © 1976 by Amos Oz and Am Oved Publishers, Ltd. English translation by Nicholas de Lange, copyright © 1978 by Amos Oz. Reprinted by permission of Harcourt Brace Jovanovich, Inc.

MUSICAL MOMENT, by Joshua Knaz. First published in Hebrew in *Siman Kriah*, 1978. English translation by Betsy Rosenberg, copyright © 1983 by The Institute for the Translation of Hebrew Literature.

A POET'S CONTINUING SILENCE, by A. B. Yehoshua. First published in Hebrew in *Kesheth*, 1966. English translation published in THREE DAYS AND A CHILD, Doubleday, 1970, copyright © 1970 by A. B. Yehoshua. English translation by Miriam Arad, copyright © 1970 by The Institute for the Translation of Hebrew Literature.

Library of Congress Cataloging in Publication Data

Main entry under title:

Eight great short Hebrew novels.

Bibliography: p.
Contents: Sideways/by Uri Nisan Gnessin—Nerves/
by Yosef Chaim Brenner—The vengeance of the fathers/
by Yitzhak Shami—[etc.]
1. Hebrew fiction—Translations into English.
2. English fiction—Translations from Hebrew.
I. Lelchuk, Alan. II. Shaked, Gershon.
PJ5059.E8E33 1983 892.4'35'08 82-14496
ISBN 0-452-00605-8

SIGNET, SIGNET CLASSICS, MENTOR, PLUME, MERIDIAN and
NAL BOOKS are published *in the United States* by
The New American Library, Inc., 1633 Broadway, New York, New York 10019,
in Canada by The New American Library of Canada Limited,
81 Mack Avenue, Scarborough, Ontario M1L 1M8

First Printing, April, 1983

1 2 3 4 5 6 7 8 9

PRINTED IN THE UNITED STATES OF AMERICA

In memory of
Philip Rahv
and
Ya'akov Shabtai

Acknowledgments

We gratefully acknowledge the services and the support of The Institute for the Translation of Hebrew Literature, and the many kindnesses of Nilli Cohen.

Our thanks to other friends who aided this project: Yehuda Melzer, Gabriel Levin, Amos Oz, Menahem Brinker, and A. B. Yehoshua.

Contents

Introduction

BY ALAN LELCHUK*

THESE EIGHT SHORT novels were selected primarily for their literary merit, not for their historical place in Hebrew literature, and our emphasis will be on their literary qualities. The assumption, of course, is that they hold up admirably according to the highest standards of world literature. Our aim is to draw attention specifically to these outstanding writers and their distinct contributions in the novella form, without bolstering them, as it were, with that background of politics or sociology which has often been used, if not as apologetics, at least as explanation, for much of Israeli literature. That form of approach, or sentimental *parti pris*, conceived by well-intentioned friends of Israel and Hebrew literature, has, we fear, in the end only done a disservice to the literature. For it has instilled in many readers the suspicion that Hebrew fiction must be read in the context of its literary youth, against the backdrop of the country's especially hard-pressed condition. In other words, that Hebrew literature exists with an asterisk alongside it, signifying that it cannot and should not be considered independent of the fact of Israel's birth just three decades ago. This anthology seeks to correct that false view.

Perhaps another misconception to be dissolved immediately for the general reader is that modern Hebrew literature is a recent phenomenon. Not so. As we can see even from this selection of works, the literature predates the state by at least five decades. Nor was it confined, in place of origin, to that sliver of land alongside the Mediterranean. In fact, most early Hebrew literature was composed in Poland, Russia,

---

* This essay is based on several conversations between Gershon Shaked and myself that we taped in Jerusalem, May, 1981.

Germany, Austria, Czechoslovakia. This geography is significant in literary terms, for it means that many of the artists here—Gnessin, Brenner, Agnon, Fogel—were writing within the vital atmosphere of European literary modernism, and not in provincial isolation. In both theme and style, their works frequently reflect elements of modernism and reveal the dramatic sophistication of these artists.

The strain of sophistication may be viewed in such an unlikely case as that of Uri N. Gnessin (1879–1913), whose background would suggest a particular insularity and literary innocence. Son of a rabbi in the Ukraine and a student at his father's yeshiva, Gnessin spent practically his whole life in the shtetl of Potchep, traveling to Palestine for a few months in 1908 to visit his brother and departing with a distaste for the primitive land and crude society. Yet Gnessin, whose major reputation rests basically on four novellas, was anything but a literary provincial, as *Sideways* indicates. He handled the stream-of-consciousness technique, for example, with easy efficiency at about the same time that Joyce was making it famous. And in several of Gnessin's themes—the lonely fate of the intellectual, the vacuum of belief after the loss of faith in God, the protagonist who sees what must be changed for his happiness but lacks the will to do anything—Gnessin shows himself to be a self-conscious modern. For Gnessin, despite his narrow background, was much more interested in the soul of man than the social reality of the Jews. To be sure, this reclusive figure who forms one point of the triad that was the base for modern Hebrew literature—the other two being Brenner and Agnon—was more of an aesthete and purist than a *cheder* boy. Dead at thirty-three of tuberculosis, Gnessin surely needed more years to develop his brand of neoromanticism, with its muted but clearly felt eroticism and its poignant portrait of the intellectual's ennui and ineffectiveness. Yet his four novellas are achievement enough. In certain ways he is the most unique writer in our collection, a sensitive stylist who hardly ever left White Russia yet whose work was suffused with the most advanced techniques and themes of Continental literature. An unfinished writer, he nevertheless exerted a large influence over later Hebrew writers, notably S. Yizhar, who some fifty years later adopted Gnessin's style in his huge novel of the War of Independence, *The Days of Ziklag* (1958), and still later, by another two decades, Ya'akov Shabtai, in his important novel *Time Continuous* (1979).

Gnessin meanwhile had his own influences. Indeed, when a character says, in the low-keyed, sensitively translated (by Hillel Halkin) *Sideways*, "Why is it so boring around here, it's always so boring? And we're bores too," the reader hears vividly the distant melancholic melodies of a Chekhov play. Or again, when the hero Hagzar is out walking: "The cries of the crows assailed and stunned him, told him with a bitter vengeance that people like him could never take what life offered them, had no business living at all. *Ka-a, ka-a, ka-a.*" Now we are in the midst of one of Chekhov's later masterpieces in the novella. Yet certainly *Sideways* affords its own charm and power, in its careful delineation of the three Baer sisters, the fine cadences and perceptions filling the deliberate style, the social reality of Jewish village life. Of course the story rises or falls with the protagonist, and here Gnessin is entirely successful. Nahum Hagzar is a moving portrait of the stymied scholar and critic, a self-defeating creature of morbidity and asceticism, whose closest literary brother may be George Gissing's Edwin Reardon of *New Grub Street*. Hagzar convinces, in all his rueful ruminations and frustrated dreams, and if there is a Chekhov specter hovering about him, a character—and writer—could have a worse ghost.

More obviously modern, in theme anyway, was the work of Gnessin's dear friend and dear enemy, the renowned Yosef Chaim Brenner (1878–1921), a semilegendary figure of paradox and unpredictability. Brenner had met Gnessin in his father's yeshiva, and the pair quickly became best friends. Yet later, after Gnessin's death, Brenner wrote a nasty criticism of his friend and his work, describing their love-hate relationship. In temperament, work, outlook, Brenner was the opposite of his friend. Author, critic, editor, Brenner was also an agricultural laborer, an aggressive journalist, leader of a workers' movement. A follower of A. D. Gordon, the Tolstoyan Zionist who inspired the kibbutz movement, Brenner was as much activist as intellectual, doer as thinker, lover of the land as of the written word. He was, too, a severe pessimist with a great zest for life. Unlike Gnessin, Brenner, after a stint in the Czarist army, left the Ukraine never to return, arriving in London for three years in 1905. There he worked as a printer's compositor while publishing the monthly Hebrew journal *Ha-Meorer*, which attacked the hollow rhetoric of the political Zionism of that time. In 1908 he traveled to Galicia, in Poland, where he edited the periodical *Revivim*, and a year later came to Eretz Yisrael to settle for good, working as a laborer and journalist and teaching for a while at the Herzilya Gymnasia. In 1919 he began to edit *Ha-Adama*, the most influential Hebrew literary journal of its time. In November 1921, warned of immediate danger from rioting Arabs, he refused to leave Jaffa, and was murdered. Another abortive ending for a talented life.

Brenner was a passionate Zionist, believing that Palestine was the only place for a Jew to live—"If not here, where?"—but he was also, as *Nerves* shows almost painfully, a fierce critic of Zionism and Jews. A paradox, a quintessence. Not for Brenner the easy posturing of patriotism, nor the cushion of religious orthodoxy. In a word, he was no comfort then or now, to the professional, religious, or sentimental Jew. Angry, neurotic, scathingly honest and intellectual—he was all of these in the extreme. A thorn to his people, a benefactor for literature: more than a bit like another tortured literary soul. Indeed Dostoievski was an acknowledged mentor of Brenner, who translated *Crime and Punishment* into Hebrew and wrote his own flawed Dostoievskian novel about an intellectual's suffering *(Breakdown and Bereavement)*. But unlike Dostoievski, Brenner found life a hell on earth without the prospect of final redemption; for he was a skeptic whose pessimism bordered on downright nihilism. In his work it is this relentless, lacerating vision, embodied in his wounded protagonists, which energizes the fiction and imbues it with an unmistakable, powerful voice.

In *Nerves* we see many of the Brenner elements fused in the ironic monologue of the European immigrant taking his adopted family to the new land of Palestine, knowing beforehand that the journey is one of futility and ultimate despair. In his bitter, caustic remarks about the Jewish people and their destination, the antiheroic protagonist displays an antisentimentalism that is harshly effective. In his virulent report, the enemy is the sacred and the pious, from landscape and Beauty to Jews and spiritual redemption. Nothing is sacred, in short, and everything and everyone are subject to criticism. There is an underlying anger in Brenner, probably dating back to his profound hatred of his father; and it is neither diluted nor sublimated in his adulthood. This anger is itself a drama, one in which intelligence acts perversely and will nastily; in this Brenner is a forerunner of the great French master Céline. From Dostoievski to Brenner to Céline, there runs a continuous line of authorial spite. And if there is no escape for the reader from that scathing drama and vision, there is at least the authentic power of the negative erupting. Not comfort for the reader, or for himself, but truth and turmoil of some sort, are Brenner's credo, and accomplishment.

Of all the writers in our collection, Yitzhak Shami (1888–1949) is probably the least known and read today. An obscure writer all his life, Shami was a Sephardic Jew from Hebron who taught high school in Palestine, Damascus, and Bulgaria before finally settling to teach in Haifa. His published work is slender, a collection of nine stories and two novellas, written primarily in the 1920s, but they are singular in depicting Jewish-Arab and Arab life. No other Jewish writer understood so well or described so authentically the Arab mind and way as Shami, himself from a Syrian family and as fluent in Arabic and Arab customs as he was in Hebrew and Jewish customs. Not a modernist in any sense, Shami is more old-fashioned, more nineteenth-century, depending on plot and character, atmosphere and incident, for his art. But a genuine art it is. Perhaps no other tale here is quite so riveting, once the story gets going, as that of the local Arab chieftain who falls from honor because of an early misdeed in a game and becomes an outcast and dervish, falling through drugs into hallucinations and his inevitable end. Clearly we are in the hands of a master storyteller, and not a note rings false in this harrowing depiction of the Arab code of honor and prestige, a code as precise and exacting in its rules and consequences as any Jamesian code of manners and morals.

As an artist Shami is an authentic primitive, like Rousseau in painting; he is a writer dramatizing the exotic and apparently naive by means of close observation of native textures, relying more on external deed than on psychological intrusion to reveal state of mind. *The Vengeance of the Fathers* is a *tour de force* of the literary imagination, in the mode of Faulkner in *Red Leaves* or Tolstoy in *Hadji Murad*. These three tales—of an Arab leader, an American Indian, a Tartar chieftain—are triumphs of authorial control in describing the primitive character and temperament without imposing a Western system of values, and in recreating a foreign world without condescending to it or romanticizing it. But more than Faulkner or Tolstoy, probably, Shami knew his material from the inside, having been surrounded all his life by Arabs—more at home with the pipes of hashish, which he was supposed to have imbibed regularly, than with Western intellectual salons or Zionist debates. *The Vengeance of the Fathers* is a small classical masterpiece, dealing with the traditional rise and fall of the tragic hero. It is a novella unique in Hebrew literature, executed with striking narrative pace and governed by solid knowledge. Reading it, one is immediately dispatched to a distant theater of exotic games and dress, actions and dialogue, that are sensuously detailed and alive. If the first fifty pages of this epic tale read slowly, filled as they are with the necessary background of local customs and values, the reader should bear with it, for the fruits are worth the wait. Once the plot begins, the story is borne forward with skillful sweep and careening inevitability. By the time Shami is finished, the reader has encountered a strange world gradually made familiar; and just as gradually, the particular has become the general, the local universal, the momentary memorable—the surest signs of art.

Requiring more patience, and more careful scrutiny, is *In the Prime of Her Life*, written by the dean of Hebrew letters, S. Y. Agnon (1888–1970). Winner of the Nobel Prize for literature in 1966, Agnon wrote for more than half a century, beginning in 1908. His work is the most difficult to render into English, largely because of the massive ironies and biblical associations of the original Hebrew, and is at least as much a challenge to the translator as to the reader. This first translation into English by Gabriel Levin, himself a poet and the son of the late novelist Meyer Levin, seems to us to be itself a literary triumph. Certainly the reader will do well to read this novella more than once before pronouncing judgment, especially since a first reading will be devoted to unraveling the plot and the shifting point of view, difficulties of the surface not unlike those encountered in the texts of James or Joyce. Though Edmund Wilson, when he learned Hebrew, came to appreciate Agnon, he unfortunately admired the wrong Agnon, praising the folksy and religious writer rather than the ironic, sophisticated artist. Calling Agnon folksy is akin to labeling Picasso a naif and letting it go at that, mistaking the one part for the complex whole. In his endless stream of stories and novels, Agnon tricked and seduced, appearing to do one thing when in fact he was doing something quite different. Like Nabokov, he had a fondness for teasing critics and tweaking pedants, leading them on a wild-goose chase with a playful and mischievous will. Wearing a yarmulke and citing the Torah, he presented himself as a man of religious orthodoxy; his work, however, offers a much broader perspective, brimming with worldly knowledge and rich secular appetite. In truth Agnon was a cunning actor, assuming this persona or that mask, all the time fully conscious of his audience, his stage, his designs and effects.

In the Prime of Her Life, composed in 1921, is narrated mainly by the young daughter who, upon the death of her mother, proceeds to fulfill her mother's deepest wish—namely, to devote herself to her first lover, whom she never married but about whom she remained passionate. Thus begins a deeply ironic tale, the daughter reliving her mother's life and kindling passion in both herself and the former lover (who should have been her father), at the same time that her actual father, still on the scene, looks on. The music of Agnon flows slowly, with statement and repetition of theme, and then counterpoint, something like a fugue, with the ironies and multiple meanings emerging more and more upon each reading. Stylistically, too, there is a deliberate irony in the contrast between the refined cool style of the narrator and the highly charged emotions of the drama, a tension balanced beautifully by Agnon. In the delicacy of the relationships and the nuances of sensibility, we are in the subtle world of Proust; in the verbal music of the prose, with its controlled lyrical breaks, the atmosphere is Joycean. Admittedly, however, for the reader to experience Agnon in this rarefied air, he has to work hard. And even then, we miss in English the rich associations with biblical cadences and references, available in the Hebrew only. Perhaps more than any other major novelist, Agnon loses significantly in translation, a painful and ironic fate for Hebrew's greatest writer.

A final word about this master. Like any major creator of the imaginary, Agnon always knew what was real for him, those sources which nurtured his talent. These included the home of his childhood and youth, the Polish region of Galicia, and the home of his adulthood, Jerusalem and Eretz Yisrael, where he came to settle in 1909, at the age of twenty-one. Until his death in 1970, he remained in Israel, with the exception of one long break, 1913–1924, when he returned to Europe. Another source was the whole of Jewish tradition—the Bible, the Talmud, Hasidic literature, a treasury of materials which was at his fingertips in the way that the Bible and classical literature were available to Milton. Finally there were the Jews themselves and their nightmarish history, especially in this century. In great part Agnon's subject was nothing less than the end of the Jews and Jewish life in Europe, and it may be said that his work is the most moving history we have of a time and a people. He foresaw with remarkable prescience the enormous tragedy in his best novel, *A Guest for a Night*, one of the great novels of twentieth-century literature. All the more ironic then that that novel remains largely unread in its pale English translation, and, like the body of Agnon's work, remains unknown to most Western readers.

The work of David Fogel (1891–1944) presents a sharp contrast to that of the previous writers and is a clear bridge to contemporary literature. Fogel lived only a brief time in Palestine, 1909, before returning to Europe, his beloved continent which tortured him all his life. A Russian exile with an un-Jewish temperament, Fogel nonetheless had a painfully Jewish life; he was incarcerated first as an enemy national by the Austrians after World War I, was next held by the French in a detention camp for the same reason during World War II, and finally disappeared for good in a Nazi concentration camp in 1944. All this time he sought to escape his Jewishness, and even as he wrote in Hebrew, he paradoxically wanted to live as a cosmopolitan in Vienna and Paris. Known mainly for his excellent poetry, Fogel wrote three pieces of prose, two novellas (the other being *In the Sanatorium*), and a long novel, *Married Life*. It is especially unfortunate that the novel remains untranslated into English, for its story of a pathological love affair between a small Jewish intellectual and a sadistic German baroness, set in Vienna between the wars, is of serious psychological and literary interest. Married, sick with tuberculosis, Fogel lived a fractured life, keeping a diary in Yiddish, writing literature in Hebrew, speaking French, German, Italian, and Russian. His was a secret, painful, bizarre life.

Facing the Sea is the first prose work available to the English reader, and the occasional awkwardness of the translation arises from the awkwardness of the original Hebrew, a kind of Germanized Hebrew with many archaisms almost unknown to the reader of modern Hebrew. Despite the occasional linguistic difficulty, however, *Facing the Sea* will undoubtedly surprise today's reader, for its world of rich sensuosity is a very modern one indeed. It is also a strongly felt and masterfully executed piece of work. Fogel's world is sensual rather than narrowly sexual, embracing objects of nature as well as people, suggesting inward feeling by strokes of landscape. Staged in a seaside resort on the Riviera, *Facing the Sea* is about a group of Europeans between the wars who come together for a holiday of bodies and depart a flock of fatigued, disappointed souls. It is a kind of Lost Generation fable, expressed exquisitely through the sensibility of a poet. In fact it should be read more as an impressionist poem—stirring the senses and bypassing logic for feeling —than as conventional tale using plot beginning, middle, and end, with exposition and flashback to fill the reader in. The movement is poetical, proceeding by means of associations and imagery, an apparent random field flung down that, slowly, accumulates and attracts with stunning force. The quality of the sensuality is also appealing, for it is a flower blooming for its own sake, and not, as in many an American garden, for some ulterior puritanical purpose. The sensuality and poetry are part of a complicated moral vision, a vision conveyed without self-righteousness or tendentious motive, a vision beyond that imagined by the moralists or hedonists. *Facing the Sea* belongs best perhaps with the early films of Fellini or Antonioni, where spiritual exhaustion and decadence hover about all physical pleasure, where beauty and sadness are indissolubly linked.

Of the three living writers in our collection, Amos Oz needs the least introduction to an Anglo-American audience. A member of a kibbutz since his early teens, an articulate representative of the first Sabra, or native-born Israeli generation, Oz was the first contemporary Israeli writer to earn an international reputation through his stories and novels, a reputation enlarged by public lectures abroad and outspoken dovish politics at home. In his homeland, too, he enjoyed great early success, and for good reason: his works are rooted in the rich life of the young state and frequently deal with and reveal a piece of that hot, convulsive history. His most famous work is probably the novel *My Michael*, yet in our estimation, Oz has accomplished his best work in the stricter form of the novella. In *Unto Death*, for example, he shows a fertile historical imagination in the spare moral allegory of a band of medieval Crusaders pillaging their way across twelfth-century Palestine. And in *Late Love*, he has created a first-rate parable of Jewish paranoia after the Holocaust. Intensity being one of Oz's fortes, the novella seems the fitting form for governing his energy and dramatizing his intelligent themes.

The choice here, *The Hill of Evil Counsel*, published in 1976, displays Oz's fondness of history, here realistically conveyed. Set in the British Mandate years of the 1940s, the story allows the author to recall his own childhood in Jerusalem and weave autobiography with fiction. This background is sketched with fidelity and skill, evoking the tense atmosphere of British occupation and Jewish underground activity. Oz's selection of the young Hillel as the protagonist for surveying the material of the story is shrewd, for it permits the background of external intrigue—the underground working against the British—to be set off with considerable irony against the boy's personal struggle, a conflict of feelings torn between his romantic Polish mother and his rational German father. Oz shows a superior talent in manipulating the public intrigues and private defeats without losing either proportion or emotion. All told, the work shows a sense of underlying structure which is organic, arising from the story and not imposed from without. History is experienced here as a living force pressing on human lives, charging the family tale with an extra dimension of meaning.

Yehoshua Knaz, the least known of our living writers, is also in mid-career. Born in 1937, Knaz is a quiet figure, living modestly in Tel Aviv, an editor of *Ha'Aretz* (the *New York Times* of Israel) and a translator of French classics into Hebrew. The author of two novels, he has also published a collection of novellas, the title story being our *Musical Moment* (1980). Here, too, the choice of a young boy for narrator is crucial to the story's success, and Knaz handles this oftworn voice with tonal delicacy and mature understanding. The boy plays a dual role, that of hero and witness: a critic of the bourgeois society surrounding him, and an actor in his own drama of self-development. Knaz avoids the familiar trap of sentimentality inherent in such stories about little boys with their violins and dominating mothers; at every turn in the story, he takes a deliberately antisentimental road. Two points stand out. One occurs when he reads an article on the violin, but not the sort one might expect in such a story:

> I suppose one ought to consider the excellence of such famous instruments as the Ira Stradivarius played by virtuosi . . . but as for the cheap variety in the hands of pupils—a harmonica would be preferable! In the latter case of violin we have to bear with a mournful scream, a sniveling plea for mercy that is enough to induce a severe case of melancholia.
>
> Yes, melancholia. The nightmare of the Jewish Ghetto screams out of these fiddles. The Diaspora Jew practically venerated the violin. It was his sine qua non, Yidel mit'n fidel. In every Jewish household, the beloved son, whether he was gifted musically or a complete imbecile, had to "saw away" on his violin, for the pleasure of his mother, who found her greatest fulfillment in the violin. Come what may, the violin prevailed. Trials and tribulations, every kind of care and woe, debts, installments, bill collectors—and the violin!

This is enough to convince the boy of the rightness of his own feelings, and he decides, with derisive pleasure, to repay the violin and his mother for all the trouble they have caused him. Indeed, it is the mother who becomes the archenemy of her son, and who provokes in him the will to leap from boyhood to manhood. For beneath the surface of the story line there is the deeper inner story of this rite of passage, this wrenching of innocence. In looking at objects of Jewish sentiment with a detached eye of critical realism, Knaz aligns himself with another cool surveyor of Jewish family life, Isaac Babel. Like Babel, Knaz catalogues and excoriates the little bourgeois world of the hero's European family with pitiless honesty, even as he approaches the inevitable wounds of the young man with painful preciseness. In part because he sacrifices neither judgment nor sympathy, Knaz achieves a purity of tone and depth of feeling that affect the reader with Babel-like resonance. Much like Schubert's sonata "Musical Moment," the violin piece which haunts the hero, so the story itself becomes a musical moment, staying and expanding in the reader's mind long after the last page has been read.

A. B. Yehoshua was born in 1936 in Jerusalem, where he grew up and was educated, and after serving in the army, he lived for four years in Paris before returning to an academic career in Haifa. In that serene city overlooking the sea, he has taught literature at the university for more than fifteen years. But Yehoshua's stories and short novels are anything but serene or academic in theme, style, or effect. His vision and his methods, in novellas such as *Three Days and a Child*, *Facing the Forest*, *Flood Tide*, *Early in the Summer of 1970*, *A Long Hot Day*, *His Despair*, *His Wife and His Daughter*, and *A Poet's Continuing Silence*, are wholly original. Both by themselves and taken together, they constitute a serious achievement, perhaps the outstanding achievement in the genre of the novella of any writer today. Though Yehoshua has recently switched to novels, just completing his second, it seems so far that the shorter form suits this author's talent perfectly, as evidenced by his string of powerful successes.

Composed in 1964, *A Poet's Continuing Silence* is not merely an excellent example of his splendid talent in this difficult form, but it is also, as Saul Bellow has noted, one of the best literary tales of the last twenty-five years. Like the arresting novella *Teach Us to Outgrow Our Madness* by the Japanese writer Oé, *A Poet's Continuing Silence* deals with a father-son relationship where the troubled son forces a profound disturbance and challenge upon the father, in this case an aging poet who has grown arid and silent in recent years. This challenge jolts the father's conventional feelings and reasonable expectations. But like Oé, Yehoshua is after more than the challenge to his characters; he is also probing and provoking the reader, and *his* conventions and expectations. For in the last analysis, it is up to the reader to raise himself to the puzzling meanings of the tale, to figure out and fill in and create for himself the emotions with which to break through into this harrowing, inexplicable world.

Yehoshua arranges his world, moreover, by means of a style fitting his material—that is, by systematically avoiding traditional forms of realism or antirealism. By careful fits and starts, by pauses in paragraphs and incompletions of thought, by emphasized silences and long distances between intention and deed, the story lurches forward, sideways, backward. From meaning to incoherence to surprise feeling. In tone and angle, sentences and gestures, the difficult, unique atmosphere is assembled, established, like Pollack dripping blobs of paint here and there to force the viewer to see anew. The arresting style is a kind of anti-stream-of-consciousness, where psychology is evidenced through situation and gesture, not contemplation. Like Beckett in his plays, Yehoshua is a master of gesture and tone, a creator of an atmosphere conveying old age, dying, fatigue, hopelessness, despair, with startling authenticity. To our mind no other living prose writer has drawn the anatomy of despair and solitude as effectively as this accomplished Israeli.

Never once during this radical performance is there a break in credibility, so controlled is the tempo and tone of the tale. This is all the more a feat if we consider the challenge to the writer himself—to resist precedent and welcome uncertainty. To be against certainty and predictability seems, in fact, a positive credo here; against certainties of plot or character, and predictabilities of meaning and feeling, the accepted comforts of the reader. And yet for all of this authorial resistance to convention, *A Poet's Continuing Silence* concerns this familiar relationship of father and son and elicits from it new feeling and powerful emotion—more than one would think possible from so unconventional a telling. In pursuing his original way of voicing our contemporary situation, Yehoshua is not, like so many today, a literary con man or pop artist using clever techniques or ingenious gimmicks for essentially uninteresting purposes. He is not aiming to dazzle us with gymnastics of style or ego, or tease us with secrets that do not ultimately exist. A mature artist trying to break through to deeper circles of feeling, to meanings beyond the cerebral or stale, to a style that approximates his enigmatic, moving vision, Yehoshua is the genuine article, a writer in full control of his marvelous gift.

These eight short novels, in sum, add up to an achievement high enough, as we have suggested earlier, to place the Hebrew novella on a par with the novella of other literatures. It is rather surprising, if not astonishing, to note that the level of imaginative Hebrew prose is already so high, given that Hebrew as a resurrected language is less than a century old. This achievement is perhaps all the more impressive if we consider the relatively modest number of great short novels existing in other, older literatures, such as French, German, Italian, English, and American. Especially so, since the literary art of storytelling, with one obvious, colossal exception, has not been a strength of Jewish culture through the ages (unlike Hebrew poetry, which has its noble history). That exception, of course, is the Bible, the source of many great stories and varied literary styles, which serves as the permanent portable library of the Jews, in all their wanderings and exiles. Thus the present accomplishment is, in a way, further testimony to T. S. Eliot's thesis about the powers of tradition—in this case, ancient culture and modern European letters—that are necessary for nurturing the individual talent.

Bibliographic Note

A LL ANTHOLOGIES MUST, of selective necessity, exclude works of accomplishment, and this volume is no exception. The editors wish to make a point of naming some of those works, absent here, worthy of the reader's attention. S. Yizhar was born in 1916, in Rehovot, Israel, and is the foremost writer of the Palmah period, before and after the War of Independence in 1948. A Faulknerian romantic with an obsessive attachment to his native wild landscape, and to his own convoluted rhetoric, Yizhar has written, besides his outstanding long novel *Days of Ziklag*, many strong stories and at least one beautiful long novella, *Midnight Convoy* (1950), about a small platoon of young soldiers trying to make a road at night for a convoy of trucks, during the 1948 war. For many, *Midnight Convoy* will be too slow, too concerned with minute details of the land, too excessive in its depiction of the romantic young protagonists. For others, *Midnight Convoy* is pure literary pleasure.

Aharon Appelfeld has recently enjoyed an American success. A child of the Holocaust who arrived in Israel in 1945 as an orphan, he has produced a host of novels and stories dealing exclusively with the Holocaust. His powerful short novel, *Badenheim 1939*, is a horror fable set in a tiny European resort on the eve of the destruction of its Jewish inhabitants. A newer writer is Yitzhak Ben-Ner, the author of several collections of stories, many first published in the newspapers. His best work remains an early novella, *Rustic Sunset*, which forcefully chronicles the disillusionments and guilty lusts of a brawny young hero in today's Israel. But for the limitation of space, we would also include works by two other distinguished writers, David Shahar and Amelia Kahana-Carmon.

Finally, we must mention Ya'akov Shabtai. When he died suddenly of a heart attack at age forty-six, in 1981, Hebrew literature lost perhaps its finest novelist. A playwright and storywriter, Shabtai turned to long prose works relatively late in his life, and produced, in the 1970s, a novel of enormous sophistication and power, *Time Continuous*. When he was stricken, he was two-thirds through a second novel. Unfortunately, this superb writer had written no novella to include here, but our respect and affection are made clear by our dedication of this volume to his memory.

(CANAAN, N.H./JERUSALEM, 1981–1982)

SIDEWAYS

BY URI NISAN GNESSIN

translated by Hillel Halkin

I

THE FIRST TIME that Nahum Hagzar set foot in that pleasant house at the far end of the quiet street was due to some trivial reason that was forgotten by him no sooner than it had occurred. Much to his surprise, he met there his stout neighbor, young Hanna Heler, with her unnaturally loud staccato laugh, and conversed with her for the first time, too. Yet he didn't stay long on that occasion, for he was dreaming of other things; feverishly, his coattails flapping behind him, he hurried home to await the new job and the challenging life that would begin the next day, here in this provincial town to which he had chosen to move from Vilna.

The next morning, however, turned out to be leaden and dull. The walls were cheerless, the ceiling was low, and the windowpanes were streaked as though with sweat. He sat chin in hand for a long while, biting his lips; then suddenly he roused himself, found some excuse to call on his neighbor, and went together with her to that house at the end of the street. Inside were new faces. Sitting back a bit from the round table was a lively young man in a semi-Oriental position, his two arms hugging his outthrust knee while he rocked back and forth and made everyone laugh at his jokes. This time Hagzar stayed longer. Indeed, as he passed through the entrance hall on his way out, a new peal of laughter from the room he had left so intrigued him that, after briefly regarding the gray windows, he turned around and rejoined the company inside.

His third visit to the house was prompted by the same young man. One morning the latter dropped in on him for a while, and after a friendly chat suggested that they pay a call on Rosa. By then Hagzar knew that his new friend was the only son of one of the town's leading citizens; donning his coat while thinking of Rosa's pretty face and her pale, pure smile in the misty glow of the shade-spreading lamp, he reflected, not for the first time, what strangers all these people still were to him.

Subsequently he stopped by several more times. He often saw Ida, the pale lycée student, and her older sister Manya, who planned to resume her studies soon as well and was forever wandering in and out and looking for something while humming jerkily under her breath. Rosa was rarely there, except when once or twice he found her laughing prettily and with infectious gaiety at the jokes of the lively young man.

The mother of these three sisters had passed away early in the spring of that year, and their father, Simha Baer, was away on an extended business trip in the Ukraine. At the time Hagzar's large wicker trunk, which was filled with books and manuscripts, still stood unopened by the door, exactly as it had arrived from Vilna two weeks before, for he had not yet finished arranging his room. He had come to the provinces hoping to find the leisure to carry out his many literary projects, and afterwards to travel in Europe, as had always been his dream.

Before long the trunk was opened and he had set to work. He had four pupils to tutor every morning, the hours of which were divided among their houses; afternoons were free for his own pursuits. That summer a Hebrew journal published a long article of his on Hebrew literature, replete with copious citations. Much of the summer was taken up with founding a local literary society, a long-standing ambition of his; in addition, he was hard at work on a second article, upon completion of which he expected to be paid for both contributions together. In fact, he was already making plans for studying abroad the following year; yet after some brief financial negotiations with the editors of the journal, he was forced to admit that he had made a slight but regrettable miscalculation—and so he turned his attentions instead to the composition of an outline for a major series of essays on the modern Hebrew novel, which boded no end of work.

Afterwards, when autumn came and—buttoned up in his bulky overcoat and wearing his high boots—he had to knead with his feet several times each day the thick batter of mud into which the town square was transformed, he occasionally passed Rosa in the street, acknowledging her when he did with a brief nod of his head. Once, however, when they chanced to be going in the same direction, he learned from her that they had a mutual . . . well, not exactly a friend, but an acquaintance: Gavriel Carmel, who had himself been a teacher in the same town several years before. In those days Rosa had been staying with an aunt in the country and had come home only infrequently, so that she and Carmel did not meet more than a few times. Hagzar, for his part, told her that his friend had been abroad for at least two years now, and that he himself had lost all track of him, having last seen him in Vilna before his departure.

On the same occasion he was also informed that Ida had been his friend's pupil. And so that evening found him sitting at the round table in the pleasant room, where he had not been for many days, while Rosa stood beside him, one hand on the back of his chair and the other on the red tablecloth. By the misty glow of the shade-spreading lamp the two of them studied the brave, youthfully chaste face that looked up at them from a page of the handsome album. Hagzar's own face, which had worn a slight smile before Rosa opened the album, was now an image of excitement concentrated on the two large, innocently self-assured eyes that stared back at him from the picture. How distant this face seemed to him—yet how it drained the blood from his own. The trace of laughing mockery upon it, which seemed reminiscent of something and cut to the heart's quick—that subtle trace that kept reappearing and vanishing into the mystery of those unsullied lips, reappearing with triumphant insolence and vanishing, as though tauntingly, with the cunning of a cat—that laughter haunted him, like the forgotten end of a dream.

Later, while calculating that the photograph must be at least eight years old, he listened to Rosa chatter on about Carmel: how fond he had been of her little sister Ida, whom he had helped prepare for the lycée; how unrecognizable he was in the picture; and how her middle sister Manya, who was two years older than Ida, always used to hide from him, ha ha . . . There followed a melancholy silence in which the oil lamp burned and the samovar boiled on its yellow stand and was poured bubbling out into glasses, while Hagzar sat quietly staring at the other lamp, the one reflected in the dark glitter of the window by the night outside. By ten o'clock his boots were sinking one by one into the mud of the strange, dark street, his body bent slightly forward as he thought of the warm room and its misty, penumbral glow, of his distant friend Carmel, of Rosa with her kind, intelligent eyes, and of life as a scroll that was pleasantly being unrolled. For a moment too he recalled the weak, suffering groan that had reached him as he stood in the dark hallway at twilight—that groan that had seemed, as it were, to solve some problem in arithmetic—and the vexed, secretive whisper that had followed it. He thought of plump, dark-eyed Manya, and of Ida, weak and pale; and upon arriving home he went straight to work, humming a mischievous tune.

After that he began coming often, as a rule in the evenings when Rosa was alone in the room. Jumping up from her dimly lit corner to greet him, she would silently hold out her small, kind hand to him and heighten the penumbra of the lamp. The corners of the room became dimmer, the tall flowers grew indistinct, and the windowpanes gleamed blackly through the parted curtains. Their harmless chatter flowed quietly between them, although by the time he had to leave, the sound of his laughter might often be ringing out loud.

The lively young man was seldom seen anymore. Once or twice he dropped by with an older sister; they sat, joked for a while, and departed. Hagzar no longer felt that these jests were malicious. On the contrary: the young man was careful to hurt no one's feelings and was certainly no worse than most youths his age. If one compared him to Rosa, who took part in these contests of wit, Hagzar pleasurably observed, with an almost feverish passion, she was far the more venomous of the two: her barbs were so nimble and never failed to strike home. Yet such evenings left him ill-at-ease, and having walked the guests to the door he gladly forgot them at once.

As soon as they were gone Rosa would begin to talk volubly about herself, Manya, Ida, her father, or whatever else was on her mind. Her speech had a feverish intensity, which she broke now and then with a softly enigmatic laugh while regarding him with confident affection. Hagzar rose at such times to his feet, tucked his hands behind his back beneath the skirts of his frock coat, and paced step by step across the soft carpet, absentmindedly enjoying each squeak of his shoes as they sank into the pliant fabric. When Rosa had finished, it was his turn to confide his thoughts to her, and so they chatted and laughed, or perhaps even sang quietly to themselves or went out for an evening stroll.

Occasionally they were joined in the room by plump, virtuous Manya, whose small, dark eyes had a look in them of mocking suspicion. Placing her open book before her on the table and slipping her hands beneath her black smock, she sat wordlessly on the edge of the couch as if proudly waiting for something. The conversation ignored her, except that now Hagzar fingered the ends of his lead-colored mustache and wrinkled his high forehead repeatedly. The first few times that this happened Manya soon rose again and returned to her room with a bitter air of injured pride, while Hagzar continued to pace back and forth and hum snatches of old melodies to himself, unconsciously biting his bottom lip. Gradually, however, Manya's visits grew longer; as though out of spite she sat silently facing him, while he slowly took on the look of a man struggling with a toothache. He was aware by then that neither Ida nor Manya had been in good nervous health since their mother's death; yet whereas Ida had taken a leave of absence from the lycée on doctor's orders, Manya had insisted on continuing her preparations for acceptance to the school's fifth form, which had already ended unproductively several times in the past. More than once Hagzar tried talking in her presence of the unhealthy effects of too much study, which could waste the best years of one's life and "nip in the bud" the "springtime of one's youth." At first glancing obliquely up at him with half-lifted eyes, then slowly revolving toward him her full, spiteful face, whose look neatly dissected him in two, Manya casually jiggled one leg on its toes and coughed deliberately to announce that none of this concerned her in the least. As soon as Hagzar paused for breath she rose and returned to her room, while the conversation went on as before.

That winter Hagzar's literary work proceeded slowly. There were several reasons for this. The outline that he had begun for the series of essays was interrupted in the middle by a long, critical article that he had decided to write on a novel that had recently appeared, in which he hoped to focus on certain issues that, although the best of Jewish youth was concerned with them, Hebrew literature had unaccountably overlooked. Yet the literary society that he had started, which had fallen on difficult times, and a fifth pupil whom he was forced to take on, consumed nearly all his free time, so that he could only jot down some preliminary notes regarding the article's content. In addition he was busy making entries in his journal, which he hoped one day to transform into a new set of essays that he was already at work on.

That spring the brother of the three sisters, a bookkeeper for a trading firm in the south, came home for several weeks of vacation. More than ever Hagzar was a visitor in the house, which now had a different ambiance. Manya, though still as spiteful as ever, began appearing more often and at times even joined the conversation, addressing her remarks at first exclusively to her brother, and then, little by little, to the rest of the company as well. Soon Ida, an open book in one hand and a white pillow in the other, began to join them too, half-sitting and half-reclining on the couch. Friends of both sexes dropped by to talk, joke, drink tea, and toss nutshells at each other. Each time they had left, Rosa, her fastidious features and gestures prettily graced by fatigue, would complain of what bores they had all become and of how she had nothing to say to them anymore. What a wit her brother Shmuel could be, though! He had been the evening's saving grace.

Shmuel, a dandyish young man of about twenty-five with a sallow, bloodless face that could have enabled him to pass for sixteen, would regard the pince-nez that his thin, petite hands were wiping with a snowy-white handkerchief, and exclaim with open disdain:

"Small-town intellectuals!"

And Manya would look at him, curling her lips with forceful assurance, and repeat:

"Small-town!"

After which Shmuel would replace his glasses on his nose, tilt his head slightly backward, and recall with a gleeful guffaw how he had "really put" that "dumb blond" or that "fat tub" in "her place." Had anyone noticed how she had turned up that trumpet that served as her nose? Then Rosa would make a crack of her own, Manya would cast all caution to the winds, and Shmuel would interrupt them again with more of his recollected repartee. And so, in giggles, gossip, jesting, and song the time went by.

Within a few weeks the season arrived for merry walks in the marvelous woods, gay boat rides on the river, poetic campfires beneath dark, satiny skies, boisterous breachings of the silence of the before-dawn-and-after-midnight sleeping streets. Now they were joined by a newcomer, another former acquaintance of Hagzar's, who had come to look for pupils in the provinces too, although only for a few months. This was a devil of a fellow with pointy brown eyes, black Gogolesque hair, and a repertoire of comically rendered folk songs, itinerant synagogue sermons, monologues of peasants called to testify in court, and soliloquies of drunkards cadging drinks from Jewish innkeepers that reduced them to helpless laughter in the end. That summer was an unforgettable time for all of them, the memory of which lingered on for many a long month after.

And so when one day long, slender cobwebs spiraled down through the air and yellow leaves dropped from the trees and littered the paths in the parks, Hagzar trampled on them with a joyous burst of savage energy unleashed. He stood straighter now, his chest more expanded and his face more alert. In another week or two the skies would cloud over; the wind would howl; windowpanes and tin roofs would rattle once more in the gloom: hurrah! His mood would be defiant then; his mind free of fetters; his heart brimful; his work crowded with satisfying new discoveries . . . Yes, a week or two would bring black nights pierced by a few quivering streetlights, torrents of rain, mud up to the ankles . . . but that dear, pleasant house would be warm and well lit. Beneath its spread of red velvet the couch would be spacious and soft; the lively eyes of the three pretty sisters would glow with a tender light; Rosa's pleasing chatter would flow self-indulgently on; Manya's deliberately spiteful outbursts would interrupt him as usual, break off in the middle as they always did, and resume again; and pale little Ida—Ida with her wondering look and her soft, lovely braid, who stubbornly refused to sit in his lap or rest her dear head against him until he grabbed her by her soft, warm underarms, which were no longer the arms of a child, and placed her there forcefully—would docilely cling to his chest like a newborn lamb, her dear, rich, smooth hair his to play with as he pleased.

One autumn day Hagzar went to the public library and borrowed an absorbing new book which he took that same night to the pleasant house and read aloud there in a single sitting. When he went the next day to return it, Rosa accompanied him in the hope of finding "something else just as nice" which they might read the following night. The sky was covered with clouds. The wind raged, the mud reached their ankles, and raindrops spattered down.

At first they formed a trio for these readings. Gradually, though, Ida joined their little group too. Palely holding her white pillow, she would enter the room and sit listening silently in one of the corners with her arms crossed before her. Manya sat on the couch's edge, one arm draped over the windowsill, while Rosa leaned against the back of the rocking chair, swaying slowly with it back and forth. Ensconced in red velvet, Hagzar read clearly and with controlled emotion from the volume that he held in his hands. Sometimes Manya asked a spiteful, disjointed question, which he did his best to answer without showing his distress. Sometimes Rosa challenged him too. In the beginning he deferred to her by blithely, almost shyly agreeing, yet soon he took to arguing back. And when she refused to back down—not with any great show of logic, to be sure, but with an adamance that spoke for itself—he concluded that she was a person with a mind of her own and rare properties of soul such as belonged only to those who have been through a great deal in life. If then he thought of that lively young man and of Rosa's venomous barbs, he had to admit that she was deucedly attractive. If only, he mused bitterly, women's souls were not such closed books to him, and this were not always fated to be the case, since his relations with the opposite sex were one irreparable mistake from the start.

For a moment he thought of his stout neighbor, whose buxom arms collided with his own whenever they walked side by side. Like the shadows of owls on frozen, moonlit nights, fleeting images arose and vanished in his mind. Though it made no sense at all, when he looked at Rosa's pure, noble face her eyes reminded him for some reason of his own gray cat, which liked to sit perched on the red commode in his bedroom. Curiously, the thought of this amused him. Rosa had stopped rocking with the chair; her eyes shone and her cheeks were slightly flushed. Her voice, which trembled when she spoke with the excitement of the pleasures of the mind, brought him back to himself. At once he began to refute her, none too logically himself, stopping repeatedly to ask:

"Do you follow me? Well, do you?"

And when she did not he turned to face Manya, who sought at first to return his direct gaze. Soon, however, she had to lower her eyes; yet immediately this annoyed her; so that spitefully she stared back at him again until he began to falter and felt suddenly so stupid that he forgot what he was saying and turned back to Rosa once more, who still refused to concede the point, which compelled him to start all over again from the beginning.

Upon returning home late that night he climbed into bed and lay there reviewing the day's thoughts and feelings and his hopes for the months ahead. He wished the winter would come. He was eager to get back to his work again, which had lately been neglected—although the fault was not his own but that of the circumstances in which he lived. As soon as the month was out he would rent a larger room in which it would be easier for him to concentrate, and everything would fall into place.

Thus the autumn went by. And one morning when the first gleaming coat of new snow lay upon the broad, empty streets and the gleeful caw of the crows sounded over the low, whitened roofs, Hagzar and Rosa, wrapped in a long woolen shawl, walked down the long street together until they came to a farmyard. A large, chained dog began to bark at them, while a fat sow squealed from beneath a summer cart that lay lamely in the middle of the white yard. A tall, sun-bronzed peasant woman came out to greet them. Her sleeves were rolled back and the edge of her apron, which was slick with grease, was tucked into her waist. With her tongue she kept searching for something in her gums or between her teeth, while burping repeatedly with a harsh, ringing sound that was accompanied by a smell of half-digested herring and onion.

Rosa addressed her by her patronymic. She spoke to her briefly, and they followed her to a large, low-ceilinged room with simple but ample furnishings, a clean white floor, lots of flowers, and a high bed standing in one corner beneath a mountain of pillows. Numerous pictures of generals on horseback galloped over the walls, and a few gloomy icons hung darkly in the corners.

That same day Hagzar moved in. In the evening Rosa and the girls came to visit. They praised the room and joked with the peasant land-lady, laughing especially when she paused on her way out, pointed with a finger to the pillowy mountain, and declared:

"I do believe you'll sleep well here . . ."

Then they took Hagzar back with them to their house. They read, talked, sang, and went out for a stroll again until it was well past mid-night.

The next morning was overcast. Yesterday's snow had turned into a gray gruel on the ground. The winds pounded on the shutters. Hagzar felt as though his soul were incubating within him. For a long time he sat on his new bed with his feet tucked beneath him and one hand supporting his head. Then he rose, turned up the collar of his buttoned frock coat, and paced slowly back and forth in the room, his left hand holding the collar in place while his right hand braced his left against his chest. After a while he sat down at his desk and remained immobile there with his pen aimed at a blank sheet of paper. Yet when he began to write, the round, curlicued, carefully formed letters raced hand-somely across the page. His face grew intense and excited. His breath came and went irregularly, and his movements were nervous and quick. With dizzying speed he filled lines and whole pages, and he did not stop to rest until he had finished a large and crucial section of his new article. Only when he had marked the final period with a large, black inkstain and had drawn a black line beneath the last sentence did he throw down his pen on the table with a sigh of relief. He leaned back in his chair, clasping his head from behind with both hands, and sat there with his eyes shut as though he were frozen stiff.

That evening he was hurrying home from the house of an acquaintance in order to get back to work. There was a bite to the distilled air outside. The last of the snow was turning gray on the eaves of the roofs. Far on the horizon the sky was streaked with a pale, congealed red. He strode vigorously over sharp, frozen clods of mud, thinking of how gay and relaxed spiteful Manya had been the day before. He thought of what he had written that day, and of what he planned to add to it that night, and felt heartened by the winter with its sleighs, its gleaming roofs, its raucous crows, and its snows that came from afar. When he decided to look in on the three sisters he found Rosa setting glasses out for tea. He rubbed his hands pleasurably together, stamped forcefully with his foot, and exclaimed in a triumphant voice:

"So it's winter after all, Rosa!"

II

Though the winter had barely begun, Manya was already hard at work. Having failed to gain admission to the fifth form the previous spring, and having spent the whole summer "in a perfect fit" about it, she was determined to take the examinations for the seventh form the following spring, it being senseless to try forever for the fifth. For a tutor she had engaged the same young man who was a former acquaintance of Hagzar's. To be sure, he was due to leave town soon, though no date had been announced for his departure; yet meanwhile a good deal about him was known in the pleasant house, both regarding his down-at-heel past with its tale of penury, privation, mad binges, police vans, artist friends sent to Siberia, and more yet that was shrouded in mystery, and the glorious future that lay strung out before him on a long chain of light, life, space, freedom, achievement, and renown. (In addition Manya alone knew of a certain pistol shot in a dark orchard and of a shirt-sleeve with a bullet hole that he still happened to possess.) In any case he was a fine sight to behold when, his curls tumbling over his forehead, he sat perched like a drunk on the edge of his chair in the middle of the room with one hand on his knee and the other in the air, poised to fall on his second knee as soon as the Delphic mood possessed him and he began to quote from Nekrasov with a windy, excruciating sigh:

"*Ekh, priyát'el! I ty, vidnó, goré vidál . . .*"

"What a rascal of a fellow!" someone would be sure to exclaim then.

On winter evenings, sitting by himself or together with Rosa in the drawing room, Hagzar would listen as the insistent, slightly vexed drone of study coming from Manya's room repeated for the thousandth-and-first time, so it seemed to him, some perfectly trite phrase or cumbersome but trivial formula that was frequently interrupted by an irritable "the-devil-take-it!" At such times Ida, who had recently been forced by her health to stop attending the lycée again, might pass before him on her way out of Manya's room. Her face pale and annoyed beneath its head of mussed hair, her faithful pillow in one hand and her heavy book open in the other, she would direct a silent, melancholy smile at him, as if to say:

—You know, and I know, that the poor child is wasting her time . . . but what good would it do to tell her?

Then she would slip into the other bedroom, whose half-ajar door opened onto the drawing room too, lie down diagonally across the two beds that stood there side by side, and read. Rosa would sit on the ledge of the stove, her knitting or a book in her lap, and Hagzar would sink deeper into his corner of the couch, or pace back and forth in the room, while they chatted and joked and fell silent again before beginning to hum some old tune. Sometimes, still swearing by the devil, Manya entered the room to inquire what time it was and worry why her tutor had not come yet. Hagzar would stare at her face, which warned against trespassing, and at her full, handsome shoulders beneath the blouse of soft muslin that caressed her alluring back, and would seek an excuse to converse with her; yet Manya, for some reason already on the defensive, would stare suspiciously back at him and answer as sharply as she could. Once, the Lord knew why, he asked her what her dreams were and who the lucky young man in them was. With wounded hauteur she turned her back on him, replying to him from the doorway in a harsh voice that seemed to bore upward from a hidden cavern in her chest:

"He's not like the likes of you, I promise you that . . ."

Which made him break into an uncharacteristically loud laugh.

In the weeks before the Russian holidays Ida made a supreme effort to return to school, so as to be able to be promoted with her classmates, and succeeded so well that she even finished the term with honors. Yet soon afterwards the pains in her head and chest grew worse again, and often Hagzar found himself standing by her bed with a glass of water in one hand while Rosa quietly rubbed down her bare arms and chest with pungent spirit and Manya searched for something along the window-sills and under the couch with a stifled groan. In a barely audible voice Ida chattered by fits and starts; she whimpered about her dead mother, about skies like none she had ever seen and some great storm at sea, and about something else, something terribly important, that everyone kept taking for himself and leaving nothing of for her. She went on hysterically, laughing and crying at once, until Rose had to beg her in a frantic whisper to calm down and Manya's movements grew still more exasperated.

At such times Hagzar grunted and twitched fretfully, alternately sipping cold water from the glass in his hand and sprinkling it over the pale face that was suddenly frozen in a spasm of new distress. Such crises did not last long, however. Soon Ida dozed off and they returned to the drawing room, where everything was as before. For a while they sat there in silence, letting the tension drain; then Manya went to her room while Rosa curled up on the stove ledge again and Hagzar settled into the couch. The door to the bedroom remained half-open, so that the shade-spreading lamp cast a dim light over the end of one of the beds and caused it to gleam in the dark. From her sickroom Ida continued to groan in her sleep, while Hagzar and Rosa sat talking and laughing in quiet tones before falling silent or breaking into hushed song.

At about nine o'clock Manya's tutor would arrive. Now the intervals of silence were themselves intermittently broken by his rude oaths that drifted out of Manya's room to dissipate in the hushed space of the drawing room. Later he might appear for a while to sit and banter with them, or to challenge Hagzar to wrestle. Sometimes he asked Hagzar whether he remembered this or that friend before turning to the others and relating to them with relish some comical incident from the time that the two of them had briefly shared a room in the city of H.

"One night when we were starving," he would begin gustily, savoring his deliberately coarse speech, "I went to see a pal of mine, a real sport. He was busted himself but he offered to stake us to some sausage and a small loaf of bread. So I took the grub and brought it back to Hagzar. The professor was lying in bed when I came, licking his chops. 'On your feet,' I said, 'it's chow time.' You should have seen him jump out of bed. 'What? Did you say food? Excellent, let's have it. But . . . *sausa-ge? . . .*"

Everyone burst out laughing.

The tutor raised his voice and concluded with brio:

"And what do you think happened in the end? My vegetarian friend ate a sandwich of bread on bread and went right to sleep!" With a merry cry he turned at last to the hero of his story. "I can see that by now you've had better sense drummed into you, eh? Come, let's wrestle!"

And seizing Hagzar beneath the arms, he sought to throw him, while the latter struggled to squirm free and cried quits. Then all laughed again and talked some more and enjoyed themselves until late into the night. Even Manya grew gay and spirited, and her eyes shot sparks.

Yet when the tutor rose to go at last and Manya chose to walk him part of the way, a brooding silence descended again on the room, a silence that pressed on the heart like a soft caress, and squeezed, squeezed away at it with a mild, gently narcotic pain. Hagzar and Rosa sat dreamily, waiting to hear the noisy creak of the front door and the squeak of boots being hastily removed—which were sometimes followed by a low, defiant voice singing chestily from Manya's room:

> *Ekh, ló-opnul obrùch*
> *Ókolo maznítsy:*
> *Trai-trrai-ti-ra-rai* . . .

When it was finally time to bid Hagzar goodnight too, Rosa put on her large woolen shawl and, shivering a bit from the cold, accompanied him along the empty street that ran in front of the house. Sapphire crystals winked and glittered from the pure blanket of snow that had whitened the world. A dusky, reddish wreath festooned the moon. The trodden snow underfoot turned to slush with a merry squish and a light, amusing puff of smoke materialized with each breath. Hagzar talked in muted tones while she walked by his side and thought as she listened of how kind he was and of how agitated he grew each time he had to grope for a word; he was a person, she felt, who lived in a splendid world, and thought splendid thoughts, and had work that was splendid too. Guilelessly she began to tell him about the Bible tales she had studied as a girl with her brother at some rabbi's; about the stories of Mikhailov-Scheler that had supplanted them as she grew older and become her constant companion; about books in general, for which she had such a passion; about her friends, who made fun of this; and about the strange sense of remoteness, the missing sympathy, that she felt nowadays when she met them. The more she talked, the more enthralled she became with her own account, every detail of which seemed so splendid to her, so full of life and enhancing of her own past, that she actually began to believe with all her heart that she too had had a past without knowing it. Not until her words began to fail, yielding to little gasps of weary, jagged laughter, did she notice Hagzar's frequent grunts, which he struggled ineffectually to emit in token of his interest in her tale. Then her speech lost the last of its flow to ever longer silences, until it trailed off completely in the end—although not before one last, pitiable grunt on his part had prompted her to laugh weakly and to conclude as well as she could:

"Yes, time certainly has flown . . ."

By February of that year it began to thaw. In the morning hours the sun peered out, causing the snow to soften, the rooftops to drip, and the dazzling ponds to fissure and crack; yet toward evening fingers froze once more, jaws stiffened, and tasseled icicles re-formed along the eaves. It was an hour at which Hagzar liked to visit the leafless park in the center of town. The snow lay in milky-white drifts there and the branches of the trees were stiff and bare. Crows screamed over the bright, desolate expanse. He wandered untrammeled along the winding paths, tracing sinuous lines with his stick in the virgin snow and some-times stopping to amuse himself by scrawling words in it.

Once he went for a walk in the park with Rosa. Her face was prettily flushed and the sound of her laughter rang like a child's at play. The golden fringes at the ends of the white scarf that she had tossed back over her shoulders blew against the snug collar of her jacket. Hagzar was in a quick, gay mood that day. They laughed at everything they saw and spoke about, most hilariously of all at Rosa's account of a dream that had woken Manya from her sleep the night before. Just imagine: darkness all around her, not a person in sight, so quiet you could hear a pin drop—and all of a sudden:

"This drunken rascal of a fellow appears. He chases after her with a revolver, and begins to shoot, ha ha . . ."

It really was so absurd . . . at which point Hagzar stepped to one side without warning, spread his arms wide, and flung himself with a playful cry backward into the pure snow, which collapsed beneath his weight. As soon as she recovered from her fright Rosa burst into such gales of laughter that she scared all the crows, who filled the park with their caws and noisily shook clumps of white snow down from the treetops. Hagzar looked into her bright eyes and called from where he lay with gay pathos:

"Man overboard! Why don't you save me, Rosa?"

Rosa laughed even harder. She bent until her flushed, bright face nearly touched his own and seized the hands he stretched out to her. Slowly he pulled himself up, digging his heels into a hollow of snow and muscularly gripping her small palms; yet before he could regain his footing she stumbled herself and would have pitched helplessly forward had she not quickly grabbed his waist and sunk her head with a merry shriek into his overcoat at a point beneath his chest. He seized her beneath the arms and continued to hold her there for a moment after helping her up—until a sudden shiver ran through him at the changed sound of her laugh, which had grown strangely contorted, and he released her. Then, without looking back at the "snowman" that his fall had made, the two of them walked home in silence.

On the way Rosa teased him with a strange venom, reminding him with fleet hints of things long repented and best forgotten, such as the time he had clumsily tried to undo the kerchief on her head while they had sat by the window of the drawing room looking out at a stormy night. Mockingly she mimicked his helpless cry of alarm when she had been about to fall in the park, his pointless, repetitive grunts. When he finally left her for the house of a pupil, his legs took him back to the park instead. He climbed the circular railing of the gazebo that stood at one end of the long, straight promenade running from the old castle to a view of the stream at the foot of the park and of a spreading willow tree beyond it. He leaned against the shaky grating, staring down at the round wellhouse by the stream and at the nearby bin of frozen ashes left over from holiday pig roasts. The white willow was a blur in the thick mist. The cries of the crows assailed and stunned him, told him with a bitter vengeance that people like him could never take what life offered them, had no business living at all. *Ka-a ka-a ka-a.* He suffered from the childishness, or worse yet, from the simple blind idiocy, of the eternal student, which was why he drew a line between his own inner life and his life in the world outside. *Ka-a ka-a.* Lies, lies. A person was one and the same, forever and aye. Whoever he was in the street outside he was also within his own walls . . .

After a while he left the park and started back through the marketplace. Breathless men hurried by him and a tall, stocky woman wiped her nose on the back of her hand. At home he took out his notebooks, dimly aware of a throbbing lump in his chest that made him want to cry, and sat down with them at his desk. For a long while he stared at them, nibbling at the cap of his pen while grunting at odd intervals with an effetely nasal sound. And when the spindly, crooked, rat-tailed letters ran from his pen at last, their sickliness so filled him with loathing that he broke off in the middle, threw himself on his bed with a suffering noise, and lay there for hours grunting and tossing in turn.

Yet soon it was nearly spring and the days were filled with light. Patches of soft blue showed through the clash of silvery cymbals in the sky. The sun was new and warm again; golden puddles gleamed underfoot and glimmering streams bubbled gaily. The newly let-out cows rubbed against the walls of the houses, seeking their stored warmth. Hagzar cut back on his lessons. Whenever he could he went for long walks through the paths and fields, splashing pleasurably through the slick bogs from which a damp glitter arose, breathing in the soft decay of the rutting earth as it warmed, surrendering himself to the steamy mist exhaled by the fat, rank soil.

Now little Ida often dropped by. She was still pale and not yet all over her illness, but there was color in her face and she seemed prettier; her chest had filled out and she was taller too. Wrapped in her shawl she would knock on his door and announce with a fetching smile that she simply could not have stayed indoors a minute longer. It was so, *so* good to be out in the fresh air now. One might almost . . . *ah!* And Hagzar would sit her down by his side and stroke her hair and ask whether Rosa was free yet, and had the three of them lunched, and what was Manya doing, and was her tutor there, and would she please tell Rosa for him that he would soon come himself.

He and Rosa now went walking a great deal outside of town. Light-heartedly they leaped over the ruined snow that still lay piled in the ditches, chatting gaily as they sank into the slick mud of the dark, steaming fields. By the time they tramped home again they were pleasantly numb and their fingers were frozen to the bone; shivering they warmed themselves indoors and swore how good it had been. Sometimes they found Manya standing before the door, half-whistling, half-puffing some Russian tune, the lapels of her black jacket that she had draped over her back held with one hand at the throat.

"Whistling, eh?" Hagzar would jeer drily.

And Rosa would smile while Manya looked spitefully back at him and puffed through her lips even more.

Yet when she was alone in the house with Ida, Manya spoke often about spiritual suffering that no words could describe; about doubts that preyed on the mind; about gifts gone to waste and dark nights of the soul; about the horrors of drink and the lower depths; about great cities; about freedom, life, and strong wings; and about the need to escape— yes, to escape in the name of all that was holy since she could not go on living like this anymore.

Sometimes her tutor still appeared. Despite the gleam in his restless eyes and his hair that was as charmingly rumpled as ever, his face was drawn and he walked with an unsteady gait. Wearily he harangued them, smelling of brandy and beating his chest with one fist. Not for the first time he declared that only a worm would spend all its days in the dirt; anyone with the breath of life in him, with a bit of pluck and independence, would leave a swamp like this as fast as he could. Where was he bound for then? For a moment a lock of loose hair tumbled gorgeously down. Ha! They needn't worry about that. Wherever he fell, he would always land on his feet . . . and meanwhile, was he really such a bad sort to have around?

And he would dramatically raise one hand and declaim with artistic flair:

> *Myórtvii v gróbe mírno spi*
> *Zhíznyu pólzuisya, zhivói!*

Who among them did not know those immortal lines of Nadson's?

At such times Hagzar would glance at Manya, who sat perfectly still while the faint reflection of her tutor's smile struggled over her face, and decide that she was not nearly so attractive as he had once thought. On the contrary: her features were on the coarse side and even annoyingly dull. One look at the rapt stare with which she regarded that chest-thumping brute was ample proof of what a dunce she was.

Later, on his evening walk with Rosa, he would murmur to her how detestably mean he found Manya, how put off he was by her vulgarity, how depressed she left him feeling each time. Gradually he shifted to how quickly young people grew up nowadays, how nothing ever stayed the same, and how little there was in human life to hold on to. Even when you considered what still might lie ahead . . . to say nothing of what you had already seen, heard, and knew . . . even then life always seemed to slip sideways and to come to nothing in the end. Was that all there was to it?

Did she understand him?

Was it?

And Rosa would cough a gentle cough and murmur shyly and not at all clearly:

"Mm-hmmm."

Which made him turn even more crimson. His breath came in spurts, one hand pawed the air, and there was unspoken anguish when he said:

"Lately I . . . it's not just that I can't write . . . it's . . . everything. And yet it's not anything either, eh? It's just that the more you look at things, the less they are what you think. Something is wrong with them . . . or perhaps nothing is . . . and yet there you are . . ."

Generally he broke off at this point to add after a while in an exasperatedly tormented whisper, raising and lowering his shoulders in despair:

"Unless that's simply how it's meant to be . . ."

At which he spat loudly and exclaimed under his breath:
"Phheww . . . the devil knows!"

And fell silent. An evening gloom cloaked the dull fields and was
woven into the cold mist that arose from them. Here and there a solitary
willow still stood out. They walked without breaking the silence, treading the soft earth. Now and then he hummed through his nose a quiet,
plaintive air that her thin, quavering voice took up. Once she stopped to
tell him that her fingers were numb and that she had forgotten to bring
her gloves. Yet when he tried putting one of her hands in his pocket, the
pocket proved too small, so that his own hand was left outside, holding
the sleeve of her coat. Soon they felt how unnatural this was, since it
forced them to walk with a limp. After a while she pulled her hand free,
and they walked on humming to themselves.

III

Simha Baer came home before Passover. For several days Hagzar stayed
away from the house. The day after her father's return Ida dropped by.
Her face was pale and wistful, as in the old days. She flitted from one
thing to another, did not stay long, and giggled when she left that her
father was eager to meet him.

Then Manya came by. She kept glancing out the window, inquired
about some book whose name she instantly forgot, whistled, promised
to come back again soon, and dashed home. When she returned she sat
by the window again before remembering that she had left her father by
himself and must attend to him. Soon she came back a third time, yet
before long she spied her tutor passing by on his way to her house. She
ran out to greet him and disappeared for the rest of the day.

But Rosa did not come at all, which left Hagzar feeling as once he had
felt when the mailman had delivered a letter to her and she had sat
reading it silently to herself in his presence before slipping it into her
pocket without comment. An injured, contrary mood settled darkly
over him and spewed its bile of loneliness into his blood.

That night he paced endlessly up and down like a man with a toothache, from time to time emitting a sickly, irascible cough that sounded
more like a groan. And when he went to bed at last, pulling the blanket
over him, the despairing thought assailed him that his surroundings had

won in the end, and that the mark they had left on him could never be removed.

The next morning he rose early, thinking of his work. The crooked, rat-tailed letters flashed before him and he stalked the room some more, trying to shake off the scaly sensation of tedium that afflicted him at such times while groggily pondering a dream he had had in which he had finished a long article and was about to set forth on a European tour. At last he picked up an old essay and leafed through it, absently searching for a certain passage that never failed to bring a modest smile to his lips. He thumbed the notebook rapidly, threw it down, picked it up again, put it down once more, and finally opened it a third time and let his glance fall on a page. Slowly his face brightened. His eyes began to glow and his steps grew quicker; feverishly he tugged with shaky fingers at his mustache while making little, resolute grunts in his chest. When his legs wearied at last from their forced march he sat down to work at his desk, humming little snatches of a tune beneath his breath; yet just then the mailman came with a postcard, whose arrival so pleased him that he read it over three times. He rose and paced some more until his head spun, then put on his coat and went out.

In the distance he saw Rosa coming toward him in the company of Hanna Heler. She greeted him like a long-lost friend, and he extended the postcard to her with a sheepish grin before turning in his dry manner to Hanna and advising her to peruse it as well, since it appeared to pertain to her too; they might look at it all, he replied, when both asked at once how much they should read of it. So Rosa read the whole card out loud, already smiling before she began, while Hanna stared at her with a wide-open mouth in whose wings a smile waited too. Then both shrieked with laughter and Hagzar joined in heartily. Now they all knew that Gavriel Carmel, who was once a tutor in this town, had written from abroad to announce that he wished to see his Naples one more time before he died, to which end Hagzar should prepare for him:

1) Attractive quarters; 2) Attractive young ladies; 3) Two or three pupils if possible.

Still the same joker as ever!

Then Hagzar retraced his steps with them and listened to Hanna assure him that she remembered Carmel quite well: a tall, dark young man who had seemed to her rather odd but certainly clever enough. The three of them chatted until Rosa went her way, and Hanna hesitated a moment before accepting Hagzar's invitation to come back with him to his room. There she kept rising every few minutes to go and sitting down again, the tower of dark hair on her head describing a weak arc around her ample bosom with each loud, staccato laugh. And when Hagzar rose to walk her to the door the thought crossed his mind that she was in fact a dear thing and really very feminine at that. For a second he thought of Manya's dull stare, of her irritating whistle, and of her jacket draped around her back. Outside the sun was celebrating spring. Rivulets of water splashed gaily by, puddles gleamed like gold, metal shovels scraped against the ice. Roly-poly children frolicked and sang, and Hagzar cried with roguish glee:

"How much light and life there is, Hanna! No, I won't allow you to go home now."

Soon they were walking in an orchard high above town. Fresh blades of grass pushed up through the earth and the sodden trees stood resurrected from their sleep. The scattered tin roofs and white churches beneath them shrank and all but vanished in the great expanse of open fields that ran in all directions as far as the dew-bright woods that ringed the broad horizon. The scent of the wakened hills in their lungs roused them too. They grew gay, and he cuffed her lightly on the nose in a giddy burst of affection and called in a whinnying voice:

"Ho, Hanna!"

Which made her laugh loudly and ask if he had taken leave of his senses and would he please—but how strangely in earnest she seemed!—"act his age." Yet in the end she had to slap his hand and order him to behave. Then his face lost its shape and his eyes darted moistly.

"But a kiss, Hanna . . ." he lisped, cocking his head to one side. "What's wrong with one little kiss?"

Again her laugh rang out, propelling the top half of her forward: she could not, for the life of her, control herself any longer, she would simply split her sides, so help her! What kind of strange creature was he? She would give a pretty penny to know who had taught him such tricks. Was it Rosa and her brood? And to think that she had always thought . . . well, well!

For a moment she looked at him reproachfully; yet his flushed, sheepish face forestalled her with a guilty smile and he seized her full palm with a timorous hand and stammered out:

"But what have I done to you, Hanna?"

Followed more boldly by:

"After all, why not?"

And then in jest:

"A person might think that I had bit you!"

With which he was in fine fettle again. They wandered along the bare paths, laughing each time they collided while vigorously trampling the dead growth beneath their feet. He strode now in triumph beside her, his right arm the master of her shoulder and hair, thinking distractedly at the same time, exactly why he did not know, that with Rosa, let alone Manya, such a thing could never have happened, even though life was the same all over and all the women in the world were simply one great woman in the end.

Hanna Heler returned the squeeze of his hand and looked up at him brightly. Soon they found a fallen log to rest on . . .

Later that day Hagzar descended with large steps the several stairs leading up to Hanna's house and stopped at the bottom of them to regard the fair sight of the broad, empty, reposeful street, the low houses alongside it, each neatly in its place, and the tranquil, pure, untroubled sky above. He thrust out his chest and turned with slow, sure strides to go home. Before long he felt as though a thin layer of something were peeling away inside him—peeling, flaking, and breaking up into small bubbles that slid quickly upward to press against his chest and burst into his throat. With surprising ease they tumbled out and he muttered to himself with satisfaction:

"So it's done then."

The words sent a rush of blood to his cheeks. He quickened his pace and clapped his hat on his head with one hand. Stubbornly he growled:

"And yet what nonsense, though!"

Despite the speed with which he walked it was already evening by the time the marketplace was behind him. Coal fires gleamed redly in some of the stores. Farmers urged home their horses, shutters slammed with a metallic bang. He slowed down again, locking his hands behind his back and dragging his stick in the mud. From time to time he squeezed a stubborn cough from his chest, and when he reached home he shut the door behind him and repeated out loud to the still, dark room:

"Yes, what nonsense!"

He glanced at the house across the street, whose drawn curtains were lit from within. He removed a box of matches from his pocket, cast it on the table, made his way in the dark to his bed, and sank into the mountain of pillows upon it; then he rose and walked about the room until his knees were weak and his chest began to ache. An enervating slackness spread through his limbs and his brain felt stupidly blank. Again he collapsed on the pillows and lay there a long while without moving, feebly musing how pointless was the life of self-denial and how some people were born to it nonetheless—which seemed to console him, so that he fell asleep thinking of the subtle, soapy odor given off by Hanna Heler's white breasts.

On his way home one day during the Passover holiday he passed by the pleasant house and saw Simha Baer and Rosa sitting together on the bench that stood in the front yard by their gate. He greeted her without stopping; yet she jumped quickly up from her seat and called to him to come in. Where had he disappeared to lately? She introduced him to her father, made room for him on the bench, and coughed gently all in one breath. Hagzar stammered an embarrassed apology and sat by her side, while Simha Baer proffered a hand, stared down at the ground, and said as though explaining to himself:

"Aha . . . so this must be your Hagzar . . ."

Rosa laughed embarrassedly too and confessed:

"Yes, papa, it's our Hagzar."

Whereupon Simha Baer grunted contentedly and began to inquire into Hagzar's past and present life. He listened carefully to the answers with his head studiously bowed, picking mildly at his bearded chin, until something appeared to please him and he broke in:

"I . . . just a minute there, slow down . . . why, you must be Leivik Hagzar's son, is that right? Whew! Why, your father and I used to play tag together when we were small boys. On Goat Street in Mogilev, where we lived."

Did he know Leivik!

"But . . . just a minute . . . tell me, wasn't Rabbi Shmulka, may he rest in peace, your uncle? Of course he was." Did Hagzar remember him? That was a fine Jew? Who could forget the funeral he was given when he died? Not an infant stayed home in its crib . . .

Hagzar sat on the bench for nearly an hour, answering Simha Baer's queries and listening to him reminisce. The mellower her father's mood grew, the less inhibitedly Rosa laughed and the more her eyes shone with pleasure. At last, enjoying his own joke, Simha Baer inquired which synagogue Hagzar attended and had he said his evening prayers there—adding without waiting for an answer that it would have broken Rabbi Shmulka of Mogilev's heart to have lived to see his nephew's sinful ways. What a Jew that man was, what a Jew!

Simha Baer rose, excused himself, and told Hagzar to come by more often.

Then Hagzar and Rosa strolled up and down the street, in which the mud had dried. Rosa's spirits were high. Laughingly he twitted her that God was less wicked than she, since He at least had sent him Hanna Heler for his loneliness, and when she laughed back he talked about Hanna some more. Did she know that the two of them met every day and never had a dull or cross moment? Then he discussed his friend Carmel, whom he hoped he would not disappoint. She listened keenly as he told her about Carmel's life, about the relations between them, and about his pleasure that his old friend from *heder*, and later, from Vilna, was soon about to arrive . . .

Besides which, nothing really was new . . .

Subsequently he began to visit the house again daily as once he had done; yet now he made a point of first saying hello to Simha Baer. Generally the latter could be found sitting between the table and the window with a floppy silk skullcap on his head, peering over the tops of his glasses at a book that he held away from himself at arm's length. He welcomed Hagzar warmly, laid his book on the table, carefully folded his glasses, placed them on the book, pulled out a handkerchief, blew a trumpet blast into it, and commenced by declaring "we-ll now" in the tone of an experienced man of affairs who is adept at getting along with the "younger set." Then he would chat with Hagzar about this or that latest fashion, spoofing it with a knowing air and humorously quoting scriptural chapter and verse, or citing rabbinic texts, in proof that it was nothing new. Finally his hand crept back toward his glasses and he familiarly ended the audience by replacing them on his nose.

"Well now . . . I don't imagine that you came here in order to be preached to by an old man like me. If you're looking for the sisters, you'll find them in the cloister . . ."

And, pleased with his recondite jest, he returned to his book.

In the "cloister," the large room that had been their father's until he had recently bequeathed it to them in order to banish their "reign of terror" from the drawing room, Hagzar would find the three sisters together with Hanna Heler, who had taken to slapping him sonorously on the back when they met. Uncomfortably he tried making small talk with Rosa; yet she sat with her face twitching moodily and refused to respond. Then he sang along with the others, sprawled out with them on the beds, talked until he was hoarse, and returned home in the early hours of the morning to grunt, spit, mop his brow, and grunt some more. Only the comforting thought of the approaching spring and of the imminent arrival of his friend could induce him to go to bed in the end.

At last Carmel came. In the beginning, Hagzar spent whole days and nights with him. Carmel lay on his back amid a wreath of blue smoke that spiraled up from the fat cigarette that spluttered between his lips, while Hagzar sat by his side, or paced stammering and laughing up and down, both enjoying his own excitement and wishing that there were less of it. Now he saw his long stay in town in a new, rewarding light that made him feel much better about it—although each time he asked Carmel to tell him about Europe, an urgent, almost physical desire arose within him to finish his work and depart for there at once. The more casually he tried listing the obstacles that had detained him so far, the more annoyed with himself he became at his inability to explain them, especially as they all had seemed so perfectly clear beforehand . . .

Yet afterwards, when Carmel became a steady guest in Simha Baer's house, where he liked to loll on the couch puffing lazily on his cigarette while Rose crossed her arms beside him, the lips chill-cornered on her dear, sad face, and Manya sat across from them, hardly speaking but whistling often at odd times, and Ida half lay on the edge of the bed with a wistful longing in her eyes, Hagzar could feel his skin crawl. His head and chest ached, and he talked such a streak of loathsome, incurable rot that he had to escape to Hanna Heler's in the end, cuffing her nose to make her laugh and then returning home to grunt and brood some more. Once he found Manya's tutor there, talking loudly and horsing around. He pinned Hanna's arms behind her back and taunted Hagzar, who sat behind a large newspaper reading an ad placed by a doctor in Vilna.

Later that same day he stood by Ida's bed with a glass of water in his hand. A smell of valerian had been in the room when he entered; Manya bent over her sick sister, rubbing down her chest, and told Hagzar that Rosa was not in. Ida laughed and cried, too weak to open her eyes. She gasped like an animal and made delirious sounds, until a sudden tremor seized her and she cried:

"To hell with it! The ship is sinking . . . and I . . . only wanted . . ."

Manya was a nervous wreck. Seething with pent-up anger, she burst out:

"She went traipsing off just like that . . . with Carmel!"

Whereupon Hagzar felt a pain like a blow in his chest. The hot blood rushed to his face and stung his eyes. What was he doing here? He stood reeling beneath the memory of Carmel's smug smile, of Hanna Heler's arms pinned behind her, of the boisterous laugh of Manya's tutor as he held them. The ad placed by the doctor in Vilna flashed before him. Then came mighty Vilna itself with its halls of learning, its bookstores, its public library in which he had worked, its long, monumental nights of writing in his room there, its companions whose dreams had resembled his own. He felt that he was going to choke. Something hummed in his ears and he could hardly see. Dazedly he laid the glass on the chair and stumbled toward the door. Not until he was out in the fresh air again did his vision clear. His temples throbbed and his heart went on pounding as he walked down the street to the end of the town and continued beyond it. He ambled slowly now, staring with melancholy detachment at the long, endless railroad track that stretched flatly out before him, quite faint and desolate in the heat of the day.

NERVES

BY YOSEF CHAIM BRENNER

translated by Hillel Halkin

1.

A PERFUMELIKE SMELL, which came from the low clumps of acacia trees, or "mimosas," as some liked to call them, scented the air of the small Jewish colony in southern Palestine. In the expanse of sky before us a golden shaft from the setting sun at our backs gilded a cluster of faint, calm clouds; other clouds, as calm and faint, were limned not with gold but with long, narrow swathes of orange embroidery. At its far end the sky shone in docile light with the silvery-black sheen of myrtle leaves. The colors changed from one moment to the next. They ran together, blended, renewed themselves, and vanished in the end.

Next to a lone, straight cypress tree, which rose from behind the acacias and some yellowish prickly pears that were stiff with needles and their usual heavy turgidity, I and my companion—an ordinary-looking man of about thirty with a set of strong sloping shoulders and a coarse-featured, acne-studded face, who because he was ill had not gone to work this September day, the heat of which was worse than midsummer's—turned from the path we were walking on and strolled toward a chain of hills that ran along the gleaming horizon. The distant ruins of an ancient castle ten or twelve miles to our right seemed suddenly close by.

We walked silently for a while on level ground. The dry, sere fields still spoke of summer, yet in the graying vistas out over the corniced cliffs there was already a hint of the approaching fall. My friend turned to look at the plain behind us, where the low, red sun continued to blast indefatigably away. The trees at the colony's edge were far from us now and indistinct.

"Those trees . . ." Though he broke the silence abruptly, the low pitch of his voice, ironic and serious at once, softened the suddenness of it.

"Eh?"

"I was saying . . . those trees . . . do you see the tops of them? If I were writing a travel journal, or a 'Letter From Palestine' of the kind that's in fashion nowadays, I'm sure I'd begin: 'Our Jewish colonies: a fleeting yet irrepressible smile quivers through their still too few tree-tops . . .'"

"Quivers?" I repeated the word, a favorite of his when playing the nature lover. Generally he hedged it with sarcasm, but now it was impossible to tell whether this was the case or not.

He swallowed the bait. "Exactly! I'm talking about the tops of those trees. How old would you say they were? Not more than twenty-five years, I shouldn't think. The oldest trees must remember . . . yes, twenty-five years ago there was nothing here at all . . . nothing but sand and dunes . . ."

"But why do you keep coming back to the tops of them?"

"The tops, is it? Because they can see a long way. Perhaps they even see the great cities from here. (Did you know, by the way, that your innkeeper's son has the good fortune to be off to America next week?) You know, the great cities, the ones beyond the sea . . ."

"What about them?"

"What about them? Millions of people made them. For centuries men built them, rebuilt them, accumulated treasures in them . . . so that . . . so that today they stand on solid ground. If you're born in them, you're somewhere. There's even a grandeur about them. Do you remember those monumental railway terminals? Those magnificent parks?"

"So?"

"Whereas here we live in self-imposed poverty. A village barely twenty-five years old . . . and lived in by whom? Ha. Why, just today your innkeeper said to me: '*I* should let my son grow old in this hole like myself? I'd see him dead first . . .'"

A bird whose Hebrew name neither of us knew flew brilliantly by, flashing green against the blue sky, and disappeared.

"But the sad thing about it," he went on in his secretive voice, which was tinged not with irony at all now, but with a peculiar sort of earnestness, "is what our treetops see, or should I say foresee, right around them. Let's say they can forget the great cities. Let's say they can't even see them and needn't compare them with our pitiful Jewish village.

They still can't help noticing their surroundings. And I tell you, my heart goes out to them . . . my heart goes out to anything that is forced to put forth branches before it has time to strike root . . ."

"A prophecy?"

"Not even an editorial. Surely we've seen for ourselves."

"Seen what?"

"Villages! The old ones, I mean, not those here. Those that belong, that have their own sun to shine and their own rain to fall on them, that aren't a quarter-of-a-century old . . . and whose inhabitants aren't exiles from their father's table either . . . who . . . still taste the fleshpots of Egypt in their mouths . . . but who . . . well, they may be filthy beggars themselves . . . oh, I'm sure of it: they are! . . . but at least they're not the outcasts of the earth. When I think that those treetops are doomed . . . and always, always, the same wrteched Jews on the run . . . what misery!"

The evening gong sounded from the village.

"And do you know what else I wanted to say?" He was in a talkative mood. "Here more than anywhere (do you think that on our way back we might rest for a while on that little hill?) . . . here of all places, where our ruin, the ruin of our people, is most obvious . . . here I've had some of the best days of my life . . . which . . . which at times I've actually thought was taking on direction, some meaning. If only they didn't blather so much back there about the sweet land of our fathers! I'm sure that's why new arrivals in this place are always so depressed . . . it's like waking from a dream. To this day—it's been a year and a half now —I can't get those first moments out of my mind: so this is what our promised land is like! . . ."

After a moment's silence he went on:

"Nerves? You say it's just nerves?" (In fact I had said nothing at all.) "Well, maybe you're right . . ."

On our way back a while later, after the sun had set, we sat down to rest on the hill, which was covered with sparse grasses and a hedge of more thick, jointed prickly pears. As always our conversation jumped from one thing to the next. When it returned to the subject of nerves and their symptoms, however, my friend stretched out one booted foot in front of him, matched it with a second that was wrapped in rags, and began to speak in an uncharacteristically emotional tone. The story that he for some reason chose to tell me did not follow in any evident way from what had come before. Indeed, it began with a few vague sentences that were hardly coherent at all; yet little by little it showed signs of making sense—or so, at least, he thought, for he kept encouraging me each time he paused in his tale:

"Don't get up yet . . . Stay a while longer . . . You see, I'm over it now . . . I'll get over this rambling too . . . One gets over it all in the end . . ."

2.

"It was on my way over here from New York.

"Funny, how I say 'it was'—as though there were really an 'it' here that 'was' . . .

"But in any case . . . in any case . . . 'it was' is the wrong way to begin. If I'm going to tell it in such a fashion I should probably say 'there were'—because this much is true: a number of things did happen, and perhaps the whole point of it was . . . that in some way they were connected . . . even if for the most part I must say that I didn't understand them . . . but one never does when traveling with people . . . that is, with people who are traveling . . . does one?

"It happened on my way over here.

"I had decided to come to Palestine. Why? What for? What did I think might happen here? That's all beside the point.

"After all, I've been through all this with you before. Like anyone who has bothered to think a bit about his own life, I had long come to the predictable conclusion that its riddle was insoluble, and that a sequel to it would emerge only in my last moments . . . if at all . . . which is to say, that there was no sequel. And it wasn't just the sequel: my life until then made no sense to me either . . . nor did the rest of the world, or what I was doing in it, or what I might have been doing previously or had I been somewhere else (look at that silvery-gold moon, how it quivers! What day of the Hebrew month is it today?)—to say nothing of who had stuck me in it to live on its earth and breathe beneath its sky, to warm myself in its sun and shiver from its cold (mind you, I'm not cold now, it's just a manner of speaking), to stir each time another of its springs returned and feel sad again with each dreary autumn. (Excuse me for sounding poetic!) But the strange part was this: there was absolutely nothing I could do without thinking about that last destination after which there was nothing . . . that had to come and of which I was constantly aware . . . that destination that was followed by an infinity of dreamless sleep from which one never awoke and that utterly blotted out all else. (But why are you laughing? Is it at my language or simply at my having taken all this so seriously? Anyway, watch out for that prickly pear, will you, before you get stuck.)

"In a word, that last destination, after which there was neither heaven nor hell, love nor hate, beauty nor ugliness . . . and that still, as hard and stupid as life was, one never wanted to come . . . because it was the last thing that would come . . . So you see, it wasn't as if when I decided to come here I didn't know all these . . . these shamefully trite things (shamefully trite and yet true!) . . . And I also already knew (after all, it wasn't really so long ago, was it?) that even though I knew them, I was like all sentient beings forced against my own will to obey my own will . . . yes, my own will . . . And . . . like everything, sentient or not . . . yes, like you too . . . to somehow fill that terrible, insatiable void that can never be filled until the end . . . if then . . . because who really knows . . .

"For eight years I lived in New York (you're not sleeping? you're still listening?), and before that in the Ukraine where I was born. In New York I worked in a sweatshop, casting buttons into the void, that is, sewing them onto tens of thousands of pairs of pants every month. (I assure you, I can't imagine a more disgusting place or job!) The fact is that I knew perfectly well that all those buttons could hardly make a dent in the void, to say nothing of filling it . . . though at the same time I was aware that this was not the fault of the buttons, and that if instead of them I tried casting oranges picked in the groves of the promised land (assuming that there were oranges to pick when I got there and that I didn't come down with malaria), the Void of Fear, to call it by its proper name, would not fill up any faster . . .

"Yet still I came running here . . . because, you see, I was still in thrall to life . . . ach, what foolishness! I mean to the possibilities of life, do you understand? That is, to the hidden, veiled power of life that rules us against our will and that sometimes manages to make our quest in life seem almost pleasant . . . Which meant that I couldn't, didn't, want to free myself of the seemingly irrational desire for something else, for different possibilities, other places . . . which is of course the trick life plays on us in order to stay attractive . . . So that what I knew, which was substantially no different from what was known by the author of *Ecclesiastes*, was one thing, and the course taken by my life quite another that had nothing to do with what I knew . . . that had to do with certain simple necessities: buttons, paychecks, distributing radical newspapers, a pair of shoes here, the torments of sex there, every hour of every day something else . . .

"Do you know what I sometimes think? Perhaps what kept quivering inside me and impelling me all that time to come here was simply a yearning for natural beauty (after all, I never got to sit on a hill like this after a workday in New York), and also perhaps for a place to call my own, which as a Jew was something I had never had from the day I was born, not even under the marvelously sweet skies of my Ukraine with its marvelous *shiksas* . . . who might sneak up on you while you were swimming in one of its marvelous rivers and throw your Jewish clothing into the marvelous water, ha ha! So that for all I know—but what do *you* think?—I may have been living all that time with the hope . . . of finding a foothold, any hold, in our picturesque ancestral corner of Asia, in which Bedouin, the great-grandchildren of Abraham the Hebrew, pitch their tents to this day and bring to the well real camels as once did his bondsman Eliezer . . . and in which (which of course is more to the point) third- and fourth-generation children of Polish-Jewish money-lenders are learning to follow the plow . . . So that I thought that there . . . I mean here . . . how does Moses put it? 'Let me cross over and see that goodly land, its fair mountains and the Lebanon' . . ."

"Well, what do you think now? Did you find your foothold?"

At once, however, I felt it was wrong to have interrupted him. My own voice sounded vulgar to me, a crude dissonance.

He absentmindedly plucked a doubled-edged blade of grass and began to roll it between his fingers.

3.

"I was telling you about . . . leaving New York.

"I suppose you know that I didn't travel directly. There were a number of detours on the way. I spent a few days in London; I also made a side trip to Berlin, taking the train from Antwerp. I traveled fourth class, which was uncommonly crowded, and my state of mind at the time, if I remember it correctly, was uncommonly depressed too.

"This depression had accompanied me from London. It wasn't caused by the Jewish ghetto there, although that can be depressing enough . . . but then I myself was coming from East Broadway and was hardly pampered in this respect. No, what depressed me was a specific incident

—which had I read about in the newspaper I would have soon forgotten, but which instead I happened to witness with my own eyes . . . and at a time when my nerves were not in the best of shape . . .

"Let me tell you about it. In the flophouse in which I was staying in a crowded, ground-floor common room there was a new arrival, a Jew from Bialystok, who was sleeping in a garret upstairs. His history was known to all of us: he had arrived in England with a large family, which having neither sufficient funds nor sponsors in the country was refused permission to land. When the ship docked in Liverpool he managed, by some Jewish ruse, to smuggle himself ashore, but his family remained aboard ship and was sent back to Germany in the end. This Jew was a bit of an odd fellow: broad-shouldered and thick-bearded, but a total child in his speech and behavior, total. Despite his desperate situation (he was a smith, and a Jew doesn't have a ghost of a chance of finding metalwork in London) he joked and clowned all the time like a boy. He had us in stitches with his antics and his stories of how he had illegally gotten out of Russia and into England. This didn't last long, though. By his second week the wisecracks had come to an end. He grew very quiet, and one night, after hearing that his family had been deported, he went up to his tiny room, shut all the windows, turned on the gas stove, and lay down. He was found in the morning in a state of perfect rest. But perfect.

"Well, you can imagine for yourself . . . I had been traveling night and day, by land and by sea, with so little to eat and drink that sometimes I spent hours at a time in a state of total apathy, without a single feeling or thought, an apathy that could only belong to a life already over (only now and then the thought would pierce my brain before melting there like an icicle: 'From shore to shore . . . he has reached his shore . . . and I?'). Yes, you can imagine the state I was in when, after several days like this, by the end of which I had grown perfectly indifferent to the base physical part of me and its ordeal, I entered the wrong railway car by mistake—it was a few stations before Berlin—and found a Jewish family sitting in one corner by the door with all its possessions scattered over the floor. It consisted of a mother, a woman of about thirty-six or -seven whose dress and appearance I need hardly describe to you; her younger sister, a lady of about twenty with not unattractive but passive, lusterless eyes and a body that seemed gross and awkward although it was actually thin; and five girls, the eldest of whom could not have been more than eleven . . . yes, seven people in all. Their packages and bundles were more than I could count; the largest of them, it appeared, had been divided up so that everyone could carry his share of the load. A loaf of white bread that had been picked apart by some-body's fingers protruded from one end of an unbuttoned pillowcase.

" 'Look, Mama, a Jew!' cried the eldest child in Yiddish when she saw me.

" '*Ja, eine Jud-d-de*,' echoed the Germans in the car with a peculiar intensity, the tripled consonant sounding like both a groan and a laugh at once.

"The mother, however, did not seem happy to see me. Indeed, she had already reached the stage where even the possibility of such an emotion no longer existed. A Jew? Fine, a Jew. What more could the non-Jews do to her? Soon she would be in Berlin; of what use would another poor Jew be to her there? She didn't even bother answering when I asked her where she came from.

" 'Brest-Litovsk,' her oldest daughter answered for her.

" 'Not Bialystok?' I asked.

" 'Who said anything about Bialystok?' exclaimed the girl in an irri-table singsong, whose unmistakably pungent Lithuanian accent was like a parody of adult speech.

"But I had already gone too far in my fantasy that this was the same family that had been turned back from English shores (and whose father had arrived at the one true shore) to abandon it now. The fact that the cities weren't the same, that this family was traveling with an aunt whereas the other one wasn't, made no impression on me. An embar-rassed, ambiguous pity—is there any pity worse than that?—welled up for them inside me.

" 'I didn't mean to ask what part of Russia you came from. I meant where are you coming from now.'

" 'But where are *you* coming from?'

" 'From London.'

" 'I'm from Yondon too,' beamed one of the smaller children from over the top of a bundle, while the sunny eyes of her eleven-year-old sister (because her eyes did have sunshine in them, that I must tell you, although it was sunshine that you didn't see at first, that you only noticed later) appraised me less harshly. You're laughing? But I tell you, she was as pretty as white satin. And what wild, lustrous hair! I'm sure that no one had washed it or combed it for weeks . . .

" 'From Yondon,' said the younger one again.

"As if I hadn't known all along!

"So that now, neither the fact, which I soon discovered, that the woman had been a widow for years . . . nor that the reason for her deportation was not insufficient funds but a chronic eye condition . . . nor that her sister was turned back because a single woman could not enter England by herself . . . none of this made the slightest difference. My mind was made up: it was the same family! At once I hurried to bring my bag from the car I had been sitting in. I felt almost enslaved to them, as though it were somehow my duty to serve them. That's nerves for you!"

"A very Jewish case of them," I said sympathetically.

4.

The fourth-day sickle moon hung high above the little colony when we got back. At first, after sunset, while we still sat on the hill, its large, thin, pale half-ring had waxed more and more golden with the gathering dusk until to its right appeared a brilliant first star that was followed by thousands of others all over the sky. The higher it rose, though, the more the golden moon paled.

We reached the main street. My friend's one boot no longer dangled from his foot; he had taken it off in the darkness and was holding it in his hand. The sickle moon had widened and turned to silver, no, to quicksilver, to silvery darts dipped in frozen smoke. Dim lights flickered within the colony's houses, each a world in itself. Through shut windows the inhabitants could be seen spinning the daily cloth of their lives.

My companion grew agitated.

"Yes," he said almost in a whisper. "You were right. Jewish nerves! What a people . . . and yet it can get used to anything. In fact it's happiest in the ghetto. I don't mean that literally . . . although in a certain sense . . . outside of the ghetto it simply isn't at home. Take this peace here, this serenity, this beauty. Of course, no one is going to get rich from it. But if only one knew how to live as a human being, to suffer what human beings must and to live . . . this would be the place for it!"

"Despite what your treetops see?" I couldn't help asking.

"Ah, them . . ." He stifled a sigh. "That's true. But still . . . if only we were capable . . . I mean really capable of making something of this place. Because all places anywhere belong only to those who put their lives into them. Which isn't to say . . ."

There was a long silence, after which he continued irrelevantly:

"You were talking about that family. How many there must be like it in port cities all over the world. So many stray sheep . . . or blind horses . . . all of them. Still, I would like to know where it is now and how it is faring. And the most curious part of it—are you listening?—was that to begin with they didn't trust me one bit. I remember it perfectly: a few minutes after we had introduced ourselves I produced the remainder of a Dutch cheese from my bag and began to eat it in front of them so as to be able to offer it to the children—and their mother wouldn't allow them to touch it! Well, I thought, she's standing on ceremony, so I took from my pocket some small, Belgian copper coins that had holes in the middle of them, strung them like pendants, and began handing them out to the children, in order to rid them, as I saw it, of their apathy. (I suppose I must have imagined that the whole world was drowning in apathy.) 'I really don't need them . . .' I apologized to the mother. She looked at me as at some kind of profligate and said, 'If you don't need them, what makes you think that we do?' But the final blow was that when we finally reached Berlin—it was already evening —and I tried helping them with some of the bundles, which despite their small size were twice as large as the children who were carrying them, they, the children, began to scream for their mama.

" 'Watch out for him!' the woman shrilled morosely at her sister.

"Luckily for me, though, something soon happened which proved to her that even if I wasn't entirely in possession of my senses (in fact I was anything but) I was at least not a professional crook. At one point we had to pass through a narrow gate where one surrendered one's ticket to an inspector. Since I was unencumbered by luggage I had already passed quickly through ahead of them when I heard her wailing behind me:

" 'God help me! I gave him all our tickets! What will become of us now?"

" 'Weren't you continuing on to Russia?' I asked.

" 'Keep an eye on our things!' she called to her children without answering me.

"She ran to demand her tickets back from the inspector, who had no idea what she wanted and didn't reply. A crowd began to form in a circle around them. A Prussian policeman appeared. The shouting woman became more and more frantic, until even my intervention seemed providential to her.

" 'Where were you bound for? For what destination were your tickets?'

" 'For Vienna! The tickets were for Vienna. I gave them to him . . .

I thought they must realize . . . that they would let us go on . . . my God, what have I done . . .'

"I approached the inspector and tried out every German lesson that I had ever taken on him. I had no idea whether he was being polite or curt with me, but in the end I did manage to establish that the woman's tickets were good only for Berlin.

"What had misled her? It turned out that she had managed while in Belgium to obtain free tickets for Berlin from some Jewish charity (she had had in her possession a letter of recommendation from a relative of hers, a prominent official with another charitable organization in Jerusalem, which had stood her in good stead), as well as a written request to a sister charity in Berlin to pay her fare the rest of the way. In her naiveté, fully confident that she was now a celebrity who would be recognized all along her route, she had surrendered her tickets like the rest of us—until her sister pointed out that without them they could not travel further and she threw herself on the inspector. I tell you, she was the incarnation of the Wandering Jew!"

"And of nerves," I put in.

He laughed and said:

"Don't think that all this didn't have its bizarre psychological effects on me either. After I had accompanied her the next day to the charity in Berlin I spoke to the secretary there, a Teutonic Jew, perfectly correctly —believe me, my German was impeccable!—but a strange nervous tickle kept running through the soles of my feet and I found myself composing little vignettes in my head, from which I felt as though the brain had been surgically removed, such as the following:

"I: (Introducing her) *Mein Herr!* This unfortunate woman set out for London with her husband and five children . . .

"He: (Turning to face me) *Was?* With her husband? But it says here that she is a widow!

"I: (Pleading) Yes, a widow, *mein Herr*, a widow! She really is a widow now, because her husband, her husband . . . (The woman treads on my toes, compelling me to lower my voice) . . . You understand, the poor soul mustn't be caused any more pain . . . but in her situation . . . her husband has reached shore . . . (She pokes me in the ribs, increasing my confusion) . . . I mean the father of these orphans died in the wilderness . . . that is, in London . . .

"He: (Losing patience with me, the devious Russian Jew) *Was schwatzen Sie so?*

"I: (Stubbornly, secretly desiring to punch his nose, as I generally desire to do when addressing important people) *Mein Herr*, these are the five biblical daughters of Zelophhad!

"She: (Beginning to scream at the top of her voice) You mustn't believe him, your Grace, you mustn't believe a word of it! This man who says he wants to help me is mad. I've been a widow for the past five years. A widow! My husband passed away in Brisk. In Brisk! Here, read this letter . . ."

This imaginary dialogue might have gone on and on had I not put an end to it with a gesture of my hand that brought him, the narrator, back to his story.

5.

"And so the woman got her ticket to Vienna with another letter of recommendation to another charity there, and that was the last I saw of her in Berlin. (Speaking of Berlin, though, that city put me back on my feet. My second night there, to be sure, was spent at a meeting of the Hebrew language society at which a number of local authors delivered themselves of addresses; various other distinguished Hebraists were present too—not exactly my idea of great fun! But it snowed every day there . . . yes, real snow . . . and I tell you . . . if I weren't afraid of exaggerating I would say that I can still smell that snow to this day. I had eight whole days to myself there!) . . . Where was I? Ah yes, I didn't see her in Berlin anymore. Just imagine how I felt, then, when no sooner had I boarded the ship in Trieste than my eyes fell on all those little packages and bundles! Next to them was my family, which had decided to visit its relative in Jerusalem.

"I could tell you things that happened on that trip, but I won't try your patience. There was only one other Jew aboard ship beside the family and myself, a stout, stooped yeshiva boy in his mid-twenties who was a native of Safed, and who appeared to be, judging by the looks of him—he had those slanting, typically Oriental eyes that glisten like the skin of some wet, dark reptile—an apprentice rabbinical emissary or fund-raiser of some sort. He was returning to Palestine from Europe and appeared to be out of sorts, no doubt because business had gone poorly . . . and yet that isn't what . . . listen: if you didn't see that woman with her rheumy eyes, which were not her best feature, and her blistered lips, the toothless space between which had turned black from rot, lying on her bundles in her white *jaquette* that was too big for her frail body and her kerchief, under which she forgot to tuck back the wisps of thin hair that occasionally escaped from it, looking like a sick cat with all her starving children crowding around her in their variously colored rags that hadn't been parted from their bodies in weeks . . . well, you missed a heartrending sight. Add to that the freezing nights outdoors on the deck of the ship, the dry bread that was their sole diet, the cuffs of the sailors, the abuse of the other passengers, to say nothing of still further adventures—I don't mind admitting to you that the splendors of the Mediterranean were not exactly foremost in my mind . . .

"The morning we docked in Jaffa I was in an especially eccentric mood. The night before that, which was the last of our voyage, we had been joined by a new passenger, a young man who had embarked the previous day in Port Said. This young man . . . are you listening? Have you ever paid attention to the faces of some of our predatory Jews who haunt the cities of the Orient . . . I mean those cocky, energetic, wolfish ones with their oily black hair and their sharp little mustaches that curl up at the edges? Have you noticed how they prowl when they walk, as though stalking prey? I tell you, I can spot at a glance which of them are merely pickpockets and sharks, and which also deal in human flesh— and as soon as the person in question boarded the ship (I assure you, an agreeable, pleasant fellow to look at!) and ran his eyes softly over the oldest daughter of the family, I knew in exactly which category to place him . . .

"That whole oppressive night this newcomer kept reminding me of an episode that had taken place the day before. What was so oppressive about it? Well, you see, it was . . . or rather, I should say . . . yes, I remember: in Port Said the deck space was filled by groups of Egyptian pilgrims on their way to Mecca, so that there was not even room to sit anymore, let alone lie down. There was a tension in the air, yet together with it an odd feeling, a kind of carefreeness . . . what? Ah yes, the episode! Wait a bit and I'll tell you all about it.

"It happened in Alexandria. That was as far as our ship went. From there we had to take the train to Port Said, where we would board another steamer for Jaffa that belonged to the same line.

"It was dawn when we arrived in Alexandria. Arabs in long gowns that looked like dresses assailed us on shore and begged, practically threatened us, to let them carry our bags. But why bother telling you all this? You've traveled the same route and seen it all too. To make a long story short, then, we were standing there confusedly, uncertain how to proceed in this strange, primitive, deafening place, when we were approached by a Jew with a limp who warned us not to give our bags to any Arabs, as the price they would demand from us in the end would be more than the worth of the luggage itself.

" 'You can trust what he says!' said another, assertive voice that belonged to a younger person, who according to the cap he wore on his head was a bellboy at some hotel. 'You have to watch out for swindlers everywhere here, but this man is absolutely dependable.' He pointed at the lame Jew. 'Did you say you were bound for Palestine? You must be Zionists then. Lots of people are headed there these days. I'm a Zionist too, that makes us brothers. Here, I can show you letters . . . but tell me, what's new in Russia?'

"I hardly need tell you that that was all we needed to hear. At once I, by now the family's adopted father, felt a surge of affection for this new brother and permitted the lame Jew to order an Arab to load our luggage into his wagon and bring it to the train station. We ourselves proceeded on foot through the streets of Alexandria, which were as filthy as only the streets of an Arab city can be, staring at the nargilleh smokers in the cafes, at the veiled women with their shawls, nose rings, and breathing tubes, and at all the rest of that Oriental clutter. Near the railway station the lame man caught up with us and asked us for half-a-franc apiece, that is, for four francs all in all—'which includes the customs tax that I've already paid for you.' Unlike the woman—my head was spinning from the journey and lack of sleep, which had apparently robbed me of all powers of resistance—I did not think the price unreasonable. True, the Jew had paid the Arab driver only a quarter-of-a-franc for his services—but had we had to carry our own bags we might have missed the train connection, and consequently the ship in Port Said, which sailed toward evening. All that we needed was to have to wait a week in Port Said for it to return! Whereas now, though we were four francs poorer, we had at least arrived in time . . . in fact, there was still half-an-hour until the train was scheduled to leave. We could thank our lucky stars for that.

" 'Do you know what the tickets to Port Said cost?' asked the man.

" 'As soon as the ticket office opens, we'll find out.'

" 'I hope you'll be able to fight your way through the crowd. You do have Egyptian money, don't you?'

" 'No. Only Austrian.'

" 'But it is at least gold?'

" 'No.' Our faces fell. 'Silver.'

" 'What do you propose to do then? You'll have to change it for gold. Look, here comes your Zionist, why don't you ask him. Perhaps he can offer some advice.'

" 'Our Zionist,' that is, the bellhop, seemed surprised to see us. As far as our plight was concerned, however, he would be only too glad to help. If we gave him the money, he would even purchase the tickets himself. How many of them did we say we needed: eight?

"By now the ticket office had opened and was besieged by a throng of people, some wishing to board the next train, some later ones, who stood on each other's feet and even shoulders. Without counting the money that I gave him—all told, some sixty or seventy Austrian crowns—our benefactor quickly took it and headed for the ticket window. Prompted by the woman, I followed closely behind. While we waited he began to perform some complicated calculation in Egyptian money that turned into such a confusion of pounds, guineas, and piastres that my tired brain could not possibly absorb it, while continuing at the same time to warn me of the danger of swindlers and showing me a letter from Cairo that was, he claimed, an invitation to speak before the Zionist association there . . . only this letter, when I read it, turned out to be another sort of document entirely, sent to somebody else three years before! I could feel my heart sink and my knees begin to shake, but I forbad myself to lose faith in the man—who for his part now developed such confidence that he began to tell me about a trip he had once taken with Herzl to Uganda . . .

" 'But how can that be?' I asked. 'Since when was Herzl ever in Uganda?'

" 'Believe me,' he insisted, 'he was there.'

"We were already close to the black ticket seller. Everyone was pushing and shoving, but the bellhop somehow managed to elbow them all out of the way (including the apprentice emissary from Safed, who was himself engaged in a fracas with some Egyptian women), and began to talk through the window in French. '*La course . . . la course . . .*' I could hear him say. Yet the ticket seller for some reason handed the money back to him, so that, making an annoyed face, he said:

" 'I'm afraid we'll have to run and change it.'

"Perhaps it was a display of pan-Semitic goodwill on the ticket seller's part that he now pointed at the bellhop and said in English to the emissary, who stood in line behind us, *'No good'*—but there was no time for me to digest all this, because I was already running after our Zionist as fast as I could. The Russian woman's sister, seeing me run, began to run on her clumsy legs too. The woman herself began to scream . . . by which point, however, the bellhop was already in the streets of the town with me hot on his heels in pursuit. The strangest part of it was that even now my addled brain refused to admit that our money was actually in danger! As swift as a leopard he bounded up the steps of banks, none of which seemed able to help him, ran back down them again, and cut across streets and alleyways, while I followed him with the last of my strength, for I was on the brink of exhaustion and a good deal weaker than he. In the corridor of one bank—it seemed to surface from nowhere like an underground creature's—I caught sight of the profile of that same young man who was later to join us on the ship from Port Said.

Suddenly the bellhop stopped running.

" 'Keep going!' I said. 'We'll miss our train!'

" 'Don't worry,' he answered. 'I promise you that you won't.'

And indeed just then he found a moneychanger to perform the necessary transaction. I took what he gave me without question and off we sped. 'We've got only a few minutes!' he urged me. I flew back toward the train station through the bizarre streets of Alexandria as fast as my legs could carry me. My shirt stuck to my sweaty skin; I doubt if I would have found my way back at all if the woman's sister, now accompanied by that same young man from the bank, who had already managed to attach himself to her as yet another guardian angel, had not spotted me on a street corner.

" 'Hurry! Hurry! Only ten minutes to go!'

"The ticket seller now informed me, however, that the money I had received from the moneychanger was twenty-one-and-a-half francs short of the sum needed to buy the eight tickets.

" 'What?' I protested, waving my arms. 'I was told in so many words that I would even get change in return!'

"The ticket seller waved his arms back. 'I told you the man was no good.'

"When I finally held the tickets in my hand, the family and its bundles were still spread all over the waiting room of the station. Good lord, only five minutes left! They were not minutes for weak hearts, believe me. But the crowning touch was that just as the train was about to depart, our offended Zionist stuck his head into the car. How could we have run out on him like this without even paying him for his pains?

" 'Haven't you cheated us enough?' I asked. I honestly could not understand him.

" 'What?!" And he launched into a harangue on Egyptian currency rates, all the time swearing with an injured expression that he hadn't taken a penny for himself. If we were determined to exploit him, however, he was helpless to prevent it.

" 'Thief! Chiseler! Crook!' screamed the woman.

" 'Listen to her! That's what comes of doing favors for Jews.'

"The train began to move. He leaped from the car and vanished.

"I made up the loss from my own pocket, of course—but it wasn't it that grieved me. I gritted my teeth with a feeling of impotence. There was a dry, bad taste in my mouth. When the children began to munch their stale bread I had to turn my face to the window. The sun beat down outside. It was summer in the month of January. Egypt . . . Egypt and Canaan . . . Sheaves were being gathered in the fields . . . 'And lo, my sheaf arose and stood upright, and your sheaves gathered round it and bowed down to my sheaf' . . . Cairo!"

6.

"In Cairo—where you had to change trains by means of various strange and endless under- and overpasses while so many porters clung to you at once and begged to be given your bags that you were forced to shake them off like flies, crying 'No, no, no!' all the time until you were hoarse in the throat—I caught sight of that underground creature again. I, carrying five packages and two small girls, and their mother, who with the rest of the family and the bundles was not far behind me, were trying to find our train. Which of the many around us was the right one? There seemed to be no one whom one could possibly ask . . . when suddenly we heard a voice politely declare—and in Yiddish:

" 'Not that one! The one on that track over there.'

"Like a true gentleman he helped the woman's sister into the car, where she found seats for us all; then he rose and excused himself, saying that he had business elsewhere in another part of the train. Were we aware, by the way, that he had been with us since Alexandria? He had spent several weeks there. Originally he was from Buenos Aires . . .

did we know that in Spanish the words meant . . . *what?* Someone had tried to rob us? You couldn't be too careful of such people. On the other hand, there was no certainty that it was a deliberate swindle. Currencies in Egypt were a nightmare and the difference between silver and gold was indeed great. What did we propose to do, though, in Port Said?

" 'What do you mean, do? Our tickets are good for Jaffa.'

"He knew that. But Port Said was not exactly a port. You had to be rowed out to the ship in lighters, for which the Arabs fleeced you but good. For us and our belongings they would probably ask three francs apiece, perhaps even four. He himself had already suggested to the young lady . . . who hadn't objected . . . if we wished, he would be happy to be of service. He would take only twelve—no, ten francs—for the lot of us. This wasn't his first trip and he had connections . . . was it agreed? He would even include in the price the cost of bringing our things from the train station to the shore.

" 'No thank you!' I interrupted him in a fury as soon as I heard the word 'shore.'

" 'No is no . . . but I'm afraid you'll regret it . . .'

"The prospect was not encouraging. Worse yet, the fear crossed my mind that perhaps our ship had already sailed . . . in which case we were lost. Yet in the depths of my despair I made up my mind to trust no one any further, and upon our arrival in Port Said to carry our bags to the ship by ourselves. Of course Port Said had a port—why should anyone need lighters? As for missing the boat, either we did or we didn't . . . if only the children would stop crying . . .

"But why bore you, old man, with my psychology? Port Said had no port after all, and one did need lighters to get to the ship, to say nothing of the distance from the train station to the shore, which was no small trek . . . in the middle of which—are you ready for a fairy tale?—we encountered a man whose name I never learned (I imagine he can still be found there), a hotel employee too, who exclaimed that it was beyond him how anyone with God in his heart could pass us by and not offer to help. At first we didn't believe him either, but he simply grabbed our things . . . yes, grabbed them by force . . . and put them and the children into his hotel cart. 'From poor Jews like yourselves I won't take a penny more than three francs for everything, including the lighters . . .'

"The water was clear and calm, the sun shone down, and it was pleasant to row out in the lighter. The children's spirits revived. Our guide did not leave our side and argued all the way out to the ship with the Arab boatmen, who accused him of taking money from us in order to hold down their wages, while he in turn complained that they had no God in their hearts . . .

"At last he saw us safely aboard ship—and then, once and for all to silence the Arabs, who still insisted that he was secretly in our pay, he reached into his pocket and paid the three francs himself. An improbable story? I told you it was. But nonetheless true. Perhaps he was doing penance for something that day . . . who knows . . .

" 'I only wanted to do'—so he said—'my human duty.'

"The woman, for her part, kept repeating over and over:

" 'The man was an angel from heaven . . . an angel from heaven . . .'

"I myself, once I had regained my composure, fetched a bit of water, washed the sweat from my hands and face, peeled myself an orange, took a piece of bread to go with it, and made a brave attempt to eat. (Not that I was hungry, although I hadn't tasted a single thing all day.) Yet with the first bite I took I was overcome with dread all over again at the contrast between the two men whom we had met by accident that day, the dread of the contrast between 'no good' and 'good' . . . No, I don't mean good and evil in relation to me or the effect it had on me, or on that wreck of a woman with her five children who was the symbol of Jewish homelessness and misfortune . . . What I mean is . . . good and evil, and all that they imply, in themselves . . . Good and evil as two different worlds, two essences . . . with an infinite abyss between them. Good lord, how infinite it was! And how tragic human life was, how hard, how hard it was to live!

"The slice of bread stuck in my throat and the tears began to come nonstop. They were hysterical, those tears, yet at the same time quiet and unobtrusive. Some Christian Arabs, on their way to the Holy Sepulchre, stared at me with the knowledge that I was a sufferer in life, and that Allah had not been kind to me . . .

"Simultaneously, the new passenger who had joined us in Cairo was busy telling the Russian woman's sister some ridiculous tale about life in Buenos Aires, followed by another concerning the sultan's harem in Constantinople, to which she listened with mixed fear and delight."

7.

"Where was I? Yes; in the harbor in Jaffa, and in my eccentric mood.

"The peculiar thing about this mood was that it was in a sense the opposite of what is said to happen to people who are on the verge of disaster or even death itself. Before death or disaster, so I've been told, one's whole life passes regretfully before one: if only one had it to live over again, how differently one would live it! Whereas my own state was the contrary: suddenly I was filled with an enormous love for everything that had ever happened to me, with an especially great, perfectly satisfied love for the events of the past several weeks—and with an almost ecstatic sense of expectation for what lay ahead. I was about to land in the promised land, after which nothing else mattered . . . after which everything would take care of itself. It was necessary only to set foot there . . . which I would do today, or at the latest, tomorrow. There was Jaffa in plain sight . . . what joy! On the first- and second-class decks the passengers were already staring through their binoculars at the majestic veil of gray haze that hung over the mountains of Judea in the distance.

"Incidentally, I forgot to mention that I myself was not planning to disembark in Jaffa at all. On the advice of a friend from New York, who had been here some three years before, I had decided to spend time first in the Galilee, and only later in Judea, and so had bought a ticket for Beirut . . . none of which prevented me, however, from experiencing all the emotions that would have been appropriate had I been about to land now.

" 'It seems strange that we should have come all this way together and now must leave ship separately,' said the Russian woman's oldest daughter to me with all the intimacy of an eleven-year-old child. How endearing her Lithuanian accent had become to me with its confusion of "sh" and "s"! To this day I am sure that if my desire to take her in my arms, to hold her there and kiss her a thousand times, had not been so powerful, and—so it seemed to me—so obvious at the time, I would have gone ahead and done it. But my blood was on fire . . . and so I slaked my thirst by patting the cheek of her nine-year-old sister instead. Life is sometimes like that, you know. The other three girls, starting with the one who had told me on the train that she was from 'Yondon,' were eight, seven, and six years old respectively. The woman had been a widow for exactly five years!

" 'Wait, it's far from certain that our ship will be allowed to dock in Jaffa,' cautioned the rabbinical emissary, who—in spite of his long ear curls, his even longer black gown, and the round fur hat of extreme Orthodoxy on his head—had gotten to know us well enough to lay aside his monkish exterior and reveal himself as a jolly fellow who spent hours gossiping with the women and grew so friendly with the traveler from Buenos Aires that he even traded dirty jokes with him.

" 'Nonsense,' said the Argentinian. 'It's true that the port in Jaffa is rocky and can't be safely entered in a storm—but the sea is calm today. If you want to worry, you'd do better to worry about the fact that our Russian passengers don't have an entry visa.'

" 'But why,' inquired the emissary, 'should I worry about that?'

" 'Why? Surely you're not so foolish as they to believe the rumor that no papers are necessary at all anymore, neither a *tazkara* nor—'

" 'But I myself am a Turkish subject!' declared the astonished apprentice fund-raiser. 'What is there for me to fear?'

"And while talking he reached a hand into his pocket and brought out some documents to prove his point.

"The Russian woman rushed agitatedly over to me. Did I hear what they were saying? She would not be allowed to land . . .

"In the meantime we were requested to assemble for a medical inspection. The devil knew what it was for—some sort of quarantine perhaps, or other new rule . . .

" 'Oh my God,' shuddered the woman. 'What will happen when they see my eyes?'

"The inspection, however, turned out to be a lark. The whole business was carried out so comically, with such a disregard for the most elementary appearances, and seemed such a mockery of proper official procedure (the doctor, who had been up all night playing cards, was too lazy even to walk the entire length of the line and contented himself with a cursory glance at three or four of the hundreds of passengers before quickly returning to his cabin) that hopes could not fail to be aroused that Turkish landing regulations were equally uncomplicated.

"So that when the entire family had descended into a lighter that carried them toward shore until their last shouted farewell could no longer be heard and I was left by myself on deck with sunbeams glancing all around me off the eternally breaking waves (I won't deny what's true!) and Jaffa beckoning in the distance (and how pretty it can be from a distance!), its rooftops climbing and falling like the steps of some great parapet, I felt—I swear to you I did!—whisperings of glory in my heart. How could it even have occurred to me that they might not be allowed off the ship, that Jews might possibly be turned away from the land of Judea? I don't mean to say of course that I wasn't perfectly aware even then of all the painful falsehood in this cliché (what on earth do we and the land of Judea really have to do with each other?) . . . but I was happy, I was wrapped in the gossamer threads of a dream the likes of which have never touched me a second time before or since . . . And I was forced to acknowledge once again that ancient truth that even though one 'knows' that all things are equally unimportant and ultimately even the same, one cannot, as long as one lives and breathes, ignore the differences between one man and another, one place and another, one life and another, and one human condition and another . . . and that despite my intellectual awareness, I could not help feeling different emotions at different times that might be worlds apart from each other, that might sometimes be of the simplest, most humanly universal variety, and at others of the most mysteriously bizarre . . . because I tell you, there *are* mysterious combinations of circumstances in this life, my friend . . ."

A bareheaded adolescent girl stepped out of one of the houses in the colony and crossed the narrow street, humming to a popular Arab melody the words of a Hebrew "folk song" written by a poet in Europe:

> *Pretty golden bird, fly far away*
> *Find me a husband for my wedding day.*

From a courtyard opposite a voice that could have been either a man's or a woman's shouted in a mixture of Arabic and Yiddish through the night air: *"Rukh, rukh min hon! S'tezikh tsugetsheppet?"* The little colony's large synagogue looked down on us with its broad but dark windows. Beneath them some local citizens stood discussing their affairs. "It's time I fired Ahmed," one of them said. "I've never seen such a thief in my life." This sentiment followed us until we neared a ditch by the side of the street from which suddenly appeared the silhouettes of two young pioneers, one dressed in a costume of dark cloth, the other wearing a blouse, torn linen pants, and no shoes. From somewhere came the words, "Innkeeper, here's seven piastres," from the ditch the refrain of a comic song about two Zionists. The notes quivered until interrupted by a soft Polish-Jewish voice that said: "Tomorrow it will be exactly four months since I arrived in this country." "And how many months will it be since you've been out of work?" laughed a second voice that was Russian by its accent and that, we now saw, belonged to the pioneer of radical mien, who appeared to be enjoying his own joke immensely.

The evening was still not through.

8.

Nor was my friend's story.

His happiness lasted for all of two hours.

At any rate, no more than that.

"When the lighters returned, the woman and her five children were in one of them. The boatmen, annoyed at having to row them back again, angrily threw their belongings, which by now were soaking wet, over the deck. All five girls began to cry out loud. The woman lashed out at them savagely and said nothing. It was too awful for words.

"Worse yet: the woman's sister had already entered the country! She too had no papers of course, but the traveler from Buenos Aires had somehow managed to get her safely through—and it had all happened so quickly, and the customs house had been in such an uproar, that they had not remembered until it was too late that their purse with all their money was in her possession. Now she, the mother, was left without a cent. Her sister was ashore and she had been brought back in the lighter. A pretty predicament!

"What now? What could she possibly do? Where was she going to go?

"The sky had fallen on her. The ship gave a lurch and set sail for Haifa. Soon the first mate would come by to check our tickets. As far as Haifa there was no problem, I would pay for their fare myself . . . but what would happen then?

"The first mate passed by without noticing them. Perhaps he felt sorry for them. Was there another piece of bread somewhere? All morning long I had been too excited to eat; now I had to swallow something to keep up my strength, to prepare for new tribulations; only once more the bread stuck in my throat—I could neither get it down nor spit it out.

" 'There were Jews standing there, Jews,' the woman began to lament once her own silence had grown tiresome to her, 'and not one of them had any pity. Not one. All they wanted to know was why did I get off at Jaffa, why didn't I get off at Haifa. I wish I had never heard of either Jaffa or Haifa!'

"And turning to the girls:

" 'If you don't shut up this minute I'll throw you all into the sea!'

"The apprentice emissary tried to calm her. It was a woman's way to scream, but really there was nothing to scream about. He too was getting off in Haifa, from there he would travel to Safed. And in Haifa he had a brother, a hotel owner, who would no doubt come to meet the ship. This brother was a Turkish subject too and would certainly be glad to come to her aid. In general it was, as far as he knew, far easier to land in Haifa than in Jaffa. In this respect the Jews who asked her why she hadn't disembarked in Haifa were right, their mistake being that they hadn't realized that she was coming via Trieste. They must have thought she had sailed on a ship from Russia, which would have docked at Beirut first, then Haifa, then Jaffa. But now all would be all right. If only she promised not to scream, he, the apprentice emissary, would do his best to help. If by any chance she had a little to money to give him . . . that is, she would give it to him and he would give it to the official at customs, who would understand exactly what it was for. Five francs per person should be enough, perhaps even one napoleon for all of them. Yes, one gold napoleon, or better yet, two halves would do the trick. With it in his palm that Turk wouldn't know up from down . . .

" 'A napoleon? How much is that? Ten francs?' wailed the woman. 'I haven't got a single sou. Even if they do let me land in Haifa . . . in Jaffa I could find my sister . . . but in Haifa . . . my children and I will starve to death . . .'

" 'There, there,' I said. 'Once we're in Haifa we'll find some way to help you.'

"I had left some twenty-five francs and a few sous, which I immediately handed to the emissary in order to work what magic he could with them.

" 'A napoleon is enough!' he said.

"So in the end I gave the remaining five francs to the woman 'for a rainy day,' and kept the leftover sous for myself. My eleven-year-old darling took her frozen hands out of the sleeves in which she had been keeping them and threw me a special look. She stuck her hands back into her sleeves, but that look gave me strength, gave me strength . . . so that again, for all the hopelessness of the situation, for all its radical sorrow, it seemed to me that it was definitely worth living and that there were things worth living for . . . Yes, that it was actually pleasant to be alive. This phantasmal notion came and went in a moment, but as long as that moment lasted it made sense. It too of course could not have withstood the scalpel of the intellect, that icicle of the consciousness of reality as it is, not to mention the nothingness that comes after as it is . . . Yet at that moment I wanted to cry out with all my being: Yes! Yes! Yes!"

9.

"You're not tired of listening? The fact is that there's not much left for me to tell you. To describe to you the emotions with which we boarded the lighters in Haifa and began our short trip to the shore . . . for that I have neither the inclination nor the skill. We felt like a man jumping straight into the ocean as we descended the ramp of the ship. (Yes, I too disembarked in Haifa in the end, since to Beirut was another night's voyage, which was by now beyond my powers of endurance—and besides, I wanted to see what happened to my family.) Soon our fate would be sealed: either the official in charge would accept our baksheesh and allow us into the town or he wouldn't . . . ah, the promised land! The promised land! How precious it seemed just then.

"Because of the swarm of passengers the woman's five children were separated at the last moment into two different lighters. I sat in the first of them with the two oldest daughters, while she and the younger ones followed at a considerable distance behind us.

"We neared the shore. I could see Jews standing there, on dry land . . . how lucky they were to be there already, to have that legal right. What more in life could be desired?

"A tumult of shouts reached my ears. My heart was in my throat. What now?

" 'Relax, Jews, relax!' a heavyset, butcherlike Jew with a flaxen beard and a Turkish fez on his head cried out to us from the shore. 'There's free entry here.'

"I couldn't believe my ears.

" 'Free?' The apprentice emissary, who was the first to leap ashore from the lighter, winked at the bearer of good tidings. 'But that's impossible . . .'

"He and his brother were so busy exchanging winks that they forgot to kiss each other.

"I followed behind him with the two children at my side. In the second lighter, which was still far out in the bay, I could make out their mother's terrified eyes. No doubt the nightmarish thought had occurred to her that the incident with her sister might repeat itself, that I and the two girls would bribe our way past customs and that she would again be left behind . . .

" 'Mama, Mama!' shouted the eleven-year-old with all her strength. 'Don't worry! Here no one gets sent back!'

"The heavyset Jew grabbed our things. 'It's settled then. You'll be staying at my hotel.'

"And in my ear he whispered:

" 'A slight misunderstanding. It's not completely free. You'll need a visa. I'll explain it all later . . .'

"The apprentice emissary had already disappeared.

" 'Did they take money from you?' The Jew who rushed up to me now appeared to be Rumanian and was, I soon learned, a hotelkeeper too. 'Those vampires! Entry is totally free here, it doesn't cost a thing. I wouldn't advise you to go with him, he'll make you pay through the nose . . . but what is the matter with you, young man?'

"My tears now were no longer the half-hidden, intermittent ones that I had shed in Port Said over the abrupt transition from our unmitigated bad luck to the fairy-tale goodness of that miraculous Jew. I simply felt empty inside, weak in all my limbs; my head was about to split in two and there was a terrible scream in the back of my mouth. I saw the Russian woman with her children drawing nearer to shore with an insane look of excitement on her face, coupled with the refusal to believe that she was actually safe; I saw Jews, who looked much the same as Jews elsewhere, standing on the soil of the Holy Land, the land I had dreamed of since I was a boy; I saw the pure blue waters of the bay as they rose, fell, broke from faraway worlds upon this promised shore . . . this shore that made me think of the Jew in London who had come to that other shore, and of his 'daughter' who had landed in Jaffa with the man with the little, curled mustache . . . It was too much for me, it churned in my guts and flooded my face with hot, gasping tears . . . ah ah ah ah ah!

" 'They didn't allow us to land in Jaffa!' panted the happy woman, reciting her adventures to the Jews gathered around her.

" 'Here they allow and in Jaffa they don't?' asked one of the bystanders. 'The law should be the same everywhere.'

" '*Terkele shiksa,*' said the Jew with the flaxen beard.

" 'But look how this young man can't stop crying!' said the second hotelkeeper, half marveling at me, half making fun. 'Ai, ai, ai!' he mimicked. 'Fool, what is there to cry about?'

"I suppose the way I must have looked just then more than justified his addressing me in such affectionate terms.

" 'Oy,' I whimpered like a naughty child in front of them. 'We're in Palestine.'

" 'So much the better then, why cry?' persisted the hotelkeeper.

"The bystanders broke into smiles. 'He's crying for joy . . . for joy that he's here . . .'

" 'He cries easily,' sniffed the woman with a shake of her head. A last drop hung from the tip of her nose; all else appeared already to have evaporated, and she was once again the person she had always been.

"I wiped away my own tears . . . why attempt to deny it? A warm trickle of happiness filtered through me as I looked now at my little friend, who refused to budge from my side, now at the shore. And each time I looked at her—who knew what lay in store for her?—I understood again what I had already realized that morning, that is . . . that as long as we are alive . . . whatever happens to us does make a difference, it does . . . and that the unbridgeable abyss between the two men we had encountered the day before in Alexandria and Port Said was present also in our two comings ashore: that of the woman's unlucky sister in Jaffa, and that of the child who had landed with me there in Haifa. I tell you, looking at that shore, I understood as though in a vision that—for the time being, anyway—it was the closer of the two . . . closer than the one reached by that middle-aged child in cold London. While as for sheer beauty . . .

"Listen, do you know what I'm going to tell you? Both of us hate all those empty words about beauty that are bandied around us day and night, both of us know that they are meaningless and sometimes even tempt us to deny the existence of beauty altogether. Say what you will, though, I wouldn't know what else to call it . . . it was beautiful then. The great sea was ravishing, and the bay in Haifa doubly so. You see, I really did believe in beauty then . . . in the beauty of nature . . . of the cosmos . . . of something even higher than that. But of course that too was only nerves!"

10.

The dark alleyway beyond the synagogue, through which we at last headed home, was deserted; no one besides us was out-of-doors anymore. The moon had dropped down the other side of the sky until its sickle shape lost its tint of frozen smoke and shone again with a golden brilliance. Soon, however, it disappeared behind a patch of cloud wafted by the light, steady land breeze, and was gone.

Despite my companion's poor health and recurrent difficulties with both his booted and his bootless foot, we had continued to stroll that night through the colony's few, silent streets—but regarding the characters in his story, and the fate of the family once it was safely ashore, I could not get him to say another word. Perhaps he himself had no further knowledge of them; perhaps—though why hide it from me?— he had parted from them that very day. In any case, our conversation passed on to other things, which we discussed with much feeling too.

Yet when we finally returned to our inn, which belonged to a local citrus grower who was by no means poorly off, my friend's malaria began to act up again, and he lay down fully clothed and soon fell asleep.

"He doesn't eat much and he certainly doesn't have much to say," complained the innkeeper to me about him after he had apparently dozed off, "but we're up half the night because of him. He keeps crying out in his sleep . . . I suppose he has bad dreams, eh? It must be the malaria . . . and to think that people like him want to be pioneers . . . and gripe that us farmers don't give them work!"

"Malaria?" knowingly asked the man's oldest son, the one who was about to set out for his uncle in Chicago. "Quinine and castor oil, that's the ticket!"

While the innkeeper's wife set the supper table the talk went from malaria to other current diseases. Some neighbors dropped in to chat and changed the subject to the opening of new shops and the question of bank credit, which they protested went only to those who did not really need it. It was nearly nine o'clock. The innkeeper's daughter, who was finishing the last grade of the local school, sat studying French beyond the oilcloth at the far end of the table. They talked, yawned, drank coffee, and ate pickled herring just as they always had done.

THE
VENGEANCE
OF THE
FATHERS

BY YITZHAK SHAMI

translated by Richard Flantz*

---

* *I would like to express my indebtedness to Professor Gershon Shaked for access to his notes and introduction; to Professor Ezra Spicehandler for looking over the manuscript of the translation; and to Dr. Sasson Somekh for some hints on Arabic forms in this book.*

R. F.

CHAPTER ONE

SINCE OLDEN TIMES, with the blossoming of spring, the *Mo'ssam* [1] has been celebrated in the hill-country of Samaria.

During this season the *fellaheen* [2] are able to stop work for several weeks. The winter labors are done and the grain is now green and tall and can grow by itself, nourished only by the gentle spring breezes. May Nebi Moussa, whose season this is, protect it from hail or *khamseen*. [3] True, it's time to start plowing and sowing for summer crops, and the few fig trees scattered around the ridges need hoeing and weeding, and the olive trees seem to cry out: "Free us from these bonds of earth you heaped around our trunks at the beginning of winter to protect us from the frost. You all wearied of your sheepskins and now wear them inside out, while we stifle here in the heat!" But all this work is not pressing and can be postponed, the last rain will be soon enough, and Nebi Youssef who is buried in Nablus—the peace of Allah be with him —presides over the last rain and its fertility and blessing. It will be worthwhile to visit his tomb, light a candle, and chant the Friday prayers in his mosque when his holy flag is carried out to be taken to the *Mo'ssam*.

Only the frivolous—the curse of Allah upon them!—the young renegades who live in the *Sahal*, [4] near the Jewish settlements, where they work as hired hands—only they have begun to reject the old tradition

---

[1] The festival of pilgrimage to the tomb of Nebi Moussa (the Prophet Moses).
[2] Peasants.
[3] Hot east wind bringing a heat wave lasting up to a week.
[4] The coastal plain.

and to scoff at the sanctity of this pilgrimage. True, they may follow the *Sanjak*,[5] as it leaves the shrine, but then they slip away, returning to work the very same day. It is murmured, in the mosques and at the town gates, that they openly deny that the tomb is Nebi Moussa's, and even argue, as the Jews teach, that the Prophet never crossed the Jordan. But who is so foolish as to believe such inanities? There are idiots of all kinds in the world, idolaters and fire-worshippers who deny the mission of the Prophet. Nor are all those who live in Nablus wholly pious. The *effendis*[6] and estate-owners—many of them like their alcohol, and eat in secret on the fast days of the blessed *Ramadhan*.[7] No redemption for such as they—they will pay the penalty. Not all the terrors of hell shall purify them of their defilement . . .

Those of the coastal plain—the Prophet will surely forgive them their errant ways, and not injure the land on their account. They, after all, have a long way to come, and to do double work, to till their own plots as well as the fields and orchards of the Jews. The Jewish *Hawadjas*[8] don't even pick their own legumes: they come to the villages and offer high wages for a day's work, and even give away the gleanings. Any wonder then, that some villagers sell their souls to the devil and neglect the holy day? The *Sahal*-dwellers are shrewd calculators. Sharp, cunning bargainers. For them each day has its price. A full pilgrimage takes at least ten working days. Ten *rials*[9] is a considerable amount of money, not to be thrown away in the streets. And if they don't go they can profit from the Jewish and Christian holy days, Passover and Easter, which fall while most of the *fellaheen* are traveling to distant places. Their womenfolk bring curds, whey, sour cream, eggs, and vegetables to town, sell the spring blessings at a good price, and return home with heavy bundles of coins in their sleeves and bodices. The men pick up the dinars by the handful, stuff them into jars, and bury them deep in the earth. When they have stored away enough, they open them all, pay another wife, divorce one wife and marry another, or even kill an enemy and pay out the blood-money. And finally they also make the pilgrimage to the grave of the Prophet in Mecca,[10] drink the holy and purifying

---

[5] The holy flag.
[6] Officials, or people of high position.
[7] Month of fasting during which eating is prohibited during the daytime.
[8] Masters.
[9] A coin about 20 grams.
[10] The grave of the Prophet Mohammed is in Medina. In Mecca there is the Ka'aba, the holy rock, which pilgrims visit. Such pilgrimages conclude with prostrations at the tomb in Medina.

Zamzam [11] water, don a broad white shawl, and return home, each a perfect *hadj* [12] who has purchased his world for ever.

But the hill-dwellers can confidently leave their homes and meager farms to the children and the old folk, and go off to join the celebrants. A week of little work brings in no earnings. When the work season ends in the hills the *fellah* has little to do. Many loaf around idly even when work is available. In the hills there is no call for working hands, and those who go off looking for work in the nearby town generally don't even earn enough to pay the price of a *pitta* [13] and a night's lodging at a *Khan*. [14] In bad times, when money is scarce and all sorts of creditors and tithe collectors descend on the *fellah*'s neck to suck his very blood and marrow even before his grain is ripe, the best thing is to flee to the hills and hide until the storm passes. The *mukhtars* [15] and the *sheikhs* [16] will know their jobs, and will turn the creditors away with a curt "Go, and return when blessings descend again."

The pilgrimage to the *Mo'ssam* and back involves no great expense, praised be the Creator! Every believer whose heart is whole with Allah and his saints can afford it. If Allah has blessed him with beasts he can delight himself and the rest of his household. There is no lack of fodder for the donkeys and the camels: everything is green everywhere—the edges of the fields beside the fences, and the rocky hillsides, are all covered with grass and thistle, rich, juicy, and fattening. The camels chomp it all up lustily, more nourished by it than by the handfuls of hay or dried beans they had been fed on during the winter. Nor are provisions for people necessary. The blessings are abundant, and the *wakfs* [17] of Nebi Moussa, Nebi Dawoud, and Ibrahim Al-Khalil and of all the other prophets provide for the pilgrims, whether rich or poor. In every town and village through which they pass, the pilgrims find laid out for them troughs and tubs full of rice and curds, colored with saffron and bubbling in boiled butter, food that melts in the mouth. Every grain is separate, like the golden pine nuts with which they are garnished. No-

---

[11] The waters of the Zamzam: the holy spring in Mecca to which healing powers are attributed.

[12] A Moslem who has made the pilgrimage to Mecca.

[13] A flat cake of bread.

[14] Hostelry.

[15] Officials appointed by the authorities.

[16] Elders, respected sages.

[17] Religious foundations, whose revenues maintain the place. Holy to the respective prophets (in this case Moses, David, Abraham).

tables and paupers alike plunge their hands into the mixture, roll it into little balls between their fingers, and eat to satiety. The glutton and the very poor fill their bowls and jars as well, and the greedy, quite shameless, even pour some into the folds of their garments. Whole sheep simmer in huge pots, and anyone who reaches out a hand can get some. True, swearing and blows, quarrels and fistfights, are everyday occurrences beside the fleshpots and water jars, and occasionally conclude in bloodshed and stabbings. For this reason many of the wiser pilgrims forego the free meat and rice, so as to keep away from these lovers of strife. They prefer to reach their destination a day or two earlier or later. But who would be so foolish as to miss out on the pilgrimage because of such trivial annoyances? After all, is it to be expected that such a large host of armed men, many of them young and hot-blooded, could travel together such a long way without stick being raised or dagger being drawn almost of their own accord, out of sheer habit?

Actually they're just big happy children, all excited about making this pilgrimage together and about meeting their brethren from near and far, from Jerusalem and Hebron, from the Negueb and the North and the East. Like children they kick and scratch at each other over nothing, simply in fun and mischief. Mostly it all depends on the leaders of the processions. the flag-masters, who are also the *sheikhs* of the young men. If these show a strong hand, and if their eyes take in everything and hold all their wild and hotheaded young men in tow, if their ears are sharp and can distinguish from afar between fervent song and screams of pain calling for help from kinsmen or neighbors, if they're always ready to spur their horses into a gallop quickly enough to separate the fighters in time—then you may be sure that with the help of God and his prophets the caravan will continue on its way according to plan. The swords will return to their sheaths, the raised stones will be thrown away, the angry eyes will smile again in reconciliation, and the stragglers will catch up with the caravan. The dispersed circles will reunite, enclosing the troublemakers as in iron rings, all feet will step out more forcefully, a mighty song will burst from their mouths, and even the hills around them will respond, carrying the song from man to man in a powerful echo.

The leaders of the young men—if the devil, the enemy of all the faithful believers (may Allah blacken his face!) does not sow the seeds of discord, jealousy, and competition among them—can make the journey much easier. Upon them depend the splendor and glory of the *Mo'ssam*. Their good name will attract or repel streams of pilgrims, and although they are elected by the sons of the most powerful esteemed town families, who can control the flags and the *wakfs*, the *fellaheen* may either recognize their authority and follow their banner or break up into small groups and, like herds without a shepherd, celebrate the feast by themselves.

And since so much responsibility rests on the flag-master, not many are willing to take on this office which, besides headaches and troubles, also involves great expense. The flag-master is expected to supply whatever provisions the pilgrims of his town lack, out of his own pocket. He must also bring to Nebi Moussa gifts which will redound to his honor and that of the flag he bears. From the day the pilgrimage is officially proclaimed, one week before the journey begins, his house must be wide open to the many visitors who come, from dawn to midnight, to congratulate him on his appointment and to consult with him about arrangements for the pilgrimage.

By the banquets and feasts he provides, by his concern and his welcome, the visitors will judge him. If they find him generous, if he succeeds in winning their hearts, they will return his abundance: they will accept his authority and assist him in his task.

In our days it is hard to find devoted nobles who are ready to give their all to the will of Allah and His prophets. Year after year, on Proclamation Day, the young men have to tramp from street to street, from house to house, carrying the flag of Nebi Youssef and singing as they go, in search of a valiant young man who will consent to be their leader. Only after much coaxing, many promises, and much anger do they finally succeed in catching someone.

Nimmer Abu Il-Shawarab was the only man in Nablus who scrupulously observed the customs of the fathers. A courageous and generous man, devoted since childhood to the prophets and the saints, on the upkeep of whose tombs he had spent much gold. The treasurers of the mosques could tell many stories of his generosity and charity. All the young men of Nablus would have responded to his call, despite his hot temper and reputation as a proud, angry man who insisted on obedience and brooked no opposition. His excitability and stubbornness often got him into serious conflicts and unpleasant situations, from which he managed to extricate himself only with the help of police officers who were among his many devoted friends, and of his family's connections with the authorities in Nablus and Jerusalem. Once he knocked a Bedouin *sheikh* off his horse for riding through a street without calling out the customary warnings "Your back . . . Your face . . .

Watch out! . . ." Once he almost broke the ribs of the water-carrier for spilling some water onto his shoes and clothes. And once he had thrown the *cadi*'s [18] white headdress to the ground in public, trampling it with his foot and cursing him and all those who had appointed him *cadi*. Yet despite these traits he was respected by all, and admired for the way he stood up for the deprived, the poor, and the orphaned, and for not currying favor with anyone. It was only because they loved him and wanted to spare him having to spend more than he could afford that the young men passed him by each year in their selection of a flag-master, and informed him of their choice only after the event.

On this Friday morning the young men marched through the Nablus market, singing lustily, with the flag of Nebi Youssef fluttering before them. The procession halted in front of the shop of Hadj Derwish, seller of silks. The flag-bearer stepped out of the circle, ceremoniously approached the shop with measured gait, waved the flag before the entrance several times, extended it and said:

"Together with Allah and Muhammed His Messenger, may your esteemed person carry the banner of Nebi Youssef son of Yakub son of Ibrahim Al-Khalil the Merciful, the glory of the son of Amram!" [19]

Hadj Derwish's face turned pale with alarm. In his bewilderment he stammered out several words. For a long while he continued sitting cross-legged on his rug, holding the mouthpiece of his *narguileh* [20] in his trembling fingers, unable to bring it to his lips. He looked like an animal at bay looking for a means of escape. Finally he recovered a little and rose. A flap of his *abbayeh* [21] overturned the *narguileh*, scattering the red-hot coals. Then he searched for some time among his rolls of silk and drew out a brightly colored kerchief. He bowed to the flag and tied the scarf around the pole as a sign of refusal. Then he turned his face away like a man who has done his duty, lowered his eyes, and became wholly absorbed in gathering up the remains of the charred tobacco.

The flag-bearer, adamant, refused to accept this answer, and waved his flag again. At that moment his arm was seized, and remained raised in the air, motionless. Abu Il-Shawarab had broken through the circle. He grasped the flag, hastily untied the silk kerchief, threw it in Hadj Derwish's face, and yelled:

---

[18] Judge.
[19] Joseph son of Jacob son of Abraham. The son of Amram is Moses.
[20] Water-pipe.
[21] Loose outer garment.

"Shame on such generosity! Go home, my friends! I shall carry your flag! And tonight we feast!"

Abd Al-Razek the Fat, whose legs were as thick and solid as an elephant's and his shoulders as broad as the beam of the olive press he sometimes turned with his donkey, threw his body about so violently that his black *abbayeh* slipped off and fell to the ground. He approached Abu Il-Shawarab, kissed him on both shoulders, pounded him affectionately on the back, and exclaimed loudly:

"May you live long among us, O Abu Il-Shawarab! Blessed are they who do good in this world and the next. By Allah, you are worthy to carry the flag! Thrust forth your arm!"

He clapped powerfully on Nimmer's hand, and all the young men acclaimed the choice. Many heads turned to cheer him, and the roar of their voices and merry hand clapping flooded the street. Arms reached out to him, embracing him and slapping his back and hoisting him up onto the shoulders of the crowd. They refused to let him down, despite his objections and pleas. Singing and carousing they carried him through the street of the leather workers, and then through the street of the confectioners, who filled their hands with sweetmeats and threw them over the heads of the cheering throng. Many of them hurriedly took their pots off the fires, spread a sack over the entrance to their shops, and joined in raucously with the merrymakers. As they advanced they were joined by more participants: *fellaheen* who had come to town for the Friday prayers, Bedouin in town for market day, blind men, children, paupers, and curious idlers. A shepherd who had been driving his lambs to the Friday market herded them all into the first *khan* he came to and ran to catch up with the revelers. When he reached them, he drew out a flute and stuck it in his mouth. His cheeks expanded, and from the reed came a stream of thin, sweet notes, like the chirruping of the first birds at dawn. These flute sounds, when poured out among the hills and waterbeds always made the calves dance and the kids skip over cliffs and stones to gather around the shepherd. Here they had the same effect. Sleeves were rolled up, trouser sashes bound, and soon a long line of dancing men, with hands thrust into their neighbor's belts, were raising their feet in a wild dance.

Abd El-Kadr the potter, whose legs were agile from constant work at his wheel, really showed his mettle this day, and led the dancers. He stamped both feet down with all his might, twisted them around, lifted them both with a sudden leap and a yell, and brought them down to earth again, now landing on his toes and now on his heels. Behind the crowd came the vendor of *suss*,[22] with his large jar of sweet drink tied to his back. With one hand he jangled the copper trays above his head ring, trying to attract the attention of Abu Il-Shawarab who, mounted on the shoulders of Abd Al-Razek, waved a red kerchief above his head to spur on the dancers; with his other hand he opened and closed the tap on his jar, giving out free drinks. With every glass he poured he roared: "To the honor of Sheikh Il-Shawarab and the glorious flag!"

When the burning sun began to send beads of sweat pouring down their faces and backs from dancing the *debka*,[23] in which all the limbs take part, the men began to increase the tempo even more until the dance reached a furious pitch in the square before the mosque. Here they began to disperse, and hurried off to the wells to bathe in preparation for the Friday prayers.

Thus did the young men of Nablus celebrate the election of Abu Il-Shawarab as their *sheikh* and flag-master.

CHAPTER TWO

All that week Nimmer Abu Il-Shawarab was busy day and night with arrangements for the pilgrimage. Visitors streamed to his large house outside the town walls, with the rotting horse's skull stuck over the front gate for luck, and the two huge hands and the seven-pointed candlestick against the evil eye painted on the front wall facing the Jerusalem road. The large empty field beside the house swarmed with people, who bustled and milled about it like busy ants. Coffee sellers, primers of *narguilehs*, wood cutters, water carriers, and barefoot boys carrying hot coals to and fro in response to an incessant stream of calls. Along the three remaining sides, long tents had been pitched, with rugs and carpets spread inside them for guests to sit on. In the middle of the field, two burning oak trunks leaned on each other, spreading smoke and flames in every direction.

Even the adjoining olive grove became a resting place for camels and horses, its fence smashed and its hedge destroyed. *Sheikhs* of distant villages and leaders of the desert Bedouin came on their mounts to

---

[22] A sweet soft drink.
[23] Arab folk dance.

discuss arrangements for a united pilgrimage with the flag-master. They could have said their say and returned to their villages and tribes that same day, but it was not easy to evade the sharp eyes of Abu Il-Shawarab. With him one could not just drink a cup of coffee and then leave. "God forbid you should disgrace me in the eyes of my people," he would scold. "By the Lord of the *Ka'abah* and the heads of the prophets, the pots are all full and the beds are prepared. If you have important business in town that may not be postponed, be it as you say: go in peace and leave your beasts here to assure me of your return. I have ordered my servants to give them water and fodder. Sleep here tonight, and tomorrow—Allah is great! My house is your house, and all you see here is yours!"

Usually he did not manage to finish his speech. His two little sons, all dressed up in their shining new silk caftans and red shoes, would run out of the women's room facing the garden, close the door behind them, and dash across the field as the beaded fringes of their *tarboushes* [1] waved in the air. Finding their father, they tugged at his *abbayeh* and cried:

"*Yaba!* [2] Grandmother says you should come in right away. Many women have come to visit us and they are asking for you."

Abu Il-Shawarab turned warmly to his sons, curled the ends of his long moustache that reached to his ears, and replied, suppressing a smile:

"Tell me, you little bastards, what gifts have the women brought? Curtains? Candles? Neither the one nor the other? All right then . . . Let them wait a little, I'll come soon!"

"No, Father," the boys shouted together, clinging to his arms. "Grandmother says we should bring you back with us."

Abu Il-Shawarab submitted, and walked with them, with slow, dignified steps. He ran his hand over his shaven chin, approached the door, paused for a moment, coughing aloud so that the women inside might hear him and have time to cover their faces. Then he lowered his eyes and went in.

The groups of chattering women sitting in the room suddenly fell silent. Abu Il-Shawarab distinguished at a glance between the women who had come to visit his women as friends and well-wishers, and the needy, who had come because fate had forced them to turn to a man for assistance. The sight of their embarrassed silence softened his fierce

---

[1] Brimless cone-shaped hat, mostly red in color, worn by Arab town dwellers.
[2] Father.

expression. His large black eyes gazed at them with pity. To encourage them to speak, he addressed his old wrinkled mother who had risen to her feet on his entry, waiting anxiously for what he might say. The *tarboush* she wore, with gold coins sewn all over it, gave her the appearance of a man.

"Mother of Nimmer!" he said. "Send a girl to bring *narguilehs* and coffee for our visitors, that they may rest."

His mother hastened to obey his command, but the women held her back and tried to prevent her from going. The eldest among them began speaking all at once, trying at the same time to hide behind her back.

"There is no need! May the lord prolong your days, Abu Il-Shawarab! May your pilgrimage be blessed! By the joy of your sons, *Insh-'allah!* [3] It is not for coffee that we have come . . . That can come later . . . First promise to do what we ask . . . We have come to beg you to do something for us . . ."

Now the women poured out their sorrows at great length. With tears in their eyes they told him of their griefs and sufferings, of the spells and enchantments that had been laid on them by their enemies to make their husbands hate them and their wombs barren, of the evil eye cast on them by their neighbors. For the breaking of spells no prophet is more powerful than Nebi Moussa, peace be with him! Many are the women who by his grace have been saved from the evil designs of malicious rivals, may their eyes rot! . . . The spell must be cast onto the prophet's grave during the morning watch when the cock crows for the third time, and with the aid of God the all-powerful its effect will be totally nullified . . . But the supplicants themselves could not take part in the pilgrimage, their husbands would not allow them to. The husbands were taking their younger wives, may they be cut down in the prime of their lives and may Allah poison their lives as they have poisoned ours! We are to be left locked up at home. But Abu-Nimmer, the flag-master, can be a mouth for us before the prophet, may Allah pray for him! He will not turn us away empty-handed.

Each of them then reached into the bodice of her dress and drew out a small parcel containing a magic charm, which they had found on a threshold, in a hole in the wall or in some other hiding place. With extreme caution, as if handling a dangerous object that was liable to blow up and destroy the whole house, they all handed the bundles to Nimmer's mother, whispering and mumbling all the while, so that she

---

[3] May Allah will it!

might pass them on to her son. Then, with the aid of their teeth they undid the rolls of coins tied in their kerchiefs, and each hesitantly drew out a gleaming silver coin which they also handed to the mother of Nimmer.

"Take this, Abu Il-Shawarab, and remember our errand," the women said to him. "May Allah bless you and keep you and may you never know distress in your house. Spend part of the sum on the gift for Nebi Moussa and the sacrificial camel, and with the remainder buy a large five-pointed candle and light it for us at the prophet's head. Were we not afraid that the additional load would be a burden to you, we would have brought the candles ourselves. Apart from Allah and you there is no one on earth who will have pity on us. Despair and distress have driven us to ask you for aid, O generous one!"

Abu Il-Shawarab listened in silence to every word they spoke, nodding his head and beating on his thigh with his hand. He truly felt their woe, so much so that his eyebrows darkened and he pushed aside the cup of coffee his mother filled for him each time she passed by him. When they had finished, he passed the mouthpiece of the *narguileh* from side to side, and answered in a sorrowful voice:

"Upon my head and upon my eyes . . . Know this: all will be well, *Insh'allah*. Almighty Allah will see your afflictions and will aid you . . . Put your trust in Him and in His prophet . . . I, of course, will carry out your errand as best I can . . . May He bring you complete healing and have mercy upon you and calm your hearts!"

And without looking at them he got up to leave. As he rose he gave the charms to his mother, telling her to put them in the traveling bags. Then he slowly opened the buttons of his vest, drew out a small velvet purse that hung around his neck, hidden in the folds of his gown— baring as he did so a bronzed chest covered with long, bristly black hairs —and calmly dropped all the coins into it; then he opened another purse that was stuck in his broad belt, and in their presence added double the amount out of his own money. Then he turned his broad back toward the door leading to the inner corridor, and left, followed by numerous blessings.

Outside he was already the center of impatient demands. Groups of noisy, angry men, barechested, barefooted, their hairy legs covered with the dust of the roads, were rushing around between the fire and the tents, their angry eyes flittering around in search of Sheikh Abu Il-Shawarab.

These were the donkey- and camel-drivers, just back from the tomb of Nebi Moussa after having brought the wives of the *effendis* and the most esteemed families there. Entering Nablus, they had raised a furor. "People, hear us!" they had cried. "You're all asleep here! And while you sleep the sneaky Hebronites have taken over the entire market square in front of Nebi Moussa's tomb, and there's not even room there for another stall. Even the big *khan*, where our beasts shelter on days of wind and storm, is overflowing with them!"

The streets had burst into an uproar. Like madmen, the street peddlers and vendors and the sellers of drinks and sweets and *pitta* and pastries, all of whom had been hoping to make some profits at the *Mo'ssam*, surrounded the newcomers and dragged them forcibly to the house of Sheikh Il-Shawarab, that they might report to him personally about the abominable and unprecedented shame done to the people of Nablus by the criminals of Hebron.

They jumped about and yelled, gnashed their teeth and waved their arms. Most irate of all was the tall *suss* vendor, who ran about from one group of men to another, his face all excited, spittle running down his chin. He raised his head, with its long black braids which ran down both sides of his face, shook them threateningly at those distant rogues, and screamed:

"Abu Il-Shawarab must get us out of this mess. We have placed our trust in him and now we've missed out, we're too late . . . He's responsible, and he's the one who must make this good. And if he doesn't, we'll take what's coming to us by ourselves! By force! We'll run them out like dogs, we'll cut them apart with our swords!"

Abu Il-Shawarab heard snatches of this tirade. With a firm, calm stride, arms folded behind his back, he approached them and stood among them. He surveyed them, his eyes gleaming with the satisfaction of a commander who can enjoy his troops' mischief and is confident that his slightest gesture will be enough to calm them and bend them to his will.

The voices at first were wild and confused. Although he had already grasped the gist of the matter, Abu Il-Shawarab silenced them with a wave of his hand and invited them to a meeting. He called the main speakers to him and, giving them a place up front, then sat down among them himself. He had placed the *suss* vendor on his right, and now sat with his elbow on the other's knee, as friends do, his ear turned to him as if poised to listen, and then called on the eldest of the group to report everything he had seen.

As he listened, Abu Il-Shawarab expressed his anger and commiseration with frequent shakes of the head and loud exclamations of surprise. Then he took counsel with them about the measures to be taken to thwart the plans of the treacherous Hebronites.

It was finally decided that the vendors and bakers would set out for Nebi Moussa with their wares that very day, to find and make room for those coming after them. In the meantime, Abu Il-Shawarab would go personally to the chief official of the *wakf* and get a written order to the authorities at Nebi Moussa, demanding that the customary quota of space due to the men of Nablus be properly set aside. This order would be sent ahead by a courier from Abu Il-Shawarab's own entourage, in order to forestall violence.

Now everyone was calm again. Even the vendors, who stood to lose most from the alacrity of the Hebronites and had at first questioned the value of turning to Abu Il-Shawarab, now stopped muttering among themselves and gazed at him with expressions of trust and hope, ashamed of their excessive doubting and bitterness. To prove this to him, they quickly drank down the coffee he poured for them and left hurriedly, promising to carry out all his orders to the letter.

He accompanied them to the road leading to the town, again instructing them to avoid unnecessary strife. "Start out peacefully, and be ruled by reason!" he lectured them. "And if that doesn't help, wait until I arrive . . . We set out the dayaftertomorrow, and until then the world won't collapse, and everything will work out for the good, *Insh'allah* . . . He who heeds not the rod of Moses will heed the whip of Pharaoh . . ."[4]

All readily assented, feeling he had spoken justly and to the point. At the crossroads the men dispersed, agreeing to meet at the Jerusalem *khan* before the call to evening prayer. From there they would set out immediately so as to still have light on their way to Ramallah. Only the *suss* vendor stood aside, still dissatisfied. When everyone else had left, he turned to the flag-master and muttered:

"It would have been better, Abu Il-Shawarab, to send a hundred horsemen ahead of them . . . I would have gone with them, to overturn their wares, smash their cheating scales, and cast them out from where they sit. I know these curs . . . they will greet our people like barking dogs, and will mock our elders. You'll see: our people of Nablus will end up sleeping on the ground, children and all, without shelter under the open sky . . ."

Abu Il-Shawarab's face darkened. The creases in his brow deepened,

---

[4] An Arab proverb.

his large eyes narrowed in anger as he studied the vendor from head to toe. His heavy hand was already raised to slap him across the cheek and smash his teeth, but he suddenly changed his mind and restrained himself. Curling his moustache he spoke in a voice that shook with suppressed rage:

"Hurry, fool, and tell the *mukhtars* of all the streets I want to see them. Then get back to your work. The day is hot and people are thirsty. And you too—have a couple of glasses of your drink and cool yourself off a bit . . . Hurry, and say to the *mukhtars:* Abu Il-Shawarab hopes you are in good health. There is a matter he wishes to discuss with you, and he awaits you in the coffeehouse!"

Having spoken, he took a silver coin from his purse and threw it at the *suss* vendor's feet.

The *suss* vendor, feeling he had gone too far, bent down to pick up the coin and thrust it into his wide belt, which had many loops and niches in it for glasses and cups. He bowed his head in submission and hurried off on his errand, the trays hanging from his belt swinging and clanging as he ran.

Sullen and fuming, Abu Il-Shawarab returned home. He stopped by the fire, stirring the coals with a pair of long tongs, while scolding the man boiling the coffee, who sat on his calves like a camel, for not taking proper care of the fire.

As he spoke he felt an evil mood rising within him. Wherever he looked he saw a mess: the whole field was littered with bones and scraps of food, and not one of the servants or visitors had bothered to remove them. Beside the fence lay an old hairless dog, happily munching at a fat bone held between its forepaws, which it gnawed now with one side of its jaw and now with the other. The sight made Abu Il-Shawarab tremble with rage. He felt like killing the dog. Bending down slowly, he picked up a large smooth stone, and threw it straight at its head. It was a death blow. The dog made one big leap, yelped once, and fell, its head hitting the ground. Abu Il-Shawarab turned away in revulsion and remorse, and then stood looking at the sooty lamps that hung from the ropes. Then he started taking them down from their rings and placing them on the ground.

He heard the voice of the *imam*[5] singing out from the nearby mosque, calling the faithful to afternoon prayer. Chanting voices from the tops of distant mosques took up the song. Abu Il-Shawarab shook his head

---

[5] Prayer-chant leader.

in bewilderment, as if waking from a dream, and began walking quickly. Picking up a clay jug from among the water jars, he strode among the tents looking for a clean space to pray in.

Beside the tent where the bedding was kept he stopped. He bent down, jerked violently at a rug, and the entire pile of pillows and blankets arranged on it scattered to the ground, where their many-colored floral designs gleamed in the sunlight. Moving away a little, he spread out the rug, sat down, took off his red shoes, and tucked in the edges of his caftan. Then he rolled his trousers up to his knees, and his broad sleeves up to his shoulders, baring his muscular brown arms. He poured a jet of water on each of his limbs in turn, and the inscriptions tattooed on his arms gleamed blue. He hastily washed his feet with the remaining water in the jug and shouted for a boy to bring him another jar, and did not cool down until the boy had poured its entire contents over his head.

The cold water restored him. When he began his series of prostrations on the rug, he already felt quite calm and at ease.

Concluding his prayers, he ordered the boy to saddle his white stallion. Then, he quickly leaped onto its back, and galloped down the long road leading to the coffeehouse to meet the *mukhtars*, whom he would take to the house of the head of the *wakf* to discuss final arrangements for the pilgrimage.

CHAPTER THREE

The day of the pilgrimage arrived. Mount Ebal and Mount Gerizim lay like huge camels deep in the slumber of dawn beside their burdens, their long necks clinging to their bodies against the morning chill and their heads still hidden in mists and clouds. A shudder of awakening suddenly ruffled their backs, rippled along their thighs, and brought them rushing to their feet.

Long thin fingers of light glinted out from behind the Mount of Curses opposite it.[1] Quivering, they burst through the clouds of fire and magic, cut through the dimness, and differentiated things from each other. On the ridges the scattered houses gleamed white, like snails in crevices of rocks, and daylight rose over the many winding paths that crossed and

---

[1] According to Numbers 11:30, Mount Ebal and Mount Gerizim.

recrossed each other and vanished from sight only to reappear alongside the valley floor.

The entire valley, from Abu Il-Shawarab's house to the square of the mosque of Nebi Youssef, was covered by thin wisps of mist which rose from the many rivulets hiding among the tall bushes and grasses. From afar the valley looked as if it were part of the fertile slopes of Mount Gerizim bejeweled with glittering spring flowers on which pearls of dew trembled in the fresh spring breeze. Now it was filled with many-colored *kefiyehs*,[2] headbands, and *abbayehs*, as masses of heads mingled and separated, covering the ground like swarms of mosquitoes over a river. Their noise and din, their snorting camels, whinnying horses, braying donkeys, and screaming children, filled the air of the valley with a prolonged cacophony. The wind carried the sound in every direction. Like a current of raging water they poured in waves over the hills and slopes, wound around the city from one end to another, knocked up the late risers, dragging them from their warm beds and swallowing them into the flow.

These were pilgrims from more distant places, men of the Galilee, the Jezreel Valley, and Bedouin from Beit-She'an. They made their way among rocks and cliffs to join the main stream of the pilgrimage, which began from the hill country around Nablus. They had come a long way and had a long way to go. Having arrived at the town in the evening to allow their weary beasts to rest, they had slept under the open sky, filling the streets of the town and the empty fields around it. In the morning they began to spread like locusts, in large groups, leaving the places where they had slept and scattering all over the town, some invading the mosques and others filling the coffeehouses. The poorer ones gathered around the baking-stoves and oil presses, gratefully warming themselves by their heat and smoke. Many jostled around the vendors of *pittas* and *sakhlab*.[3] Shivering from the cold, they drew red trembling hands out of their *abbayehs*, curled them around the hot cups, and drank the warmth into their bodies with a whistling sound.

Today, though this was not the general custom, the shops had opened before the shadows left the roofed markets, before the faithful had had a chance to make *istftakh*, the first sale of the day, which determines the day's fortune. Scores of beggars and cripples tramped in their filthy rags from shop to shop, calling for alms; the town beggars stood in silence,

---

[2] Large kerchief with which Arabs cover their heads, held in place by a looped cord.
[3] A kind of hot drink.

swinging censers of incense around the shopkeepers with one hand while with the other hand they stretched out pails to receive in miserable silence whatever was given them, a neckbone and an onion, a dried *pitta* or a moldy piece of bread.

Busiest of all were the gypsies and the poorer Bedouin, thin and shriveled figures with eyes like embers. Beating on drums, jangling the copper rings and green beads hanging from their hoops, they sang of the glories of Nebi Youssef and Nebi Moussa, the heroes of this day, and of the great reward to be earned by all who took part in this pilgrimage. They forced their listeners to pay them generously, and insisted on handsome sums. Anyone who refused was punished on the spot with derisive rhymes composed there and then about his miserliness. Many merchants had been stung before, and now acted cunningly to avoid such trouble. As soon as they heard the singers approaching they hurriedly turned their backs to the street and fell into attitudes of prayer, continuing to prostrate themselves until the singers had gone.

One of these new arrivals, a tall, white-faced man who was as thin as a rooster, had stood since dawn at the main crossroads in the town center, his pointed chin resting on his staff. His gown, a patchwork of many colors, hung over the wreck of his body, beneath which poked his long thin legs. One of his hands was pressed to his breast, and the other was stretched out to passersby. He did not move aside even for loaded camels or galloping horsemen. In a hoarse dry voice he repeated a monotonous chant, beginning over again even before he had finished:

"I beg of Allah . . . and of the delight of Allah . . . and of the possessions of Allah . . . and of the generosity of Allah . . . I have vowed a vow to Allah . . . and to Youssef and to Nebi Moussa beloved of Allah . . . Who will have mercy on a poor sick exhausted man . . . four rials to be blessed by Allah . . . the price of a beast for the pilgrimage to Nebi Moussa the generous one of Allah . . . and the recompense and the payments be upon Allah!"

He solicited no one and at first made no movement. Only his eyebrows, which looked very black underneath his white forehead, moved and trembled nervously each time he was forced to repeat the sad and poignant request.

And suddenly he had a fit. His eyes expanded and turned red and bulged out of their sockets. White spittle flowed from his blue lips, from which fever had taken the redness. In a mad frenzy, he cast off the rag that covered his body and stood there naked, his protruding chest, in which the thin ribs were coiled like springs, rising and falling in rhythm like bellows, his features contorted. In insane fury he tossed his head to and fro at a feverish pace. He raised his voice, cleared his throat, and repeated his cry in terrible and desperate screams.

The onlookers who had gathered around him in a circle stepped back in horror, and then stood there as if rooted to the spot. Soon they were joined by many more passersby, finally blocking all traffic. Those furthest away stood on tiptoe to stare and listen. Hearing him repeat his inordinate request for four rials they shook their shoulders pitifully, calling out "May almighty Allah have mercy upon you and fulfill your request," and moving off, some making a detour to avoid the crowd.

A hunchbacked Egyptian vendor of fodder and beans appeared. He looked like a dressed-up turtle and was known for his wit and his hatred of beggars, whom he chased away wherever they crossed his path. Now, to make fun of this beggar, he filled his hand with beans and hid them in his gown. Then he quietly approached the pauper, making strange movements all the while, like one who is looking for a lost purse that only a moment ago was lying in his lap. Suddenly his face lit up, as if he had found it and with a show of great generosity he handed the beggar a large quantity of beans.

All the onlookers burst out laughing. The wretch who had been tricked threw the beans away from him in disgust, snorted loudly, and started rolling around like a wheel, to the delight of all present.

For some time they cavorted around him. Suddenly there was an outcry, and men began to push and fall on top of each other. The closely packed crowd split open; men who were being shoved and trampled began to curse and swear, clenching their fists and looking around for whoever it was that had started shoving his way, ready to beat him to a pulp. But on recognizing Abu Il-Shawarab, they all drew back, their curse unspoken. Shamed, embarrassed, they retreated before him on all sides.

Curling his moustache, the way he did when he was angry, Abu Il-Shawarab stood there unspeaking in the cleared circle, which grew narrower and narrower as more men pushed closer in their eagerness to see what he would do. His eyes darted about in search of the hunchback, who, realizing in time what would happen to him, sneaked stealthily through the throng and hid behind a wall of backs. When Abu Il-Shawarab saw that he could not find him he shook his head. With slow, heavy steps he approached the beggar, shook him by the shoulder to stop him rolling about, and kissed him on the back of the hand. To ensure that the beggar heard what he had to say to him, he repeated his words several times, in a loud voice:

"May your strength be preserved! And may Allah aid you! Hear this, Father! Allah has opened unto you the gate of salvation!"

Thrusting his hand into his belt, he took out four pieces of silver and pressed them into the beggar's hand.

The pauper suddenly stopped his contortions and snortings. His reason seemed to have returned to him. His maddened eyes stopped rolling about. As he looked straight at the face of the benefactor, his entire soul seemed to be rejoicing. For a moment he stood there in absolute silence. Then he gathered the remains of his strength, as if about to do a great deed. He wiped the spittle from his chin and threw himself to the earth and, lying prostrate, he buried his face in the hem of Abu Il-Shawarab's *abbayeh*, while his trembling hands embraced the flag-master's knees.

Abu Il-Shawarab, deeply moved, whispered:

"Poor man! There is no endurance nor strength save in Allah."

He bent over him, placed his arms around him, and lifted him from the earth like a feather. With his arms still around him, he said:

"Praise Allah, the Blessed and the Supreme, and pray to the Prophet! Now run and find yourself a mount while there is still time. We move off in an hour!" Letting go of him, he straightened up and turned to the onlookers, at whom he roared:

"May your houses be ruined! Why stand here in idleness? Where are my men? Come here! Put this man's coat on for him. Take him from here and see him on his way: one or two of you go and hire him a donkey or a camel, whatever you can find, put him on it and let him have some rest. Look after him well, as I command you—and then catch us up in the square of the mosque."

The onlookers hastened to do his bidding. Many vied with each other for the right to carry out the command. The strong arm of Abu Il-Shawarab separated them. Well pleased now, and smiling broadly, he selected two and put the pauper in their charge. The remainder he sent off to tell the pilgrims in the town to hurry, and to alert those in the more distant streets who had not yet been informed. Only when the entire crowd had dispersed did he too hasten home, to change his clothes, don his weapons, harness his horse, and take his place at their head.

Leaving the central market, he could hear the dull, incessant din that came to his ears like distant thunder bursting against the summits of the surrounding hills. The sounds grew louder and louder. From moment to moment they broke against the stone walls and overflowed on all sides like the waves of a stormy sea. The dim gates and alleys, the domes and the archways, the minarets and yards of the mosques all responded with a prolonged echo that made him tremble.

The voices enveloped him, inflamed his blood and cut into his flesh like the teeth of a saw. He moved quickly through the throngs of children and adults streaming past him on all sides like clouds of dust in a sandstorm, panting, rushing, stumbling, becoming entangled in the skirts of the frayed *abbayehs* of those in front of them, quickly getting up again, thrusting the edges of their caftans into their belts and running on.

Abu Il-Shawarab wanted to reach home by a shortcut on the far side of the road, but was prevented from doing so by the masses of people pressing along it with their donkeys and mules and camels. He pushed through the waves of people moving slowly beside the narrow gate of the town, found a way out of the gate, and was suddenly in the clear. His gaze rested on the mountains and hills and valleys all around, and he stood rooted to the spot in amazement, unable to take his eyes off the many sights that presented themselves to him all at once.

All around the valley, along all the roads and paths leading to the town, streamed hosts of pilgrims from the nearby villages. They flowed toward the square of the mosque, singing joyfully. Flags, gleaming and many-colored, waved and fluttered slowly above their heads, and the blades of drawn swords glinted as they struck against each other in the dance. Men carrying spears and daggers walked slowly backward, facing the drummers, the players of cymbals and lyres, and the dancers, who advanced with short measured steps. Those in the lead turned about in all directions shaking their heads and gesticulating wildly to urge the dancers, the singers, and the players to even greater exertions.

From the hillsides and the rock paths clusters of dervishes and *hadjs* now descended to the main road, over which clouds of dust were rising. They belonged to various sects. Some had come from Shiloh and Levonah, some from Pharoton and Salem, from Horata and Orata. On they came, barefooted ascetes with tangled hair, naked except for a narrow belt covering their loins, men wearing sackcloth, their skins covered with blisters and pockmarks, *hadjs*, in a magical mixture of headgear of all hues; lily-white, olive-green, saffron-orange, and poppy-red. Before them came bearers of implements, carriers of incense-burners, and players, some strumming the one-stringed *rebab*, some blowing crude flutes, their bare feet skipping from crag to crag as they advanced.

As soon as they reached the open space they separated into groups, arranging themselves in circles or columns. Here the spirit suddenly descended on some of them, and they began to prophesy in terrible screams. Like swarms of bees smoked out of their hive they whirled and turned about, flinging their bodies to and fro, throwing themselves to the earth only to bounce up into the air again like balls; they crawled on all fours, stood on their heads, regrouped and again performed their extraordinary feats. Many poked spikes into their cheeks, from one side of the face to the other, or stuck long nails into their nostrils, crunched broken glass between their teeth, and walked barefoot on blades of swords, which they had stuck points upward into the earth for this purpose.

The crowd roared in religious intoxication and excitement, with loud praises of Allah and his Prophet and of those who do His will and perform His miracles upon the earth.

The excited crowd thronged around the group of dervishes who had now formed a circle and were all swaying to and fro, prophesying and gesticulating around their master, Abu Alhidja. Abu Alhidja was mounted on a white horse, with a white sheepskin spread over the saddle and another draped negligently over his back. Two black snakes curled around his arms, their raised heads and forked tongues darting out toward his tangled beard, their alert eyes turned toward his in sparkling fury, while their flat heads and necks swayed to and fro to the rhythm of the flute in his mouth.

The tall figure of Abu Il-Shawarab, which had been advancing slowly, now appeared beside them. From here on he was unable to make further progress. The disciples and admirers of Abu Alhidja filled the entire road from one end to the other. They had stripped themselves naked, their faces were blue, their eyes bulged, their wild and tangled masses of hair mingled with their beards, and blood streamed from their mouths, as they rolled about and repeated in hoarse cries the phrases spoken by their master.

Abu Alhidja gave a signal. In response, all dervishes prostrated themselves on the earth, facedown, shoulder to shoulder. He pulled at the reins, and his horse, froth dripping from its mouth, rose on its hind legs and swayed from side to side without moving from the spot. The rider kicked the horse harshly in the belly and pounded on its head with his fist, and it lowered its head, bent its legs a little, and, like a swimmer diving into the water, flew off like a streak of lightning over the prostrate people, its hooves pounding on their backs.

Abu Alhidja reached the end of the line of backs, pulled up, and shouted a command to his people. They got up as one man, teeth clenched and lips white with pain. Not one of them batted an eyelid. With blanched faces, shaking knees, dizzy heads, and trembling hands they looked around, as if searching for something to hold on to until their strength returned.

The walls of onlookers, who had watched all this with bated breath, now moved forward in terrible waves, like sheep pushed by a storm, and rushed to the dervishes, to kiss their hands and receive their blessing. Abu Il-Shawarab was carried along with them, pushed and shaken, stumbling and recovering, until he reached Abu Alhidja, who had completely lost interest in what was going on around him and was now totally engrossed in his snakes. He patted and caressed them, unrolled them from his arms, and calmly put them into a leather bag hanging around his neck, which he then closed and replaced in his lap.

Abu Il-Shawarab fervently and devoutly kissed the hem of the camel-hair robe of the master of dervishes, bent his head to the other's knee, and asked for a blessing from him. Abu Alhidja recognized the flag-master, leaned over him, and kissed him on the shoulders. The merry eyes in his yellow face twinkled as he whispered:

"May your fortune be great and exalted! *Ma-sha-Allah* [4] . . . There are many pilgrims this year, their numbers are like locusts, may Allah increase them. The flag of the Prophet will fly this year from the highest stair . . ."

And with a sly crease of his eyebrows he added:

"We are already roasted and charred from the sun, yet you have not yet dressed or called out your people. It is time to bring out the holy flag in all its splendor and to set out on our way. Hurry home, complete your arrangements, and return quickly. We shall stop here and await your return."

"Yes, my father!" replied Abu Il-Shawarab. "You speak truly. But the blame for the delay is not ours. The men of Nablus have been waiting since morning at the gate of the mosque, and I too am ready: behold, I return!" With this, he hurried off through the crowd of heads

---

[4] So God has made it!

that had been turned inquisitively to them to overhear their conversation, and which now immediately withdrew to clear a path for him.

It did not take Abu Il-Shawarab a long time to emerge among the horsemen who stood mounted in the olive grove beside his house, waiting for him. He galloped toward them, stooping slightly over the neck of his white stallion. With one hand he straightened the silk *abbayeh* he had just donned in honor of the day, which fanned out in streaming waves down to his new red boots.

As soon as the horsemen saw him they affectionately pounded on their horses' necks, which were raised high in the air, their small ears almost touching their riders' chests. At a prancing trot they rode toward Abu Il-Shawarab and surrounded his white stallion, which was also gaily caparisoned in honor of the day. The stallion seemed to be aware of his own importance and splendor. Proudly raising his head, he shook his ears, as if to show the other horses the red silk scarf tied around his forehead, with roses and carnations braided around it in a wreath. He turned lightly and haughtily to the sides, shaking the red fringes of the saddle blanket which hung over both sides of his belly. He dilated his nostrils, threw up his head, shook his mane, stamped his hooves several times, and waggled his ankles to let the sunlight fall on his horseshoes of polished steel that gleamed like silver.

Abu Il-Shawarab and his escort rode slowly down through the breaks in the high fence which separated the grove from his grounds. Women, their faces half-veiled, leaned out from the windows and the roof of his house and showered sweets and flowers down on them. Without glancing at the women, he turned left and paused for a while beside the row of tents now being dismantled and rolled up by their owners.

The tents came down to the ground one after the other. A shadow passed over his face as he gazed with contempt and anger at these men who were so concerned over their property. Then, lowering his pointed eyes, he slapped his horse and galloped off along the path leading to the main road.

Behind him he heard stifled cries of weeping and prolonged wailing. He stopped, turned his horse's head, and looked back. His two sons were running after him with outstretched arms, weeping and sobbing. They caught up with him and hung on to his stirrups, raised their tear-stained faces to him and pleaded:

"*Yaba!* Take us with you to Nebi Moussa!"

Abu Il-Shawarab bent down to them, moved and bewildered. He picked them up and seated them on his horse's back, in front of him.

Then he took out a kerchief and wiped their eyes and noses, and spoke to them, trying to calm and console them with affectionate words. He gave each of them a coin, kissed them, and prepared to set them down and send them home.

The boys started sobbing and crying again. Abu Il-Shawarab lost patience with them, and angrily slapped the eldest on the cheek. The boy continued weeping and wailing. He was about to hit him again when the rider beside him, who could be clear-minded in this crisis, grabbed his arm and stopped him, saying:

"No! No! Ya Nimmer, leave them be. Thus spoke Ahmed the Bedouin, Allah grace him: 'Let not woman or child weep before you set out on your way.'[5] Let them ride with you a little, as far as the gate of the mosque, at least, to gladden their hearts."

Abu Il-Shawarab remained adamant. The rider raised his head high in the air, replaced his silver sword in its sheath, and tightened the clasp to the handle, making it fast. Then he reached out his hairy arm and without saying a word took the children from their father's arms one after the other, placed the younger one in front of him and the elder behind him on his horse's back, and rode off with his spoils.

All the other horses leapt off after him, only to pause, skittish, at the stretch of water running alongside the road. One of the horses, however, jumped across fearlessly, and then all the others rushed across after him, in haste and confusion, as if ashamed of their needless fear.

The riders lined up in columns, drew their weapons, and waved them above their heads. The blades glinted in the sunlight. The eldest man in the group drew himself up to his full stature, and turned about to look for Abu Il-Shawarab, who in his modesty was riding toward the rear.

The sharp eyes of the elder soon found the flag-master. He wrapped his horse's bridle around his arm, turned the horse around, and rode back through the tightly packed rows of riders. Reaching Abu Il-Shawarab, he cried out:

"Advance, *ya sheikh* Al-Shawarab, and ride at our head! This day is your day, and from now on your word commands us!"

At first Abu Il-Shawarab refused. Not moving from where he sat on his horse, he curled his moustache and said:

"May Allah forgive! There is yet time. When I carry the flag, then will I ride at the head and it will not be held against me as a sin . . .

---

[5] Ahmed the Bedouin was a renowned Egyptian mystic and dervish. His words may be intended to prevent a woman or child putting the evil eye on one setting out on a journey.

There are elder than me among us. Go you and ride at our head. How may I raise my face to you, when you are older than my father?!"

The old man replied:

"Lead us! Allah will forgive you! By the beard of the Prophet, we will not march one step if you are not at your post!"

Abu Il-Shawarab was compelled to accede to his request. He left his position and began moving forward. Drawing his long, sharp-edged sword, he wound his shawl around its handle, whirled it around his head several times, turned this way and that, and proclaimed:

"Hear me, believers and servants of Allah! Prepare for the pilgrimage! Spur on your animals and set out on the road. Long life and peace be with you!"

The riders moved forward, cutting through the milling throngs that swayed and bent and straightened like waves in the open sea. From rooftops and from behind fences women burst out in loud cheering. The air rang with the beating of drums they held under their arms and with the shouts of their songs.

When the road was cleared somewhat of men, groups of women suddenly appeared, with babies on their shoulders, their veils slightly raised, revealing their blue-painted eyelids. They glanced aside suspiciously as they ran, to be sure that no man could see them. Quickly they darted past fences, gardens, and vineyards, climbing through hedges and trampling on fields of grain, running without a pause until they reached the orange orchards surrounding the square of the mosque, which they reached before the riders, who were advancing slowly. There they again lowered their veils, and stood craning their necks. Later arrivals shoved through them, pushing them aside with curses and screams, kicking and elbowing in an attempt to force a way through to the front rows for a good view of all the proceedings.

In the distance Abu Il-Shawarab and his horsemen appeared, and the criers proclaimed their arrival in loud song. The thousands of men and children who had been squatting on the ground, crammed tight up against each other, quickly rose to their feet. Caught up in the excitement of the pilgrimage, they began to sway and rock, knocking into each other, mixing and milling together.

In the center of the square Abu Il-Shawarab gave a signal with his drawn sword—and the drumming and clashing of cymbals ceased. The criers fell silent, and there was a stillness like the calm before a storm. The many flag-bearers hurried into the square from all sides and lined up in columns. Rows of horsemen charged at the crowd with drawn

swords, crying: "Make way! Move! . . . Back! Make way for the glorious flag!"—and people looking for their animals or their relatives
moved back for the moment. All eyes turned in anticipation to the gate
of the mosque.

When the top of the red-gold flag flashed through the dark gate of the
mosque, like a crescent moon bursting through layers of thick cloud, the
crowd burst into applause. Those with musical instruments began to
play, and a cry of rejoicing and cheering burst from the mouths of all
present, so loud that the horses began to panic and scamper. *Sheikhs* and
hadjs and *dervishes* all called out:

"*Allah wakbar! Allah wakbar!*"[6]

The women emitted sharp broken ululations of joy, which were cut
by a quick repetitive knocking of their tongues against their lips. They
threw showers of sweets and raisins down upon the dervishes who, the
veins in their necks standing out blue and contorted, snorted and frothed
as if they were being strangled while they mumbled the prayer of
union.[7]

The name of Abu Il-Shawarab was on every tongue. Lithe as a cat he
leapt off his horse, handed the reins to the rider beside him, and ran
straight ahead to the flag. He lowered his sword, bowed his head, took
the flag from the *imam*, and waved it in the air. The flag unfurled. It was
of black velvet, with a band of gold the width of a finger sewn round
its edges, and passages from the Kor'an embroidered in gold thread on
both its sides. He placed the end of its silver pole into the ring on his
belt that had been specially designed for this purpose. Then, proudly
raising his head, he marched with measured tread toward the other
flag-bearers.

They advanced quickly toward him. At some distance from him they
turned aside, made several circles around his flag and touched it with
theirs, encircling it and crowning it with a wreath of flags, but always
with care that its top remained higher than all the other flags.

The riders crossed swords with a clang, the drummers beat mightily
on their drums, and the rite was over. The circle of flag-bearers broke
up: each of them returned to his own group or sect or village troop,
which meanwhile lined up in readiness to set off, all of them facing the
road to Jerusalem.

---

[6] "God is mighty!"
[7] Perhaps the prayer of the oneness of God: "There is no God but Allah and Mohammed
is his Prophet".

Glowing, radiant, with sunbeams dancing on his sword blade and flag, Abu Il-Shawarab walked quickly toward his horse. As he placed the flagpole into the saddle ring and mounted his steed, the armed men waved their pistols and rifles in the air. A wild burst of shots exploded in the air all at once, accompanied by loud cries of cheering. Then the whole camp moved off, progressing slowly and heavily, through the valley, singing as they went, until they reached the foot of the *'Amud* where, as had been the custom since ancient times, they stopped for some time and burst into a renewed spate of dancing and games in honor of the forty prophets of Israel buried in its folds. From there the procession wound onward, like a huge dragon, among thick sycamores and olive trees which at times hid them from view.

The many spectators who had accompanied them to this last station, though it was not the custom to do so, stood here for a long time to gaze with wonder at this splendid procession, the like of which not even the eldest person present could remember. Many of them slapped their thighs and clapped their hands, nodded their heads up and down, and sang in response to the song of the pilgrims, which reached them from beyond the groves of gray-green olive trees. Only when the echoes died down in the quiet of the hills did the crowd begin to disperse. The shopkeepers and merchants began rushing back to town, wondering how they could have so forgotten themselves as to leave their shops untended all this time; the visitors who had neglected their beasts hurried to the *khans* to feed and water them. Bustling, noisy, all talking at once, they hurried back to town, with many tales of praise about this wondrous and unique pilgrimage.

The only ones who were silent and angry were the young women. On this day they had allowed themselves some laxity with the precepts about covering the face and not raising the voice. The celebration had finished so quickly: the spectacle was over, and they again felt their enslavement. Ahead of them stretched a long line of gray, monotonous working days, with no spark of joy or consolation to illumine them. Again they would have to close themselves up in their homes and continue bearing the yoke; again they would have to suffer in silence at the hands of their rivals and mothers-in-law, to submit to having their every movement watched and used as a pretext for hints and slanderous remarks against them to their husbands, who severely punished any wrong move or error, and beat them for the slightest motion of their eyelids, or for any superfluous dallying by a window or a door.

Sad and dismal, full of apprehension, they made their way back mutely along the sides of the roads. In their anger they kicked and scratched their children, lowered them from their shoulders and made them scurry along behind them. At the town gate they covered themselves properly again, hid the hand drums under their arms, and, dark as outcasts, moved on with a groan, slipping away like shadows into the dark narrow alleys of the town.

CHAPTER FOUR

After two days' march along winding roads, with stops at every village and spring, enthusiastic dancing at every crossroads and at all the tombs of the saints, and a night's sleep under the open sky, the pilgrims reached Jerusalem at dawn, while the star of the shepherds was still twinkling on the horizon. Despite the early hour, and their weariness, they did not enter the city in silence. On reaching the deserted and still-dim road leading to the Damascus Gate, Abu Il-Shawarab rose upright among the riders, who had been riding along without order, and commanded them to line up along the sides of the road, so as not to allow the pilgrims to scatter. Then he alerted the flag-bearers and the musicians. He divided them into groups and placed them in position, and galloped off down the entire procession, spacing it out in an orderly manner, separating those who were too close together, and spurring on the stragglers who had sat down to rest by the roadside, forcing them to their feet and even waving his staff at tired beasts who were advancing with lowered heads, hitting them occasionally to make them move along smartly.

To add to the splendor of the procession and make a greater impression on the Jerusalemites and Hebronites, Abu Il-Shawarab ordered his assistants to take the two expensive carpets—the gift of the people of Nablus to the mosque of Nebi Moussa—out of their wrappings. The men tied the carpets to each other by their fringes and then draped them over either side of the camel that had been selected for the sacrifice. Then Abu Il-Shawarab called to the shepherds, who led forth the cattle and sheep and goats which were to be given as offerings. The horns of these animals were painted crimson. The shepherds brought them along the sides of the road and herded them into the space in front of the riders.

A light breeze blew, the last stars faded, rays of light glinted on the points of the spires and the teeth of the city wall, the lights of the streetlamps on the corners paled, and atop the dome on the Temple Mount there spread a reddish glow.

Filled with the excitement and greatness of the occasion, his head high, Abu Il-Shawarab reappeared on his horse in front of his followers. He turned toward the Valley of the Giants, where they were to meet with the pilgrims from Jerusalem and Hebron. A wave of pride rolled through him as he gazed first at the city before him and then at the milling procession behind him awaiting his command to set out.

Abu Il-Shawarab took hold of the flag and waved it. Immediately the drums, the cymbals, and the flutes burst into clamor.

At the head of the musicians stood a Negro with a goatskin bag from which a pipe protruded. He blew and gurgled through it with all his might, contorting his face, baring his teeth—and began walking forward. The stream of pilgrims moved off after him and burst into the city. The sound of their raucous song could be heard from far off. Windows shook to the noise of their marching feet. Swallows nesting in the crevices of the city wall rose in panic and flew about emitting cries of alarm, sweeping around in circles as if fleeing a storm. For some time they hovered above the heads of the pilgrims, shaking their wings in wonder, and then flew off into the distance.

On both sides of the street doors and gates grated and creaked. The residents of the houses, barefoot or hurriedly shod, pressed out onto the sidewalks which were still wet with dew, some marveling, some yawning, others watching the arrivals with curiosity. Sleepy faces peered out from windows and balconies. They all watched in wonder, for a long time, not moving away until the tail of the procession had left the city on the other side.

The pilgrims moved away quickly from the narrow path and turned left to the wide thorn-covered field, opposite the German Colony on the way to Hebron. The riders had barely managed to put down stakes to tether their horses, and the dancers and singers had hardly found a place to rest awhile among the brambles, when several horsemen appeared at the edge of the valley and sent out a courier to say that they requested a meeting with Sheikh Il-Shawarab. Abu Il-Shawarab remounted his horse, and advanced toward them. Several paces away from them he dismounted. The other horsemen did likewise. With a sweep of their hands they unfurled the *kefiyehs* covering their faces. The men stood looking directly at each other for some time.

The eldest among them drew himself erect and then bent his thin neck before Abu Il-Shawarab. He placed his hands on the other's shoulders, fell upon his neck, and kissed both his shoulders, and then, smiling joyfully, said in a loud voice:

"The blessing has come to us, and a thousand greetings be yours! May your feet be blessed within our bounds. All this land is yours, and all that is upon it—and we have first call on hospitality, we your brothers of Hebron, with Abu Faris at our head. We have been awaiting your arrival since morning . . . Give orders to your people, and set out to greet the flag of our lord Ibrahim, the Friend and the Merciful . . ." [1]

A shadow passed over the face of Abu Il-Shawarab as he heard this, and he replied, curling his moustache upward:

"The flag of Ibrahim the Friend—may Allah pray for it and may manifold peace be upon it! We and you are the guests of Nebi Moussa, may Allah value his generosity! . . . The provisions our people of Nablus are carrying will be enough to provide hospitality for you, and more . . . Our camp and yours are now on the lands of the people of Jerusalem, and neither of us is the first among guests . . . If we have come into your bounds as you say—then it is *your* obligation to come and welcome *us* and greet *our* flag . . ."

The elder turned angrily away, raised the flaps of his *abbayeh*, and prepared to ride off. He cast a penetrating and furious glance at Abu Il-Shawarab, and added:

"Hear this, Nimmer! He who honors others obtains honor . . . Were you noble, nobility would show in your face . . ."

Abu Il-Shawarab did not remain to hear more. He had already turned his horse back toward the inquiring chiefs and dignitaries of his own camp. He rose straight to them. One of his men, seeing him pass and grasping his mood, gave a signal to some others, and they all galloped after him until they reached a many-branched fig tree, whose soft leaves still covered its buds and quivered in the morning breeze. There they stopped and waited with bated breath for the rest of the inner circle.

Abu Il-Shawarab told them all that had happened. The men all shook their heads in amazement, pursing their lips in contempt. Abu Il-Shawarab was furious. His face was flushed and his moustache trembled, and his voice choked as he tried to speak. Finally he folded his arms and said:

---

[1] Ibrahim Al-Khalil—Abraham the Friend (of God). Also a name for the town of Hebron.

"They're puffing themselves up like Ethiopian cocks. They want to shame us . . . We have not even met Abu Faris yet, and he is already trying to exalt himself above us . . . Every dog barks in his own garbage and in the gate of his own yard . . . Our flag will go to greet theirs only when our camel mounts the spire of the mosque, not before. But *you* are the rulers and wisdom and understanding are yours: consider what lies before us, and give your counsel . . ."

Everyone turned expectantly toward old Abu-Zaid. The elder drew himself erect on his horse. Smoothing his pointed beard with his bent bony fingers he spat out:

"The curse of Allah upon the troublemakers . . . Your answer to them was frank and correct and its weight is as gold . . . We are of greater repute and honor than they . . . The smallest shoe among us is worth the price of their heads . . . We must not give in to them in the slightest thing. If they have made light of the respect due to guests, it is our duty not to yield an inch. Go and tell all our people to scatter across the entire valley!"

In a flash all the leaders rode off swiftly toward the rest of the procession and blocked the waves of people pouring across the track toward the sounds of voices coming from the horizon. Galloping backward and forward to the right and to the left, they drove the pilgrims like shepherds assembling their scattered herds, each leader calling his own people to him and then leading them toward the plain. When they were all spread out far across the plain, the order was given for them to stop and rest and refresh themselves with a meal.

The drums were lowered to the ground, the flags were furled, the masses of people sat down and the armed men took off their weapons. Some of them spread their *abbayehs* or sheepskins on the ground to lie on, or folded them under their heads. Others squatted on their heels, or lay on their stomachs, leaning on their elbows. All movement in the camp gradually died down, until it stopped utterly and there was a stillness, like the stillness that comes when night spreads its wings.

Abu Il-Shawarab roamed around on his horse, riding around the plain and observing everything. He told the cooks and their assistants to pour the rice and meat they had cooked that night into pots and basins for serving. He summoned the camel drivers, who made their camels kneel while they opened the saddlesacks they were carrying and gave the horsemen grain for their horses. He moved quickly from group to group, loudly berating those who had still not managed to find a resting place. When all, people and animals alike, were completely engrossed in their eating, their champing teeth sounding like grasshoppers in fields of grain, he rode back to his officers and led them to the large tent that had stood waiting since morning at the end of the plain, with its flaps rolled up.

They all dismounted several paces away from the tent and tied their horses to its pegs. For a long while they stood by the entrance, each trying to persuade the other to accept the honor of being the first to enter. On the carpets and pillows which lined the floor of the tent they all spread out contentedly forming a half-circle, their faces to the camp and their backs to the road. Calmly, serenely, they lit their pipes and lethargically puffed out smoke with half-closed eyes, as if asleep.

Now the procession from Hebron, which had been making its way slowly along the winding valley paths, approached the plain. From the hilltop came an incessant flow of heads of people who, mounting the crest, rose to full stature, only to be pushed down the hillside by the masses of men. Through the clouds of dust spreading around them bobbed the necks and heads of camels, the pack saddles on their backs shaking to and fro like boats upon the waves. Among them swayed the horsemen, the tops of their flags, spears, and lances crossing and recrossing, their polished blades gleaming like a wide wreath of fires. The path down which this crowd now poured seemed to be moving and alive. In the rear came the carriers of implements, beasts of burden and the stragglers, followed by a long line of carriages and carts. As those in the van reached the space where the path met the edge of the plain, they stopped in bewilderment, not knowing whether to turn off onto the plain or to continue along the path.

What had astonished them was the sight of the Nablus camp, which stretched across the plain as far as the eye could see. Not one of the Nablusites made a move to greet them. Some were holding large chunks of meat which they chewed at their leisure, others were shoving large handfuls of rice into their mouths, the grease dribbling through the spaces of their *abbayehs* and down their chins and beards. The horses of the leaders stood tethered around the tent, their heads inside feedbags. The Hebronites exchanged glances of amazement, their mouths ajar and their shoulders shaking. Those in the foremost lines turned about and called for their spokesmen. Those further back found themselves inexplicably stopped, and anxiously asked each other why. Meanwhile more people kept streaming down the hillside, adding to the confusion and din. Angry voices were raised, and grumblers and slanderers had a field day. Those who tried to calm and quiet the uproar only added to the clamor. People crammed in the middle of the crowd called to those in the front to move forward again, urging them on with curses and oaths. Those in front angrily pushed them back, and called in desperation for their leaders.

The leaders of the Hebronites, who had moved aside to take counsel, did not hurry forward. Abu Faris, seeing the confusion their absence had caused, interrupted the discussion and ordered his officers to take up positions at the heads of their groups. His order was not heeded, so he charged forward alone into the agitated crowd, leading his piebald horse behind him. Waving his staff above his head he ran back and forth in a frenzy, ordering the crowd back to form ranks with proper spaces in between. Those who didn't obey him found themselves leaping aside with a scream, staring at him in wonder as they rubbed their shoulders, which now burned with the blows he had rained upon them. Others, seeing this, moved back quickly to avoid him, and by the time he reached the forward lines the whole camp was properly lined up in a single column.

A hush of anticipation followed. Abu Faris stood unmoving, his forehead creased, as if considering what his next tactic was to be. His horse nuzzled its moist nostrils in his hand and knelt down, as if inviting him to mount. At this, Abu Faris seemed to wake from his stupor; the shadows of doubt that had darkened his face were driven off as if by a lightning flash of decision. The pupils of his eyes, which had been staring vacantly ahead, focused sharply again and gleamed like steel, fired by a fierce determination. His entire bearing bespoke anger. Mounting quickly, he surveyed the horizon. Then he turned, called his flag-bearer to him, snatched the flag from him, brandished it high in the air, and signaled to his officers to come to him. His signals did not reach them, so he sent out couriers to them, with terse commands. Not waiting for the couriers to return, he called out an order, and the entire host moved off at once with rapid steps.

As they passed the place where the Nablusites were camped, Abu Il-Shawarab and his officers emerged from their tent and stood beside the path, waiting for the Hebronite leader to approach them. Abu Faris did not turn toward them, but when he recognized them his eyes flashed, his pale face contorted with rage, and the sparse hairs of his gray beard trembled with hatred. Muttering a fierce curse between his teeth, he turned around to face his own people. In order not to have to see the

Nablusites, he unfurled the large flag and placed it on one side, to block them out from view. He himself seemed to shrink and be swallowed up among his riders.

Abu Faris rode around the entire Nablus camp and then led his followers onto the plain too, setting up camp at some distance from the Nablusites, in an area they had not managed to occupy. As the masses of people poured toward him, he directed them to positions on the upper slopes, where he grouped them close together, to increase the space between the two camps. In this space he assembled his horsemen and, deploying them as a barrier, strictly ordered them not to allow anyone to cross from one side to the other.

He instructed them to wait here until the Jerusalemites arrived. Meanwhile, the Nablus horsemen also rode up quickly and took up positions in front of their own lines. The horsemen of the two camps now faced each other as if before a battle.

Many Hebronites as yet knew nothing of the dissension between the leaders, and now moved toward the wings, hoping to cross over and mingle with the Nablusites, as was the custom. To prevent this, and at the same time to impress the Nablusites, Abu Faris selected ten of his best riders, divided them into two groups, and sent them out to the two wings. He himself rode down the entire line, straightening it here and there, and by means of a rope, divided it into two equal lengths. In the center he placed a rider. Having completed his preparations, he drew his sword, and signaled the riders to begin the horse race.

The riders, their legs against their horses' sides, and with spears raised high above their heads, charged at each other in a powerful gallop, shouting wild battle cries as they rode. Taking care not to cross the line, each rider tried to strike a rider of the opposite side on the head with his spear; as the combatants approached each other they all lowered their heads at once, pulled hard at their horses' reins, and pulled up; then they advanced again with loud cries, only to stop and withdraw again. They retraced their steps and stopped, breathing heavily, their faces toward the horizon and their spears on their shoulders.

The Hebronites challenged the Nablusites to take part in their games. Ten riders from Beit She'an, who were considered part of the Nablus camp, came out. They held palm fronds, with which they struck their big horses, and their raised sleeves revealed muscular arms lined with blue veins taut like strings. They gazed contemptuously at the Hebronite camp, which was half the size of their own, and sneered at their short, scrawny horses. Lined up, their horses capering proudly, they looked quite confident of their victory, as they carelessly struck their red boots with the palm fronds, their entire attitude one of scorn.

At a sign given by Abu Faris the original competitors now left the line and were replaced by ten other riders, of the Negueb Bedouin. The aridity of the desert and its blazing sun were evident in the charred dark skin of their faces; from behind the colorful *kefiyehs* protruded sharp noses, bent like beaks of birds of prey, and eyes that gleamed like burning fires; their small horses, lithe as snakes and fleet as deer, snorted and whinnied impatiently, biting at their reins and stomping their hoofs. They galloped several times up and down the entire line, and then returned to stand at the starting point in silence.

The goats in both camps, not easily subdued by commands, broke through lines of horsemen, ran madly about, some rearing up on their hind legs, some even climbing up onto camels and other high places to get a better look at the proceedings. Excited people, jammed together, noisily shoved and bustled about like bees. Suddenly they all fell silent, to watch the contest with bated breath.

The competitors threw down their staffs, drew their swords, and whirled them around their heads. Then, replacing them in their sheaths, they grasped their spears and galloped off as one man, their white *abbayehs* fanning out and lifting in the breeze like sails, while clouds of dust rose from under their horses' hoofs and enveloped them up to their waists.

The contest went on for a long time. The Negueb horsemen, who clung to their saddles like cats, ran the Beit She'an riders to the line scores of times. Shrewdly calculating the strength of their opponents' mounts, they kept up a murderous pace, until the big heavy horses were trembling with exhaustion and their broad backs were foaming with sweat. Their red eyes bulged out of their sockets, and froth mixed with blood flowed from their mouths and nostrils. Only then did the Bedouin charge at their opponents, with a roar suppressed through gritted teeth. Several paces from the line they suddenly swung from their saddles and hid under their horses' bellies—and in a flash swung up again to sit upright on their steeds. Before the Beit She'an riders could recover, to raise their spears for a renewed attack or to retreat, the Hebronites were upon them. Savagely snatching the headbands off the Nablusites' heads, they threw their trophies up into the air and caught them in midflight on the points of their spears, and then dashed off toward their own camp with their booty.

A thunderous uproar followed. Had a storm arisen among the thousands of trees in the nearby woods, its noise would not have been as loud as the one that now greeted the riders. This was a sound of triumph and pride, a wild and prolonged roar of victory and joy, which burst out among the Hebronites who thronged around their champions, kissing them on the shoulders, slapping them on the back, shaking their hands violently, even lifting them from their saddles and affectionately stroking the necks of the thick-maned horses, whose hair was now dark and gleaming with sweat as their riders led them proudly by the reins through the dense lines of people.

The Nablusites stood there dumbfounded. The unexpectedness of this total defeat left them staring at each other in disbelief, as if waiting for some event that might deny the spectacle they had just witnessed.

The defeated riders walked back with eyes lowered, as if looking for a place to hide with their shame. The people from Nablus heard the cheers rising from the Hebronite camp and felt themselves disgraced. They writhed in agony and bit their lips in anger. Then, roaring like wounded beasts, they started running forward in disorder, rushing toward the Hebronite camp to take their revenge. Fists clenched, heads thrust forward like bulls about to butt, the spate of their fury increased as they ran, until the Hebronites, frightened by the sight, fell silent and began to retreat.

But just as the flame of their wrath was about to ignite the surroundings, Abu Il-Shawarab swept down on his horse into the narrow space now separating the two camps. Waving his sword above his head he called on his people to stop, and on hearing his raging voice they all turned aside. Even the more impudent and violent among them, who raised their eyes to him for a moment, quickly lowered them again in shame. Slackening their grips on the daggers in their belts, they sullenly retraced their steps.

His rapid ride had brought Abu Il-Shawarab very close to the Hebronite camp, which now seethed over the plain like leaves of a tree on a stormy day. Suddenly he caught sight of Abu Faris rushing around desperately in an attempt to control his own people, who were fleeing in panic in all directions. In all the confusion he had lost his headdress, and his bald pate gleamed in the sun. On seeing Abu Il-Shawarab approaching him he reined in his horse, straightened up, and raised his head high with a victor's pride, looking for all the world like a cock ruffling his feathers at the sight of a rival encroaching into his territory, at which he stretches out his throat, follows the intruder with his eyes, and waits for the slightest movement on his antagonist's part before falling upon him and latching on to his comb.

Abu Il-Shawarab looked straight into his eyes for a long while, in ominous silence. He felt as if a wave of hatred had struck at his heart. The wave rose up to his throat, strangling him. His face paled and his moustache trembled. Completely overwhelmed by his sudden and violent rage, his eyes dilated and blurred. It seemed to him that the arrogant face of Abu Faris, mocking and scornful like that of an old fox, was becoming vague and distant. All he could see was the closely shaven skull, bluish-white like an ostrich egg. The skull now began circling around him like a point of light, exciting his eyelids until they hurt, yet drawing him toward it as if by magic cords. He felt such a fierce and burning hatred for this skull that the thought flashed through him that he had to smash it with his sword, as one smashes the head of a venomous snake. Still watching the skull, the hand in which he held his sword suddenly tightened around the handle, while his other hand pounded fiercely on his horse's head. His thighs pressed tightly against the horse's belly. The horse shuddered, reared up, and raised its forelegs, ready to leap upon the other horse. But at that very moment he was thrust aside, to fall back and stand motionless, quivering from the force of the unexpected blow. Abu Il-Shawarab almost fell to the ground, but managed to drop his sword and the reins in time to free his hands and grab the horse's mane. As he swayed in the saddle, his foot groping for the stirrup, he turned to look at the rider who had ridden up so suddenly and given his horse that powerful kick which had turned it aside. This rider had dashed on and then turned about in mid-gallop, and now stood in the narrow space between the two flag-masters.

The rider was Abu Za'id. When the uproar began he had seen Abu Il-Shawarab rush forward in his lone attempt to hold back the furious Nablusites, and had ridden up to assist him. When order was restored he had turned to go back. But as he rode around the fringes of the camp he had caught sight of the two leaders bristling on their horses' backs, necks forward, faces pale, looking as if they were about to swallow each other alive.

Though not lacking experience in such affairs, Abu Za'id was startled at first. He reined in his horse and stood stock still as if trying to find a way to prevent this mischief. But when he saw the movement of Abu Il-Shawarab's hand he roused himself from his bewilderment, stuck his spurs into his horse, and rode straight at the two adversaries. He passed between them like an arrow, pushing them both aside at the same time, and then returned and placed himself between them. Shaking his shoulders and his head, he said:

"Allah preserve us from your inflictions . . . Return to your camps and do not bring disgrace upon us . . . The Jerusalemites already await us on the main road . . ." Controlling his own anger, he turned to Abu Faris and said:

"Order your riders to return what they have plundered . . . I will be warrant: the riders from Beit She'an will not escape, nor will they evade Arab justice . . . The ten suits of clothes due to you as lawful prizes for your victory, as well as the *kefiyehs* and the *abbayehs*, you will receive from me . . ." To assure him further he pounded his breast with his bony hand, and then offered it to the other to shake. Then he turned to Abu Il-Shawarab and whispered in his ear:

"Avoid evil and anger . . . They defeated us fairly and justly, and we have no grounds for complaint against them . . . Your people are a rebellious lot, and such is not the way of Arabs . . . By Allah and by his Prophet, were it not for my respect for your father, I would already have left here with my people."

Like a sleepwalker who is suddenly woken while he walks confidently toward a dangerous pit, Abu Il-Shawarab started with a sudden shock of horror. He passed his hand across his brow several times, as if to wipe away the dreadful sights still hovering before his inner eye. He remained there like this for a long while, staring uncomprehendingly at Abu Za'id. When the buzzing in his ears finally stopped and his reason returned to him, he lowered his head in embarrassment and bit his moustache in remorse. Like one caught in a crime he moved his lips as if struggling to say some words that might be suitable to the occasion, that might wash him clean and prove his innocence. But his empty brain could think no thought or find any words and he could feel only one desire—to get away from here. He turned the horse's reins, struck them down quietly, and moved away hesitantly with averted eyes. After several paces he beat violently upon the horse's back and broke into a furious gallop, and did not stop until he was deep inside his own camp, among his own people.

Many of his people had set out to search for him in the midst of the surging crowd. Seeing him return they all hurried to him, impatiently and vigorously pointing toward the road. On reaching him they all began to urge him to order the camp to move on.

Abu Il-Shawarab wiped the beads of sweat from his face. Shading his eyes against the blazing sun, he studied the road all the way to the horizon.

Wherever he looked he saw heads crawling and creeping forward like vast masses of insects: Allah! Allah Who has created men like locusts! Like locusts they covered the fences and the fields and the path, and like locusts they emitted an incessant bustling sound.

At the outskirts of this host rose a huge many-colored flag, made of silk, with gold and silver and embroidery, like a gigantic sail flying on the open sea above dancing waves. The golden crescent stuck on top of its pearl-studded pole glinted in the distance, and around it fragmented colored circles of light gleamed like butterflies fluttering against the sun. A host of smaller flags flew ascending and descending as the horsemen bore them toward where the hill path opened into the plain.

Here the lines of flag-bearers opened out and formed straight silent columns. From behind them emerged an old man dressed all in white, whose thin body, bent with age and weakness, had until then been surrounded by dozens of horsemen riding slowly beside his white horse, leaning toward him in concern, supporting him on either side, and controlling the pace of his horse lest it walk too fast, nodding their heads to everything he said with a smile of agreement.

Abu Il-Shawarab recognized him, for this was the Mufti of Jerusalem.[2] Escorted by the most important of his notables, the venerated leader now waited to greet the two camps of pilgrims. Abu Il-Shawarab felt his heart beat with apprehension. Highly agitated, he began rushing about senselessly, and then called to his men:

"Hurry, ride quickly and catch up with me!"

In the ensuing confusion he turned his horse, assembled his horsemen, and took his place at their head. Like a screeching flock of cranes rising to the skies, they flew off in a disorganized group toward the path.

As they approached the path, the Jerusalemites brandished their flags and welcomed them with low bows. The Nablusites followed suit. They drew their swords and whirled them about with all their might, and then dismounted. With halting steps that testified to the quantity of hard riding they had done, they approached the welcoming party. Falling on each other's necks, the two groups of leaders kissed each other on the shoulders.

Abu Il-Shawarab took the Mufti's hand, which was as thin and narrow as a child's. As he brought it up to his lips, the Mufti seemed to

---

[2] Religious leader.

awake from a reverie, shaking his head as if surprised. Then he drew Abu Il-Shawarab toward him, trembling. Raising himself slowly, he tried to dismount. Abu Il-Shawarab grasped his intention and prepared to lift him from his saddle in obedience to his wishes. At that moment, however, he felt himself elbowed aside. He stared in amazement at the back of the man who had shoved him aside, and tried to identify him. Just then he heard the other's voice raised vehemently:

"Allah forfend! Preserve you, and forgive you . . . By your head and the flag of Al-Khalil which I bear, we will not let you move from where you are!"

The old man listened to this with a gentle smile of pleasure and affection. Blushing like a young girl, he straightened the edges of his yellow silk cloak, which spread around him like waves of radiance. Then he bent over and kissed the speaker on the head, twice, the motions of his beard moving in time with his toothless mouth as he showered instructive blessings upon him.

Leaning intimately on the Mufti's saddle with both arms, Abu Faris brought his mouth up to the old man's ear and whispered something to him. As he spoke he seemed to be puffing himself up with pride, for he kept casting sidelong glances at the Nablusite leaders, glances full of self-satisfaction which seemed to be aimed at showing them his own importance. Noticing that Abu Il-Shawarab was devouring him with his eyes, his face beamed. Ostentatiously ignoring the Hebron flag-master, he continued to talk at great length, shaking his head and arms vigorously in accompaniment. Casually, as if unaware of what he was doing, he insinuated his body between Abu Il-Shawarab and the Mufti, tapped the old man's horse gently and aroused him to walk, and slowly walked beside him, talking all the while, not subsiding until he had led the Mufti aside and brought him into the midst of the Hebronite camp.

Abu Il-Shawarab, who had watched all this with growing apprehension, now leapt up as if stung by a scorpion. Arching his body backward, he rapidly raised one foot, and for a moment it seemed as if he was about to pounce on Abu Faris. But then he reached a decision; his arm which had tautened like a spring dropped to his side. Gnashing his teeth, he firmly restrained his resentment and turned toward the horse. The veins in his temples throbbed violently. Groping like a blind man because of all this agitation, he rested his head on the saddle and remained standing beside his horse for some time, his trembling fingers drumming on the animal's neck but incapable of grasping it. It took him many deep breaths, concentrating all his energy and willpower, to regain some self-possession.

When, somewhat recovered, he was mounted again, he could not refrain from waving a threatening fist at Abu Faris and calling out:

"Just you wait! We'll meet again! By Allah, I will bring upon you a day you'll regret . . ."

These threats, spoken in a harsh, penetrating voice, were applauded by his companions. But they were also overheard by a Hebronite horseman who happened to be standing nearby. Hoping to impress his leader with his loyalty, this horseman rode quickly to Abu Faris, his face wearing the expression of a bearer of important tidings. Sidling up to the Hebronite flag-master, he reported the threats, with substantial additions and flourishes. Then still watching Abu Faris's face to see what impression he was making, he asked him what tactics he thought they should employ to put some sense into the Nablusites' heads.

To his informer's surprise, Abu Faris calmly shrugged his shoulders in disdain. His gray horse capered playfully about like a dancer, and with the same kind of frivolity Abu Faris answered:

"Our salvation is Allah . . ."

By age-old custom and precepts of conduct the three chief flag-masters—of Jerusalem, Hebron, and Nablus—must not show any ill feelings they might harbor for one another when they meet to lead the *Mo'ssam*. The honor of the prophets whose flags they bear and the customs that have been passed down for many generations forbid any act of revenge or blood feud during these days. They must control their emotions and make the pilgrimage together, riding to the tomb of Nebi Moussa side by side.

When Abu Il-Shawarab heard the great drum of Nebi Moussa from the Jerusalemites' camp, he hurried toward his own musicians, who were already lined up beside the path waiting for the signal to start "work." On reaching them he waved several times, then galloped off toward his riders, who were standing around in small clusters, whispering secretively or arguing rebelliously, while others silently ground their teeth in anger, their faces inflamed with shame. He yelled at them to disperse and to start the camp moving and beckoned to two of them to accompany him. The two he had called asked him to wait a little and moved about slowly and sullenly as if looking for something. Abu Il-Shawarab bit his lips impatiently and rode off without them. After having ridden several paces, he changed his mind and turned back.

Now the instruments of the Hebronites began to play in cacophony and the many musicians in the other camps responded with even greater volume. The blind men walking in the middle ranks twisted up their frozen faces which had been staring toward the skies, like dreamers, and their bodies swayed in unison. As if suddenly pushed by a single invisible force, all the pilgrims moved off at once, advancing slowly, clanging their cymbals. The drummers, marching ahead to show them the way, now approached Abu Il-Shawarab, who stood in the middle of the road. They made a half-circle around his flag, beating lustily on their drums. Those behind them quickly followed suit. They bowed devoutly, and their cymbals clashed like the wings of locusts. Soon they were joined by the flute players, behind whom came the dervishes blowing their *rababas*[3] with closed eyes, emitting hoarse cries through their overgrown beards. Through this din thumped the separate, dull, yet penetrating beat of the Jerusalemite drum, resounding across the plain like thunder-claps.

The massed crowds moved from the plain to the road, like currents of a river sending its rushing waters cascading down to the sea. Abu Il-Shawarab paused, raised himself on his horse, and looked around him. When he saw that the two other flag-masters were already standing side by side, he waved his flag and clanged his sword, ordering his deputies to ride ahead and clear a path for him. The upper part of his body drawn strangely erect, he rode with a cold self-importance through the groups of Hebronites, who had been the first to leave the plain. He ignored everyone as he rode: those who denied his leadership, those who stared at him with long offensive stares, and also those few who truly and wholeheartedly wished to greet the flag he was carrying.

To all appearances perfectly calm, he cantered up to the mounted pair of flag-masters, who had been whispering and smiling together for some time. On his arrival they immediately fell silent and quickly drew apart. With intrigue in their eyes, they both leapt onto their horses, and turned their cold gaze upon him.

Abu Il-Shawarab felt a premonition of dread. Their presence stifled him. But he remained calm. With the resolution of a fearless man who offers his arm to the bloodletter, he fulfilled the obligation he had taken

---

[3] A double-tubed flute.

on himself. Gravely, with studied movements, he bowed slightly to them, touched his flag to theirs, and muttered a quiet blessing under his thick moustache. Then, without favoring them with another glance or waiting for their invitation, he took several paces forward, set his horse into a slow, confident trot, and pressed forward into a position between the two horsemen: this being the most important place, the one reserved by custom and tradition for the master of the greatest and most esteemed flag of the three, or for the one whose following of pilgrims was the largest.

At this Abu Faris gave a start, as if he had been touched by something foul. His body arched like a bow, and with a venomous smile flickering around his thin lips, he angrily reined his horse back. To the surprise of all the horsemen, he moved away from Abu Il-Shawarab's right and rode around him. With an expression of flattering humility on his face he then urged the Jerusalem flag-bearer—the host and lord of this district—to move forward and take up the middle position.

An astonished silence followed this insult. All heads turned at once toward Abu Il-Shawarab and his deputies, whose faces flushed and then paled. Then a mighty tumult burst out, indescribable in its fury.

The Nablusites, who had by now gathered at the scene of this incident, all clenched their fists and waved them at Abu Faris and those of his people who stood around him in a narrow circle. The horsemen dismounted, and all of them rushed at him, screaming. Loudest of all in his imprecations was the *suss* vendor, who seemed to have appeared out of nowhere and now hit out blindly with head and elbows. Panting as he struggled to extricate himself from the grip of the Jerusalemites who held him back, he screamed: "Let me at him! I'll break his skull for him! By Allah, I'll smash his skull . . ." The exhortations of the Jerusalem flag-bearer and his companions who tried to mediate between the disputing factions went unheard in the general uproar.

Suddenly everyone fell silent as the Mufti himself appeared on the scene and raised his arms. Walking quickly to Abu Il-Shawarab, he lifted his head up to the Nablusite leader and spoke to him at length. Speaking cautiously and gently, to pacify the irate flag-master, he solemnly made him a public promise that the flag of the Nablusites would lead the procession as it entered Nebi Moussa, even though the Hebronite flag was of greater importance and degree. Not waiting to hear Abu Il-Shawarab's acceptance, he then proceeded to scold the Nablusites, angrily chastising their rebellious cries of opposition to his proposal, which arose anew again and again. Then he went over to the Hebronites, took Abu Faris by the arm, and led him to the Nablus camp, and there rebuked him for his conduct, which he characterized as ill-mannered. Then, to resolve the dilemma and satisfy both sides, he himself took the Jerusalem flag, placed Abu Faris on his right and Abu Il-Shawarab on his left, and ordered his own flag-bearer to divide his horsemen among the two camps. This done, he gave the order to set out, and rode on in silence at the head of the procession, toward the city.

The compromise imposed upon them against their wills pleased neither side and it certainly did not check their anger. The story of the new insult to their flag spread quickly among the Nablusites, taking on more offensive proportions and collecting many commentaries and invented additions as it traveled. The Hebronites too, seeing their own flag displaced from its customary position, grumbled about their leaders for not having stood their ground to defend their honor; at the same time they blamed the arrogant Nablusites, at whom they stared with hatred. Like some drinkers who, loving strife, begin to nurse in their imaginations the thought of the brawl to come from the moment they agree to drink together, the thought increasing in force as they drink more and more, so did the resentment and indignation of both sides increase as they approached the city.

The masses of onlookers who packed the streets and the walls, the outskirts of the city, and the fields abutting on the path gazed with no little apprehensiveness this time at the hard, angry secretive faces of the advancing pilgrims. Some, anticipating the worst, withdrew in alarm. Others hid hurriedly inside shops and waited with pounding hearts to see the end of this procession, for it looked more like a horde of savages setting out for plunder than a solemn march of pilgrims assembled to celebrate the performance of a sacred commandment . . .

The thousands of spectators, who had been drawn by curiosity or love of entertainment and were now trapped among the pilgrims overrunning the city and filling all the roads to such an extent that it was impossible to escape them, this year witnessed strange and wonderful sights, many of which they would remember long after with no few tremors. The procession advanced in complete disorder; horsemen pushed those who walked; men on foot cursed and screamed at those mounted on donkeys and camels who pressed forward through the crowd; the throngs belonging to the two opposed camps moved forward in closely packed lines, each camp apart, as if each person in each camp sought shelter from those around him. Every face wore an expression of violence, a kind of bestiality ready to explode at any moment; their hostility was only too evident. As if driven by an invisible force the stragglers ran after them, trying to catch up, constantly turning their heads to look back in fright, then looking intently ahead, and listening for the slightest sound of danger.

Even the many rings of dancers, so alike in their dress and their movements, did not mingle with each other as had been the custom for generations. Their motions this time had the barest semblance of a dance, and their cheers too came only from the mouth, not from the heart. The clashing of swords and the banging of shields in the dance made them sense the call to battle. The poison bubbling out of their hearts corrupted the atmosphere. Whenever a ring of dancers happened to draw close to another, all the participants immediately retreated and stopped dancing. With looks of contempt and disgust in their eyes they would demonstratively move apart, push aside those who stood in their way, and leave the place, muttering sullenly as they went.

In this manner, almost in flight, they passed the North Wall and toiled up the slope of the Mount of Olives with its steep and curving paths. Here the "middle men," dancers bearing shields, began to take up positions facing each other for the sword battle—but before they could even make several turns to show their mettle, the signal was given to stop the dance and to move on. The leaders of the rings of dancers seemed to be competing with each other to see who would get the obligatory dances finished first, and on the weary slopes of the Kidron Valley, arms and hands drooped, and the last sounds of song and music faded and died.

Now they all quickened their pace, hoping to arrive in time for the parting ceremony, and to see the Mufti send the pilgrims off with his blessing, and watch him present to the flag-masters the gift sent by the Caliph to the mosque of Nebi Moussa. All wished to be present when the escorts parted from the pilgrims, a moment that was to be preceded by songs of glory and praise to the Prophet and to conclude with wild enthusiastic dancing. Out of breath, covered with sweat and dust, they arrived at the spring of Siloam, whose clear waters now flowed abundantly after the recent heavy rains, pouring and frothing between green fields of grain where curling stems rose unmoving while the tiny budding ears bristled and leaned forward like needles. As they walked they dipped their hands into the streams, to bring handfuls of water up to their dry lips and dusty tongues, or to wet their skulls, which blazed under their heavy headwear. Many soon found themselves being pushed back by throngs of people coming back from the ceremony and marching back to the city. Shoved and surrounded in this way, they were forced to mingle with the returning escorts and even to retreat. For a long while they strayed this way and that, unable to see any of their companions or leaders. It was only with great effort that they succeeded in wrenching themselves free from the streams of men descending upon them like a storm which rolled aside everything in its path. Then the survivors could stop to look back at the cowards who had given up the struggle and left the pilgrimage. These now looked very small indeed in the distance. Indignation swept through them when they looked around and discovered to their astonishment that great gaps had been torn in their ranks, reducing their number by half.

Shamed, sad, like people who have been invited to a banquet and find on their arrival that those present have already finished the dinner without them, they stood bewildered, surveying this place which had just been so full of cheering people. They looked around as if seeking something more, but on seeing in the distance the wild and unruly masses of pilgrims moving forward like untended herds, they anxiously began running after them, almost in panic, pushing and shoving each other along the mountain paths and into the desert to catch up with them.

CHAPTER FIVE

From here to the shrine of Nebi Moussa was some twenty-five miles. Allah, wanting to placate his favorite, and mitigate the punishment which He had imposed on him in His anger, had promised Moses before he died that He would not leave him alone in the distant desert, to be visited only by heat and dust. He had therefore instructed the faithful, through the mouth of the Prophet Muhammad—peace and prayers be with him!—to attend at his grave every year, during the month he had died in, for seven successive days of feasting and dancing, and had commanded the three most important flags[1] to visit him at his shrine with much splendor and ceremony. To make the pilgrimage less of a burden, He had moved the grave several parasangs[2] closer to the places of habitation,[3] and had made the road leading to it pleasant and easy, so

---

[1] Of the three major districts—Hebron, Nablus, Jerusalem.
[2] A "parasang" is a Persian measure of length, usually 3 to 3½ English miles.
[3] According to an Arab legend, Moses was originally buried further away, but Allah had moved the grave to where the mosque now stood.

that even old people and children could make the journey without difficulty. Half of it He had set between mountain ridges in a long continuous descent, so that your feet moved forward of their own accord without any effort, and the remainder on the flat and level plain. Marvelous sights greeted the pilgrims at every step. He had gathered pools of cold water from the rains and preserved them in crevices among the rocks, not allowing them to evaporate, to quench the thirst of birds and pilgrims alike. With carpets of grasses and fragrant flowers He had decorated the desolate desert for this brief period, for the sake of those who performed His will, giving them refreshing sights to restore their souls and dissipate their fatigue, inspiring them with renewed vigor.

In the normal course of events, the flag-masters lead their camps on without any unnecessary delays. They complete the journey in less than six hours, hoping to bring their followers to the tall white wall surrounding the great square shrine with its towers and wings and domes by the time the *muezzin* on the minaret chants the call for evening prayer.

Experienced leaders, who know their people and care for them as a father for his children, have always tried to conclude this part of the pilgrimage in daylight. This way they have time to find resting places inside the buildings for the women and the children and the sick, to see that the distribution of meat and rice is conducted properly according to the quota, and—above all—to spend what remains of the day resting, so that their charges may regain strength before the lighting of the torches [4] which will illuminate the desert with dancing flames while celebrants prance around them to the sound of hundreds of drums and other instruments, at the beginning of the noisy and enthusiastic dances which will continue all night long.

As storks train their young to fly, now taking to the heights, screeching and encouraging the fledglings to join them, now returning, to flutter around, support them by their wings, and push them forward, so do the leaders circle around their groups and urge them to walk faster. Now they pass them at a gallop, with gleeful cries; now they mingle among them or drive from behind, occasionally lending a hand with an animal that has collapsed under its load or coaxing stragglers on with all kinds of tricks and proverbs. As they give themselves over completely to joy and fun, the road leaps out to greet them and they arrive with the speed of a dream at their destination.

---

[4] The hosts light torches in the desert and on mountaintops to show the way to wanderers and to invite them to the festivities.

Since the imaginations of the participants are very active all this time, in years to come they will generally recall only the most prominent or impressive event of the pilgrimage, forgetting all the other trivial details. But the incidents which precede or cause such an event are so powerful that they too become engraved in the memory for ever. Such was the case this time too. The strange occurrences and amazing sights which attended this pilgrimage determined the atmosphere and created the framework for the awful spectacle that followed, all the parts and links of which were flooded with the red glow of a single flame.

As told by extremely reliable eyewitnesses from among the *hadjs* and dervishes, seers of things present and future, it appears that while the flag-masters were standing calmly and peacefully side by side with their flags held high, and the Mufti was reciting the holy and venerated opening prayer of the Kor'an, far down in the valley two crows rose from among the tops of the olive trees. Screeching bitterly, they fell upon each other, gouging and scratching one another with their beaks until large quantities of feathers fell around the flags like autumn leaves. After weaving circles in the air several times, forming a covenant with the agents of hell, they drew tight the ring of enchantment and disaster above the pilgrims' heads and flew off swiftly and silently, to vanish eastward beyond the mountains.

And from that moment onward the pilgrims were caught in a snare from which there was no escape. The Devil had driven his nose-ring through their nostrils and now led them as he willed, using them as tools for the perpetration of his schemes to make the pilgrimage a failure. His chief agents, disastrously for themselves, were Abu Faris and Abu Il-Shawarab.

After the Mufti and his entourage had left these two, they lost all their self-control, revealing to all present their true faces, which were full of hatred and cold calculation. The passion for honor and revenge burning inside them darkened the light of their reason, dragging and driving them from error to error, to insane and inconsistent actions.

Just as fish darting about around an open net instinctively follow one of their group who swims into it—so did the throngs of pilgrims become entangled in the hellish fabric woven by their leaders, with their whispered and muttered barbs, their contemptuous treatment of each other, the venom that pervaded their movements and comments whenever they passed one another, the fractiousness and contradictions in the commands they gave, and the perversity in their hearts which spread like an epidemic to infect the thousands of sunstruck heads of men who followed them with eyes closed as if smitten with blindness, inflaming the blood lusts latent in their souls.

Very soon they all lost their way and forgot their objective. The desire to destroy, to injure, to raise riot, became the only driving force in all the camps.

The invisible Devil, who had been working all that day with all the means at his disposal, had now also taken the sun as an ally, using it to close the circle of disaster around the world by bringing to ripeness all the notions of hatred that had not yet fully taken shape.

That terrible day was a day of stifling heat. Even before completing half its journey the sun had lost its luster and taken on that dull silver hue that presages the *khamseen*. At the fringes of the mountains there were still a few patches of shade here and there where the pilgrims could find some relief, but as soon as they descended into the Jordan Valley they walked into an east wind that blew from the desert as if from the mouth of a white-hot furnace. The wind swept before it gusts of sand and dust, whirling them around as in a devil's dance. The blazing and charged waves of air stretched the pilgrims' nerves taut, poured fire into their arteries, and worked up a storm in their hearts.

As beasts of burden plodding along lethargically may suddenly run amok for no reason at all, tearing off their harness, flinging off their loads, kicking and biting at each other—so did the pilgrims clash at every step. Trivial incidents, which during any other pilgrimage would have been passed over or laughed away, developed into unending series of quarrels, which often flared up into a large-scale brawl.

When the shouting and screaming brought the leaders of the two opposing camps running to the scene of the incident, they made no effort to soothe the vexed spirits. Instead, fuming with anger themselves, they either stood there with folded arms like impartial observers or, pretending to be separating the antagonists, misused their status in order to favor their own side. Thus they would grab the arms of someone on the opposing side only if he seemed to have the upper hand, allowing the weaker antagonist, of their own side, to hit him freely.

Prominent among these ugly waves of hatred, bobbing up everywhere, was the *suss* vendor. On this day there was almost no one who did not become aware of his presence and his strength. His name was an abomination in the Hebronite camp. In every cluster that formed around a brawl or a dispute he could be recognized from afar, by his mop of hair that bristled on his head like a hawk's comb, and by the dark paint around his eyes which had spread with his sweat to smear his cheeks and neck. As long as all he did was to push spectators about or place himself in the middle, shouting abuse at the Hebronites and giving indirect assistance to the Nablusite hotheads, the Hebronites tolerated him and treated him cautiously, careful not to provoke him further. But when his cries of derision grew more numerous than their blows, some of the more daring Hebronites ganged together and cunningly inveigled him into a spot concealed from the sight of his fellows, where they surrounded him and began to rain blows upon him. He, however, did not call out for help. Skillfully swinging his staff—a split pomegranate branch with a rounded head—he drove back his attackers, breaking their ring and making them flee. By the time some Nablusites saw him and rushed to his aid he had completely extricated himself and came striding proudly toward them. Still cursing his attackers violently and calling them by all the known names of abuse, he tore a long strip from the lining of his caftan and bandaged his bleeding forehead with it. Then, straightening his *abbayeh* and waistband, like a triumphant cock preening his feathers after a hard battle, he stepped forth with head held high into the midst of his townsmen, who stood staring at him in amazement and awe at the bravery he had just displayed.

And so he became the leader of all the Nablusite hotheads who wanted to revenge themselves on the world at large and to terrify everyone they met. As their chief, he devised numerous tricks. He conducted attacks, aroused brawls, and infected all his followers with his own blazing temper and rebellious anger, the result being that the malice and impudence of this wild gang soon broke down all barriers of order and discipline.

In this chaos of quarrels and brawls which burst out time and again with ever greater frequency, the flag-masters found that they no longer had any control over the conduct of the procession, and could not have stopped the rioters even if they had really and truly wanted to. Almost without realizing what was happening, even the more moderate people suddenly seemed to have lost the ground under their feet, and all of them rolled down into a deep abyss of savage strife among brothers, conducted with bared teeth and clenched fists and immeasurable cruelty.

Things went so far that at the well of Maaleh Adumim a fierce struggle took place between Hebronite donkey-drivers who were drawing water for their animals and a group of Nablusites who had come hurrying rowdily after them to try to capture the place for themselves. Yelling fierce battle cries, calling on the name of Allah, the new arrivals snatched up the reins of the drinking animals, beat them, and scattered them in all directions. The Hebronites were not tardy in retaliating, and fell upon their attackers with hoarse cries. Men fought and kicked each other, many of them rolling on the ground, screaming and striking until the water in the troughs was red with their blood. This shameful incident aroused many hearts against the Nablusites, and drew in its train other acts of revenge and infamy.

This year, as in previous years, the proprietors of the Al-Akhmar *khan* welcomed the flag-masters, and then brought them to a shelter behind the building where they could rest, serving them the banquet that had been waiting for them here since morning.

Abu Il-Shawarab and his officers sat down on the mats around the steaming, fragrant dishes. A little later Abu Faris arrived with his party. They too allowed the *khan* owner to lead them to the shelter. But when they saw who was seated inside their expressions changed visibly and they quivered with hatred. Without discussing this among themselves, they all turned about at once and strode off, loudly and angrily, the spurs on their boots jangling as they walked. In vain did the bewildered and insulted proprietor plead with them. They denied him the benefit of their presence, and refused to eat or taste anything in his establishment. Glowering, they shook their heads coldly at him, mounted their horses, and commanded their followers to continue on their way and bypass the *khan*.

When they had traveled far enough so as to no longer hear the din of the Nablus camp, they stopped to rest on the slopes of a reddish hill that was covered with adonis and poppies which bent on their stems with the east wind that blew against them from the desert around Jericho. Here the tired Hebronites lay down to rest, some simply sprawling where they dropped, without moving a limb, while others crawled into the elongated shadows of their camels to find shelter from the blazing sun.

If they were angry when they lay down, they were doubly angered when they were suddenly brought to their feet to see groups of Nablusites who had deliberately left the road and were now rapidly leading their heavily laden animals with shouts through the field where they lay, maliciously disturbing their brief rest. A general pandemonium spread everywhere with nothing to inhibit it, like water pouring down a slope. From all sides came curses, oaths, frightened cries of women and children, and angry voices yelling "Hit them!" "Without mercy!"

Abu Faris and Abu Il-Shawarab did not lift a finger to try to stop the uproar. They circled around the hillslope like wolves seeking prey. In reply to the desperate pleas addressed to them, and to the just demands of the Jerusalemites that they put an end to the dispute, they only shrugged their shoulders and flung back in response: "Let's see if *you* can stop this!"

The few policemen accompanying the procession were also powerless to quell the riot. In their attempts to restore order they did not have the courage to burst in among the combatants and use firm measures against them: they contented themselves with spoken appeals, and most of the time ran about helplessly in all directions. Finally their Turkish officer lost patience with the effort, and with a furious expression on his face blew a long blast on his whistle, assembled his policemen, whispered something to them, and then they all galloped off on the road to Jerusalem to request reinforcements.

This simple and daring tactic, together with the untiring efforts of the Jerusalemites, had some effect on the milling crowd, bringing back a modicum of reason. The brawling petered out, and gradually the circles of angry men, which had been whirling about like lakes into which a rain of stones has been hurled, dispersed and quieted down.

All this wrangling had cost them a lot of time. Instead of reaching the mount at the customary time of the evening offering, to pray the third prayer of the day in public assembly, they now arrived at its foot, exhausted and scattered, just before evening, when the setting sun was at the height of a camel and his rider above the horizon. And when they reached the top of the mount, it seemed as if the shrine of Nebi Moussa, with its precariously tall tower, its rounded domes and arched windows, was enveloped in flames from the setting sun, and that the bare hills around it were alight in a bluish-orange hue, like burning sulphur, their long shadows spreading across the plain.

While waiting for the stragglers, the first arrivals moved about wearily, busying themselves with gathering stones and piling them up in little hillocks for markers, and with repairing the many piles that had become scattered since the previous year. Old men and young, fearful of being late for the sunset prayer, hurriedly formed circles and moved aside, while the red glow of before-dusk rested on their faces, which were contorted with exhaustion and sorrow. Silently they took off their *abbayehs*, spread them out on the ground, and stood on them barefooted, with folded arms, in long rows, erect and frozen, like the cliffs and hills beneath them, then bowed and prayed fervently, all bending in unison, like ripe corn when the wind blows through it. When they had completed their whisperings and prostrations they stood up again with a sigh, shaking their heads with concern as they rejoined the many gangs who, forgetting the customs and ignoring the reverence due to their elders, now passed by them, without pausing to wait for them until they had finished their prayer.

For another half hour people kept coming from among the hill-slopes. The camels, sensing that they were soon to arrive and receive their fodder, held their heads erect and joyfully shook the bells hanging around their necks. With no prodding from their owners they moved forward and clambered with broad strides to the top of the last hill that bounds the plain where the mosque stands. Their owners hurried to catch up with them, and everyone advanced more quickly. Going down the hill on the other side, the owners finally caught up with their camels, grabbed their reins, and, pouring out their wrath upon the animals with blows and curses, held them back and forced them to a halt.

According to custom, they were supposed to wait here for the final rite during which the flags were brought into the mosque of Nebi Moussa by the flag-masters at the heads of their parties. So an increasing crowd of people continued to gather here, and one could discern among them many whose faces were filled with the savage anger that had burst out earlier. Their fury and excitement were manifest in their very postures and movements. Of their own accord they divided up into two camps with a large space between them, and a great bustle of movement, marking the final preparations, swept over them like a stormy wave. Now their leaders passed among them with officious speed, moving them excitedly backward and forward, hitting them to get them to form up into columns, the bounds of which each leader determined as he wished. The din increased with the bleating of sheep and goats and the snorting of camels that were also being pushed about. The hundreds of drums and other instruments which pounded out their sounds in total disorder made the earth tremble and startled the horses and the mules, increasing the clamor and filling the hearts of the pilgrims with rage and resentment at the conflicting commands which could in no way be carried out.

And suddenly, like a wind blowing among the trees of a forest, a whisper traveled from mouth to mouth: "There they go! There they go!" Fear and anxiety appeared on every face. Now all the screaming stopped and each man easily found his proper place. The pilgrims divided their camps into three sections: those on foot first, behind them the riders, and last of all those in carriages. All eyes turned in a single direction, all hearts pounded fiercely, and with bated breath they drew themselves erect and gazed disbelievingly at the spectacle unfolding before them.

From the opposite hilltop the flag-masters descended slowly on their noble steeds bedecked in checkered trappings. The flags they bore did not budge, and descended in folds around their poles, which were as long as masts. In the center, a step ahead of the others, rode Abu Il-Shawarab, cantering proudly and freely, his face beaming with the joy and pride of victory. On his right and a little too far back rode Abu Faris, courageously bent over his steed, like a tiger about to pounce. His legs were drawn back, his stomach drawn in, and he and his horse looked as if they had been glued together. His thick eyebrows arched over his flashing cat's eyes, which stared unmovingly ahead and clearly expressed his dark decision of intrigue.

They reached the very heart of the camps which still stood, immobile as walls, waiting for the flag-masters to ride past them so that they could turn and follow them. The *suss* vendor was standing at the head of a column of Nablusites, beside the sacrificial camel. Girding his loins and thrusting the ends of his *caftan* into his belt, he somersaulted onto the beast's neck and from there climbed up, nimble as a squirrel, to stand erect on its back. When the flag-masters were some twenty meters from him he bent his head backward a little, pressed his hand to his temple, and declaimed in a loud voice:

> *"Nimmer, Nimmer, on his white stallion proud,*
> *His sword a lightning bolt, his flag—a cloud,*
> *Eagles chose him to lead their ring*
> *Roaring lions have crowned him their king,*
> *Those who love him rest in his shade*
> *His enemies fall before him and fade!"*

"Ai! . . . Ai! . . . Ai! . . . Support him! Praise him! Follow him!" came the cries from the Nablusite camp. In wild enthusiasm they roared and cheered, greeting their leader and their flag with a triumphant song. Then again they cried: "Ai! Ai!" and "Support him! Praise him!" with increasing fervor and deafening roars.

Abu Faris started laughing—strange, contemptuous short bursts of laughter. His left leg began to tremble, knocking with his spur on his horse's thigh. The well-trained horse looked from side to side and did not move from the spot, and soon his master calmed down. He had understood that the time had not yet come to act, and looked about stealthily to see if his secret intrigue had not been discovered. On seeing in Abu Il-Shawarab's face the expression of one who is confident of his own power and high degree, he restrained himself, disguised the fury and contempt in his eyes, and again put on an air of unconcern and scorn, as if what had happened did not affect him in the slightest.

In the Hebronite camp, tears of indignation and shame could be seen on many faces. The *suss* vendor had aimed his pointed barbs well, and they lodged deep in their hearts.

But their downfall did not last long. Soon enough a redeemer was found among them, who removed the disgrace and returned it sevenfold upon their foes. A man arose from among their rear ranks, tall as a giant. As he walked forward he threw the flap of his *abbayeh* over his shoulder with pretended casualness, freed a hand, and motioned to one of his companions to kneel down. Taking off his shoes, he climbed up on the other's shoulders. Then, taking his *kefiyeh*, which he had rolled up like a snake, and waving it around his head in all directions to draw the attention of all present and to tell them to be silent, he too declaimed, in a lion's voice:

> *Soon will come the day of redress*
> *With wrath overturning distress*
> *Then the faces of the oppressed will all shine*
> *And the faces of the robbers be shamed!*

"Raise him! Raise him! . . . Again! Again! . . ." roared the Hebronites. Hundreds of arms reached toward him, grasped him, lifted him into the air like a feather and held him high, cheering all the while. They did not cease calling out even when their leaders urged them to move off. Only when their limbs grew weary and their throats hoarse did they respond to their leader's commands, and moved off with much noise and clamor.

Then the dervishes enthusiastically began singing a sacred song:

> *To you, the Prophet Moussa,*
> *We will pour out our hearts,*
> *Our bodies—your redemption,*
> *Our souls—your compensation.*

Moussa kalim Allah [5]
Like a father who watches our growth
Like a craftsman who suckles our art,
Purify us to seek early your shrine
Pour on us your spirit so fine,
Moussa kalim Allah.
In your flame we are consumed
To your tomb we are attuned
Shade us in your shelter,
Bathe us in your spendor,
Moussa kalim Allah!

Their intoxication spread to all the pilgrims, and thousands of wild voices responded to the song, which merged into a single fierce and prolonged shout, savage and sad as the desert. Heads swayed to the rhythm of the singing, and it seemed as if the entire plain was singing and swaying with the people and the animals and the flags and the swords.

Twilight deepened, the last gleams of day began to fade and slip away from the wide enclosure, which steamed with the evening, emitting its heat in thin, pale, mistlike clouds. In the midst of these moved the flag-masters, their shapes already blurred. Some had already completely vanished from sight and only their flags could be seen, stretched like moving sails in the misty air.

Darkness had descended on the walls and the wide-open gate of the shrine. When the flag-masters were some three hundred lance-lengths from it, Abu Il-Shawarab, excitedly sensing the importance of the event he was about to take part in, drew in his reins, stood up on his stirrups, and looked back to see if everything was in order among his followers. At that moment he heard the sound of a stick whistling through the air a little to his right, followed by a pounding of hoofs: the red horse of Abu Faris, who had been riding behind him, shot past him like a flash of fire; the unfurled Hebronite flag swelled out in front of him, fanning him with wind as it flew on, like the flapping of a mighty wing.

Astonished at first, Abu Il-Shawarab stared at the flag as if unable to believe the terrible sight he had just seen. But his sharp eyes had recognized Abu Faris, and now a sudden clarity flashed through his brain and set all his limbs aquiver. At one glance he took everything in, and

---

[5] "Moses [who] speaks with God."

understood the whole of Abu Faris's cunning and perfidy. His blood boiled and hummed in his temples, his eyes darkened, and he struck himself hard on the head. He let out a mighty roar: "Perfidy! . . . " dug his spurs deep into his white stallion until the blood flowed, and, bending slightly forward over his saddle, slashed down with his reins.

The stallion, sensing his master's agitation, burst into the speedy gallop for which he was famed. Neck down, tail flying, he seemed to glide through the air without touching the ground. Very soon he had caught up with the horse ahead of him, and ran so close to him that the legs of the riders were touching. Several paces away from the gate he succeeded in passing him by a whole step, and then Abu Il-Shawarab thrust his drawn sword in front of the eyes of his opponent's horse, without touching him. The red horse reared and drew back. Before he could start riding forward again Abu Il-Shawarab had blocked his path and forced him to stand still on the spot.

The two animals of different breeds stood there staring at each other in hatred, and a dreadful and ominous silence ensued. Then Abu Faris shrugged his shoulders impatiently, beat upon his horse's neck with all his might, changed his position, and struck his horse again with the intention of evading Abu Il-Shawarab and passing around him.

Abu Il-Shawarab grasped his intention and moved his own horse around to block his path again. Coming close enough to his rival to touch him, he stammered in a hoarse, strangled voice:

"Get back, traitor! . . . And if you don't . . ."

"Your mother's cunt!" hissed Abu Faris, and gave him a hard shove in the ribs with the end of his flagpole. Abu Il-Shawarab swayed and groaned in pain, but quickly recovered. Trembling with rage, his mouth ajar and his eyes dilated, now totally in the grip of one of those frenzies that bring a man to sin, he rose up on his stirrups and bent toward his enemy. He grabbed the flag in an attempt to wrench it from Abu Faris's hands, and the flag tore. Abu Faris reached for his belt, to draw his revolver, but Abu Il-Shawarab was quicker, and thrust his sword into the other's breast with all his might.[6]

"To me, my men! The son of a whore has killed me! . . ." Abu Faris gurgled, and spoke no more. He fell on his face, his head landing on the neck of his killer's horse. A stream of blood poured from his mouth onto

---

[6] Author's note: Some 25 years ago [this book first appeared in 1928] an incident like this actually occurred. In a riot over the flag the Hebronite flag-master and two of his followers were killed, and several Nablusites also fell.

the saddle, and sprayed onto his face and clothes. The stallion gave a start and moved away, and the lifeless body turned over and fell to the earth, landing with a dull thud.

Abu Il-Shawarab stood rooted to the spot, bewildered and astounded, staring at the dark form lying in the sand in the growing pool of blood which now divided into two streams advancing toward him like snakes. Suddenly a huge mounted figure rose up beside the dead man, large as an elephant, and began wailing in bitter, heartrending tones: "The Muslims are finished: the end has come . . . ! My brothers! . . . Help! . . . Help! . . ." And from further away, in the other direction, came a loud cry: "Flee, Abu Nimmer! The dogs are after you! . . ." Abu Il-Shawarab shrank in fear. Without knowing what he was doing he brandished the flag he was holding and sent his horse galloping toward the gate of the shrine before the shadows, now advancing upon him like wolves, could reach him. By their flashing swords and their angry cries he knew the danger he was in, and understood that he would be hopelessly lost if he did not get away from them quickly. Casting a quick glance to the side, he placed the flag by the gatepost and galloped on to the right, in the direction that was clear of people. The wails, the cries for help, and the shots cutting through the air behind him increased his fear and the speed of his flight, and his horse flew along the treacherous paths among the hills as if borne on the wings of mysterious forces. To Abu Il-Shawarab it felt as if he were flying down into some deep abyss. Only when the noise of pursuit was far behind him and he found himself surrounded by darkness did he stop his horse for a moment. He leapt to the ground, put his ear to the earth, and listened attentively for its secret pulses. When he was sure that no pursuers were coming after him he got up again, his knees shaking. Still breathing heavily and sweating profusely from every pore, he pressed his trembling hand to his chest to calm the dreadful pounding of his heart. Concentrating all his senses in his ears, he laid his head sorrowfully on his horse's neck and hugged the animal the way a terrified child presses close to his mother's breast.

"Allah's decree!" he muttered over and over between compressed lips, in an attempt to overcome his weakness and distress, and to grasp the torturing thought which kept fluttering through all the other dark visions of chaos that flew about in his brain like withered leaves on a stormy day. The words, however, neither penetrated to his heart nor restored his strength. He struggled to exercise the thought and free himself of it, but he could sense it roaming through his soul, hovering above him and burning his forehead. He closed his eyes and tried to catch it, and sank into a kind of idea for which there is no concept.

Several minutes passed. They were like hours to him. His consciousness returned and he shuddered like a man falling from a great height in a dream. Something like a giant flame lit up in front of him, illuminating all the dark and secret places of his soul. Hitting himself on the head with both hands, he roared like a madman:

"Coward that I am! What have I done to myself and to my people? . . . Why did I flee? . . . O the glory! . . . O the shame and disgrace! . . ."

The more he thought about it, the more his blood streamed to his temples, and he was filled with self-contempt. His entire being sobbed silently, and a great remorse consumed him. But now a new idea seized him and filled him with enthusiasm, and being by nature very changeable, he decided that he must return immediately to the field of conflict, even at the cost of his life.

The natural instinct which guides creatures that are in danger spurred Abu Il-Shawarab to be cautious. With trembling hands he took off his *abbayeh*, cut it into long strips with his sword, and bound his horse's hoofs so that its galloping might be silent. The darkness which encompassed him on all sides encouraged him in the hope that he might succeed in stealing back into his own camp, even if his pursuers were still roaming about and lying in wait for him to return.

He tried to mount his horse again, but the horse's chest was rising and falling like a bellows from having run so much; its breath came in snorts and the sweat poured from it, moistening Abu Il-Shawarab's hand, which slid gently along the horse's neck. He could not mount. Knowing that there were still many obstacles ahead of him for which he had to conserve the horse's strength, he grasped the reins and began walking, leading the horse. He advanced silently and with great caution, his eyes darting around him as if trying to rip apart the mists now rising across the plain like dense white steam from the Dead Sea that glinted like steel on his left and from the Jordan slumbering on his right in its gray *abbayeh*.

After walking in the sand for about an hour, his legs now weak and unsteady, he finally caught sight of the white rows of hills. He stopped beside the steep path which gleamed in the darkness, and considered whether to continue along it or to change direction. He decided to make the rest of his way directly through the huge rocks which rose above each other like a camel caravan that has stopped to rest by the wayside. These rocks, he hoped, would give him cover. He crawled forward among them, crouching, with feeble steps. Slowly, very carefully, feeling his way forward with his hands, he climbed to the ridge of the hill whose peak rose to the clouds.

Although his hands and knees were soon scratched and bruised all over by the thorns and clumps of rock he kept bumping into, he ignored the pain and kept on going. But whenever his horse's hoofs dislodged some stones his heart went tearing after them, trembling in his chest as he listened to the noise they made rolling down the hillside. Then he would take a deep breath and bend forward again to continue crawling forward.

With great effort he reached the peak and climbed onto its hump-top alone. There he lay down and blinked, molded his body to the shape of the hilltop, and scanned the surroundings. Strain his eyes as he might, all he could see was a deep chasm descending into invisible depths, and behind it a dark wall, terrifying in its stillness. And more than he could see he sensed that the descent on this side was steep, and that more peaks, higher than this one, rose ahead of him.

"It's a bad way I've chosen," he thought to himself, and his spirits fell. "My horse will never get down this cursed slope."

Nevertheless he continued to crawl on. With the stubbornness of an ant he circled around trying to find a path. He stopped being careful, and stepped out with broad steps, until he stumbled and fell into a pit.

Through the darkness he saw the ravine he had almost fallen into, next to the pit. Although the sweat was pouring from him, he suddenly felt terribly cold all along his spine. Gritting his teeth he dropped heavily to his knees, and, leaning with both arms over the brink of the ravine, he mumbled in a tone of self-derision:

"Serves you right . . . Maybe now you'll learn . . . Why be stubborn?"

The despair mounting in him, he retraced his steps and reached his horse. He wound the reins around the horse's head and placed his hand on its back, to let the horse lead him. The horse understood him and began to descend. Now digging its hoofs into the ground and slowly dragging its body forward, now twisting itself around rocks, the horse made its way painfully down the slope.

When they were finally on the plain again, Abu Il-Shawarab hurried the horse on and turned it toward the path he had left earlier. No sooner had he entered the fissure that was like a tunnel than the horse shuddered, stepped backward, and jerked its ears up: only a few steps away a figure seemed to have risen out of the bowels of the earth, clearly visible since it was darker than the darkness of the night. The figure moved, and then spoke in an urgent whisper:

"Nimmer! Is that you? . . ."

Abu Il-Shawarab recognized the voice, and his fear vanished. Like a drowning man who has been offered a lifebelt he ran straight to the other man, fell upon his neck, embraced him, kissed him, and held him tight, not letting him go while he pelted him with questions.

The *suss* vendor stood there bewildered and unmoving. He was stunned by this fierce outburst of love from a man so much higher and more exalted in rank than himself. The flag-master's frightened voice, and his tone of suppressed sobbing, made the hard heart of the *suss* vendor tremble, as air in a dark room trembles when pierced by a large beam of light. An inner joy such as he had never known flooded through every corner of his soul and overflowed its banks. Placing his hand under Abu Il-Shawarab's arm he held the flag-master firmly and led him back to the horse. Grasping the bridle, he led the two of them quickly onto the plain, mumbling fragmented and disordered pieces of information:

"Pray to the Prophet! . . . The disaster is great . . . All the blame is being placed on you . . . The riot was enormous . . . There are many killed and wounded . . . I knew you'd be lying in wait so I escaped to try to find you and tell you . . . Flight is one half of bravery . . . that dog's head who leads the Jerusalemites, the *Hadj*, cursed be his father— he wails and laments over the corpse of Abu Faris, as if he were his own brother . . . He goes among the groups and the camps carrying the torn flag of Al-Khalil, and crying for vengeance . . . You have been shamed in the eyes of all the camps . . . Even the Nablusites will not shelter you . . . The soldiers who came from Jerusalem have arrested all our leaders . . . They're searching for you along all the paths . . . Allah has hidden you . . . It is your duty to escape . . . If you don't get away in time, you'll rot in the bloody prison at Acre, or you'll hang in the streets in Stamboul . . ."

On hearing all this Abu Il-Shawarab drew his arm out of the other's grip, made a gesture as if defending his soul, swayed like a drunken man, and fell helplessly to the ground.

His head dropped to his knees and continued falling toward the ground. He buried his face in his hands. A despairing groan burst from his throat, the savage moan of a man who has been defeated by a mighty power from which there is no escape. Then he fell silent, and a terrible stillness filled the air.

Shocked and confused, the *suss* vendor gazed around him with eyes peeled. He heard no suspicious sound, and calmed down a little. Then he turned to Abu Il-Shawarab, bent over him, touched him pityingly on his trembling shoulders, and tried to lift him.

"Enough, my brother," he whispered. "Listen to me, what is past is past . . . Everything comes from Allah, praise Him and exalt Him! . . . What is said is written and what is thought is decreed . . ." Seeing that his words were having no effect on Abu Il-Shawarab, he went on in a more energetic tone:

"There's very little time left . . . Rise, and cross the Jordan before the moon comes up and reveals your tracks . . . With Allah's help, in a week or ten days you'll get to Wadi El-Arish . . . There nothing can harm you, and the blood-avengers and the government won't be able to touch you. In a year or two things will settle down, Abu Faris's family will be reconciled to their loss and will agree to accept a ransom. That's my advice to you . . . Let's make an effort now . . . I'll arrange everything. I promise to watch out and let you know everything that happens. Get on your horse. Ill accompany you to the Jordan crossing. From there I'll head left to Nablus . . . It'd be best if I disappeared too. Those dogs, may Allah not have mercy on their fathers' bones! They're surely planning to do me harm . . ."

He grasped Abu Il-Shawarab around the waist and raised him from the ground. Noticing that Abu Il-Shawarab's *abbayeh* was not over his shoulders, he took off his own and wrapped it around his leader, and then held the horse's stirrup to help him mount.

For a long time they traveled in their hasty flight, like animals fleeing before the hunters. To conceal their tracks they left the paths and wended their way among the pools and waterholes, over crystals of salt that crackled under their feet and twinkled and faded like stars in the dark sky. They passed beside the swamps and the mouth of the Jordan, pushing their way through reeds and bulrushes and many other marsh plants that fastened around their legs and waists and impeded their progress.

When they drew near to the crossing the *suss* vendor turned his sheepskin inside out and began crawling forward on all fours. He cautiously inspected the entire area, looking, as he moved, like a jackal stealing through the fields. While he was doing this, Abu Il-Shawarab remained hidden among the bushes, waiting fearfully for his return.

The *suss* vendor came back, walking erect, and Abu Il-Shawarab took courage, left his hiding place, and mounted his horse. Straining to overcome the trembling of his voice, he spoke to the *suss* vendor, instructing him of the messages he was to bear to his family and household. When he had finished speaking, he continued standing on the spot, gazing blankly into space.

"Hurry now," the *suss* vendor urged him, offering him his hand in farewell. Abu Il-Shawarab felt a flush of joy, and kissed the other man on the head, wept on his neck a little, and then spurred his horse on.

Several times he turned his head back as he rode, to gaze at the immobile figure of the *suss* vendor. When the figure had completely merged into darkness, he sighed deeply and continued riding forward, sorrowing and bent under the desperate suffering and agony of men exiled from the land of their birth . . .

CHAPTER SIX

Abu Il-Shawarab suffered innumerable hardships in the course of his flight. Fearing people as he now did, he kept away from inhabited places, making large detours around villages and tent camps. Like a hyena, he would hide by day in crevices among the rocks or in caves on mountaintops, whence he could get a glimpse of what lay ahead of him, and when darkness came he would continue on his way. For entire nights he traveled through deep valleys, crossed ravines, or slowly climbed up mountain slopes, leaning on the hind part of his horse. Fearing the bright moonlight too, he would flee into the deepest shadows, and here, in these waves of expanses which rose and fell yet stood still and petrified, not obstructing the vistas of the horizon extending into infinitude, he and his steed would lose their importance, and appear tinier and more lost than ants.

When troubled by hunger he would turn aside for a while to one of the camps of the Bedouin shepherds which he encountered here and there, scattered over some field like large black wings. Even though it was dark he would cover his face and head well with his *kefiyeh*, showing no more than his glinting eyes, which wore that special film of weariness and sorrow, and would glance hastily over the faces of all the men around him. Having asked politely about the health of all present, and having listened carefully to the reply of each, he would draw out the hand which had been grasping a weapon under his *abbayeh* all this time, and in a sad and shamed voice would make his request, asking directions for his journey and waiting expectantly for them to offer him their hospitality, all this without descending from his horse. Only when they had coaxed him profusely, assuring him that he would offend them and turn them into pursuers if he didn't accede to their invitations, did he agree to join them around their fire, and to wait until they had kneaded and baked their flatcakes for him.

Not one man of all those who offered him their hospitality in the course of his flight asked him questions about his past or the reasons for his journey or his estrangement. By an unspoken agreement they circled wide around this point, which was shrouded in mists and riddles. On seeing his stubborn stance and his endeavors to change his voice and to cover his presence and his traces, they deliberately ignored him, turning their eyes away from him and not even examining him surreptitiously under their eyelids. All of them were naturally aware that he was estranged because he was fleeing. No man travels alone into far parts in the darkness of night unless some disaster has come upon him. And such occurrences are not unusual among men who carry arms. In these cases it was clear that the hosts were duty-bound to support the pursued, to hide him and shield him and assist him and not to inform upon him to the blood-avengers, who would surely be not very far behind. They would supply him with provisions for himself and his horse, as generously as they could afford, and one of them would then accompany him some of the way on, calming and assuring him faithfully in his own name and in that of his entire tribe that his secret would be as safe with them as in a deep well, and that not even the birds in the sky would wrest it from them or discover that he had passed through their bounds. Before taking leave of him, his escort would give him directions, telling him of secret and forgotten paths he could follow where no one would be able to find his traces.

Since he had to circle around the entire Negueb in order to avoid traversing the Hebronite lands, his journey took twice as long and his troubles increased. Because of his ignorance of the terrain here, he got lost in the Edom desert around the arid southern coast of the Dead Sea. For two days he saw neither man nor a spot of green which might signify a waterhole, nothing but occasionally some whitish thorn bushes, rust-eaten and covered with salt crystals that glinted like frost. They looked more wretched and desolate than the desert itself. Their mucous, sticky juice increased the stale and bitter taste in his mouth and dried up the juices of life in his horse's veins. On the second day, as he was rising over a high hill in the heat of noon, his horse, already weakened by hunger and thirst, suddenly bent its back, slipped down to its knees, rolled over, and fell on its head. It lay on the ground, its dry, swollen tongue hanging out like a withering cactus leaf, its chest contracting and expanding like a bellows. In vain did Abu Il-Shawarab rush around the animal, tearing his hair like a man who has lost his senses, in vain did he cut the saddle straps and roll the saddle away with his foot, kissing the horse on the forehead, embracing it around the neck and calling it a string of affectionate names and endearments. The horse only raised its head slightly, gazed at him through its sorrowful and dripping eyes that had already lost most of their spark, as if pleading and saying:

"Master! You can see for yourself that my end has come! Why torment me? Let me die here in peace and let this be the reward you give me." Then its legs jerked aside, its hairy thighs moved a little, and it died quietly.

Abu Il-Shawarab buried his face in the ground. With sand between his teeth he howled and moaned, emitting strange sounds that belonged to no language. His burning eyes blazed as if consumed by fire, and his blood pumped through his veins with a strange heat.

When the horse's movements had ceased entirely, Abu Il-Shawarab crawled silently forward and bent over the animal's carcass, as if to take leave for the last time of the very source of his own powers. When he finally decided to get up and continue his journey, his soul and hopes were broken to fragments, and he had neither the strength nor the desire to gather them together.

In the company of a camel caravan that he met, which was conveying its animals to Egypt, Abu Il-Shawarab traveled the desert of El Arish and then further south. After several days he reached the bank of the Suez Canal. Agitated and frightened, like a night bird that is suddenly flung out of its dark nest in the middle of the day, he mingled with the vast throngs of men rushing and pushing toward the whistling steamboat that was about to sail to the nearest railway station on the line to Cairo.

CHAPTER SEVEN

Abu Il-Shawarab's exile in the capital of the Nile-lands was a long one, a time of many difficulties and troubles, injuries and disasters, disappointment and despair. The changes in his condition and the deep emotional shocks that followed them left their mark upon him and brought sharp changes in his character. To grasp something of their nature it is necessary to unravel the complex web of fate and describe the events in the sequence in which they happened.

During the first days, after the torments of his flight, the weeks spent in deserts and places remote from any habitation, Abu Il-Shawarab found a resting place in a small narrow room overlooking the Nile. He had rented the room in a large *khan* consisting of a vast number of cubicles and crannies, like an anthill, in one of the poorer sections of the city. Here—in the whirlpool of the city, in the incessant noise of masses of refugees and exiles from different lands and of different races, among sad displaced peasants in broad blue gowns who had left a homeland not their own to oppressors and bloodsucking landlords to escape empty-handed to the distant and enchanting city of promise and to try their fortune there as porters and street-cleaners, doormen or pickpockets— here his presence aroused no wonder or astonishment. No one here saw him as a special kind of creature to be suspected; no one annoyed him with talk or pointless questions or interrogated him about his past or the reasons for his flight.

The few Nablusites living in Cairo, his "brethren in misfortune," received him with understanding and with the joy and loyal friendship so characteristic of bitter and afflicted refugees when they meet on foreign soil. The news of his arrival and of the reason for his flight spread like wildfire among them. It touched and moved each of them profoundly. The wondrous event, already enveloped in mists of legend and bravery, captivated their imaginations. In the cruel intrigue of chance from which there can be no escape each one of them saw his own reflection and the story of his own life. Before long they all found him, one by one, and came to the place where he was staying, to visit him and congratulate him on his escape.

Several of the more desperate characters, who had long since cut themselves off from their past and their future, became very frequent visitors. Among these was Abd El-Kadir, a man with many adventures and outrages behind him. He had been the terror of all the policemen in Nablus, and had won notoriety when he evaded his prison guards and jumped off the roof of the jail, carrying a friend on his back. He claimed to be one of Nimmer's old acquaintances, and now attached himself to him as guide and mentor. He and his friends took him under their wing and offered him the benefit of their experience. They also tried to cheer him and disperse his gloom, and to keep him from thinking about either past or future. To this end they sought things which could delight and divert him. They altered the shape of his moustache and beard and changed his clothing beyond recognition, to protect him against any unexpected dangers, and they did not leave his side. The hottest hours of the day, when the air quivers as if on coals and the sunbeams pierce through it, they would spend squatting in the shady yards of the white mosques, or lying outstretched and immobile in groves of palmtrees that rose wearily against the slumbering noon. In the evenings they would wander through the lively bustling streets, visiting various coffeehouses and taverns, to listen to the chants and songs, finding the expression of their own feelings in the verses of the poets, whose burden was separation and longing, loneliness and wandering, and in the marvelous voice of the famous songstress whose song was like a stormy waterfall. Their passions, long restrained within familiar bounds, were violently aroused by the singing and the dancing. With tears in their eyes they would plead in whispers with the waiters in the coffeehouses, until they got what they wanted. Then, their nostrils dilated with lust, their faces wearing the expressions of thirsting beasts, they drew deep into their lungs the smoke of the *narguilehs* which had been spiked with *hashish*, in which they sought the oblivion longed for by the most miserable and unfortunate of souls. When quite intoxicated they would get up to all sorts of mischief, often starting up quarrels with real or imaginary enemies. And sometimes they would sink into melancholy over their own griefs, often bursting into outcries of pleading and wailing. Their nonsense would go on into the last watch of the night, and with the gray light of dawn, when their eyes were half closed with weariness and their tongues were already babbling meaningless and fragmented syllables, they would accede to the Negro proprietor's persistent demands that they go home. With neither grace nor dignity in their movements, they would get up silently and unwillingly, for their limbs as well as their souls were held down and enthralled by the marvelous visions and joys fluttering about in their minds. One moment signs of sorrow and suffering would darken their brows, and they would clench their fists at the black emissary of hell who was disturbing them out of their paradise and interrupting the choir of angels in their song. The next moment, their faces would light up again with the same smile full of heavenly joy, and they returned to weaving their marvelous dreams of delight with trembling hearts. Thrusting their arms out into the air to imitate the flight of the swallows that were cutting swiftly through the air like arrows, as if having cast off all the troubles of the earth, they left the coffeehouses and walked, swaying and stumbling and slipping on the clay paving stones that gleamed in the morning dew, as if gliding over the waves of the sea that raised their froth in the liquid purple of dawn, and climbed the steep and winding stone steps leading to Abu Il-Shawarab's room. Locking the door behind them so as not to be disturbed by voices coming in from outside, they sprawled out like dead men on the floor mats in a drunken slumber of deep oblivion whose twilit state would continue into their waking on the night of the next day.

And even though Nimmer Abu Il-Shawarab knew well that only now, after his flight, his real struggle was about to begin, and that he had to prepare himself and devise stratagems to get out of the trouble he was in, he was in no hurry to begin any decisive action, and made no real effort to prepare the ground for negotiations with his enemies. Tired, full of doubts and remorse and hopelessness, absolutely certain that everything that had happened and would happen was predetermined and necessary, he saw no point in forcing things. In addition, his secret fear that his last hopes might be disappointed weakened and terrified him. This terror grew stronger even than his torments of doubt and his suffering. He could find no way of ridding himself of this terror other than by fleeing it into vain illusions, and postponing by every means possible the day when he would have to meet it face-to-face.

Giving himself the excuse that he was being cautious in order not to make an error, and was really advancing slowly toward his goal, he yielded to the advice of his new acquaintances, who counseled him to sit tight and not show any sign of life, to blot out his existence as far as possible until the blood-avengers became reconciled and would agree to accept ransom. He disguised his terrible weariness and his great longing for rest and oblivion and turned his thoughts forcibly away from the events that had besmirched his life. He didn't even want to know a thing about the verdict that had been passed on him in distant Nablus, in that other world from which he was now divorced. The entire affair seemed to him so complicated that even to touch it might be dangerous. Having found that here in this refuge no harm was likely to come to him, and feeling confident in his circle of acquaintances, who would protect him from his pursuers, he allowed slumber and inaction to take over his being. He drove away all thoughts of past and future, and found contentment in the fact that he was alive and breathing freely under a free sky. As for the future—*Allah karim!* God is great! With patience and endurance the berry leaves turn to silk. The hasty fails and the patient is saved.

Meanwhile there was the enticing web of this exciting city, with its driving passions and its wild sensual delights coursing through tens of thousands of heads numbed by the blaze of the sun and streaming undisguised through all the streets like the clouds of black flies hovering over the muddy waters of the tributaries of the Nile. Nimmer gave himself up wholly and unthinkingly to the pleasures and delusions of his acquaintances. With them he found delight in the game of *tabla*,[1] in *hashish*, and in cards. For days on end he sat bent over with his friends and other dice-players, learned the tricks of their trade at a filthy table in an out-of-the-way coffeehouse, and played cards with them. He smiled at their crude and dirty jokes, took part in their shouting and quarrels, and delighted in the tricks performed by traveling wonderworkers and dervishes with trained monkeys and dancing snakes.

When success did not smile upon his games—and this happened to him too often—and when his thoughts of remorse, which were hidden like sleeping scorpions in some secret corner of his heart, began to awake and sting him with their venom, he was quick to seek refuge from them in *hashish*, behind gray mists of smoke in dark and moldy cellars. All his troubles, all his images of horror, would evaporate then, to turn into shadow plays and dances of flashing lights. The thick stone walls surrounding him on which his forehead struck like a fly trapped in an empty bottle collapsed and fell before the rings of smoke emerging soundlessly from his mouth. Broad and radiant paths stretched ahead of him, leading to banks of streams where date palms whispered, dripping with fragrant aromas, and the singing of birds rose to the summits of the distant hills of Samaria with a blue dome of sky above them, and among their ridges shadows and glimmers played and interspersed while sunbeams wove and circled around their crevices like the burning embers reflected in one side of the *narguileh* bowl. At such sights Nimmer's head would droop forward a little, and his eyes would close as if in sleep. A sense of

---

[1] Backgammon.

bliss and contentment filled his heart, and reached his mouth in the shape of a smile, moving his lips which had turned pale with the sweet intoxication.

As his friends had expected, here in the kingdom of magic and dreams in which his spirit walked even when he was awake, the bitterness that had filled his entire being during his first days in the city began to melt away, and in its place came a kind of calming equanimity, the pleasant fatigue of a man beginning to recuperate after a long illness. In this state of stupefied convalescence, his eyes, though broader and bigger because the pupils were always dilated, became blurred and frozen, with a longing for sleep always upon them. In all his words and gestures, in his every movement, could be sensed a moderation and a confidence which stemmed from patience and faith. A film of hallucinations enveloped his senses, which were imprisoned in chains of sleep and intoxication. For him the light of the sun was no brighter than the ordinary light of the moon, and everything was equal and quiet in the dimness and silence.

Nevertheless there were days when this veil of hallucinations and mists was torn as cobwebs are torn when touched by a cleansing hand. Then the darkness was shattered and wakening came, and with it amazement and thoughts of remorse and horror in a sobriety which brought no good. By the cold and sober light of day all the shadows of deception and illusion stole away, baring and destroying the bridges of false hope he had built in his imagination over the abysses of horror that were now again exposed to his sight. Shame penetrated into his innards, licking his bowels like the flames of a fire. He felt shamed by his cowardice and his idleness, by his wasting his money on games and revels, and by his neglect for his family. He was disgusted with himself for roaming about not doing a thing, as if there was no burden or suffering on his shoulders. The emptiness of this strange waiting for the favors of time was suddenly despicable to him, and pointless and impractical as well. His reason, clear now, showed him many contradictions in this policy, and repeatedly gave him one cold, clear piece of advice: the only way was for him to take the reins of his destiny into his own hands, to forcibly break free by his own efforts. To bring this about, he first had to get out of the powerless condition in which he now found himself, to build up his strength and be as he had been before, to struggle fearlessly against all obstacles and to bring this affair to a conclusion as quickly as possible.

Under the influence of these hasty and excited conclusions, Abu Il-Shawarab began doing some confused and surprising things. With the carelessness and impatience of spoiled children who have not learned to restrain their desires and are willing to give up everything they have to get what they think they want, he would give himself over to numerous idle projects which flashed momentarily through his mind, or to dubious though daring deeds. As soon as they occurred to him they would capture his imagination, and he would send desperate letters to relatives and friends and people of influence in Nablus. In these letters he would pour out all his grief, describing the poverty of his condition in the land of his exile, his longings for his children and family, and complaining about the unconcern of his friends, the "brothers of the wealthy who surrounded the tree and picked its fruit when it was at its prime, but now that it withers they leave it for the cold and the heat to devour." And he would curse "treacherous time," which made friends forget friends, and separated lovers. He would conclude by giving them instructions, telling them which officials to bribe, and which of the notables of Hebron to approach with suggestions of mediation and compromise. Begging them to stand beside him in his time of trouble and not to torment him any longer with prolonged hoping, he would conclude:

"Let no ransom seem too high to you. Don't bargain. Pay whatever the exploiters demand, sell my possessions, mortgage my properties. How many watermelons does a camel break? The main thing is to put an end to this thing, and the sooner the better; there is no power and no might save in Allah."

The days of waiting for a reply either went by too fast or crawled slowly along like blind men trying to make their way through deserts of bare and level sands, and during these days fear and hope ruled him alternately and he swung between them like a ball. Unclear premonitions of disaster agitated his breast, he felt sudden and inexplicable pangs of dread, and then he flailed about like a fish which, attracted by a worm, leaves its home and is trapped. He was horrified by his hasty and unconsidered act, and regretted the stupidity that had made him give away his shelter. At other times he would suddenly be filled with confidence and faith in his stars and in the success of his project, and his heart whispered to him that very soon now his exile would be over.

During these periods of belief it was all so clear, so beyond any doubt, that he would hurry to his room, pack his belongings, settle his accounts with the proprietor of the hostelry, and rush out, with an excited sense of liberation, into the bustling streets and narrow winding markets of the city. There he would happily examine the wares on display, asking prices and selecting the best articles which he wanted to prepare as presents for his relatives and friends. This wonderful belief which took root in his mind and radiated from his face did not fade even when he saw the frank contempt with which his friends greeted his boasts that his affairs were getting straightened out and that, Insh'allah, in a little while he would be going home, putting an end to this life of idleness and games which he was sick of. He was unmoved even by the pointed comments of Abd El-Kadir, an experienced man well versed in the ways of the world, who in his devotion to Nimmer did not want to see him deluding himself, knowing that the fall that comes with disillusion is more painful.

Abd El-Kadir preferred to express his doubts in hints or barbs or even stubborn silences of disregard and obvious disbelief. But once, when he could no longer bear Nimmer's talk about his dreams, he decided to throw all the bitter truth mercilessly in the other's face. Sweeping aside the backgammon board, he said angrily:

"Listen, Nimmer! This rice needs a lot more water yet! I know those Hebronites. It's easier to drag a silk *abbayeh* out of a cactus plant than to get out of their clutches. The more you mollify them and chase them and yield to them, the more they'll raise their heads high and refuse and be stubborn, and bark like dogs beside their garbage. My advice to you is this: don't delude yourself with vain hopes. Don't grasp at cobwebs. What's past is past. Send for your family to come here, and forget everything. Earn a living as best you can, and don't walk around fuming and miserable like someone with an onion under his nose. You were a drum and you're broken. Praise Him Who changes and is not changed and exists for ever!"

Abu Il-Shawarab made no reply, but his hands and lips trembled with excitement and sorrow. All that long evening until very late at night he sat on the low stool, lost in thought, drinking many cups of coffee and surrounding himself in a cloud of *hashish* and tobacco smoke. Finally he dropped to the floor and fell asleep, like a man rolling into a deep, dark pit.

CHAPTER EIGHT

Months passed, and there was no change in Nimmer's situation. The mediation attempts made by a number of Nablus notables bore no fruit, despite their diligence and haste. The Hebronites, as Abd El-Kadir had anticipated, dragged out the negotiations interminably, so as to gain time to implement their secret intrigues, for they held zealously to the time-honored tradition of blood vengeance, as inscribed on their flag: "A hundred reversals but never defeated." They did not reject the ransom offers made to them, nor did they refuse the first gifts, those known as "to go down to the well and to leave the camel," sent regularly by the murderer's family as a basis for postponing the revenge. The heads of their families even accepted the invitations of Nimmer's peace emissaries and came to dine at the banquets these had prepared with the intention of softening their guests' bitter resistance and coaxing them to concessions and forgiveness, and of discovering their peace conditions and the sum of the ransom they wanted. The Hebronite worthies came with their boys and their horses to where the cushions were laid down for the banquet in one place or another. Here they fell upon the meat and the rice, vociferously demanding fodder for their animals, making the best of the situation until the moment came for serious discussion, at which point they would put off their hosts with half-promises and vague replies and a variety of excuses. "Go back to your homes and come back another time," they would tell the intercessors. "We must wait until all the relatives of the murdered man discuss this again, for they, finally, are the ones who have the last word on this important matter." Realizing that their efforts had all been in vain, the negotiators would lose patience, and sadly and hopelessly head back to their homes.

The strategy of the Hebronites was at once simple and daring: to impoverish the murderer and his family as much as they could, to trouble their rest and not allow them to tend to their affairs. As for the blood vengeance—its time would come. The true Arab "takes blood vengeance after fifty years and says 'I've been quick!' "

This devilish plan of theirs was very successful. From the incessant stream of emissaries coming to them from Abu Il-Shawarab, they received ample proof that the murderer was in Egypt, and that he had become as soft as wax. They could knead him as they wished. The more Nimmer's intercessors continued their activities in his name and with his permission, squandering money without keeping accounts, giving bribes right and left, and offering concession after concession, the greater grew the arrogance and the greed of Abu Faris's family. They grew so excessive in their demands that even the tolerant Abu Za'id, the last intercessor, who had seen many things in his long life and knew how to restrain his feelings under the frozen mask of his thin face, which was creased like the trunk of an ancient olive tree, lost his patience and self-control on hearing their insolent conditions. Unable to bear their intrigues any longer, he threw aside the cushion he was sitting on, rose to his knees as if preparing to get up and leave, and after casting angry glances at the company seated there, spoke in a quavering voice:

"Pray to the Prophet! Extortion will not fill your pitchers; you will gain nothing but a mote of dust . . . By this white beard, I have never in my life been so mocked and ridiculed . . . I have been among you for more than a month now, and I know your intentions: you do not want peace, you want blood. You don't want to put out the fire, but to inflame it further. And what good are words? But know this, by the beard of the Prophet!—if you send me away empty-handed no one of Nimmer's family will come again to bow his head to you or offer you hand of peace . . . The hammer you are swinging now will find an equal anvil beneath it . . ."

Abu Za'id took his time folding his *abbayeh* and fixing his belt, with the clear intent of giving them a chance to thoroughly consider the consequences of their stubbornness, and to change their minds in time. But all he saw was the deep hatred engraved on their faces, the bitterness and malice expressed in each of their movements. Getting up with a painful decision, he muttered a few quiet words of parting, and strode toward the doorway of the house.

The next evening, even before Abu Za'id reached home, the news of his return and of the failure of his mission was already circulating among Nimmer's relatives. A little later, even though the hour was late, they all gathered in an upper chamber of his house and waited expectantly for his appearance, hoping to hear all the details from his lips. Abu Za'id, weary and violently angry at Abu Il-Shawarab and his family who had coaxed him to get involved in this disgraceful affair as a mediator even though he had known from the beginning that only shame and failure would result from his mission, came upstairs and spoke to them at length about the vile plots and intrigues of the Hebronites. Full of contempt and disgust he outlined all the details of the Hebronites' deceitfulness, and demanded of his listeners not to demean themselves again by making more offers of concessions, none of which would be of any avail. And when one of those present asked hopelessly what to do about Nimmer, who in his suffering in exile was sending them streams of letters containing pleas which would melt a heart of stone, Abu Za'id replied with a meaningful shrug of the shoulders. He forcefully condemned their weakness and exaggerated pity, and stirred up their injured pride, until all present were convinced he was right. Finally they called for writing materials, and wrote a long, resentful yet conciliatory letter to Abu Il-Shawarab in which, among stern words of moral instruction, they told him the whole truth without any pretenses, thoroughly and finally destroying any grain of hope he might still have had. In the margins of the sheet Abu Za'id added the following words:

"Listen to the cup and it will bring you to ruin. You have sent us many words and involved even me in the mess caused by your hot temper. I have just returned in shame and empty-handed from the Hebronites, that treacherous breed to whom the only great thing is a camel. During the days I spent with them I learned their spirit and grasped the meaning of their intrigues, the curse of Allah be upon them! They want to impoverish you down to the last loaf of bread, to strip you of your last shirt, and to use your money for bribes, to hasten the judgment and to tumble you into a deep pit. Your hands are now in cool water, don't put them into boiling water. Turn your back on them until the blind man regains his sight. Chains are for men, weakness and panic for women. No counsel or reason can help against the decree of Allah, from Whom we come and to Whom we all return."

Nimmer was totally engrossed in shuffling the cards, which were dirty and swollen from sweat and use, when the letter carrier, who knew where he regularly sat in this coffeehouse, made his way among the tables and handed him the letter. The friends he was playing with shook their heads on seeing his hands suddenly start trembling and his face alternately flushing and turning pale as he read. In bewildered silence they watched him crumple up the letter between his fingers and throw it aside with a curse. Then he got up and picked it up again, tore it into pieces, and put the pieces in his lap. When they saw the expression of despair contorting his face and the misery in his eyes, the questions died on their lips and they turned their heads away without saying anything.

For some time Abu Il-Shawarab sat frozen on the spot without moving, like a terrified bird seeing its nest being destroyed and its offspring killed, while itself unable to screech or chirp or flee. Finally he pulled himself together forcibly, and put on a smile of scorn and contempt, which looked more like a contortion of agony than a smile. With uncertain motions he took up the cards again, tossed them from hand to hand, and invited his friends to renew their interrupted game.

He shuffled and dealt, made a mistake in the count, and suddenly lost patience with what he was doing. With a fury rising in him, he flung the cards away from him, and they scattered in all directions. Leaping up like someone suddenly awakened, he struck his head on the lamp hanging over his chair. Pressing his hands to the injured place, he rushed, bent over, to his room in the hostelry, to be alone with his pain.

Like a wounded animal hiding in its cave to lick its injuries, Abu Il-Shawarab dropped down on his mat in the corner and sat there, his hands around his knees and his head leaning against the wall. He sat there like this, depressed, all his previous thoughts and plans evaporating like smoke, until evening.

Late at night he crept out of his room and walked wearily to the moldy cellar. With a dry mouth and chafed lips he thirstily drew in the *hashish* smoke which obliterates all griefs. With the deep breaths he took to fill his lungs with the powerful smoke, he felt it also penetrating to the left of his breast, where with gentle featherlike strokes it calmed the swelling that had risen up to his throat to stifle him. And then came the expected relief and expansion. His tense and acutely responsive nerves relaxed. The rustling of ants tingling on his back and under the roots of his hair stopped. Waves of delight, warm and clean, poured over his skin, his thoughts became misty, and all fear and despair vanished, present and future merging into a serene, comfortable, and painless experience, and in white visions that cannot be expressed he rocked like a child relieved of its suffering, who falls asleep, calmly and quietly, in his mother's lap.

CHAPTER NINE

Autumn and winter passed, and the summer and autumn after these, and nothing happened to give Nimmer even a gleam of hope.

He continued living his life of waste and idleness, given over entirely to intoxication, revelry, and oblivion. Each day was like the day before, each night like the nights preceding it. The coffeehouses and the singing were his entire world, *hashish* and cards his joy and vision. Accustomed as he was by nature to being considered a leader always surrounded by a circle of admirers who went with him everywhere he went and hung on to his every word, here too he behaved magnánimously, surrounding himself with sycophants of all kinds whose tongues were milk and honey in their flattery; through these he made the acquaintance of the songstresses, and met secretly as well as in the open with the beautiful Khasibah, the nightingale of the East, the rising crescent of song. With these Egyptians and with his Nablusite friends he spent his days and evenings in games and pleasure, and his nights in the intoxication of *hashish*. At the last watch of the night he would totter home, stumbling and tripping at every step, or, as happened most often, supported by Abd El-Kadir, who dragged him along against his will while appeasing and calming him and trying to coax him to stop his shouting and cursing and wild behavior, because of which they had just been thrown out of the pleasure house by the policemen patrolling the city, to be shamed and scorned by believers.

Living this way, he wasted the remains of his property. The money he had soon dwindled and seeped through his fingers; want and poverty began knocking on his door, showing him their terrifying faces. The proceeds from his house and other possessions which his relatives had sold for him the year before were already gone, and the other remnants of his properties were quickly decreasing. He was coming to the end of the last money that had been sent him, and for some weeks now his relatives had been unable to raise more money and had even stopped replying to his letters. His Egyptian friends were quick to sense the change that was soon to befall him, and were the first to turn their backs on him and to begin to avoid him.

Nimmer was the only one who did not sense the need to find out how things stood with him. He had no desire to examine the changes occurring around him. With a bitter stubbornness that distorts the reason he continued acting as he had till now, increased his rash spending, and tried to keep the worries which gnawed at him from being seen by those who surrounded him. The only thing he did to extricate himself from his situation was this: during the few hours when he was sober he would draw up a mental list of all those who owed him something, recalling dubious loans made a long time ago. He would grasp at these as a drowning man at a straw, rejoicing as if he had discovered a treasure. In his mind he wrote them threatening letters, firmly demanding what was due to him. In his tiredness and laziness he postponed the writing of these letters to another time. Then, under the influence of *hashish*, which confuses illusion and reality, it seemed to him that he had already sent them off to his debtors, and he waited impatiently for the replies with the assurance of a child.

But finally the days came when poverty became his daily lot. His mind froze at the thought of the day when his money would be entirely gone, and he would be forced to forego the heavenly drug which had become the life and soul of his spirit. Just the thought of this would set his whole body trembling like the papyrus reed in the hot east wind; a cold sweat would moisten its neck and drip down his tingling back. In dread of this horrible possibility he became lost and hopeless, and like a man standing before the gaping jaws of a terrible beast, he decided to sacrifice everything in order to extricate himself from this situation.

It was then that Nimmer suddenly changed his whole attitude. He put aside his stubborn rebelliousness and reconciled himself to the inevitable—to go and look for work. Having seen that most of the exiles from his town earned their livelihood by selling Nablus soap in the streets, he decided to grasp at this last hope and to try his hand at it.

Abd El-Kadir was astonished when Nimmer told him of his decision and asked for his help. Nimmer's face, in this, his first admission of his plight to someone else, wore an expression of indescribable weakness and despair. He looked like a man who no longer cared what people thought of him or what would become of him.

The next morning Abd El-Kadir accompanied him to the warehouses of the soap agents, where Nimmer discussed arrangements with the officials and bought several sacks of soap, a pair of scales, and some baskets.

The men in the warehouses apparently knew Nimmer, for they received him with wonder and pity, and gazed at him questioningly. As he walked out the door bent under his load as if carrying the burden of agonies on his back, they accompanied him with sympathy in their eyes. Nimmer knew what they were thinking, through that heightened power of observation that is the possession of those who have settled their accounts with the present and in whose souls there is a bitterness unto death.

In a dark and gloomy mood Nimmer carried his merchandise to his room, dropped onto his mat, and hastened to cross the border into intoxication and oblivion while it was still day.

The next day, as soon as he awoke sober, he leapt up decisively from his mat. He quickly took off his silk caftan and donned the blue robe worn by all vendors. Outwardly calm, he picked up his baskets and scales and weights, slung them over his back, and with quick rough strides and lowered eyes he crossed his street and headed for the Old City of Cairo.

He lasted as a vendor for several days. His efforts, his stubbornness, and his struggle against his weak will during this brief period were like the flame of a lamp in which there is no more oil, glimmering and lighting up before it finally goes out. Very soon he grew weary and impatient with his work, doing it as if compelled by a demon.

In the mornings, before the heat of the day, he had no sooner loaded his heavy basket on his aching and burning back and crossed a number of streets, shouting his wares, than he began to lose breath and feel weak. The sweat started to burst like water from all his pores, wetting his blue robe and making it stick to his skin, inflaming his face and burning his eyes. His legs were suddenly as weak and soft as rags, and he felt as if his bones were folding up with every step he took. His arms trembled under the heavy weight he was carrying, and as the trembling increased the basket would slip off his shoulders, even though he held on to it with all his might.

Sticking to his decision to succeed in this enterprise and not to stop selling until he had made enough for his day's needs, he would drag his burden on with the remains of his strength, stopping for breath at every step. But after several moments his stubborn will would evaporate. Hesitant and bewildered, like a man caught out in a crime, he would look around for a shady place in which to drop his goods and himself. When he found a cool dark coffeehouse from which came the sound of the little wooden discs pounding fiercely and joyfully on the backgammon boards he quite forgot his wares and the purpose for which he had come out. With his neck thrust forward like a camel when it scents water he would rush to the doorway of the coffeehouse, and with the motions of a prisoner liberated from his chains he would unencumber himself of his load, push it aside with his foot, and drop helplessly into the concavity of the stool.

For a long time he would sit there like a silent statue, his dull eyes fixed on the lifeless bodies circling to and fro on the board according to the blind and mysterious luck contained in the fall of the black numbers inscribed on the bone dice. In this game he saw his vision of everything, of the world and of himself, of the things that had happened and that were to happen to him. In the combinations of numbers which depended on chance, which defeated all reason and always at the last moment confounded all certainties, he thought he saw the iron hand of fate that suddenly descended upon a man at the height of his fortune, thrusting its fingernails into his neck to defeat him. In the desperate plight of the lone disc caught in territory not its own, where all others blocked it and injured it, he saw the adventures of the exile torn from his homeland, his wanderings and his hopeless efforts to extricate himself from the circle of traps surrounding him on all sides, while in the total siege which led inevitably to a final departure from the field he saw the last surrender to the invisible forces from which there is no escape.

In this way the best hours for selling passed in idleness. Those playing when he sat down had already finished, other players had taken their places, and also gone, and Nimmer still sat absorbed in the depths of his visions. He stared into space without seeing a thing, dazed and stupefied by the incessant knocking of the wooden discs which still continued their circuits in his head, like a miller's horse circling around the wheel, stamping its hoofs and turning around itself even in its sleep.

When he finally decided to get up and leave the day was already over. The light of the sun, white as chalk when he had come in, was orange when he left, and on the horizon the sky burned like beaten sheets of blazing tin. On these summer evenings people walked around like powerless shadows, weakened by the hard struggle against the heat of the day; the Europeans drove their pale and tortured ladies, who looked as though they had withered in the hard climate of this land of heat, in carriages and motor cars. The streets were crowded with people streaming to the banks of the Nile in search of some air and moisture to refresh their spirits. Through and among them rolled a long line of carriages and cars with no spaces between them. Haughtily reclining in them were the wealthy elite of the land, pashas and their deputies, beside their wives who wore veils up to their noses. Beneath their foreheads, which were white as alabaster or brown as bronze, their eyes blazed with fire at one moment and closed under indolent heavily lashed eyelids the next. Down the long avenues lined with tall palms standing still as if bewitched, this reveling Babel moved and hustled in a single direction, carrying with it the variegated masses of Cario—Syrians, Negroes, Copts, Armenians, and Greeks. A vast misture of strange races and costumes.

All these throngs of people had come out to greet the evening breeze before the coming of night, with its hot air that was as heavy as lead. In an ever-growing babble of noise they walked among the rows of thick date palms and the eye-entrancing plots of lawn beside the river bank, where a number of orchestras, Arab and European, played a confusion of gay and boisterous tunes and heartbreaking melancholy Oriental melodies full of longing and emotion. In the intervals they would gaze with weary eyes at the streams of tepid water and at the distant horizon stretching like a sorry strip of silver over white sands, from where they hoped would come the caress of a breeze which might ease their breathing and bring them some relief.

And Nimmer, trying to silence the roar sawing through his brain like an insistent cricket, ran this way and that with his soap, simple laundry soap, among all these pleasure seekers, whose only object was entertainment and revelry and who had no time or interest in everyday needs. Inexperienced in his trade he would mix with all the other hawkers and vendors of confections and cold drinks, who were shouting their wares in deafening cries. With them he would silently press among the groups of strolling people and fearfully offer his wares, almost as if they were stolen goods. Each time he offered his soap he would feel offended and insulted deep inside his soul, both by the angry gestures of refusal with which some of those he approached responded to him, and by the way others turned their heads away and ignored him. Bewildered and agitated, the film of tears in his eyes blurring his vision, he would hurry away, making detours and then running straight ahead as if rushing to a particular place without looking to the sides. Covered with sweat and dust, dizzy and stumbling, he made his weary way as hastily as he could through desolate quarters and suburbs, to arrive at his room at dark, breathing heavily and groaning like an ox that has pulled the plow all day through rocky ground and, its yoke and harness removed, falls to the ground with trembling limbs.

For about a month Nimmer repeated his depressing and shameful attempts, with less success each day. In this short time he slipped from bad to worse. This back-breaking physical work, for which he had never been trained, completely exhausted his strength, irritated his weak and angry nerves, and did not bring in its wake that pleasant tiredness which leads to tranquillity of soul and the sweet sleep of the laborer. The contrary was the case: even when his tiredness wore off, his mind kept foreseeing evil and bitter things ahead. Things went so far that the slightest noise would fill him with fear and horror, increasing the ache that pressed permanently around his head like an iron ring.

At nights, even though all his limbs and muscles were as heavy as lead, he was unable to close his eyes without doubling his dose of *hashish*. One night his Nablusite friends found him lying unmoving on his mat, his legs spread out, his caftan off and rolled up under him, his hairy chest bare, and his eyes wide open and staring at the rusty tin lamp hanging on the wall above his feet, gazing at it without any other sign of life. His lower jaw was shriveled and contorted like a dead man's.

After a number of weeks Nimmer suddenly realized that he was ill. When he woke up and tried to get to his feet, the floor started moving and the walls danced around him; even the mat began to move horizontally, rising into the air until it almost reached his face, and then sinking slowly with circular movements. For half a minute or so Nimmer stood where he was, amazed at what was happening, his arms reaching for the collapsing wall to stop it from falling. Then he started shivering; a tremor of weakness passed down the length of his spine, and continued to his knees and then his ankles. Fear came then, and total powerlessness, and he fell to the floor with a stifled scream of dread that burst through his gritted teeth and quivering lips.

When he regained consciousness, the terrible dread of death that had frozen the blood in his veins had still not left him. He did not dare remain alone in his room. Strange visions of horror rose in his imagination. A sudden thought flashed through his mind: perhaps he was fatally ill, and was about to die. Then a bout of shuddering ran through him and again he felt he could not stay where he was. An irresistible force drove him to flee, to escape, to be in the company of people, to call for help and to do something.

Feverishly he jumped off his mat, and, with weak knees, stumbling dizzily like a drunken man, he wandered around for a long time in the hall and in the narrow corridor between the doors, until he succeeded in finding the cubicle where one of his acquaintances lived. Finding the door locked he knocked on it with all his might, until the owner and the Negro boys who served in the *khan* came rushing upstairs in alarm to see what was happening. When they finally made some sense of the garbled words he was muttering and grasped what was wrong with him, the owner of the *khan* quickly sent for Sheikh Salame the barber, who was also a doctor known for his grinding of perfumes, unbinding of spells, and annulling the evil eye. In the meantime they carried him back to his room, laid him down on his mat, and remained standing around him, helpless and confused at the sight of the contortions of pain convulsing his body from time to time, and the groans that escaped from his mouth.

Sheikh Salame, a short fat man with a wizard's beard gracing his cheeks and chin, examined Nimmer thoroughly, inspected his vomit, kneaded his stomach, and listened to his breathing. On discovering the nature and causes of the illness he shook his head and creased his brow in sorrow, and then, with a lot of fuss, went about his work. He stuck plasters on Nimmer's temples and drew blood from his ears and biceps, boiled up various herbs, gave them to him to drink, and bandaged the cuts with cotton wool. As he worked he wagged a warning finger at Nimmer, who sat on the cushions looking as pale as lime.

"This is all from excessive use of *hashish*," he said. "Your blood is spoiled and burned out: it's thick and black. Keep away from it completely, or your end will be a bitter one . . ."

Nevertheless, as soon as he felt a little better Nimmer could not deny himself the drug he so desired, and immediately returned to his former way of life. After giving the matter much consideration, he rejected the claim to understanding and expertise of this barber who prattled on so volubly, and decided that he himself knew what was wrong with him better than Sheikh Salame.

Attacks of this sort grew more frequent. Nimmer grew so used to them that they stopped having a frightening effect on him. They became such a regular occurrence in his life that he became able to sense their coming in advance. To assuage the pains, and to get himself into a condition in which he would not feel their coming or going, he would hurry to his room, close himself inside, and draw the stunning, numbing smoke deep into his lungs. More than any of the talismans and remedies given him by *hadjs* or holy dervishes *hashish* seemed to him the most tested and efficacious means of dulling the pains, blurring his suffering, and submerging the long moments of dread in the twilight of dozing.

And the more he took of the poisonous and malignant drug, the worse his condition became. He grew thinner from day to day, his skin turned gray and withered, and his posture stooped. His eyes lost their luster and became bleared and motionless. Soon his appetite went completely: hunger stopped troubling him and he forgot to eat. When he felt himself terribly weak, and noticed the stale bitter taste in his mouth, he would suddenly remember that for a long time he had not eaten a thing, and would be amazed and alarmed at his laziness and negligence in looking after himself and at his having ceased to care about his dress or to look after the cleanliness of his body and his room.

After many hesitations, coaxings, and urgings, he would berate himself into summoning up all his strength, and raise himself from a lying position. Groaning with the effort, he rested on his side, reached out a weak arm to the *pitta* by his head, brought it to his mouth without any pleasure, and nibbled at it with grimaces of nausea. When he forced himself to swallow the piece he had chewed and turned over many times with his tongue, he found it sticking in his throat, stifling him. His gullet had contracted and grown so narrow that it absolutely refused to obey his will, and rejected the bread in disgust. He was forced to spit it out again, coughing hard, with watering eyes.

He also suffered from sleeplessness. All night he tossed about on his hard bed, finding no rest for his heavy, tortured limbs. With the chill of dawn, when the *muezzin* called the faithful to the morning prayer, sleep would finally visit his eyelids, which burned and pricked his eyes as if sharp and hot grains of sand and gravel had been scattered under them. Nor was this sleep anything like his accustomed intoxicated slumber, that heavy, deep, luxuriant slumber that had come so frequently to him after the arousing of his senses. Now he slipped slowly into a numb stupor, as if sinking into a thick oily fluid. He would feel his body freezing and his mind remaining alert in his senseless body. When he finally drowsed off a little, at the end of his strength, his sleep was short and tormented, full of terrible dreams, interrupted at times by horrible visions from which he would awake screaming. Nor did the awful visions end when he awoke. They continued floating about in his mind, appearing before him in all their horror, and he could not escape them except when he was fully awake, and even then only by leaping in despair from his mat, getting dressed, and hastily leaving his room.

These nights of sleeplessness and nightmare were only a transition to more severe symptoms of illness. Soon his senses became marvelously acute, and he began having hallucinations even during his sober intervals between one bout of intoxication and the next. These terrible hours would begin at around midnight, when the din from the streets had ceased and silence reigned in the hostelry. Night after night, when this hour came, one could hear awful screams and wails and strange conversations coming from Nimmer's room.

But the sight that really gripped him and completely changed his entire life appeared one night: that evening Nimmer had left the coffee-house much earlier than usual, and headed toward his *khan*. Sweltering from the heat, weak in all his limbs, he swayed and stumbled as he walked, and then slowly climbed the stairs, holding on to the rail and resting to take a breath at every step. When he finally succeeded, with great effort, in finding the keyhole in his door and turning the key in it, he followed his custom in recent weeks and went straight to the *narguileh* and the other equipment that lay on the window shelf, and began preparing it for smoking. He bound the cord around its head and firmly attached the tube into its neck. Then he drew from his gown a piece of *hashish*, weighed it in his hand, added a little more to it, and stuck it into the wet tobacco leaves, covered it on all sides, and rubbed the tobacco in his palm with his fingertips until he'd shaped it into something like a nipple. Then he placed the *narguileh* near the head of the mat and squatted down next to it. But when he put the tube into his mouth and tried to take his first draw he suddenly realized that he had forgotten to pour water into the bowl. He got up quickly, put on his robe again and his shoes, picked up the clay pitcher, and rushed off to get water.

The taps from which the lodgers in this *khan* filled their pitchers were on the ground floor. Nimmer hurried down the long corridor and into the filthy passage next to it, where a smoking oil lamp, standing on a shelf, cast its dim light with long dancing shadows on the entire area. When he opened the low door between the passage and the slippery broken stairs leading down to the yard, three figures suddenly emerged from behind the door. They were tall men, draped in white *abbayehs*, with glistening white *keffiyehs* around their heads. With no forethought, almost in response to an inner command, Nimmer drew back and flattened himself against the wall to let them pass. As he raised his eyes to look at them he saw that they greatly resembled each other in feature and hue: all three had great black eyes that glowed and glittered like stars, long white hair that descended in manes to their shoulders and on both sides of their necks to mingle with their long beards which came down to their belts. They approached him calmly, with a solemn and dignified gait, as if they were on their way to a very important meeting and were about to pass him without even looking at him. When they became aware of his presence their faces darkened and they raised their eyebrows, and stopped their advance, standing still and unmoving as they directed their glowering and threatening glances at him.

Although Nimmer had never seen these men before and had no idea of anything they might want with him, he had an intimation of terror and sensed that he was the one they were seeking. One glance at their marvelous apparel and the glory radiating from their faces, at the way they moved across the floor without the sound of footsteps, the way they passed the oil lamp without causing even a flicker in its flame, was enough to convince him that these were no ordinary men come to lodge at the *khan* but superior creatures who had left Paradise and were walking abroad on the face of the earth to fulfill an essential and highly important mission. With awe and reverence, his entire frame trembling with dread, he bowed his head to them and spoke to them in submission:

"*Salaam Allah aleikum!* The Peace of God upon you! Behold, I am an instrument to serve you, my masters . . . What will you command me?" he pleaded in a hoarse and terrified voice. "What do you want of me? Why have you troubled yourselves to seek me?"

The aged men remained unspeaking and frozen, though they stared at him with even more fury in their gaze. Then the middle one, all aglow with wrath, took one step forward. With lips pursed and eyebrows arched, he raised one arm as if motioning Nimmer to stand still.

His broad sleeve rolled down and fell about his shoulder, exposing his raised arm to the armpit. To his astonishment, Nimmer saw that it was a dead man's arm, its bones glowing in a phosphorescent white. In his long fingers the figure held a staff, from which hung a torn and blood-stained flag, frayed at the edges. He brandished the flag in front of Nimmer's face, with the obvious intention of showing him the rips in it. Then he put it down, stuck it at his feet, leaned his head against it in sorrow, and again stared at Nimmer with eyes burning with hatred and vengeance.

Now all Nimmer's doubts and questions were resolved. He understood that these were the Three Fathers,[1] finally come to avenge the insult and sacrilege to their feast and their honor. The man with the torn flag which Abu Faris had borne was none other than the Proselyte, Ibrahim himself, there could be no mistake about it—it was him! And this was the flag with his name embroidered upon it in prominent letters . . .

"Mercy, my lord the Proselyte! I beg your protection!" wailed Nimmer, and flung himself to the ground. Prostrate, he squirmed at the other's feet like a worm, kissed the ground before him and moistened it with his tears as he thrust out a hand to grasp the hem of his *abbayeh*. The gown flared out as if blown back by a sudden gust. Nimmer crawled on in despair toward the other two aged figures, stretched out his hands to them and pleaded, weeping as he spoke:

"Khalil the Merciful! My lord Abu Youssef the Forgiver! I have sinned! Be charitable! Speak, intercede to him for me! It was not with malice that I tore his flag . . . Nothing is hidden from you, you know all, you know the truth! It was Abu Faris's fault! He was the one who started it all! Please! For the sake of Allah! Do you want to kill me? Go away from me! Take your eyes off me! . . . Allah! Allah! I've had enough! . . ."

He wailed some more disconnected phrases and great hot tears rolled down his cheeks to mingle with the spittle coming from his mouth. None of the three responded to his pleading and weeping. Suddenly he stopped his stream of words, and with the remains of his strength slowly raised himself, covered his face with his hands, and began shaking his head from side to side in despair, uttering a stifled groan from time to time.

Several dreadful moments of apprehension passed, during which he did not dare to look around him or to move from the spot. He felt as if

---

[1] Abraham, Isaac, and Jacob, who were buried in Hebron.

the aged figures were watching his every movement, and that the slightest attempt on his part to flee would arouse their ire even more. Finally
he took courage and turned his head away from them slightly, so as not
to have to face their gazes, which were striking at his eyes even through
his hands.

The Fathers did not fall upon him with their fists, nor did they throt-
tle him. He thought for a moment that he was already safe and out of
danger. He started moving backward slowly. When he was several paces
away he rose quickly to his feet. Like a tortured beast that has escaped
the claws of a predator, he sneaked away in haste, bending over and
pressing close to the walls, shuddering in horror and drawing back in
fright at every step, turning his head to look behind him, and then
charging forward again.

Reaching his room completely out of breath, he flung his entire body
at his door to open it, and then quickly closed it behind him. When it
closed he found himself enveloped in total darkness, in which red and
blue points and stars flickered and moved. Again he was filled with the
terror of darkness. He remained by the door, quaking all over and
breathing heavily, listening tensely for any sound. When his heartbeats
and the pounding in his head had subsided a little, he put his hand into
his belt, ferreted around in there for some time, until he found the box
of matches stuck away among its folds. He lit one match and looked on
the shelf and on the mat for the key so that he could lock the door. The
match went out as he moved and he had the feeling that a wind had
blown it out. The darkness grew thicker, engulfing everything. Quickly
he pulled out several matches and lit them one after another, but they
all fizzled out after being lit, or broke between his trembling fingers.

Finally he managed to light the lamp. The orange flame sent weird
and horrifying shadows and figures scurrying across the walls and floor.
In order not to give way entirely to the fear that had attacked him anew,
he stubbornly started looking for the key in every corner. Finally he
found that it was stuck in the keyhole on the outside. A strange tremor
of horror ran through all his nerves. But he went to the door. He peeped
through its cracks, bent down, placed his ear against it, and listened
carefully. Neither seeing nor hearing anything suspicious, he put his
hand on the door handle, firmly resolved to open the door swiftly and
silently, to snatch the key out and lock the door on the inside.

Just as he began doing this, the door turned on its hinges, emitting a
strange creaking sound. Nimmer's heart leapt up to his throat. His
terror mounted. Fragments of voices and footsteps came to his ears,

sounding closer and louder all the time. Hastily he shut the door, pressed himself against it with his chest, his hands, and his knees. For a long time he stood like this without changing his position. When the noise passed, and the silence of a tomb had returned, an idea flashed through Nimmer's mind a way to protect and save himself. Quietly he took off his shoes, left his place by the door for a moment, and walked on tiptoe to where the sacks of soap were stacked. He grasped one of the sacks with both arms and, struggling with all his strength, dragged it across the room and leaned it against the door. Then he dragged over another sack and stacked it on top of the first, straightening and supporting it with his head and chest. After dragging all the other sacks over, he climbed up and started pulling the sacks up one after the other, stacking them up with great effort until they blocked the entire space of the doorway.

His work completed, he turned over onto his stomach and slid down the stack, taking care lest they fall down after him. When he felt the floor under his feet and tried to stand up, he sensed a terrible weakness in his knees and had to hang on to the sacks again and lean on them to prevent himself from falling. With his sleeve he wiped away the beads of sweat that were pouring down his blazing cheeks and wetting his neck and chest, and crawled wearily to his mat. When he came to its edge he flung his body upon it, pulled his blanket up above his head, sunk his head deep into his pillow, closed his eyes and blocked off his hearing, and gave himself up to the peace of oblivion that spread over all his limbs and froze his sweat-drenched skin. This weakness also overcame his other senses, agitated his imagination, and confused his memory. Things merged and fused, and, like the colors at the rim of the western sky at sunset which combine and change to fade and melt away until they are one single hue, so all the various fragments of thought in his head combined until they turned into a single nothingness.

Minutes or hours passed while he remained in this state of paralyzed unconsciousness. Then he began to awake slowly, and a dream came, arousing him again to vain and distressing visions. In his dream, his soul had long since parted from his body and had now returned and was fluttering about nearby, except that it was very difficult for him to find its exact position. But he could clearly hear the flapping of its wings as it flew above him, and his entire body writhed and trembled in pain and fear of its coming.

"It's hiding, it must be hiding!" he thought. "It's hiding so as I won't take care, so it can jump upon me all at once. But, Allah, it's so strange!

How did it get in? I blocked the door, didn't I? It must have gone around and come in through the window." Now he remembered that a split second earlier the window had swung open as if someone had given it a strong push from the outside.

Nimmer turned his face toward the window. He clearly saw a strange white bird knocking on the pane with its beak, scratching at it with its claws, pushing at it with its wings, pressing its entire body against it while its head wept and wailed voicelessly. The pane finally cracked and the white bird thrust its body through the opening and stood on the shelf. With its beak it pulled out the fragments and splinters of glass that were stuck in its body. Then, from under one wing it drew out a dirty rag and cleaned the open wound in its breast from which blood was pouring. Rising into the air, it flew to the window, grasped the bolt, and opened it carefully. Bending over, it looked out into the darkness, and emitted a weak and broken cry. Immediately two other birds appeared, their white feathers ruffled and tangled. The first bird waved its wings at them, blinked, and shook its head as if ordering them to approach no closer until it returned. The other birds understood, and took up crouching positions, standing still and silent as if prepared to wait and watch for a long time. Then the first bird turned about and drew away from them. Stepping gingerly forward on the points of its claws to the edge of the shelf, it spread its wings and flew into the room, which it circled several times, casting about searching glances all the while as if looking for something.

"I must go away!" Nimmer said to himself, and tried to get up off the mat, but to his amazement his body did not obey him. His arms and legs seemed to have dried up and his head seemed to be chained to the pillow. He could not move any part of his body. Just then the bird became aware of his presence. Lowering its head, it flew straight at him, with claws outstretched. Reaching the blanket, it stopped, as if deliberating what to do next. Then, appearing to have come to a decision, it flew aside and landed on its feet, walked beside the mat with slow, measured steps, and stopped at Nimmer's head. Aiming its beak at his eyes, it leaned over him and fixed him with a gaze full of hatred and vengeful wrath.

At this point Nimmer screamed with all his might and awoke. He threw the blanket off his head and leapt up into a sitting position. As he opened his eyes to look around him he felt his heart stop still, as if it had died within him for a moment. But the next moment it began beating so fiercely that it seemed to him that the entire mat was shaking beneath him. In front of him, beside the sacks of soap stacked in a straight column that stood out clearly in the dimness, stood the three old men, consuming him with their blazing eyes, their pupils piercing his flesh like white-hot spikes.

Now he did not think of prostrating himself at the feet of the white-bearded men, nor of trying to escape. With clenched teeth and wide-open eyes he shrank up and bent over like a fetus in his mother's womb, his arms on his knees and his chin in his hands. From time to time a great tremor passed through his body, and he pressed himself backward against the wall, shrinking up even more and thrusting out a hand in the direction of his tormentors.

This vision of horror continued all night. When daylight appeared in the window and the room began to grow gray and then pale, the Fathers moved silently from where they had stood and slid slowly along the wall. At the window they all turned toward Nimmer, stared at him pointedly with gazes of threat and warning, and slipped through the window to vanish among the pale fragments of mist that rose above the Nile, enveloping the trunks of date palms and growing dense around their still and frozen tops.

Dawn had already risen and whitewashed the roofs and railings and walls of houses that could be seen from Nimmer's window, but Nimmer still sat on the spot as if petrified. His staring eyes gazed into the vapors moving around the palm fronds that lay open like giant fans, and at the piles of white clouds in the fringes of the east, their red and gold edges giving them the appearance of dripping blood. Though it was quite some time since he had seen any vision, and though he knew for certain that with the coming of dawn the Fathers were obliged to return whence they had come, his temples were still pounding and the blood rushed around his arteries with a strange heat. Thoughts ran through his head like autumn leaves in a storm; fragments of notions floated up, whirling in confusion. And among all the bits and pieces that fluttered through his head without beginning or end, there recurred the tormenting question which seemed to stick like a splinter in his flesh: "What does it mean? . . . What do they want from me? . . . What shall I do? . . . What shall I do? . . ."

The last of the mists had evaporated. A great sulphurous sun emerged from among the yellow desert sands, rose as from behind the veil of orange dust and sand, and flooded the room with the radiance of a flame. A long narrow beam of sunlight glittered like the blade of a spear and struck him full in his pale contorted face, which was turned in horror toward the window. Abu Il-Shawarab gave a start and swayed, as if something outside him had pushed him, or some inner voice awoken him. He struck himself on the forehead with the palm of his hand as if something had suddenly become clear to him, and jumped decisively to his feet.

"He's the only one!" he mumbled to himself, getting dressed quickly. "He'll solve it all for me! By Allah the Almighty, he will!" he kept on whispering in complete self-assurance. "I'll find him at Azhar.[2] I'll put on my best clothes so that they'll let me see him straight away. I just mustn't get into a panic. Approach him quietly," he repeated to himself with firmness.

But despite his intention to leave quietly, he charged at the door; finding it closed impassably, he flung himself violently at the sacks, as if they were his worst enemies. He pulled and shoved them with his hands, and kicked them with his feet. When he had cleared a narrow space he pushed his way through and rushed out without even turning around to lock the door behind him. Almost doubled over, he ran along the corridor, down the stairs, and was soon in the street.

The Azhar Mosque has a special quarter allotted to it at the edge of the Old City on the other side of the Nile. To reach it from his *khan* Nimmer had to cross almost the entire length of the city. He took various detours to shorten his journey somewhat, cutting across dirty winding alleys and running down long, straight streets full of dust and din and strange traffic, his belt dragging behind him, his hairy chest protruding through the openings of his thin silk lemon-colored robe, which was made with rows upon rows of tiny seams in the shapes of fringes and flowers. As he ran he talked to himself and waved his arms about, often bumping into passersby and pushing them aside if they stood in his way. These would bristle up at first: they drew back their shoulders and thrust out their chests, and slowly turned around to scrutinize him with anger and surprise in their gaze, as if ready to fight him. But when they saw him they would lower their heads in pity, and turn aside reverently without injuring or insulting him, taking him by his strange actions and wild appearance for a dervish whose senses had become muddled in the course of his devotions.

Covered with sweat like a tired horse, Nimmer finally arrived at one of the large iron gates of the Azhar Mosque[3] that stood wide open. He

---

[2] The religious university in Cairo.
[3] Mosque and study center for religious Moslems.

flew across the huge open square of white marble that gleamed in the radiance of the sun and directed his steps toward the inner halls that hummed and bustled like a hive of bees. Totally immersed in his quest, his heart beating wildly, he ran through the dozens of halls and arched foyers, among the numerous groups of *sheikhs* and disciples of all countries and races who sat on mats and carpets chanting the Kor'an in curling melancholy voices or lay silently musing and contemplating distant worlds of mystery. With the stubbornness of a dog which looking for its master completely forgets its fear of humans and pushes its way through dense crowds, sniffing here and coming back and sniffing again, Nimmer ran about among the groups of sitting and lying men, searching for Sheikh Al-Azhar[4] with wild gazes from which madness shone. He did not find him in his usual place. Turning, he moved off in one direction, then changed his mind and tried another, going around in circles and mumbling feverishly to himself, wringing his hands in distress.

A Sufi dervish dressed in rags, a tall thin man completely wrecked bodily by his many mortifications, who traveled much and spoke like a drunken man or one intoxicated with love, accosted Nimmer and attached himself to him, raining upon him a torrent of speech and then asking him what he was looking for. Nimmer, who at first had not listened to his harangue and had ignored his presence, suddenly stopped walking and stared at the dervish with silent agony and pleading in his eyes, and as if delivering his fate up to the other, placed his hand on his shoulder and told him what he wanted.

The dervish, recognizing him for a lost and afflicted man, grasped his hand, pressed it hard, and drew him along behind him. Silently he pushed a way through the clusters of men, led him along winding side corridors and past long rows of rooms that looked like monks' cells or nests in a dovecote. At the edge of the mosque, in a side wing which had corniced pillars around three of its sides, he knocked with his fist on a closed wooden door. No answer came, and he pushed it open. Without turning his face to Nimmer, who stood there bewildered, trying to pause for a moment to make himself more presentable, the dervish stepped inside, dragging Nimmer after him.

Sheikh Al-Azhar, white-haired and wrinkled of face, everything on him and around him white, raised his round pleated *laffah*,[5] which

---

[4] The president of the religious university; one of the prominent man of Islam.
[5] A kind of wrapping cloth.

shaded his face and the large book lying in front of him on a high cushion, creased his eyebrows, and gazed in stern surprise at these men who had dared to enter his library and disturb him during his studies. On recognizing the dervish, however, his face beamed and broke into an expression of concern. He put his book aside, placed his beads on top of it, and hastily raised himself from the cushions on which he was sitting, poking his small childlike feet into his orange sandals as he did so, and took several steps toward them.

The dervish bowed to him, took his hand and brought it up to his mouth, kissed it several times and then rested his forehead on it until the *sheikh* raised his left hand, and mumbling something, placed it on the dervish's head. The blessing concluded, he tapped the dervish affectionately on the shoulder and made him sit down beside him on the mat. Then he turned to Nimmer, who had been standing there all this time, pale and trembling like a leaf, asked politely about his health, and offered him his hand.

Noticing the terrible agitation of his strange visitor, the *sheikh* greeted him very warmly. To try to calm him, he attempted to divert his mind to other matters, and so to disperse the dread that was displayed on his face. He pulled a cushion from under him, offered it to Nimmer, and invited him to sit down. Then he spoke to him in a simple and humble manner, asking him about the town he came from, the *mufti* and the *cadi* serving there—his disciples once—and various other peripheral questions.

Because of the reverence he felt for the *sheikh*, and also because he did not want to be the first to begin a conversation, Nimmer answered all the questions briefly and halfheartedly. All this time he swayed and rocked to and fro as if sitting on embers, now opening his mouth and now stopping it with his hand to prevent the words which were on the tip of his tongue from bursting out against his will.

Realizing that it was impossible to calm Nimmer, the *sheikh* turned to the dervish and in a quiet voice gave him several errands to do, so he could remain alone with Nimmer. As soon as the dervish had left, he placed one arm on a cushion and placed his chin in his hand. Looking intently at Nimmer with questioning and friendly eyes, he smiled serenely at him and spoke:

"*Kir In-sha-Allah!* [6] Do you need my counsel and guidance? I will be very glad if I can help you in any way, especially since you come from

---

[6] "All will be well if Allah so wills it."

the Holy Land." And, seeing that his visitor still did not speak, as if uncertain whether he should or not, and was vainly trying to say something and then stopping as if he didn't know where to begin, the *sheikh* added:

"Speak, my son, speak! Speak it all openly, and you will feel better. I will listen to everything you say. After all, there are no strangers among us . . ." Pity and deep compassion were suddenly apparent in his voice and in all the lines of his face.

Nimmer collected all his strength, and stood up. With pale lips and a frozen gaze he silently approached the *sheikh*, extending his hands toward him in dumb pleading. He grasped the edge of the *sheikh*'s robe, brought it up to his lips, and covered his face with it. Then he retreated and sat down again on the cushion he had just got up from.

In whispers, with long pauses, and with a demented expression on his face, Nimmer began his confession. In his bewilderment and agitation words and phrases escaped from his mouth without order or sequence, but as he went on his speech became more ordered, the descriptions of events grew shorter, clearer and more precise, and thus more touching in their simplicity. With a sharp pleasure, a passion close to cruelty, he told the *sheikh* of his miseries and confessed his crime and guilt. He made no attempt to defend or justify himself, nor did he belittle his pride, his stubbornness, or any of the other bad qualities that had been his since childhood and that had always been a stumbling block to him.

When he came to the vision of horror and the terrible tortures of the previous night, he was again overcome by that dark mysterious fear. His soul swayed within him as on a storm tossed sea, his memory failed him, and he began blubbering disconnected and incomprehensible words. Suddenly, as if stabbed in the back with a dagger, he trembled, screamed, flung himself to the floor, sank his head into a cushion, and howled in agony. When, some long and dreadful moments later, he slowly raised his head to look around him, he sensed the *sheikh* leaning over him and touching him on the shoulder. Nimmer wrung his hands at the *sheikh* in despair and moaned:

"Father! Master! What will happen to me? What must I do now? What does the vision mean? What do they want from me? Tell me! Nothing is hidden from you! My soul be your atonement, tell me!"

The *sheikh* turned away from him, drew back a little, and started pacing the floor of the room with pursed lips and crinkled brow, concentrating on the problem. After a long silence, during which Nimmer consumed him with his eyes, lurking for his every gesture or motion, the *sheikh* suddenly stopped his pacing, halted beside Nimmer, and spoke to him in a soft voice which sounded as if he was gently arousing himself from sleep:

"These are wonders and the workings of Providence! There is no strength and no might save in Allah! It is a severe warning. The whole thing is clear and evident and requires no interpretation. Our Lord (be He praised and exalted!) is angry at you and wishes to destroy you. You have killed, you have desecrated the Holy and blasphemed His prophets. What have you not done?! It is a wonder that He has been patient with you as long as this and has not yet squashed you into dust. Yet He is the One and the Only, He is the judge and the punishment. Everything depends on His will and His decree and on the fate that He has determined for every creature before it was created. If He wills, He will have mercy on us even if we sin greatly, or destroy us even if we are righteous. All is written and sealed from the beginning, and there is no escape, and no changing this . . ."

"Ah!" yelled Nimmer, slapping his head and pulling his hair. "Is there no hope then? How? How? . . . What will I do now? What will I do?" He kept repeating this last question, weeping and wringing his hands all the while.

Nimmer's weeping, and his miserable thin figure shaken with desolation and dread, made a strong impression on the *sheikh*. In the pale face contorted with despair, in the feverish eyes darting about in frenzy, he saw so much sorrow and agony that he was overwhelmed with pity. His original feeling of compassion now swept through him like a wave. Softening, he gazed at him thoughtfully and spoke, as if inspired.

"What are you to do, you ask me? Don't despair. Allah's mercies are deeper than the sea. If a man were to live a thousand years he would not learn His secrets or understand even a fraction of His ways. It is true that the Proselyte is as his name is, vengeful and watchful, pursuing his enemies to the bitter end . . . You offended him and desecrated his festival and his flag . . . Nevertheless there is still a way in which you may save yourself. By submission and begging for forgiveness it may be possible for you to arouse his compassion and turn back his vengeance. Make yourself a proper flag, and a proper crown on a proper staff. Then, barefoot and living on alms, go to his tomb, kiss it and moisten its earth with your tears and ask his forgiveness. That is what you should do. Perhaps he will give heed to your prayer and remove his hand from upon you . . ."

"I'll do it! I'll go, Master!" Nimmer cried, bravely, as a spark of hope lit up in his face. "I'll prepare a flag and do everything else you say, right away. If the blood-avengers recognize me and kill me, it doesn't matter . . . For a man cannot die twice, nor can he escape death, is that not so, Master?"

"Yes, it is so, my son!" the *sheikh* affirmed with absolute certainty. "No man dies a moment before his appointed time. All the same, you must not endanger yourself needlessly. The Hebronites, whose stink can be smelled at great distances, Allah preserve you—if they recognize you, you won't get away from them alive. They'll neither respect a celebrant nor shrink from committing a crime. There's still time to think the matter over carefully. You would be best to wait for the day when the celebrants return from the grave of the Messenger,[7] prayers and peace upon him! Then, when they go to prostrate themselves at the two holy sites, the Mosque of Omar and the Cave of Machpelah, join them. Among all those people it will be easier for you to remain unrecognized and to do what you have to do without attracting undue attention. Caution is one half of wisdom . . . This way seems the best . . . I too will feel content that I have given you good advice," he added with enthusiasm. "But should disaster overtake you . . ."

"No! No, my Master!" Nimmer interrupted him impatiently, waving his hand as if to contradict the *sheikh*, and getting to his feet. "I mustn't wait even one more day. Why should I stay here any longer? I'll go, whatever happens . . . I'm not afraid of death. All that matters is that I won't see those eyes pursuing me anymore! Can I live like this? . . . No! I can't take anymore! I can't take it!" Shouting this with terror, he again spread his hands pleadingly to the *sheikh*.

The *sheikh* started pacing the floor of the room again. He seemed to be considering the question deeply. Without noticing what he was doing, he approached the cushion, picked up the book that was lying there, carried it to one of the book cabinets, then to another, took it out again, and put it back on the cushion, then suddenly stopped pacing but remained silent.

Nimmer, who had waited all this time in great concern, his eyes glued to the *sheikh*'s face, could no longer restrain himself. Trembling where he stood, he made a deep but hasty bow like one in a great hurry, sighed, and started retreating toward the door.

"Wait! Wait!" the *sheikh* finally said, shaking his head and his hand

---

[7] Mohammed.

decisively. "It may be that you are right." His voice was assured now. "The Proselyte calls you—only a blind man cannot see that. Who and what am I to oppose his will? Toward life or toward death—it is *his* secret, and what is our strength against him? Go!" he commanded, again with unexpected enthusiasm, "go toward your fate. Speed your actions, Allah be with you and lighten your suffering." Saying this, he approached Nimmer, patted him affectionately on the shoulder and took his arm, leading him out of the door and accompanying him along the corridor.

At the stairs Nimmer grasped the *sheikh*'s hand with deep emotion and gratitude, lowered his head to it, and kissed it with burning lips, then drew himself erect, shook his shoulders as if casting off a burden, and without turning to the sides rushed off headlong on his way . . .

That afternoon Nimmer completed all his preparations. He sold everything he possessed, bought the gold crown and the silk for the flag and the embroidery, and settled up all his debts with the lower world in which he had been living. Barefoot, wearing a robe of thick sackcloth over his nakedness and a tall white cylindrical dervish's hat on his head, carrying a censer of frankincense in one hand and a staff in the other, and with a tin pail hanging from a rope on his back, he left the *khan*, and before night fell he had crossed the city and was heading eastward toward the tomb of Ibrahim Al-Khalil, his destination.

CHAPTER TEN

A winter Friday in Hebron. A day of cold and drizzle. Low leaden skies, mud, slush.

A heavy mist that looked like frozen smoke lay over the town and the hills around it, on which stood strong ancient olive and carob trees. It enveloped the walls, the houses, and the minarets of mosques, and one could barely make out a number of dark shapes marking their location. By the sides of the paths, down the hill slopes, and from the vineyards on their ridges, streams of murky water rushed down, carrying silt and the decay of vine leaves to the lower streets and the houses and shops in the decline. The bare fig trees and the vines which lay lifelessly upon them, gripping their bared trunks, dripped incessantly. In the pale light of this dismal winter morning they seemed frozen in a last wail, and looked like the ribs of skeletons or the arms of corpses, signifying the sorrow of withering and decay in their contorted spasm of dying and perishing.

With deadened senses and a frozen stare in his eyes, Nimmer slowly made his painful way up the steep hill toward the point of the high spire of the Cave of Machpelah, which rose above the horizon like an illuminating beacon. The flickerings of its burning fires pierced the mist, spreading quivering orange beams full of mystery and glory. Water, with fragments of frost in it, streamed down Nimmer's long white hair and dripped from his unkempt beard onto his bare hairy chest, and from the bloated rags of his robe onto his blue calves.

He seemed not to feel the cold, not to be aware of wind or rain, or to notice any obstacle. Moving freely, as if not touching the ground, he was totally immersed in the visions present to his inner eye, his mind filled with the marvelous faith that consumes body and soul and sets the blood racing at astonishing speed. Wading in water up to his waist, Nimmer crossed the Street of the Glaziers, and then, his bare feet squelching in the mud, he walked with his long staff through the open vegetable market, where the crying of a baby from an upper story somewhere mingled with the sound of turning handmills. In the roofed Street of the Merchants, where the darkness was still thick and dense, he stopped beside a long open furnace, from the far end of which flames danced and lit up the whole cavelike space. Bent over, Nimmer stared for a long while at the baker, whose face was black with soot but full of light and movement. Thrusting his staff before him like a blind man, and knocking with it on the steps before him, he descended and entered. He approached the pile of fuel, put his pails and bags down on the ground, bent over and groped around in them, and drew out the censer which hung from chains that had coins and talismans attached to them. Then he filled the censer with incense and turned to the baker, and in a sleepy, whispering voice, asked him for some embers from his fire, thrusting the censer out to him as he spoke.

The baker stared at Nimmer in astonishment and gave him what he asked with an expression of pity and awe. For a moment he wondered if he should give his visitor some alms. Apparently reaching a decision, he pulled a hot *pitta* out from under a rolling pin, waved it in the air to cool it, and offered it to Nimmer, at the same time asking him what town he came from and where he was going.

Nimmer ignored the offering, and neither thanked him for his generosity nor answered his questions. With agitation in his face, with trembling hands, he was again busy over his bag, which he was trying to undo. He clutched it and shook it, emptying it all out on the ground, and was startled on hearing the rustle of the silk and the ringing of the golden crown as it fell out and rolled along the shelf. He ran after it with a scream, caught it as it was rolling, picked it up gently and, placing both hands around it, brought it to his lips and then his forehead, and affixed it on the pointed top of his staff.

He unfolded the flag, which gave off greenish and reddish gleams in the light of the flames. He attached it by its loops to the rings on his staff, rolled it around the staff, and placed it on his shoulder. All his preparations completed, he walked out of the place, leaving the baker amazed and bewildered, with a heavy and unclear suspicion in his heart.

From here, the Cave of Machpelah was only several streets away. Nimmer crossed the dirty, curving alleys quickly, with the remains of his strength, moving stealthily along the walls like a cat, sticking to the shadows, the cloud of incense rising from his censer and enveloping his face.

Thus he pressed through among the paupers and the cripples thronging around the entrance of the charity kitchen at the outer gate of the Cave of Machpelah. With rising excitement, his heart pounding fearfully, he struggled up the stairs, stumbled along the corridor and, pale as a corpse, his eyes glazed, dragged his quaking legs into the mosque.

The interior of the mosque was a square hall, tall and spacious, with arched ceilings and rows of marble columns and pillars. Its floor was lavishly covered with carpets from Damascus and Bagdad and fabrics from India, Persia, and Turkey, and lamps of silver and gold and crystal hung from its domes. At this hour the mosque was almost empty. The prayer of the last watch had concluded some time ago, and the men of affairs who rise early had long since completed their prostrations and gone about their business. The beggars had all hurried off to the charity kitchen to receive their daily bread, a double portion today because it was Friday. The dervishes and *sheikhs*, who had been up all this long winter night in the vigil of the Zeikar,[1] had all gone to rest their weary eyelids in the side cubicles, where they had fallen on their mats like dead men. Only the attendants still ran anxiously and busily about, filling lamps, cleaning carpets, changing the sand spread over the tombstones parallel to the markings of the graves beneath them. Then, pulling hard at the iron rings stuck on both sides of the rock that covered the cave,

---

[1] A dervish ritual of prayer, song, and dance.

they opened the aperture and lowered into its well-like depths the per-
petual lamp with its dozens of burning lights, and left it open in honor
of the day. Around the opening they lit the large wax candles, and
prepared the hall for the Friday noon prayer.

Nimmer traversed the entire length of the mosque, heading straight
for the tombs. Here, at the central shelf, in a space where no tombstone
stood, was the grave of the Proselyte. Nimmer put down his flag, set up
his pails and his candles, and began to drop, first to his knees, and then
prostrated his entire body on the ground. Lying there, he kissed the
earth, pounded upon it with his head, moistened it with his tears and
with the spittle dribbling from his mouth, and beat upon his heart with
the palm of his hand. As he did so he wailed and groaned in a voice that
sounded like the beating of a hammer against a hollow wall. All the
attendants rushed over to him and stood around him, exchanging bewildered glances as they wondered what to do.

The head attendant, Abu Hassan, formerly Abu Faris's right-hand
man, blind in one eye, his good eye always glinting with a pale watery
light while his white eyebrows seemed to be blinking with venomous
derision, now bent over Nimmer. He subjected Nimmer to a long,
penetrating gaze, then suddenly jerked upright as if bitten by a snake,
and placed his hand over his mouth as if to hold back the shout that was
about to burst from his throat. Clenching his fists and repressing a
malicious laugh behind his sparse beard, he turned around on tiptoe and
moved hastily and stealthily toward the door leading out of the mosque,
the ends of his caftan splaying out behind him and his green *laffah*
swaying on the nape of his neck like the tail of a lizard when it runs.

Not many minutes later he was running up Al-Sheikh Street, which
still lay under straying mists in a dim and slumbering stillness. At the
end of the street he turned into a broad open field that lay at the feet of
the mountains. Hundreds of beheaded waterskins lay in long rows
across it, their open necks dripping drops of reddish water. They looked
like living creatures bleeding and writhing in their dying pangs on the
muddy clay earth. Here, at the large walled house that resembled a
fortress with its round windows closed and shuttered, he stopped and
knocked vigorously with the iron hand hanging on the gate.

At his insistent knocking the bolt was finally drawn back, and to the
sound of loud cries of fear and wonder, Abu Hassan burst inside to meet
Abu Faris's two brothers, who were running to the door barefooted,
dressed only in short sleeveless gowns, followed by the rest of the young
men and boys who hurried after them in their nightgowns and gathered

in the entrance. Abu Hassan drew the two brothers aside into the courtyard, and with much self-importance and great detail told them his
secret.

"Gird your loins!" called Abu Faris's brothers. "Hurry, bring your
daggers and your staves, and catch up with us, boys!" Roaring more
commands, they rushed out into the street, their clenched fists raised
high and their protruding eyes blazing a threat. Abu Hassan ran to the
Cave of Machpelah by a shorter route to stand guard and to prevent his
treachery being discovered, which might mean his dismissal from his
post.

Abu Faris's brothers ran breathlessly to the bottom of the street.
When they reached the open square they climbed on top of the tall dome
of the wayfarers' bathhouse, from which the *muezzin* calls the faithful to
prayer. They bent their heads backward a little toward the upper stories, pressed their fingers to their temples, walked to and fro, and,
howling like frantic wolves rallying the pack to the prey, burst out in a
loud prolonged cry:

"Come! Come, brothers, come!"

Twice, three times, they called, louder and louder each time, and a
large crowd began to gather. From all the streets and lanes and alleyways
shadows of running men came charging, all of them armed with sticks,
staves, swords, and daggers. Ignorant of what had happened, they ran
about in alarm, listening in suspicion and anxiety to the sounds and calls
around them, their faces bespeaking their bewilderment and fear.

"Muslims! Nimmer Abu Il-Shawarab of Nablus, who tore the flag of
the Sheriff, and murdered your flag-master, is inside the tomb!" roared
Abu Faris's brothers to the packed crowd. "The task has been placed in
your hands, all praise and gratitude to Allah!"

Calling thus, they hastily jumped down from the bathhouse, approached the elders who stood at the front of the crowd, stopped before
them, and fixed their gazes on them, expectantly waiting to hear what
they would say.

"Get him! Get him! Where are all the brave men now? Block off all
paths of escape! Catch him! Smash him!" Many cries of this sort now
came from all sides, rolling like thunder over the heads of the crowd,
penetrating all their hearts and inflaming their blood. Agitated now, all
burst into violent uproar. Like a herd of bulls which, having smelled the
blood of one of their number, pack together in a circle around the place,
bellowing, raising their noses and their horns and then bursting into
stampede, so they all packed around the brothers of Abu Faris with

dreadful cries, brandishing their staves and clubs and swords, and then moved forward like an advancing storm.

And like the torrents that pour down from the mountains to the king's lower pool, the mob made its way to the Cave of Machpelah along numerous routes, until they filled its main entrance and overflowed onto its outer slopes. Like hungry wolves lurking around a closed pen they besieged the four gates of the shrine and ran around its ancient walls.

As they stood there panting and staring toward the deep tunnel-like openings, as if intent on smashing and destroying all the walls with their gazes, a man came hurriedly out of the mosque and ran down the stairs, blinking and making strange movements with his head as he forcibly pushed a way through the milling people in his path. Then he pulled the scarf of his *laffah* off his *tarboush*, waved it around above his head as if giving a final signal, and ran back to the mosque.

All the people there craned their necks and stood up on their toes, and a silence of anticipation lasted for a long moment. Then they all saw how from the upper gate there emerged a bent old man, thin, exhausted, bare of foot and head, the white hair of his head and beard descending in long unkempt braids on both sides of his face. He swayed as he walked, as if borne on the waves of a dream, slowly dragging his feet and knocking on the ground before him with his staff like a blind man seeking his way. It was clear to everyone that he had sensed nothing of what was going on around him.

He had descended some three or four steps when the sudden outcry of angry hostile voices erupted. As if waking from a dream he swayed on the spot, raised his head slightly, and looked around him. He saw wave upon wave of heads approaching him with snakelike movements, and above them gleamed glittering sword blades and spiked clubs. A heavy darkness descended upon his spirit, his blood pounded in his temples and burst like a torrent through his head.

Without knowing what he was doing, he turned his head as if hoping to retrace his steps, drew himself back to the wall, and leaned against its smooth cold stones. As he stood there it seemed to him as if the ground had dropped from under his feet and that he was falling into a pit as deep as the abyss.

"My God! My God!" his lips muttered, and he thrust out his thin hairy arm. The next minute he collapsed, falling on his side with a hoarse snort that escaped from the opening of his frothing mouth. All his limbs began to tremble and contract in convulsions, his eyes bulged out of their sockets, and his mouth writhed in a terrible manner. His thin fingers quivered and shook, and grasped at empty space as if trying to touch the secret unknown. Then they clenched in a spasm. His eyes became covered with a murky whiteness like smoked glass, and turned to the ground to which his body was now attached forever . . .

"The vengeance of the Fathers! . . . The vengeance of the Fathers! . . ." cried Abu Faris's two brothers, and the mob turned about and fled in dread and terror . . .

IN THE
PRIME OF
HER
LIFE

BY S. Y. AGNON

translated by Gabriel Levin

M Y MOTHER DIED in the prime of her life. She was one and thirty years of age when she died. Few and harsh were the days of the years of her life. She sat at home the entire day and never stirred from within. Her friends and neighbors did not visit and my father did not welcome guests. Our house stood hushed in its sorrow, its doors did not open to a stranger. Lying on her bed my mother's words were few. But when she spoke it was as though limpid wings spread forth and led me to the Hall of Blessing. How I loved her voice. Often I opened her door to have her ask, who is there. I was yet a child. Sometimes she descended from her bed to sit by the window. She sat by the window and her clothes were white. Her clothes were always white. Once my father's uncle was called into town, and he saw my mother and thought, she is a nurse. For her clothes deceived him and he did not realize that she was the one who was sick.

Her illness, a heart ailment, bowed her life down to earth. Summer after summer the doctors sent her to the health spas, but no sooner there than she returned, for she said her longings gave her no peace, and once again she sat by the window or lay on her bed.

My father began to ply his trade less and less. He no longer went to Germany where as a bean merchant he would travel year after year to deal with his clients. In those days and at that time he forgot the ways of the world. On his return home at dusk he would sit by my mother, his left hand under his head and his right hand in hers. Now and then she would lean forward and kiss his hand.

The winter my mother died our home fell silent seven times over. My mother descended from her bed only when Kaila entered to tidy up. A carpet was placed in the hallway to absorb the sound of every footfall, and the odor of medicine drifted from one room to another. Our entire house was burdened with sorrow.

The doctors would arrive unsummoned and then not depart, and if we inquired of her health all they said was, with God's help. Meaning all hope was lost—there was no cure. But my mother never sighed, nor did she shed a tear, and no complaint passed her lips. She lay quietly on her bed and her strength left her like a shadow.

Then there were days when hope tugged at our hearts: indeed, she must live, we thought as winter passed and the first days of spring appeared on the earth. My mother then seemed to forget her pain and we saw with our own eyes how her illness subsided. Even the doctors consoled us, claiming there was hope: spring will approach, they said, and the sun's rays will quicken her body.

Now Passover was at our doorsteps and Kaila made the necessary preparations for the holiday, while as mistress of the house my mother attended to her duties and made sure nothing was amiss. She even fashioned herself a new dress.

Several days before the holiday, descending from her bed, my mother stood before the looking glass and put on her new dress. Shadows running over her body glimmered in the mirror and the light of life brightened her face. My heart quickened with joy upon seeing how beautifully her face shone in that dress. The new dress could not be distinguished from the old one, for both were white, and the old dress was as good as new, for lying in bed all winter she had had little use for articles of clothing. I don't know in what I detected a sign of hope; perhaps a fragrance of hope blossomed from the spring flower she pinned above her heart—or was it that the odors from the medicine had faded away? A new fragrance sweetened and refreshed our entire home. I have known a number of perfumes, but such a fragrance I have never known. Once, though, I did inhale the scent of such a fragrance in a dream. Where did this fragrance come from? For my mother did not anoint her body with womanly perfumes.

Descending from her bed she sat by the window. A small table containing a drawer stood by the window. The drawer was locked and the key to the drawer hung about my mother's neck. Silently my mother opened the drawer and removed a bundle of letters which she then spent the entire day reading. She read until evening. The door opened twice, thrice, but she did not ask who was there, and when I spoke to her she did not answer. On being reminded to drink her medicines she drained the spoon in one gulp, without making a face or uttering a word. It was as though their bitterness had vanished. And after having taken her medicines she returned to her letters.

The letters were written on thin paper in a round neat hand, written in short and long lines. Seeing my mother reading I told myself that she would never relinquish the letters, for she was bound to the case and the letters by the very string around her neck. At dusk she took the bundle of letters, secured them together with the string around her neck, and kissed and tossed the letters and key into the fireplace. The chimney, though, was clogged and only one ember flickered in the fireplace. The ember gnawed through the thin paper, the letters burned in the fire, and the house filled with smoke. Kaila hastened to open the window, but my mother prevented her from doing so, and she sat by the drawer as the letters burned and the house filled with smoke, inhaling the smoke from the letters until evening.

That night Mintshi Gottlieb came to inquire about my mother's health. Mintshi was her close friend. As young girls they had studied together under Akaviah Mazal. For close upon three hours Mintshi sat by my mother's bed. "Mintshi," said my mother, "now I am to see you for the last time." Drying her tears, Mintshi said, "Leah, have courage, you shall soon regain your strength." My mother remained silent, and a solemn smile played over her feverish lips. Suddenly she clasped Mintshi's right hand in her right and said, "Go home, Mintshi, and prepare all that is needed for the Sabbath. Tomorrow afternoon you shall accompany me to my resting place." This occurred on a Thursday night, the dawn of Friday, Sabbath eve. Taking hold of my mother's right hand, Mrs. Gottlieb spread her fingers out and said, "Leah." A throttled cry stifled her words. Our hearts sank.

My father returned from work at the store and sat by the bed. My mother's solemn lips hovered over his face like a shadow as she bent forward and kissed him. Soon Mrs. Gottlieb rose, wrapped herself in her coat, and left. My mother then descended from her bed and Kaila entered to make the bed. In the evening light the hem of the white dress rustled in the semidarkness of the room.

Returning to her bed my mother drained the medicine served by my father. And she took his hand and placed it above her heart, saying, "Thank you." The drops of medicine trickled one at a time on his hand like tears. My mother took a deep breath. "Now rise," she said, "go and have some dinner." "I cannot eat," he replied. Again she urged him to eat. My father left for the dining room, and he ate his bread with tears and returned.

Regaining her strength, my mother sat up and seized him by the hand a second time. She then had the nurse sent home and instructed my father to tell her not to return. And she lowered the light in the lamp and lay still. "If only I could sleep," my father said, "I would now do so. But since God has deprived me of sleep, I will sit, if I may, by your side. If you should ask for me I will be here, and if not I will know all is well with you." But my mother would not heed his words. And he went to his room and lay down. He had not slept for many nights and now as soon as his head touched the pillow he fell asleep. I too lay down and slept. But I suddenly awoke, frightened. I jumped out of bed and rushed to my mother's side. My mother lay peacefully in bed, but, ah, she had ceased breathing. I then woke my father up and he cried with a great and exceedingly bitter cry, "Leah!"

Her soul had returned to the Almighty and now my mother rested peacefully on her bed. My mother yielded up her soul and on the Sabbath eve at twilight she was accompanied to the cemetery. She died a righteous woman, on the Sabbath eve.

For seven days my father sat in silence. My mother's footstool stood before him and on it were placed the Book of Job and the Ways of Mourning. People I had never seen came to console us. Until my days of mourning I had not known there were so many people in our town. Those who came to console us suggested that my father prepare the tombstone. My father, though, remained silent and did not answer a word. On the third day Mr. Gottlieb arrived. "Here," he said, "I have brought with me the inscription for the tombstone." Those present stared in surprise, for my mother's name was formed out of the first letter of each verse, and the year of her death was written in every line. Gottlieb then spoke to my father about the stone, but my father did not attend to his words. So passed the days of mourning.

The days of mourning passed by and the year of mourning was close to its end. That entire year a somber unmoving gloom crouched over us. My father resumed his work and when he returned from the store he silently ate his food. In my grief, I said my father has forgotten me; he has forgotten my existence.

One day my father stopped saying the Kaddish, and he approached me and said, "Come, let us go and erect a tombstone for our mother." I put on my hat and gloves. "Here I am, Father," I answered. My father drew back in surprise, as though only today noticing that I wore mourning. And he opened the door and we left.

Once on our way my father stopped in his tracks and said, "Spring has arrived early." And he passed his hand over his brow as he spoke. "If spring had not been tardy a year ago she would now be alive." My father sighed. We walked on and circled the town. Placing his hand in mine my father said, "This way."

We approached the outer limits of the town and suddenly came across an old woman, digging in her yard. My father greeted her and said, "Please tell us, good woman, does Mazal live here?" The woman set aside the spade with which she had been digging and answered, "Yes, sir, Mazal is at home." My father grasped my hand. "Come, my daughter, let us go in."

A man well into his thirties opened the door. The room was small and pretty and sheaves of paper were piled up on the table. The man's face was veiled in sorrow. "I have come to ask you to write the inscription for the tombstone," my father said. And as if it suddenly dawned upon the man who these people were, he covered the sheaves of paper and welcomed us, and he stroked my cheek and said, "You have grown a great deal." Looking at him I was suddenly reminded of my mother, for the gestures of his hands were identical with my mother's. My father stood before the man. So they stood facing each other. "Who knew then," my father said, "that Leah would leave us." The man's face brightened for a moment as my father appeared to encompass him in his grief; little did he realize my father's words were intended for me. Then, removing the covering from the table, the man extracted a single sheaf of paper and handed it to my father. My father took the sheaf and, as he read, tears covered the tears already on the page. Now the sheaf of paper and the handwriting astonished me. I had seen such a page and such writing before. Indeed, it has always been this way: seeing a certain thing, it appears that I have already encountered that very thing before. Nor were the tearstains foreign to me.

My father read the poem to its end without uttering a word, for his words were held back in his mouth. And he put on his hat and we departed. We crossed the town and arrived home as Kaila lit the lamp. I then prepared my lessons and my father read the inscription for the tombstone.

The stonecutters arrived and cut the tombstone's figure as instructed by my father. After copying Akaviah Mazal's inscription on large sheets of paper my father and I stood on both sides of the stonecutters and we chose the lettering for the tombstone. But none of the letters seemed right in his eyes. A bookshelf stood in our home. One day, having leafed fruitlessly through the sheaves of paper, my father took down a book from the shelf and his eyes lit up. He then leafed through book after book. A somber compassion enveloped our home. At that time, as my father searched for the tombstone's lettering, he all but forgot my mother. And he never grew tired, as a bird in gathering sprigs for its nest will not tire in flight.

And the stone engraver arrived, leafed through the books and letters, and found a script for the tombstone. That was during the first days of spring. The stone engraver then set about his work outside. As he struck the stone the letters grouped themselves into rhymes the way a swarm of bees will gather about the sound of a single bee hitting against a rock. The tombstone was made out of marble. The stone engraver embossed the letters in black. Thus did he fashion the lettering on the tombstone. And he glazed the heading in gold. And once completed the tombstone was erected on the ordained day over the grave. My father then rose and went to the cemetery along with the townfolk to say the Kaddish. He leaned his head against the stone and grasped Mazal's hand. And since the day we descended to the cemetery to erect the tombstone my father and I have visited her grave daily—excepting the Passover holidays, for during the holy days one does not descend unto the cemetery.

"Let us go for a walk," my father said one day during the intermediate days of Passover. I put on my festive dress and approached him. "You have a new dress," he said. "It is my holiday attire," I answered as we departed.

And once on our way, I thought: what have I done, for I have fashioned myself a new dress? Suddenly I felt God stirring my conscience and I stood still. "Why have you stopped?" my father asked. "I couldn't help thinking why have I worn holiday clothing," I replied. "It doesn't matter," he said. "Come." I removed my gloves and was gladdened as a gust of cold air enveloped my hand. We left the town.

Reaching the town's outskirts my father turned off the road in the direction of Mazal's home. Mazal hurried toward us as we entered. Removing his hat my father said, "I have rummaged through all her belongings." After falling silent for a moment he sighed and conceded, "I have labored in vain, all my searching has come to naught."

My father saw that Mazal did not grasp the meaning of his words. "I thought to publish your poems and I rummaged through all her drawers, but I could not find a thing." Mazal shook, his shoulders shuddered, and he didn't say a word. Shifting from one foot to the other, my father extended his hand and asked, "Do you have a copy?" "There is no copy," Mazal answered. My father drew back, frightened. "I wrote the poems for her, that is why I did not make any copies for myself," Mazal added. My father sighed and ran his palm over his head. Mazal then grasped the corners of the table and said, "She is dead." "Dead," my father answered, and he fell silent. The day waned. The servant entered and lit the lamp. My father bade Mazal good day. And as we left Mazal extinguished the lamp.

Now classes resumed at school and I sat over my lessons until the evening hours, when my father returned from his work at the store. We then sat hushed over our food; not a word was spoken.

"Tirtza, what are you doing?" my father asked one spring evening as we sat by the table. "I am preparing my lessons," I answered. "And have you forgotten your Hebrew?" he said. "I did not forget." And he said, "I shall find you a teacher and you shall learn Hebrew." My father then found me a teacher to his liking and brought him to our home. The teacher, following my father's urging, taught me grammar, for as with the majority of our people, my father believed grammar was the soul of the Hebrew language. The teacher taught me the Hebrew tongue, the rules of logic, and the interpretation of Man's Profits. I was left breathless. And aside from grammar, a *melamed*, a teacher of novices, also instructed me in the Pentateuch and Prayer. For my father had me study under the teacher's guidance subjects which other young girls did not know and he had the *melamed* come and instruct me in all which they did know. The *melamed* appeared daily and Kaila would bring him a glass of tea and cream cake. If the evil eye had seized upon her she would approach the *melamed* and he would whisper into her ear. And when he spoke, a chuckle in the depth of his beard would glimmer as in a mirror.

How weary I grew of grammar and its endless rules. I could not make head or tails of the meaning of such words as *bedingungs buchstaben*, *sprach werkzeuge*. I chattered like a crane a string of meaningless names. Once the teacher exclaimed, "I have labored in vain. I have spent my strength for nothing and in vain!" On another occasion he approved of my words, for I parroted his words letter for letter. I commanded my brain: away! I cried out to my memory: help me!

One day the teacher arrived while the *melamed* was still in the house. The teacher waited and waited for the *melamed* to leave. The *melamed*, however, did not go. Kaila came from the kitchen as they sat and said to the *melamed*, "I dreamed a dream and my spirit has been shaken." "What did you see, Kaila?" he asked. "I saw a small German with a red wool cap on his head." And he asked, "What did the German do?" "He hiccuped and yawned," she answered, "and since waking I can't stop sneezing." The *melamed* then stood up, closed his eyes, and spat three times in front of the teacher. Then, whispering, he cast his spell. But before he could finish the teacher leaped to his feet in anger and exclaimed, "Wickedness and fraud, shall you throw dust in an innocent woman's eyes!" And the *melamed* called after him, "Heretic, shall you scorn the customs of Israel!" And in his anger the teacher spun on his heel and left. Since that day the *melamed* remained on guard for the sound of the teacher's footsteps. But the teacher ceased to come and the *melamed* then set out to teach me the weekly portions of the Bible. For until the day in which the teacher absented himself we had not studied the portions. And I was enveloped by the spirit of grace and supplication whenever I recalled the teacher's pleasant voice.

Now it was summer and the golden locust appeared. Its strains swelled about us as it spread forth its thin wings and its golden belly glowed in the daylight. Sometimes we heard from within the muffled sound of the house locust striking its mouth against wood. My heart then beat feebly, fearing death; for such a sound heralds death.

And in those days I read the Books of Joshua and the Judges, and at that time I picked out a book from among my mother's books, may she rest in peace. I read two chapters, telling myself: I will repeat the words my mother read, may she rest in peace. I was dumbfounded, for I understood what was before me. I read on and the stories were familiar to me. Reading my mother's books I felt like the child who in hearing his mother's tremulous voice suddenly recognizes his own name.

School recessed for the summer holidays. I then sat at home and altered my dresses, for they had last been worn before my year of mourning and no longer fitted me. One day, while my father was at home, the doctor called on us. My father was pleased by his visit, for he had lived in the company of doctors during my mother's entire lifetime, may she rest in peace. The doctor told my father, "Here both of you sit at home while summer is stirring." He grasped my hand and felt my pulse as he spoke and as he leaned over me I smelled the odor of his clothes. The odor was identical with my mother's odor when she was ill. "How you have grown," the doctor said. "A few months hence I won't be able to call you child anymore." And he asked me my age and I answered, "I am fourteen." Then, seeing my dresses, he asked, "You also know how to sew?" "Let another man praise thee, and not thine own mouth," I replied. The doctor smoothed his mustache with his two fingers as he laughed, saying, "A bold girl, and looking for compliments." Turning to my father, he added, "Her face is like her mother's, may she rest in peace." My father turned and beheld me. Kaila then came from the kitchen with a pitcher of water and sweetmeats. "My, it is hot today," the doctor exclaimed, and he opened a window. The streets were silent for want of passersby. We lowered our voices as people will do when all about them it is very quiet. The doctor drained his glass of water and covered the sweetmeats with a bowl, saying, "You have been sitting here in town long enough; now you must go and find yourselves summer lodgings." My father nodded, indicating that he would follow the doctor's advice. Though it seemed that he did not have his heart in it.

Close upon that time Mrs. Gottlieb invited me to spend the remaining days of my vacation in her home. My father readily agreed, saying, "Go now." But I answered, "How will I go alone?" And he said, "I will come and visit." Kaila stood dusting by the mirror and she winked at me as she overheard my father's words. I saw her move her lips and grimace in the mirror, and I laughed to myself. Noticing how my face lit up with cheer my father said, "I knew you would heed my words." And he left the room.

When my father had gone I told Kaila, "How strangely you behaved, making faces in the mirror." Kaila appeared angry. "What is wrong, Kaila?" I asked. "Have you lost the use of your eyes?" she retorted. I then cried out, "Kaila, God be with you, speak up, don't remain silent, please, stop torturing me with all your hints and riddles." Kaila wiped her mouth angrily and said, "If you do not know, my dove, then pray take a good look at your father's appearance. Why, he is nothing but skin and bones and he walks about like a shadow on the face of the earth. When I was polishing his shoes, I thought, where on earth did he collect such mud, until it suddenly dawned upon me that his shoes were caked with earth from the cemetery. I also recognized his footprints by her grave, which he visits seven times a day."

Only then did I fathom Kaila's thoughts and the meaning of her insinuations in the mirror; if I remained at the Gottliebs my father would be obliged to pay frequent visits and consequently he would be prevented from visiting the cemetery. And so I gathered my dresses and placed them in my trunk. I then filled the iron with coals, intending to press two or three blouses before arriving at the Gottliebs. The following day my father had my clothes sent ahead with the young servant, and at noon we ate together, rose, and departed.

The Gottliebs' home rests on the edge of town, on the way to the train station. A good tract of empty land lies between it and the rest of the town. The building is a cosmetics factory and its rooms are large and empty, for in building the factory Gottlieb had told himself: I will build my factory large enough to house all those whom I will employ, my factory shall then be renowned throughout the country.

We crossed the town and arrived at the Gottliebs as Mintshi issued from the garden where she had been picking cherries. She hurried in our direction and welcomed us and ushered us back into the garden. Partchi then came at her summons, carrying two bowls of cherries. And Mintshi offered us the freshly picked cherries.

The day waned and Gottlieb returned from his work at the factory. Partchi set a table out in the garden. The light blue night enveloped us in its pleasing warmth. The moon stood in the heavens, the sky filled with stars, and the limpid songbird trilled its finest song as the train sounded in the distance. After the meal Gottlieb asked my father, "Would you care for a smoke?" "In the dark?" I interjected in astonishment. "And why should he not smoke in the dark?" Gottlieb asked. "I once read in a book that every smoker longs to gaze at the red ashes and at the cloud of incense rising from his cigarette," I replied, adding, "that is why the blind do not smoke; being blind they cannot see the ash or the smoke." "Have you not learned yet that books and all their profundities are of little use?" Gottlieb said, laughing. "In my case I first learned to smoke in the dark. Lying on my bed at night, I treated myself to a cigarette as soon as my father fell asleep. You see, I chose to smoke at night since I feared doing so in front of my father during the day. Partchi, bring the cigarettes and cigars, and don't forget the matches and ashtray." "If my husband smokes today then it is indeed a good sign," said Mrs. Gottlieb to my father. Mr. Gottlieb, though, pretended not to hear her words. "Now I will tell you what I have read," and he continued: "In bygone days if a man smoked a pipe they hung it from his nose, for they said that there was death in the tobacco, and the government penalized those who distributed tobacco in the country; and now, my friends, they have thrown under lock and key a worker from my own factory after he imported tobacco from a foreign country; our government, you see, has a tobacco monopoly." Such was Gottlieb's manner, grumbling incessantly over the action of the government. For his heart was not at one with the petty functionaries.

That night my father did not remain with us for long. "Tirtza must learn to stay in your company without me," he said. Mrs. Gottlieb then led me to a small room, kissed me on my brow, and left. The room contained an iron bed, a table, a closet, and a mirror. I lay on the bed by the window and a sudden breeze blew between the trees and I fancied I was being cradled in a hammock in the garden.

At daybreak fresh rays of light illumined my window. The sun graced the wings of birds trilling from their heights. I jumped out of bed and hurried to the well where I washed my face in fresh water. Partchi then called me to the table.

There was no joy in the Gottliebs' home. Gottlieb criticized his wife after each meal she prepared. "What is this I'm eating, straw?" he would exclaim. Since her husband was a perfumer, Mrs. Gottlieb was at pains to preserve his sense of smell, consequently she did not prepare spicy dishes. Also Partchi, the daughter of Gottlieb's deceased sister, was not welcome in their home. Mrs. Gottlieb gave the girl no peace. Mintshi and the girl's mother had quarreled and now the daughter was being punished for her mother's sins. Also Gottlieb was angry at her lest it be said his sister's daughter walked barefoot. Few visitors called upon the Gottliebs. Mr. Gottlieb met with his business associates in his office at the factory and Mintshi refrained from befriending other women from the town. In this she resembled my mother, may she rest in peace. When together they were like the two Austrians who meet outside of town; one says to the other, "Where may you be going?" and the other replies, "I'm off to the forest, for I want to be alone." "Why, I too want to be alone," exclaims the first. "Let us then go together." Thus I sat by Mrs. Gottlieb's side, her only companion.

Mrs. Gottlieb was a diligent woman. Yet she never appeared to be busy, whether attending to her affairs at home or whether in the garden. And if she paused in the midst of her work it seemed as though the task at hand was just completed and that she had arrived to see to its progress. I sought her out at least seven times a day, yet I never felt I was intruding into her affairs.

During my visit at the Gottliebs we evoked the memory of my mother, peace be with her. Mintshi then told me how Mazal had loved my mother, peace be with her, and how she had also loved him. Her father, though, had not consented to their union for he had already promised her hand in marriage to my father.

Night after night I lay on my bed, asking myself: what would now be if my mother had married Mazal? And what would have become of me? I knew such speculations to be fruitless, yet I did not abandon them.

When the shudders which accompanied my musings finally ceased, I said: Mazal has been wronged. He seemed to me to be like a man bereft of his wife, yet she is not his wife.

Now it was summertime. All day long I lounged under the oak and birch trees and stared into the blue sky. Sometimes I went to the factory and talked to the herb gatherers. They cared for themselves like the birds of the sky and their spirits never seemed to dip even for a single day. "I should go walking in the woods with them and forget my sorrows," I told myself; but I did not join them and I did not go into the woods. Instead I lay listless all day.

"Look, our friend is boring a hole through the heavens," Mr. Gottlieb said laughing as he saw me staring up at the sky. And I laughed along with him with a pained heart.

How I loathed myself. I burned with shame and did not know why. Now I pitied my father and now I secretly grew angry at him. And I turned my wrath upon Mazal also. Although I recalled the locust blows upon the walls of our home at the onset of spring, death no longer frightened me. Sometimes I told myself: why did Mintshi Gottlieb upset me by telling me of bygone memories? A father and mother, are they not man and woman and of one flesh? Why then should I brood over secrets which occurred before my time? Yet I thirsted to know more. I could not calm down, nor could I sit still for a moment's quiet. And so I told myself: if Mintshi knows what happened surely she will tell me the truth. How though will I open my mouth to ask? For if I but let the thoughts come to mind my face turns crimson let alone when I speak out my thoughts aloud. I then gave up all hope. More I could not know.

One day, though, Gottlieb left for an extended journey and Mintshi then asked me to sleep in her room. And while in her room she began again to speak of my mother and Mazal. What I expected was then unfolded to me.

"Mazal was still a young man when he arrived here. He left Vienna to tour the country towns and came here as well. He came to see the town and since coming to our town he has not left; it is seventeen years now." Mintshi spoke in a low voice and a cold gust of air rose from her words. It was the very chill which I had felt upon touching my brow against the marble slab of my mother's tombstone, may she rest in peace. Mintshi swept her left hand across her brow, saying, "What more can I tell you that I haven't already said?" She then shut her eyes as though in a dream. Mintshi suddenly started awake and fetched a diary like the diaries educated girls possessed a generation ago. "Now read this," she said, "for I have copied from Mazal's writings. I have copied all which he wrote in those days." I took the notebook which Mrs. Gottlieb had copied and placed it in my bag. I never read in Mintshi's room at night as Mintshi could not sleep with the light of the candle. And the following morning I read all that was written in the book:

How I love the country towns during the summer months. The streets are hushed, the town and its inhabitants a pot of flowers peering out with no one to behold them. Her sons are in hiding, the sun has driven them into their homes, and I walk solitary in a peaceable land. I am a student at the university and God has led me forth to one of the towns. Now as I stood in the street I beheld a woman braced by the window, and she placed on its sill a bowl of millet to soak in the sun. I bowed before her and said, "Will not the birds prey upon your millet?" I scarcely finished my sentence when a young woman appeared at the window, and she stared at me and laughed at my words. I was nearly put to shame. And lest the young woman sense my confusion I said to her, "May I have some water please?" The young woman then proffered a glass of water from the window. "Why have you not asked the man in to rest?" the woman said to the girl. "Does he not live in a foreign city?" And she said, "Come sir, come in." So I turned and entered the home.

The members of the household appeared well-to-do, and a man in his full years sat over the Gemara. He had dozed off over his books and now he awoke and greeted me and asked, "Who are you and what brings you to our town?" "I am a student," I replied after returning the greeting. "I have come to see the countryside during my vacation." They were struck with wonder by my words. "Look now and see for yourself," the man said to the young woman, "educated people come from afar to see our town. And you ask to leave us and our town. You can now banish the thought from your mind." The young woman listened silently. "So, you are studying medicine, you want to be a doctor?" the father said to me. "No, sir," I replied, "I am studying philosophy." The man was surprised to hear this and said, "I have always thought that philosophy is not to be learned in school. For the true philosopher is he who ponders over scholarly books to fathom their meaning."

The day waned and the man told the girl, "Bring me my sash, for I will recite the afternoon prayer. Don't be ashamed for I will recite the afternoon prayer." "I too will pray," I exclaimed.

"Bring me the prayerbook," he said. She then hurried to fetch the prayerbook. And he took the prayerbook in hand and opened it wide, indicating the passage we would read. "Please, sir," I said, "there is no need, the prayer is sealed within me." The man was surprised to hear that I knew the prayer by heart. He gestured toward the East where a tapestry hung on the Easterly wall, and I read all which was inscribed on the Easterly tapestry:

> *Blessed be he who shall not forsake Thee*
> *And he who shall cleave unto Thee.*
> *For those who seek Thee shall not fail*
> *Nor shall they be put to shame*
> *Those who seek and dwell within Thee.*

As soon as I finished praying I extolled the Easterly tapestry, for indeed it was splendid. My words though were like the sun's dying rays at dusk, illuminating but the fringes of the East, whereas the whole is left darksome: for I could utter but a small fraction of all the praise which swelled within me.

The woman set the table and bid me share their meal. And the dishes were placed before us and we ate. Though not abundant, consisting but of flour and corn in milk, nonetheless we lingered over our food as the man spoke of all which had befallen them.

He had once been a wealthy man, doing commerce with the landed gentry and investing his money in field crops. Such was his way from year to year. But such prosperity did not last for long, for the overlord did not keep to his end of the agreement. Money he took and crops he did not give. A bitter and prolonged quarrel then ensued between the two men. And what remained of the fruits of his labor was exhausted in legal fees.

Though bribing is a criminal offense and it is forbidden to bribe a state judge, for the gentile is also subject to the laws of the land, the overlord offered the judge gifts so that the judge would not turn the sentence against him.

"Eternity may well come to its end," he said, "and I still won't be able to finish telling you all that befell me in those days: my adversary slandered me with false accusations, and my eldest son —though crippled and exempt from serving the Kaiser—was conscripted into the army; and the selfsame overlord was a high-ranking officer in the army, and my son died under the crush of his iron fist.

"But should a man bemoan the loss of imaginary possessions? Blessed be the Holy Name for He has not removed his merciful eye from us. Though the Almighty has not entrusted me a second time with wealth and happiness, I bless the Lord daily, for we are not lacking in food. At times, though, upon calling to mind the inflictions wrought upon my son, then would I choose death over life."

The members of the household dried their tears and the woman asked her husband, "If he were alive today, how old would he be?" "What sort of woman-talk is this?" he answered. "Do not lay reproach on the Almighty, the Lord giveth and the Lord taketh, Blessed be the name of the Lord. How splendid are the words of Rabbi Meir Ben Yehiel Mikhal, blessed be his memory, concerning the passage: and he shall shave his head over the loss of his property, for it is forbidden to do so over the dead."

The oil in the lamp was nearly spent, and I rose from the table and asked, "Tell me please, is there an inn in town? For I will not be able to continue on my way tonight." The man and woman conferred amongst themselves and then said, "Indeed there are a number of inns in town but who knows if you shall find comfort in any one of them; ours is a small town and the inns are of the plainest sort, for respectable guests seldom come here; he who isn't accustomed to such conditions shall not find such inns to be very restful." The man then glanced at his wife and said, "A stranger shall not sleep outside; I will open my door to a guest."

The young woman then brought a candle and lit it and placed it on the table, for the oil in the lamp was spent. We sat together for another hour as they did not tire from hearing of the wonders of Vienna where the Kaiser dwells. I felt dearly drawn then to their way of life. And later that evening they prepared an extra bed for me in one corner of the house and I fell into a deep and restful sleep.

I heard the sound of a man's footsteps and started awake. The master of the house stood by my bed, his prayer shawl and phylacteries under his arm and the morning prayer on his lips. "Ah, sir," I cried out, "you are on your way to pray while I lie in the lap of lassitude." The man smiled. "I have already prayed," he said. "I am on my way back from the synagogue; but be at ease my son." And seeing my discomfort he added, "If you have slept soundly then lie back and sleep, soon enough the days shall come wherein there will be no sleep, but if you are wide awake then rise and we will breakfast together."

After eating I made to pay for my food. The woman and her daughter drew back in shame and the man smiled and said, "Such are the ways of the city dweller; they do not know that an act of charity is honored and that it is a holy duty to invite a guest into one's home." I thanked them for letting me remain in their home for the entire night and morning. "Blessed are you in the eyes of the Lord for your kindness," I exclaimed. As I turned to leave the man asked, "Where will you now go?" "I will go and cover the length and breadth of the town," I answered. "For that is why I have come." "Go then in peace," said the man. "But return with us at noon." "I am unworthy of such kindness," I said. And I left in the direction of the town.

I soon arrived at the Great Synagogue, which contained a rare prayerbook whose gilt letters were inscribed on deerskin parchment. The gold, though, was obscured by the smoke which had risen from those martyred in the name of the Holy One, and the smoke had seeped through and blackened the pages.

I then came upon the House of Study. The sun's rays beat against its walls. Those dwelling within had unburdened themselves of their coats as they sat by the table of worship, and they looked up and were surprised to see me enter. No sooner had I entered than they implored me to speak of other houses of learning and visions of distant places lit their eyes.

I left the House of Study and turned toward the forest. I was overwhelmed with grief as I approached the green and somber woods. And I fell upon the earth and lay on the scrub by the oak trees. The Lord's mercy did not stir from within me. Suddenly I remembered that I had been bidden to the noon meal and I rose and returned home.

The members of the household reproached me as I entered, saying, "We waited for you and you did not come. We then thought you forgot us and ate without you." "I went for a walk in the forest," I replied. "Indeed I am late and now I will be on my way." But the woman looked at me and said, "You will go nowhere before having eaten." And she promptly set about to bake me an egg biscuit. "The cantor will ascend to the pulpit today," the master of the house said. "Lo, he will pray in the synagogue; eat something and then come along with me to the synagogue; the bed we prepared for you yesterday is still in its place; sleep now with us another night and tomorrow you shall be on your way."

I do not play an instrument, nor can I carry a tune. Little is my knowledge of music, nor do I understand it. Indeed when taken to the opera I would sit and count the windows. But I now told the master of the house, "Very well, I will accompany you." I will not describe the cantor's singing, nor will I speak of what was on

my mind just then; rather I will speak of what I did upon
returning with the man.

I returned with the man to his home. And after eating we sat
outside by the doorstep. So, I told myself, have I not longed to
travel across the length and breadth of the countryside? If I
remain here one more day I will surely use up all the days of my
vacation. It is fine to see the countryside, my heart cried out
suddenly, but to sit here is even better. I was of robust health and
in those days the mere thought of rest didn't even cross my mind.
It was like another one of those notions a man appropriates before
having the faintest idea of its meaning. Alas, those days have
passed by and are gone and my rest has been swept along with
them.

The following morning I asked the members of the household,
"Tell me kindly, do you have a spare room for me, for I wish to
remain in your company for the rest of my vacation." And the
members of the household led me to their holiday *succah* built to
serve also as a room. "Remain here as long as you wish," they
said. And so the woman prepared my meals, while I in turn
taught their daughter to write and read.

Now I sit in the home of these good people. They have vacated
a special room for me, it is the holiday *succah* built to serve also as a
room. There is, moreover, a small stove in the *succah*. Now they
shall say it has no use; soon enough though winter will come and
we shall warm ourselves by its heat. And I dwell in my rooftop
room overlooking the entire town. I can see from my perch the
huge marketplace where women sally forth with their baskets
laden with vegetables. They shall sell the rotten ones, while the
good ones they shall keep until they rot too. And there is a well in
the center of the market with water gushing from its two
conduits, and the country girls draw from its source. A Jew
suddenly approached one of the maidens, desiring to drink from
her pitcher. "Jew," I called out from my garret, "why do you
drink drawn water? Is not the entire well in front of you? And a
freshwater well at that?" But the Jew did not hear me. For he was
bowed down to the ground and I dwelled in the heights.

A new voice resounded in the house. The voice of a young
woman. I folded my coat behind the windowpane to catch a
glimpse of my image before descending to see the young woman.
Leah introduced me to her friend Mintshi. I greeted her with a
bow. Returning to my room I spent the rest of the day lost in
thought, for Mintshi did not live here but in the capital. While
there she had witnessed the respect accorded to me when my

poems were extolled at a public reading. When she returned home her mother had said that a man had lived in her room. "And what is the man's name?" she had asked. "His name is Akaviah Mazal." Her heart had then beat fast, for she had had the privilege of knowing me. My God, how I held my head high. I buried myself in the Book of the Righteous, perhaps it would quench the embers of lust burning within me? I could not quench its embers, though, and I then found comfort in certain moral tales. Both the good and the bad within you shall embrace the Lord your God, taught the Sages of blessed memory. Oh, if only it were so.

How the students from the House of Study delighted in my presence. They implored me to instruct them in the ways of the Enlightenment, and is there a teacher more able than I? Today two lads came to see me and instead of reading the Talmud they pored over the contents of profane books. Standing beside me one of the boys commenced to read a German poem, and the one chanted while the other read. My students moan, they ask but to know the ways of the Enlightenment. As for myself? My sole desire is to follow in the path of the Lord all the days of my life.

What is God's path? A man sets out on his way and his strength fails him. His knees buckle and his parched tongue thirsts. He falls seven times and rises up again without reaching his longed-for destination. The way is still far and the illusions are many. The man will then say in his heart, perhaps I have strayed from the path, this is not the way. And he shall turn off the path which he first took. Now upon turning off the path which he first took, lo, he shall see a light flickering in the distance. Although he does not know yet whether indeed this is the right path, who will say the man erred in choosing a different path from the first?

Though I am a teacher of the Enlightenment I declined the young men's request. For how will I provide for myself if the lining of my purse is empty. Today I am like a thief who stumbles upon a bundle of coins, returns it to its owner, and then snatches the money back from the owner's pockets; for he is a thief and he cannot live otherwise. Thus I teach Leah and her friend Mintshi, as well as the sons of the rich. My friends mock me in their letters, and my father, seeing that I have abandoned my studies at the university, bewails my fate daily. Summer swept by and my vacation drew to an end but I did not return home.

How resplendent was my *succah* during the feast of the Tabernacles. We hung from her boughs red lanterns and gathered within the finest of the household vessels. As Leah made to hand me the Easterly tapestry a ring loosened and fell from one of its corners. Leah took the ring and slipped it on my finger. She then proceeded to untie the crimson ribbon fastened to her locks and using the ribbon secured the Easterly tapestry to the wall, reading out loud, "Blessed be he who shall not forsake Thee." I read on, "And he who shall cleave unto Thee." Suddenly we both blushed as her father and mother peered in, their faces glowing with joy. They called me master of the house as we sat together in the *succah* and they thought of themselves as my guests. Leah came to the *succah* at least seven times a day; once she brought food and another time she cleared the table. And we thanked God for exalting us toward love.

How resplendent was my *succah* during the feast of the Tabernacles. But now the festive *succah* is stocked with beans and lentils. A bean merchant has rented the *succah* to store his merchandise, while I have been forced to leave my home and abandon my *succah*, and I have rented myself a room on the outskirts of the town. My lodgings are small and peaceful. An old woman tends to my needs, she prepares my meals and washes my linen. I am surrounded by peace and quiet, yet my heart knows no peace. Mr. Mintz who has rented the *succah* is a wealthy man. His trade has spread throughout the country and Leah's father has promised him his daughter's hand. And I am but a poor teacher, a good-for-nothing. When I came from the city they befriended me. Alas, they drew near me with their mouths while their hearts were elsewere. How strange are the ways of my brethren.

Apart from teaching Leah to write and read I also taught her Hebrew. Her parents had been happy to see her learning the Holy tongue. Her father, though, came to envy her knowledge, and he drew us apart. Ah, sir, surely she will not forget all that I taught her. She will brood over the poems I have written and though she has left me she will hold fast unto my teachings.

One day I went into town and I saw Leah's father and I quickly made to leave. But he ran after me and said, "Why have you run off, I must talk to you." My heart beat fast. I knew he had nothing to say which could possibly calm me and yet I stood and listened. He is Leah's father, I thought, he will speak of Leah. He then looked here and there and seeing that no one was in sight he said, "My daughter is ill. She suffers from her brother's illness." I remained silent and he continued to talk as at first, saying, "She was not born for toil, physical labor shall be the death of her, if I don't find her peace and quiet she will die before my own time has come." He appeared to be suddenly frightened by his own words. At last he raised his voice and blurted out, "Mintz is a wealthy man, her health shall be restored under his care. That is why I have promised her to him. He will send her to the health spas and all her desires shall be fulfilled."

Ah, sir, another illness altogether lies within your daughter's heart which all the health spas shall not cure. And I said I will cure her, but you drew us apart.

As I drew away from the man I slipped off the ring which Leah had given to me. For she is engaged to another man. A sudden chill then swept over my finger.

So ended the chronicles of Akaviah Mazal.

Twice, three times a week my father arrived at the Gottliebs and dined with us in the garden. A soothing dusk enveloped the table and its vessels. We ate by the light of the fireflies. Also the red lanterns by the tracks lit the night, for the train station was not far from the Gottliebs' home. Rarely was my mother's name mentioned, and when Mrs. Gottlieb did speak of her you could not tell that she was speaking of a deceased person. Only when I became familiar with her manner of speech did I come to see that she acted out of good sense.

My father would make all possible efforts to turn the conversation toward my mother, may she rest in peace, exclaiming, "We are the miserable widowers." How strange were his words. It was as though all womankind had died and every man was a widower.

One day Mr. Gottlieb left to see his brother. "Perhaps," he said, "my brother will enter into my business. He is a wealthy man and will contribute to the factory's growth." Mintshi, who normally did not like to interfere in her husband's affairs, then told me more than she wished. All of a sudden she realized what she had done and she then seemed to ask me to forget all that she had just recounted.

For she spoke to me of that which had occurred when she had first arrived at her father-in-law's house. The groom had entered, welcomed her, and then had turned on his heels and left. Mintshi had been greatly disheartened by his mechanical manner. But no sooner gone than he returned. Mintshi stood bemused and yet saddened over what had happened. He had then asked to kiss her and she drew back, offended. Mintshi had not known then that she had been greeted at first not by the groom but by his brother, whose features were identical to the groom's.

The holidays were about to end. "Remain here until Tuesday evening," my father said. "On Tuesday evening I will come and we will return home together." He was suddenly gripped by a spasm of coughing as he spoke. Mintshi poured him a glass of water. "Have you caught a cold, Mr. Mintz?" she asked my father. "Indeed," he answered, "I have considered leaving my work." We listened in astonishment as he continued, "If not for my daughter I would wipe my hands clean of my trade." How strange a reply. Will a man leave his trade because of a slight cold? To wear a long face would only lead him to think that indeed he was ill. And so Mrs. Gottlieb said, "What then will you do, write books?" We all laughed. He, the merchant, a man of action, would sit and write books.

The train's whistle sounded. Mrs. Gottlieb said, "My husband shall arrive in ten minutes," and fell silent. Our conversation came to an abrupt halt; all of us suddenly awaited his arrival. Mr. Gottlieb entered. Mintshi stared at him and her unremitting eye ran up and down his frame. Gottlieb rubbed the tip of his nose and chuckled like a man intending to amuse his listeners. He then told us of his affairs and of what had occurred at his brother's home.

Upon arriving he had found his brother's wife sitting with her son. And he had hoisted the boy up on his lap and then he had leaped and capered about with him. They had been taken aback, for the boy had followed him about fearlessly even though he had never seen him before. Mr. Gottlieb's brother had entered in the midst of their play and the boy had stared now at his father and now at his father's brother; his eyes darted from one to the other, he stared and was dumbfounded. Suddenly he averted his face and burst into tears as he flung his small arms toward his mother, and she had embraced him as he buried his face in her bosom.

I returned home and to school. My father also found me a Hebrew teacher, a Mr. Segal, with whom I studied for many days. Mr. Segal arrived three times a week, and not liking to jump from one subject to another, he divided my studies into three parts: one day of the week I studied the Bible, one day grammar, and on the third day I studied the craft of writing.

Segal set out to explain the Holy Writings in a clear light, and he did not refrain from teaching me the commentaries of our Sages. Many good hours were spent over such commentary and exegesis, leaving us little time for the Book. He spoke to me of all the splendors which hitherto I had not found in books. Hoping to revive our language, he would also urge me, whenever I spoke up, saying, "Pray, say it in Hebrew." He spoke like an orator and he delighted whenever he stumbled upon a passage which rang close to his heart, for a prophet had spoken, and had not the prophets spoken Hebrew?

Of all the hours spent in study I cherished most those devoted to the craft of writing. Segal would then lean back peacefully, his left hand under his head and his eyes firmly shut. Ever so quietly he would read from the wellsprings of his heart, without a glance at the book. Like a musician plying his instrument during the darkest hour of the night, his heart brimming to its banks, without a glance at his notes, playing only what God had placed in his heart—so was this man.

My father paid Segal three reinesh a month for my studies. After clipping the bills together, I furtively handed them over to Segal. Segal, though, counted the money in full view, exclaiming, "I am not a doctor and need not be given my pay secretly. I am a worker and I am not ashamed of receiving a salary for my labor."

And my father toiled at his work without end. Nor did he rest at night. When I would go to sleep he would remain seated by the lamplight. Sometimes I would rise in the morning to find the light still lit by his side, for being preoccupied with his accounts he would forget to extinguish the light. My mother's name no longer graced his lips.

On the eve of Yom Kippur my father bought two candles: the one candle, the candle-of-life, he lit in the house, and the other candle, the memorial candle, he took to the synagogue. And as my father took the candle to the synagogue and I accompanied him, he said, "Don't forget, tomorrow is Remembrance Day for the souls of the dead." His voice shook as he spoke. I bent forward and kissed his hand.

We arrived at the synagogue. I peered through the lattice and saw one man greeting another in the midst of the assembly, and the one asked of the other to be forgiven. I then saw my father standing in front of a man without a prayer shawl, and I recognized Akaviah Mazal, and my eyes clouded with tears.

The cantor sang Kol Nidre and his song soared from one moment to the other. The candles flickered and the building filled with light. The men swayed between the candles, their faces veiled. How I loved the holiness of the day.

We returned home without speaking a word. The silent stars in the firmament and the candles-of-life burning in each home illumined our path. We took the path leading to the bridge, for my father said, "Let us rest by the water for a while, my throat is choked with dust." From within the rippling water the night stars peered out at the stars in the

sky. The moon broke through the furrowed clouds and a low murmur-
ing sound rose from the water. From his heavenly heights God sent
forth silence. I shall never forget that night. The candle-of-life flickered
its flame toward us as we arrived home. I read "Hear O Israel" and then
slept till the morning hours. In the morning I was roused from my sleep
by my father's voice. We left for the House of Prayer. A white scarf
covered the sky as the heavens are covered in autumn. The trees flung
their red leaves earthward and the old womenfolk stood outside, ready
to gather the leaves into their homes. From the surrounding farmhouses
thin columns of smoke rose from the dry leaves burning in the furnaces.
People wrapped in white garments swayed back and forth in the court-
yards. We arrived at the synagogue and prayed, meeting briefly in the
synagogue's courtyard between the morning prayer and the additional
service and then between the additional service and the afternoon
prayer. My father asked whether the fast was not too great a strain upon
me. How my father's voice confused me.

I barely saw my father during the holiday. For I studied in a Polish
school and we were not excused from classes during our own holidays.
Returning from school at noon I would find my father and the neighbors
crowded together in the *succah*. I would then sit and eat my meal alone,
as there was no room for women in the *succah*. But I was soon appeased
by the coming of winter. Evening after evening we would have supper
together and then bend over our work to the light of the one lamp. And
the white oval shade would cast its light over us as our heads merged
into one black presence in the shadows. I would prepare my lessons and
my father would bring his accounts into order. At nine o'clock Kaila
would put before us three glasses of tea, two for my father and one for
me. My father would then push aside ledger and pen in exchange for the
glass of tea. One glass he would drain steaming hot, and the second he
would drain cold after dropping into the glass a lump of sugar. We
would then return to our work, I to my lessons, and my father to his
accounting books. At ten o'clock my father would rise, stroke my hair,
and say, "And now go to sleep, Tirtza." How I loved his use of the
conjunction, *and*. I always grew happy in its presence; it was as though
all that my father told me was but the continuation of his inmost
thoughts; that is, first he spoke to me from within his heart, and then
out loud. And so I would say to my father, "If you are not going to sleep
then I too will not sleep. I will stay up with you until you go to sleep."
My father, though, would not heed my words. I would go to sleep. And
upon waking I would find my father still sitting over his accounts, his

ledgers covering the table. Had he risen early, or had he not slept the entire night? I did not ask, nor did I get an answer. Night after night I would tell myself: I will go now and appeal to his heart, perhaps he will listen to me and rest. But I would fall fast asleep before ever getting out of bed. I knew my father intended to leave his business and that wishing to set his accounts into order he now bent over his affairs with redoubled effort. I did not ask what he would then do.

I had turned sixteen and finished school. When the school year ended my father sent me to the teachers' seminary. He did not send me because of my talents. I had no talent for teaching, but I also showed little enthusiasm for anything else as yet. I believed then that a person's deeds and future were decided by others. And I said, it is good. My relatives and acquaintances were astonished. How in the world will Mintz make a teacher out of his daughter?

To labor is our lot and therein lies all hope. We knew the Hebrew teachers to be different from the Christian teachers, for the former were sent to a remote village where, being Hebrew, they were badgered by cruel-hearted villagefolk. In addition, one's tuition earnings were exhausted by the time one arrived at the village, for all of it was spent in travel. Still, a great number of Hebrew teachers attended the seminary.

The seminary was a private institution and Mazal taught there. Once a year the principal would travel along with his pupils to the district capital where the pupils were examined. The schoolgirls would then apply themselves to their studies with redoubled effort. For a girl was put to much shame if she returned without a certificate in hand, for the travel expenses were high and she also sewed herself a new dress before departing; and if she returned from the examinations and had failed, her rival would then say, "Why, you have a new dress. I don't believe I've ever seen it before." "It is not new," answered the girl. And the other went on, "Did you not sew it to wear for your examinations? But where is your certificate?" And if the girl happened not to be wearing her new dress she was asked, "But where is your new dress worn on the day of your examinations?" And they reminded her of her shameful lack of a certificate. This is why the girls labored at their studies without stop. If the brain did not comprehend then they drilled their lessons in by rote, for what the brain cannot do memory shall.

Now I was surprised that Mazal showed no signs of recognizing me when I arrived at the seminary. Do I not find favor in his eyes? I asked myself. Does he not know who I am? For days on end I could not keep myself from brooding over such feelings, and I studied twice as hard and was never bored.

In those days I loved to take solitary walks. No sooner had I finished my lessons than I would set out to walk in the open fields. If I happened to meet a friend on the way I did not call out a greeting, and when hailed I answered in a low voice, lest I be accompanied while all I desired was to walk alone. Winter had arrived.

One evening I set out for a walk when I heard a large dog barking and then the sound of a man's footsteps. I recognized the man; it was Mazal. And I wound my handkerchief round my hand and waved it before him in greeting. Mazal stopped in his tracks and asked, "What is wrong, Miss Mintz?" "The dog," I replied. "Did the dog bite you?" he asked, startled. "The dog bit me," I answered. "Show me your hand," he said, almost breathless. "Please," I said, "bind the handkerchief for me over my wound." Mazal seized hold of my hand with quivering fingers and as he held my hand I unwound the handkerchief and jumped up in the air, exclaiming as I laughed loudly, "There is nothing, sir! Not a dog, nor a wound." Mazal was so taken aback by my words that for a moment he could but stand frozen to the ground, not knowing whether to shout or laugh. But he quickly recovered and then he too laughed loudly and cheerfully, exclaiming, "Ah, you are a bad girl; how you frightened me." He then accompanied me home and left. But before leaving he stared deep into my eyes. And I told myself: surely he now knows that I know, he knows my secret. Nonetheless, I thought, I will be grateful if you do not remind me of that which you do know.

All that night I tossed about in my bed. I thrust my hand into my mouth and stared at the designs on my handkerchief. I regretted not having asked Mazal into the house. If Mazal had entered we would now be sitting in the room and I would not be nursing such delusions. The following morning I rose and gloomily paced about in the heat of my spirit. Now I stretched out on my bed and now on the carpet, and I was beguiled by a fickle wind of delusions. Only toward evening was I able to calm down. Like the weak-nerved who doze off during the day and start awake at night. And recalling all that I had done yesterday I rose and tied a red string around my wrist as a reminder.

Now it was Hannuka and geese were being slaughtered. One day Kaila left to ask the rabbi a question and a man well advanced in age appeared. "When will your father come home?" he asked, and I replied, "Sometimes he comes at eight and sometimes at seven-thirty." "In such a case I am early," he declared, "for it is now five-thirty." I said, "Yes, it is five-thirty." And he said, "It doesn't matter."

I drew up a chair for him. "But why should I sit," he said. "Bring me some water." And as I poured him tea into a glass, he exclaimed, "He asked for water and she gave him tea." He then poured the tea from the glass onto his hand and cried out, "Well, well, and the Easterly?" Turning toward the wall he continued, "In the house of your grandfather a man didn't have to ask such questions, for the Easterly shall hang on the wall." He then rose to his feet and prayed. I took two, three large dollops of goose fat and placed them in a bowl on the table. The man finished praying and he ate and drank and said, his lips dripping with fat, "Fat, my dear, fat." "Here," I said, "I will bring you a napkin to wipe your hands." "Rather bring me a slice of cake," he said. "Do you have a cake that doesn't require hand washing?" "There is, and enough to spare," I said. "I will bring you some cake at once." "Please don't hurry, you can bring the cake along with the second helping. Will you not give me another helping?" "Why of course." "I knew you would, but you still don't know who I am. It doesn't matter," the man said softly. "I'm Gotteskind.

"So, your father is indeed late today." I looked at my watch. "It is a quarter after six, my father will not arrive before half-past seven." "It doesn't matter," he said. "But do go on with your work. Don't disturb yourself." I took a book. And he said, "What's that you have there in your hands?" "A book of geometry," I replied. Gotteskind seized hold of the book and asked, "And do you also know how to play the piano? No? Why didn't they teach you how to play the piano?

"Why, I've just come from the pharmacy where the pharmacist told me he would never wed a woman who didn't know how to play the piano. 'Listen, Gotteskind,' the pharmacist said, 'I'm prepared to live in a small town since I can't afford to buy a pharmacy in the city.' But I failed to mention that he really isn't a pharmacist but the pharmacist's assistant. But what does it matter, assistant pharmacist, pharmacist, it's all one and the same.

"Now you'll say, why he doesn't even own a pharmacy. It doesn't matter, soon enough he'll take himself a wedded wife and from her dowry he'll purchase himself a pharmacy. 'And so, Gotteskind,' the pharmacist said to me, 'here I am about to settle down in a small town; if my wife doesn't play the piano she will surely die of boredom.' So, knowing how to play an instrument is a rare gift indeed, aside from enjoying moving its keys think of it also as a source of wisdom.

"But the hour of seven is about to strike and though I said I will go, will not your father soon arrive?" Gotteskind stroked the wisps of his beard and continued, "Indeed, your father should realize that a faithful friend is waiting for him. And so man knows least where lies his good fortune. The clock is striking two, three, four, five, six, seven. Let the clock be witness to the truth of my words." I grew weary, but Gotteskind went on, "Why, you didn't know who I was, nor did you hear mention of my name until today. And I knew you before you were formed; through my services was your mother wed to your father."

He was still talking when Kaila arrived and we set the table. "You are also versed in housekeeping?" Gotteskind exclaimed with surprise. "And you said your father will soon return. If so let us wait for him," Gotteskind said, as though having just made up his mind to wait.

Close upon the eighth hour my father returned. "We mentioned your name and here you are," Gotteskind said to my father. "Lo, the clock has struck. It will be witness to the truth of my words." And he winked at my father and went on, "I have been sent here to see you but lo and behold the Almighty has also shown me your daughter."

That night I dreamt my father gave me away in marriage to the High Chief of an Indian tribe. My entire body was impressed with tattoos of kissing lips and my husband sat opposite me on the sharp edge of a rock, combing his beard with the seven talons of the eagle. I was struck with wonder, for I was certain that Indians shaved their hair and beard. How then had my husband acquired such a mass of hair?

Four days had passed since I met with Mazal. I did not go to school. And I feared lest my father would notice and worry over me. Whenever I thought of returning to school I was of two minds. Would I not blush in shame upon seeing Mazal? Or, if Mazal was absent that day, would I not shudder at the sound of his footsteps? And, should I go, what if I arrived after classes had begun, and what if he then suddenly cast his eyes upon me? In the end I left for the seminary only to find another man reading out the lessons. I then asked one of the schoolgirls, "Why hasn't Mazal arrived today?" "Neither did he come yesterday or the day before and who knows whether he will ever return to the seminary," she replied. "Your words puzzle me," I said. "A woman's hand is in the matter," she replied. I shuddered at her words. The schoolgirl went on to tell me how Mazal had been forced to leave the school because of Kfirmelach the teacher who received from his grandmother an allowance, earned as a maidservant in Mazal's home. One day she had placed her money in an envelope taken from her master's letterbox. Kfirmelach had then unsealed the envelope and had found a letter written to Mazal by one of the schoolgirls in the seminary. It so happened that the girl's father had lent Kfirmelach money. Kfirmelach now told the man, "Forget my debts and I will give you your daughter's letter written to her lover Mazal. And hearing of what had occurred Mazal left the seminary lest the institution's name be tainted by his presence.

I returned home, relieved at not having seen Mazal at the seminary, and I did not tell myself, he has been stripped of his livelihood. From now on I shall scarcely see Mazal but neither shall I blush in shame if I should happen to see him. And I suddenly loathed going to school. I then remained at home and helped Kaila with the housework. How I recoiled in horror whenever I called to mind the aging schoolmistresses. Shall I waste my life bent over books which I cannot understand and shall I become like one of them? When I brooded so, I forgot my own work and I neglected the housework. I longed to go out, to fill my lungs with fresh air, to stretch my legs. I then rose, wrapped myself in my coat, and left. Once on my way I turned in the direction of the Gottliebs' home. Mintshi hastened toward me and she clasped my hand and warmed it in her own, and she peered deep into my eyes, eager to know what tidings I brought. "Nothing is new," I said. "I went for a walk and turned in your direction." Mintshi took my coat and seated me by the stove. After drinking a glass of tea I rose and prepared to leave, for I had heard that the tax inspector was expected for dinner and I feared lest I disturb Mr. Gottlieb in pursuing his affairs with the inspector.

The rain was upon the earth and I sat at home. I read all day long or else I sat in the kitchen and helped Kaila with the chores. My heart's desires were quelled; I knew no wrong.

At eight o'clock at night my father would return home. He would quietly remove his shoes and slip on a pair of felt slippers. The faint rustle of his slippers brought back to mind the ancient stillness of the house. The table would be set before his arrival, and when he arrived we would sit and eat. After dinner my father would return to his accounts and I would sit by his side until ten o'clock, at which time he would rise and say, "Now my daughter, go to sleep." Sometimes he would stroke my hair with his warm hand as I bowed my head. My happiness was too great to bear. Thus passed the days of rain.

The sun rose over the town and the puddles were near dry. I lay awake early one morning, unable to sleep, as I fancied something had lighted upon the world. I turned toward the window and lo, a faint bluish light shone in the window. Can there be such a light, unknown to me until now? Several moments passed before I realized that it was the curtain which had fooled me. And still my happiness did not leave me.

I jumped out of bed and dressed. Something has happened. I will go now and see what has happened. I ventured out. And I stood spellbound whichever way I turned. I peered into the shop windows and the windows glowed in the early morning light. I then said, I will go in and buy something. I did not know what I would buy, but I said to myself, I will buy something and Kaila will not have to trouble herself. I did not enter into any of the shops though, and I turned and set out toward the bridge at the edge of the town.

There are a number of dwellings under the bridge and on either side of the banks. Pigeons flitted from one roof to another and a man and woman stood on one of the rooftops, mending its surface. I called out to them good day and they returned my greeting. And I turned to continue on my way when lo, there stood before me an old woman, waiting, so it seemed, for me to ask her the way. But I did not ask.

I returned home and I gathered my books and left for the seminary. I was tired of the seminary: this house is a den of boredom; and I saw that there wasn't a person to whom I could pour out my heart; and my disdain grew and I could not stand my studies. I then said, I will speak to Mazal. I did not know how he would help, still, I welcomed the thought and toyed with it that entire day. How, though, will I come to speak to him? For I dare not approach his home, and I will not find him in the streets. Winter passed, the snow melted, but we did not meet.

Close upon that time my father fell ill and Mr. Gottlieb came to inquire of his health, and he told my father that he was expanding his factory, for on becoming a partner in the factory his brother had given freely of his own money, also the government had stopped putting any obstacles in their way, since an important minister had sought help for him after having accepted a bribe. "My dear sir," the minister had told Gottlieb, "all the petty bureaucrats, including the Kaiser himself, hunger for money. There isn't a minister in this country who won't accept a bribe. Let me give you an example," said the minister. "When we ask, what makes Mr. So and So unique, are we not surprised when we are told, why the length of his nose is five centimeters. But five centimeters is indeed the very length of every nozzle." "Heaven forbid I should condemn them," Gottlieb said to my father, "but their hypocrisy maddens me; today you shower them with gifts and by tomorrow you are a

total stranger to them. In this I admire the Russian bureaucrats, at least
they take a bribe without pretending to be honest.

"From the sick to the sick," Gottlieb exclaimed as I accompanied him
to the door. "Who is sick?" I asked, concealing my embarrassment. "Mr.
Mazal is ill," answered Gottlieb. For a short moment I longed to accompany him. And yet I checked myself and did not go.

"Is it not a wonder, Tirtza," said my father, "Gottlieb has always
been a hardworking man and he hasn't ever complained at being child-
less. Who then will inherit the fruit of his labors when his final hour has
come?" My father bade the accounting book to be brought to him and
he sat up in bed and worked until suppertime. The following morning
he rose in good health from his sickbed and that afternoon he left for the
shop while I set out to Mazal's home.

I knocked on the door but there was no sound nor any that answered.
I then said, Blessed be the Name, the man is not home. Still I did not
move. And all at once, seeing that no one was at home, my hand grew
bold and I knocked loudly.

Several moments passed and my heart grew feeble. Suddenly I heard
someone stirring within the house and I took fright. And just as I meant
to go, Mazal appeared. Wrapped in his overcoat, he greeted me. I lowered my eyes and said, "Mr. Gottlieb came by yesterday and mentioned
that Sir was taken ill and I have come to inquire of his health." Mazal
did not answer a word. He beckoned me into his home with one hand as
he clutched the collar of his overcoat with the other. Saddened, I shifted
about and he said, "Forgive me, miss, for I cannot speak like this," and
he disappeared into the far room only to reappear after several moments
dressed in his best clothes. Mazal coughed. A sudden quiet fell over us
as we stood alone in the room. "Please, sit down, miss," he said, placing
a chair by the stove. "Has your hand healed from the dog bite?" he
inquired. I stared into his face, my eyes filling with tears. Mazal took
my hand into his own. "Forgive me," he said. His voice was warm and
tender and filled with mercy. Little by little I grew less embarrassed. I
stared at the room I had known as a child and it suddenly appeared new
to me. The heat from the stove warmed my body and I felt a new and
steadfast spirit welling up within me.

Mazal placed a log in the stove and I hastened to help him. But in my
haste I thrust my hand out and knocked a photograph off the table. I
reached out for the photograph and found that lo, it was a photograph
of a woman. She wore the expression commonly worn by women who
are not lacking anything, yet her brows were knit in worry over the

uncertainty of her good fortune. "It is a photograph of my mother," Mazal said as he set it aright. "There exists only one photograph of her, for she has not been photographed since her youth, and only once was she then photographed. Many years have passed since then. Her face no longer resembles the face you see in the photograph, but I will always cherish the likeness of her face as captured in this photograph; it is as though time had passed and nothing had changed." What had prompted Mazal to speak? Was it the room's stillness, or was it I sitting by his side in the late evening? Mazal spoke at length. He told me of all his gentle mother had endured. And he said:

"My mother is a member of the Bauden-Bach family and all of the Bauden-Bachs are converts. Her grandfather, Rabbi Israel, was wealthier than all his countrymen. He had a winery and fields and villages. He gave generously to scholars and he built Houses of Religious Study. And there were many books at that time that extolled his name. For he dispensed freely both of his money and gold in honor of the Torah and in pursuit of its study.

"Now in those days it was decreed that all land owned by Jews was to be appropriated. Hearing of this Rabbi Israel spared no efforts to preserve his land, but all his efforts came to naught. So he changed his religion and returned to his home and estate where he found his wife reciting the Morning prayer. 'Lo, I have converted,' he announced. 'Hurry now and take the children to the priest.' The woman recited the Aleinu prayer, saying, 'We have not done as the heathen of the land,' and she spat three times and pressed her lips to her prayerbook, and she and all her sons rose and changed their religion.

"Close upon that time she bore a son who was circumcised by my great-grandfather, Rabbi Israel. For they kept the Lord's commandments and only in the eyes of the gentiles did they behave as Christians. And they rose in their station and received the same respect accorded to nobles. The new generation, however, forgot their God, their creator, nor did they return to their religion when the decree was nullified, nor were they God-fearing, nor did they live by the commandments of the Torah. The only commandment that they followed was to sell their leaven to the rabbi's emissary on the eve of Passover, for otherwise Jews would not touch their cornwine. Such is the law concerning leaven which is not sold to a gentile on the eve of Passover.

"My mother is the granddaughter of the youngest son. And she sat over the catechism yet all the priest's efforts came to naught. Time, though, is too short to tell of all that she suffered until the day the Lord

took mercy upon her and she found peace in his shadow. For she was
sent to a convent school and she was placed in the hands of harsh teachers. She did not follow their ways, though. And she bent her mind over
what was sealed and concealed from her.

"One day my mother found a picture of her grandfather and he bore
resemblance to a rabbi. 'Who is he?' she asked. 'It is your grandfather,'
they replied. My mother was astounded. 'What are those locks of hair
falling over his cheeks, and what is that book he is reading?' 'He is
reading the Talmud, and he is twirling his earlocks,' they answered, and
they told her of her grandfather's story. Thereafter she walked about
like a shadow and she stirred in her sleep at night on account of her
dreams. Once her grandfather appeared and took her on his knees and
she combed his beard. Another time she saw her grandmother holding
a prayerbook in her hands. She then taught her the Holy Letters and
when she awoke she wrote down the letters on a tablet. It was a miracle,
for until that day my mother had never set her eyes upon a Hebrew
book.

"And a young Jewish functionary worked in her father's home.
'Teach me the laws of the Lord,' she asked of him. 'Alas,' said he, 'I
know them not.' Just then the rabbi's emissary arrived to buy leaven.
The functionary then urged her, 'Speak now to him.' And my mother
told the emissary all that I have recounted. 'Madam,' said the man, 'pray
come to my home today and celebrate with us the Passover holiday. So
that night she went forth to the man's home and she dined with him and
the members of the household, and her heart cleaved after the God of
Israel, and she longed to follow His laws.

"That very functionary was my father, peace be with him. He never
studied the Torah and the Commandments but God created him pure
of heart. My mother cleaved unto him and together they cleaved unto
their faith in God.

"After their wedding they left for Vienna, saying, 'There no one will
recognize us.' And he lived by the sweat of his brow, and they did not
turn to my mother's father for help. My mother gradually adjusted to
her new station. My father toiled at his work. And he deprived himself
of the fruits of his own labor, his one desire being that I study in the best
of schools, gaining thereby through knowledge and wisdom a footing in
the heights of society. For he knew that he would not be able to leave
me any money to speak of on the day of his death.

"Now, in my father's eyes I had been expelled from my own property.
For had my mother not married him I would now be the son of a noble

family. My mother, though, had little designs of her own upon the world. She loved me as a mother loves her son."

The day drew to an end and Mazal paused, saying, "Forgive me, miss, for I have spoken at great length today." "Why excuse yourself," I replied, "when you have done me nothing but good; now I know that you do not hate me, for you have opened your heart to me. Oh, withhold not your words anymore!" Mazal drew his hand over his eyes. "Heaven forbid that I should hate you," he exclaimed. "I am glad to have spoken of my mother and to have found an attentive ear, for I do miss her a great deal. But since you feel I have been sparing with my words I will tell you all the more."

Mazal then told me how he had come here, yet he did not mention my mother and her father. He spoke of the hard times that he had endured. He had yearned with all his heart to complete what his mother had set out to accomplish upon returning to the God of Israel, for he had returned to his people. Yet they did not understand him. He walked as a stranger in their midst—they drew him close, but when he was as one of them they divided their hearts from him.

I returned home, my spirit thrilled. I reeled like a drunken man as the moon poured its beams and shone upon my path.

As I walked I said, what will I tell my father? If I speak of all that happened between Mazal and myself will he not listen and then be angered? But if I am silent will not a barrier be erected between us? Now I shall go and speak to him; though angry he will see that I have not concealed my actions from him. When I arrived home, however, I did not speak of the matter, as just then the doctor came to pay us a visit, having heard that my father was taken ill. I did not let a word pass my lips, for how can I speak out in front of a stranger? And I did not regret doing so, as my secret was a comfort to me.

I was at peace in my home. I did not engage in maidenly secrets, nor did I send seasonal greetings. One day, however, the postman arrived with a letter for me. And the letter was written in Hebrew by a young man called Landau. "As the lone wayfarer raises his eyes heavenward on a black night," its author wrote, "so do I now dispatch my letter to you, fair and ever-resourceful maiden." My teacher Segal appeared for our lesson as I was reading the letter. "I have received a letter written in Hebrew," I said. "I knew you would, " he replied. Segal then told me the young man was a pupil of his and that he was the son of the village tenant.

Eight days passed and I soon forgot the letter. One day I left for the seminary and lo, a woman and a young man stood there. And seeing the young man I was certain that he was the author of the letter. Later in the day I told my father and he laughed, saying, "The son of villagers." But I thought to myself, why has the young man behaved in such a manner, and why the strange encounter? Suddenly I was seized by a vision of the young man. I beheld his discomfort and how he blushed, and I regretted not having answered his letter lest he awaited my reply and was offended. Tomorrow I will write to him, I told myself. Though I did not know what I would write. My body then grew numb under the balmy weight of sleep, the sweet slumber wherein the body is peaceful and the soul is soothed.

Two, three days passed and still I did not answer the young man, and I said, it is too late to answer. But just then, as I innocently scribbled with my pen on paper, lo and behold, I found myself replying to the young man. I wrote only a few lines and reading my letter I thought that surely he did not pray for such an answer. For the matter neither did the sheaf of paper earn favor from me. Still, I sent the letter, knowing that I would not write another such letter. I will not write to him any more letters, I told myself, for my mind is not bent upon letter writing. Several days passed without my receiving a letter from the young man, and I was sorry not to hear from him.

I gradually forgot the young man and his letters, however. It had been my duty to reply, and I had done so. One day my father asked me, "Do you remember the woman and young man?" "I remember," I replied. "Well," he said, "the young man's father came to see me and he spoke of his son. The family is a good family and the young man is learned." "Will he come here?" I asked. "How can I know," he replied. "But I will do as you decide, for you have not concealed your thoughts from me." I bowed my head. God, Thou knew my heart. "So often," my father added, "we will not go to the stargazers and astrologers, nor will we ask them whether my daughter will find a groom." And he did not refer to the matter again.

One Sunday evening my father came home accompanied by a man. He bade the kettle be put on the fire and the large lamp be lit, and he also looked to see whether the stove glowed warm. They then sat by the table and talked. The man did not take his eyes off me. I returned to my room to work. But no sooner did I sit down at my work than a winter carriage pulled to a stop under my window and Kaila came and announced, "Guests have arrived, go now into the hall." "I will not go," I said, "for I have a great deal of work to finish today." Kaila however continued to urge me, saying, "It is a night that calls for celebration, your father has ordered me to make pancakes." "If so," I replied, "if so I will help you prepare the meal." "No," Kaila insisted, "go now into the hall. The man who has just arrived is a handsome lad." "Is Gotteskind also present?" I asked Kaila disdainfully. "Who?" she said. "Gotteskind," I replied. "Have you forgotten the man and all he had to tell us?" "Your memory is a marvel, Tirtza," Kaila replied, and left.

The food was ready to be served and I entered the hall and stared in astonishment, for the young man was now transformed into another person. Nor was he embarrassed as when I had first seen him. And his black goatskin hat heightened the charm of his red cheeks.

Landau soon returned a second time. He arrived in the winter carriage wearing a wolfskin overcoat and his smell was like the smell of a winter forest. No sooner did he sit down than he was up on his feet again. He had come to see the coppersmith and had passed by to see whether I would accompany him on his journey. My father gave me his fur coat and we departed.

Galloping under the moonlight along the snow-filled lanes, the horses' hooves sparkled, mingling a melody with the sound of the harness bells. I sat to the right of the young man and gazed through the animal pelt. Buried in my overcoat I was unable to speak. Landau brought the carriage to a halt in front of the smith's house and he descended and hoisted me out of the carriage and we entered. Our cups were filled with birch sap, and apples were roasted in our honor. And Landau bade the smith come to the village the following day, as the kegs in the wine factory needed mending. The members of the household listened with rapt attention to his words, spoken with the authority of a prince. I too stared at Landau and was astonished. Is this the young man whose letters were the outcry of a solitary heart? And on our way back I did not bury my face in the folds of my overcoat, as I had grown immune to the cold. For all that we did not exchange a word, for my heart was girded in silence. Landau also remained silent, only now and then speaking to his horses.

"Lo," my father said to me, "the old man Landau has spoken to me of his son, his heart is drawn to your heart, tell me and I will reply." Seeing my discomfort, however, he added, "There is still time for us to speak of the matter, after all, the young man is not about to be conscripted into the army and you are young in days." Several days passed and Landau, once again, began writing me eloquent letters filled with visions of the land of Israel. His roots were in the village; since boyhood he had known how to till its soil, and the land of Israel did not cease providing him with dreams and visions. Landau's letters gradually stopped arriving and he would often come into town on foot, driving himself to exhaustion on the way, lest he be considered fit for the King's work. At night he would roam in the market and streets with the penitents. I shuddered in anguish whenever I recalled their nightly tunes; I remembered my uncle, my mother's brother, who had come to an untimely end in the army. And I said, if only I could accept Landau I would now be his wedded wife. One day I ran into Landau on his way into town. His eyes were sunken and his cheeks worn thin and his clothes gave off an odor of cold tobacco. He wore the face of a sick man. And returning home I seized hold of a book, telling myself, I will study and soothe my sorrow. But my throat pained and I could not study. I then opened the Book of Psalms and read out loud; maybe God will think of him and the young man will not perish.

And workmen labored at the Gottliebs, building a left wing to serve as a home for Gottlieb's brother who, as partner to the factory, had come to live with him. Once the wing was completed Gottlieb held a housewarming party. Until that day Gottlieb had never held a housewarming party, for only now was the house built to his liking. Gottlieb was transformed. He also altered the cut of his beard. I saw the two brothers and laughed, remembering how Mintshi had been startled when she had first come to their father's home. Gottlieb extracted a letter from his pocket during the noon meal and said to his wife, "I almost forgot, a letter has arrived from Vienna." And she asked, "Does it bear any news?" "Nothing is new," he said. "He sends his blessings for the house-warming. Also, his mother's condition hasn't changed for better or worse." I realized they were speaking of Mazal, for I had heard his mother had taken ill and that he had left for Vienna to see to her welfare. I then recalled the day I had visited in his home, and the memory was a blessing to me.

After the meal Mintshi walked out with me into the garden. She had been restless while sitting with her sister-in-law and now she looked back upon earlier times. "Bender," she suddenly called out, and a small dog leaped toward her. I almost took fright. Mintshi patted his head with love and said, "Bender, Bender, Bender, my son." Although I disliked dogs I ran my hand over his coat and patted him. The dog looked at me with a worried look and then barked in approval. I embraced Mintshi and she kissed me.

A short distance away from us stood the mansion. The noise of children and the unceasing sound of a woman's voice rose from within. The sun set and reddened the treetops and a sudden gust of cold wind blew. "It was a hot day," Mintshi said in a low voice. "Summer is almost over. Ah, I cannot bear all this commotion. Since the day they arrived even the birds in the garden have been silenced." The dog barked a second time and Mintshi growled back, "What's wrong, Bender?" She then turned to me and said, "Have you noticed, Tirtza, how a dog will bark whenever the postman approaches?" "We do not have a dog at home," I replied, "and no one writes letters to me." Not heeding my words, Mintshi went on, "The letter that my sister-in-law sent after her departure, telling me of her safe return, was delayed, for it rolled about behind the gate and the postman had scribbled on its envelope, 'I have not delivered this letter to your door because of the dog.' Bender, my clever one, come here!" Mintshi called out to the dog, and she resumed stroking his coat.

The evening twilight enveloped us and a light glowed in the windows. "Let us go in, Tirtza, and prepare supper." As we walked back Mintshi said, "Mazal will soon return," and she embraced me. We entered the house. That evening the factory workers came to toast their masters, not having come during the day when the guests had been present. Mintshi set a table for them, and when their hearts were merry with wine they burst into song. And the factory hand who was released from prison warmed our hearts with tales he had heard straight from the mouths of the prisoners. Gottlieb rubbed the tip of his nose, as was his way. I looked at Mintshi, whose face brimmed with strength and vigor; her grief was not to be seen.

The days of celebration ended and the autumn sky hung low over the town. My father was preoccupied with his business affairs and would not come home for lunch. I then came to know full well the harsh beauty of the autumn season when the land far and wide was fortified by the sight of the copper-leafed forest.

My studies at the seminary resumed and grew more difficult. That year our teachers led us into the classroom, where we were expected to show our strength in instruction. I showed little talent. Even so, I did as I was told.

Mr. Mazal returned to town. He spoke to the local chroniclers and gathered material on the history of our town. Presently he dug in the cemetery and unearthed ancient relics. Mazal's heart was so filled with joy in his work that he did not heed the principal's summons to resume teaching at the seminary, for Kfirmelach had long been forgotten.

Close upon that time my father's sister arrived. Her daughter's hand was asked in marriage and she had come to see the young man. This particular aunt of mine was quite unlike my father, for she took pleasure in life. "I am glad, my daughter," my father said, "that you are fond of your aunt. She is a good woman and she is gracious and pleasant in every way. Yet I am not fond of her. Perhaps it is because of you that I reproach her." He then fell silent.

My aunt returned to her home during the last days of autumn. I then cut across the open fields on my way home from the train station. The train's whistle melted in the air, potatoes were unearthed from the bare fields shining under the yellow sun, and the bloodberries lifted their eyes. I remembered the tale of the bloodberries and I walked in a daze.

As I passed a farmhouse where I had bought fruit in the summer, the farmer gave me a bouquet of asters. I took the autumn flowers and continued on my way. Now as I walked home I noticed that I was close to Mazal's home. I will go thither and bid him good day, I thought to myself, for I have not seen him since he returned.

Mazal was not at home, and the old servant sat by the entrance, waiting for him. Because of her grandson Kfirmelach she had had to leave her master's house, and she had gone to live in a neighboring village. And now, on her way into town with the wheat crop, she had stopped to see how he was faring. The old woman did not let go of me as she spoke of her master's good deeds. I was pleased to hear such words of praise and as I turned to leave I scattered my flowers near the entrance to the house.

Several days later we received a parcel of gifts from my aunt. She also thought of Kaila and sent her a new dress. My father looked on and said, "So she has sent gifts. But she did not come to look after you when your mother died." Only then did I understand why my father reproached my aunt.

Autumn passed. The sky was shrouded in gray as swirls of mist whisked about from here to there and the rooftops shone under the thin drizzle of rain. A tainted grief spread over the land. The last shriveled leaves bent to the weight of the raindrops. Clouds, wind, rain, and cold. The raindrops chilled and froze and stung like thorns in the flesh. The stove was lit. Kaila spread thatches of hay on the windowsills. The stove blazed the entire day as Kaila prepared the winter victuals. Soon the snow began to fall and to cover the lanes, and bells from the winter carriages jingled in merriment. Leaving the seminary one day, I saw a group of girls carrying ice skates over their shoulders. They were going to skate on the river. They enticed me to join them and I succumbed. I bought myself a pair of ice skates and I raced over the ice with them. The frozen earth was covered with snow, the woodcutters chopped wood in the streets, and the fresh winter air mingled with the fragrance of wood shavings and cut wood. The days grew colder, the snow creaked under the soles of all who walked by. And I raced along with my girlfriends, devouring the river with our skates.

Those were good days when I skidded over the river. My body grew strong and my eyes seemed to grow in their sockets. My eyes were divested of their beclouded grief and my flesh and bones had found a cure. I ate heartily and when I sat to read a book I lost all sense of my body. Twice upon returning home I tiptoed toward Kaila as she bent over her work and I suddenly hoisted her up in the air. Kaila cried out in vain, for I clanged my skates together and the noise drowned out her voice.

But such days did not last for long. Although the sun was not to be seen the snow melted. And when I approached the river I found it was deserted. The ice had nearly melted and crows perched on the loose sheets of ice. At that time I felt sharp stabbing pains in my chest and the doctor came and gave me medicinal balms, and he forbad me to exert myself over my lessons. "But sir," I said, "I am to complete my studies this year." "If so," he replied, "your turn to teach the countryfolk will come in a year's time." And having gone that winter with the schoolgirls to skate over the ice I almost grew to love the seminary. Love grows idle when its cause passes away.

Now the house was purified for the Passover holidays. I fetched the old books from the closet to give them a good airing. Whenever I found a book whose binding was damaged I told myself, I will bring it to the bookbinders. And rummaging through the closet I found the Easterly tapestry which had hung in the home of my mother's father, and I tucked it in my bag along with the books, intending to take it to the glazier, for its glass cover and gilt frame were cracked and bruised, and the crimson ribbon which my mother, may she rest in peace, had used to hang the Easterly was also torn. And as I was about to leave, the seamstress arrived with my new spring dress. I quickly slipped on the dress and thus attired I put my hat on my head and set out with the books and the Easterly for the bookbinder and glazier. While I was at the bookbinder's Mazal entered and he stared at the books which I had brought and then at the Easterly which was wrapped in broad sheets of paper, and he asked, "What is that book?" I removed the paper and said, "One moment, sir," and I unwound the string which I had twined round my hand after meeting with Mazal and the dog, and I fastened the string to the Easterly and hung it on the wall. Mazal stared in astonishment. I read what was written on the Easterly: Blessed be he who shall not forsake Thee. Mazal bowed his head. I blushed and my eyes filled with tears. Now I longed to cry out: you have brought upon me this shame! And now I longed to humble myself before him. I then hurried and I did not tarry for long at the bookbinder's shop.

I left the shop but lo, Mazal strode beside me. I then laughed and said loudly, "Now you know, sir." My throat burned and I could hardly bear the sound of my own voice. Mazal grasped my hand. His hand shook like his voice. He looked this way and that way, and said, "Soon we shall be seen." I dried my tears and tidied my hair. "Let them look," I said, still angry. "It is all the same to me." We walked on for a short while, and, reaching the corner of my street, Mazal said, "Here is your father's house." I stared into his face. "I will not go home," I declared. Mazal remained silent. I was at a loss where to go. A host of thoughts stirred within my heart and I feared lest Mazal abandon me without my having said a thing. Meanwhile we left the town behind and approached the edge of the woods. The forest green was about to bloom and the birch trees sprouted their first leaves. A fresh sun rose over the woods. Mazal said, "Spring has come." And he beheld my face and he knew I was angered by his words. Mazal then brushed the palm of his hand over his head and sighed.

I sat on a tree trunk and Mazal grew confused and groped for words. He stared at my dress, my spring dress, and said, "The tree is still damp and you are wearing a light dress." I knew the tree was damp and that my dress was light; all the same I did not rise, and though sitting so was hard upon me I delighted in the feeling. Mazal turned pale, his eyes dimmed, an odd smile swept over his lips. I thought he would ask, has your hand healed from the dog's bite? My spirits weighed heavily upon me. But I suddenly sensed a joy which until that moment I had never known, a wonderful warmth kindled within my heart. I quietly smoothed my soft dress. It seemed then that the man with whom I sat in the woods on that early spring day had already revealed to me all that was harbored in his heart. And I was startled to hear Mazal say, "I heard your voice at night. Was it indeed you at my window?" "I was not by your window," I replied, "however, I have called out to you from my bed at night. I think of you every day, and I looked for your traces in the cemetery, by my mother's grave. Last summer I placed flowers on the wayside and you came and went but you did not stop to smell my flowers." "Now let me tell you something," Mazal said. "Such feelings will pass. You are still young. Another man has not captured your heart yet, that is why your heart is set upon mine. The men you have met were empty-headed, whereas you were not bored in my company, and so you swore to yourself, it is he. But what will we do the day you find the man who will really capture your heart? As for myself, I have come to the age when all I desire is peace and quiet. Think of your future, Tirtza, and concede that it is good that we part before it is too late." I gripped the tree trunk and a stifled cry escaped from within me. "Let us remain good friends," Mazal said, placing his hand on my head. "Friends!" I cried out. How I loathed such romanticism. Mazal stretched out his warm hand and I bent forward and kissed his hand. And Mazal rested his head on my shoulder and kissed it.

The sun set and we returned home. A spring chill, doubly potent after a sunlit day, settled in my bones. "We must talk again," Mazal said. "When, when?" I asked. Mazal repeated my words as though he did not understand their meaning. "When? Tomorrow, before dusk, in the forest." "Good." I took out my watch and asked, "At what time?" "At what time? At six o'clock," Akaviah replied. I then bent over my watch and kissed the very same numeral on the face of the watch. And the warmth of the watch which hung over my heart was very pleasing to me.

Returning home I shook in every limb. My bones shivered from the cold as I walked. Once at home, I thought, it would pass. But lo, I arrived home and rather than subside the fever grew worse. I lost all desire to eat and my throat burned. Kaila brewed me some tea to which she added a slice of lemon and sugar, and after draining the tea I lay on my bed and covered myself. But I was not warmed.

I started awake, my throat burning. I lit a candle and then snuffed it out, for its flickering red flame hurt my eyes. The wick's thin curl of smoke and my cold hands only increased my discomfort. The clock struck and I grew frightened. I fancied I was late going to the forest at the appointed time which Mazal had set. I then counted the hours and prayed to the Lord to prevent the appointed time from arriving. Three, four, five. Ah, now I must rise. But I am overcome by sleep. Why haven't I been able to sleep until now? And now I will approach Mazal, my eyes drowsy from lack of sleep. I must leave my bed and rid myself of the drowsy haze. But how can I wash having caught such a cold? I fumbled against the bedposts and finally succeeded in descending from my bed. I was gripped by a fierce cold and I groped about not knowing where I stood. Here is the door, or is it only the closet door? Where are the matches, and where the window? Why has Kaila veiled the window with curtains? Will I not slip and shatter my skull against the table or stove? Confound it! Where is the lamp? This time I won't find a thing, perhaps I have been struck blind. And now, having lost all hope of finding myself a man, Akaviah Mazal shall take me to be his wedded wife, and as one who will lead the blind, so shall Mr. Mazal lead me. Ah, why did I approach and talk to him. Blessed be the Name, I have found my bed, thanks to a merciful God. I lay on the bed and covered myself, yet I imagined myself to be still walking about. I walked for a good many hours. Where to? Lo and behold, an old woman stood by the road waiting for me to ask her the way. Is she not the old woman I first saw a month ago when one bright day I ventured out of town? The old woman opened her mouth. "Here she is," she said. "I barely recognized you, are you not Leah's daughter?" Are you not Leah's daughter, the old woman exclaimed while snuffing tobacco. She chattered on though and did not let me answer a word. I nodded my head that indeed I was Leah's daughter. The old woman went on and said, "Did I not say you are Leah's daughter, while you swept by me as though it did not matter a straw. The lambs are ignorant of the pastures where their mothers grazed." The old woman sniffled a second time and continued, "Did I not nurse your mother with the milk of my breasts?" I knew this to be a dream, yet I was astounded: my mother had never nursed at the breast of a foreign woman, how dare the old woman claim she nursed my mother. I had not seen the old woman for a great many days, nor had I thought of her, and this gave me further cause for surprise. Why then had she suddenly accosted me in my dream? Wondrous are the ways of the dream and who knows its paths.

My father's footsteps startled me awake and I saw that he was saddened. He gazed at me with loving care through his reddened eyes. I felt ashamed of my room's disorder. My new dress and my stockings lay scattered on the floor. For a moment I forgot it was my father who stood before me, all I could think of was that a man was present in my room. Filled with shame I shut my eyes. I then heard my father's voice addressing Kaila, standing by the door, "She is sleeping." "Good morning, Father," I called out, no longer ashamed. "Were you not asleep?" he exclaimed with surprise. "And I thought you were sleeping, how are you my daughter?" "I am well," I replied, straining to speak in a clear voice, but a spasm of coughing overcame me. "I caught a slight cold and now I shall get up, for my cold is over." "Blessed be the Name," my father said, "I suggest, though, my daughter, that you not leave your bed today." "No, I must get up," I cried stubbornly, fancying my father would prevent me from going forth to my groom.

I knew I must throw myself upon my father's neck, perhaps he would forgive me for having done what is not to be done. My good father, my good father! I called out from within my heart, and I took courage and exclaimed, "Father, yesterday I was engaged." My father stared at me. I longed to lower my eyes, yet I took heart and called out, "Father, did you not hear?" My father remained silent, thinking I had spoken out of my fever, and he whispered something to Kaila which I could not hear. He then went to the window to see whether it was shut. Regaining my strength I sat up in bed and said to him, "Although I caught a chill I am now better, sit now by the bed, for I have something to tell you. Let Kaila come too, I have no secrets to hide." My father's eyes bulged out of their sockets and then dimmed with worry. He sat on the bed and I said, "Yesterday I met and spoke to Mazal. Father, what is wrong?" "You are a bad girl," Kaila exclaimed, frightened. "Hush, Kaila," I retorted. "Lo, I have opened my heart to Mazal. But why go on like this, I am engaged to him." "Have you ever heard of such a thing?" Kaila exclaimed, wringing her hands in despair. My father calmed Kaila down and asked, "When was this done?" "I do not remember," I replied, "although I looked at my watch I have forgotten the hour." "Have you ever heard of such a thing," my father said, laughing out of confusion. "She doesn't know when it happened." I too laughed and all at once I heaved a deep sigh and my body shook. "Calm down, Tirtza," my father said in a worried voice. "Lie in bed for the moment, later we will talk." And as he turned to go I called out after him, "Father, promise not to talk to Mazal until I tell you to do so." "What can I do," he exclaimed, and he left the house.

As soon as he had gone I took pen, ink, and paper, and wrote: my dearly beloved, I will not be able to come today to the forest, for a chill has taken hold of me. Several days hence I shall come to you. In the meantime, be well. I am lying in bed and I am happy, for you shall dwell in my thoughts all day, undisturbed. I then bade Kaila send the letter. "To whom have you written," she asked, letter in hand, "the teacher?" Knowing that Kaila did not know how to read or write, I replied in anger, "Read and find out." "Don't foam at the mouth, my bird," Kaila said. "The man is old while you are young and full of life. Why, you are just a child, and barely weaned at that. If it weren't for

my rheumatism I would carry you in my arms. But I have thought of
your decision. Why fuss over a man?" "Good, good, good," I cried out
laughing, "hurry now and send the letter, for there is not time to wait."
"But you haven't touched your tea," Kaila said. "Let me bring you
something hot to drink, and water to wash your hands with." Kaila soon
returned with the water. The chill almost subsided, my body grew
warm under the bedcovers, and my tired bones seemed to melt into the
sheets. Although my head was hot the heat was soothing, my eyes
fevered and flared in their sockets, yet my heart was set at ease and my
thoughts were pleasant. "Look here, you've let the water get cold," Kaila
exclaimed, "and I already brought you something hot to drink. It is all
due to your endless brooding and heartthrobs." I laughed and the pleasant weariness increased. I barely managed to call out, "Don't forget the
letter," before a sweet slumber descended over my eyes.

The day waned and Mintshi Gottlieb arrived. "I heard you were taken
ill," she said, "and I have come to see how you are faring." I knew that
my father had sent for her and so I concealed my thoughts and said, "I
caught a cold, but now I am well." Suddenly I seized hold of her hand
and stared into her eyes and said, "Why are you so quiet, Mrs. Gottlieb?" "But we haven't stopped talking," Mintshi replied. "Though we
haven't stopped talking, what's really important we haven't discussed."
"What's really important?" Mintshi exclaimed in surprise. And suddenly she added sourly, "Did you expect me to congratulate you?" I
placed my right hand over my heart and thrust my left toward her,
crying, "Indeed, why haven't you congratulated me?" Mintshi frowned.
"Do you not know, Tirtza, that Mazal is very dear to me, but you are a
young girl while he is forty years old. Even though you are young you
can plainly see that a few years hence he will be like a withered tree
whereas your youthful charm will grow." I listened and then cried out,
"I knew what you would say, but I will do what I must." "What you
must?" exclaimed Mrs. Gottlieb in astonishment. "The obligations of a
faithful woman who loves her husband," I replied, laying stress on my
last words. Mrs. Gottlieb was silent for a moment and then opened her
mouth and said, "When are you meeting?" I looked at my watch. "If my
letter has not reached him yet then he will now be waiting for me in the
forest." "He will not wait for you in the forest," Mintshi said, "for he
too has surely caught cold. Who knows if he isn't lying in bed right now.
Why, you have behaved like schoolchildren. I can scarcely believe my
ears." "Is he ill?" I asked, frightened by her words. "How can I know
whether he is ill?" Mintshi replied. "It certainly is possible. Haven't you

behaved like little children, sallying into the forest on a winter day in a summer dress?" "No!" I cried out. "I wore a spring dress on a spring day." "Heaven forbid," she said, "if I have offended your pride by saying you wore a summer dress on a winter day."

I was surprised that both Mintshi and my father spoke circumspectly. Still my happiness did not leave me. While I was yet absorbed in my own thoughts Mrs. Gottlieb said, "My task is an odd one, my dear friend, I must play the bad aunt. But what can I do? I thought your folly was that of a young girl, but . . ." Mintshi did not complete her thought, nor did I ask her the meaning of the word "but." She sat by my side for another half hour and upon leaving she kissed my forehead. I savored a sort of new taste in that kiss. I embraced Mrs. Gottlieb. "Ah, little monster," she cried, "you've upset my hairdo, let go of me, I must fix my hair." And, taking the mirror, Mintshi laughed loudly. "Why are you laughing?" I asked, offended. Mintshi gave me the mirror. And I saw that its entire surface was marred, for I had etched into the quicksilver the name "Akaviah Mazal," over and over.

A week passed and Mazal did not come to inquire of my health. Now I reproached him for fearing my father and acting in a cowardly way and now I feared lest he too was ill. But I did not ask my father, nor did I have any desire to talk of the matter. I then remembered the legend of the Baron's daughter who had loved a man from among the wretched of the land. "It shall not come about," her father had said. Hearing her father's words the maiden took ill and nearly died. And seeing that she was ill the doctors said, "The wound is grievous, there is no healing of the bruise, for she is stricken by love." Her father had then gone forth to her lover and he had implored him to take his daughter as his wedded wife. So I remained confined to my bed as sundry visions washed over me. And when the door turned on its hinges I asked, "Who's there?" My heart beat feebly and my voice was like my mother's voice at the time of her illness.

And there came a day when my father said, "Lo, the doctor tells me you have regained your strength." "Tomorrow I shall go out," I replied. "Tomorrow," my father said, frowning. "Pray, wait another two or three days before going out, for who knows, heaven forbid, if the open air will not do you harm. Three days hence and ours will be a different road. Remain here until the Day of Remembrance for your mother's parting, we will visit her graveside together then. You will also find Mr. Mazal there." My father turned to go.

His words puzzled me. How did he know Mazal would come? Did

they meet? And if so, was it out of good will? And why had Akaviah not come to see me? And what is to happen? I was so excited that my teeth ground against one another until I feared that I would fall ill again. Why had Akaviah not answered my letters? I cried out. And suddenly my heart was silenced, I ceased mulling over my thoughts, and I drew the covers over my hot flesh and I shut my eyes. The day is still far off, I told myself, now I will sleep and the Lord will do what is good in His eyes.

What happened afterward I shall never know, for I lay on my sickbed for a great many days. And when I opened my eyes I beheld Akaviah seated in the chair, and his face lit up the room. I laughed embarrassedly and he also laughed, and it was the hearty laugh of a good man. Just then my father entered and cried out, "Praise be the name of the Holy Name!" He then strode toward me and kissed my forehead. I stretched my arms out and embraced and kissed him, "Oh Father, Father, my dear father," I exclaimed. My father, though, forbad me to utter another word. "Calm down, my joy of joys, calm down, Tirtza, be patient for just another couple of days and then you shall talk to your heart's content." Later in the afternoon the old doctor arrived. And after examining me he stroked my cheek and said, "You are a courageous girl. So this time you have regained your strength and now too all the medicines in the world won't harm her." "Blessed be the name of the Lord," Kaila cried out from the doorway. Winter was over and I was saved.

I was married on the eve of the day following the Ninth of Ab. A mere ten people were called to the bridal canopy. A mere ten and the entire town buzzed, for until that day such a simple wedding had never been witnessed in our town. And after the Sabbath we left our town for a summer resort, finding lodging in a widow's home in the village. The woman prepared our meals, both supper and breakfast, whereas at lunchtime we visited the dairyman's house in the village. Three times a week a letter arrived from my father, and I too wrote often. Wherever I found a postcard I would send it to my father. Akaviah did not write other than sending his regards. Though a different nuance was always to be found in his greeting.

A letter arrived from Mintshi Gottlieb, for she had found us lodgings. And she drew the general outline of the house and its rooms on a sheet of paper. Mintshi wished to know whether to rent the lodgings, assuring us thereby of a home upon our return. Two days elapsed and we did not answer Mintshi's letter, and on the third day there were peals of thunder and flashes of lightning and all morning a hard rain poured. The mistress of the house came to ask whether to light the stove. "But it is not winter today," I said, laughing. And Akaviah told the woman, "If the sun has gathered its heat unto itself then the heat from the stove shall indeed be sweeter seven times over."

"Today," Akaviah said to me, "we shall answer Mrs. Gottlieb's letter." "But what shall we say?" I asked. "I shall teach you how to put reason to good use," my husband said, "and you shall know what to answer. Mrs. Gottlieb has indeed written to us a letter telling us that she has found us lodgings, nor were we surprised by this, for we are indeed in need of lodgings, and the apartment is indeed agreeable, and the woman is a woman of good taste as well as a friend, which gives us all the more reason to trust her words." "In that case I will write and tell her that the flat appears good in our eyes." "Wait a moment," Akaviah said, "someone is knocking. Ah, the mistress of the house is here to light the stove." And the woman kindled the fire with the wood which she had brought. She then told us how she and her forefather and the fathers of her forefathers were born in this very village. She would never leave the village, here was she born, here she grew up, and here would she die. She could not see how settled people could leave their birthplace and wander to the far corners of the world. "If you have a home then be honored and dwell within it. And if you said, I like my friend's garden, then why not plant yourself such a garden? Why should the air be foul in your own neighborhood while it be good in your friend's neighborhood?" My husband laughed at her words and said, "Her words are true."

It stopped raining, the earth, however, was not dry yet. The fire blazed in the stove and we sat in our room and were warmed. My husband said, "We have had such a good time that we nearly forgot about our future lodgings. But listen to what I have to propose and tell me whether it seems right in your eyes. You are familiar with my house, and if it is too small we could add a room and dwell within it. Now we must write to Mintshi Gottlieb to thank her for her labors." We wrote Mintshi a letter of gratitude, and to my father we announced our decision to move into Akaviah's house. My father did not favor our plans, for Akaviah lived in farmers' lodgings. Yet my father made repairs in the house and he also built us a new room.

A month passed and we returned. My home won over my heart. Although no different than the other farmers' homes, a different spirit dwelled within it. A flowerpot and a freshly baked cake, prepared by

Mintshi for our homecoming, gave off their odors as we entered. The rooms were pretty and comfortable, for the hands of a wise woman had adorned them. An adjoining servant's room had also been built. But there was no maidservant to serve the house. My father sent Kaila but I promptly sent her back. We then ate in my father's house until the day that we should find a young servant. And we would arrive at noon and return in the evening.

After the holidays my father left for Germany where he intended to complete his business affairs and consult doctors. And the doctors directed my father to the city of Wiesbaden wherein he remained for some time. Kaila then came to our home to help me with the household chores.

We soon found a young servant girl and Kaila returned to my father's house. The girl came for only two to three hours a day and no more. How will I manage all the housework by myself, I thought. I soon realized, though, that it was far better to have the servant come for a few hours than for the entire day, for she would leave after completing her duties and there was then no one and nothing which prevented me from talking to my husband whenever I so desired.

Winter came. Wood and potatoes were stored within our house. My husband labored at his book chronicling the history of the Jews in our town and I cooked fine and savory dishes. After the meal we would go out for a walk, or else we would remain within and read. And Mrs. Gottlieb gave me an apron which she had sewn for me. Akaviah beheld the wide apron and he called me the mistress of the house. And I was happy in being the mistress of the house.

But not all times are the same. I began to resent cooking. At night I would spread a thin layer of butter on a slice of bread and hand it to my husband. And if the servant did not cook lunch then we did not eat. Even preparing a light meal burdened me. One Sunday the servant did not come and I sat in my husband's room, for that day we had only one stove going. I was motionless as a stone. I knew my husband could not work if I sat with him in the room, as he was accustomed to working without anyone else being present in the room. But I did not rise and leave, nor did I stir from my place. I could not rise. I undressed in his room and I bade him arrange my clothes. And I shuddered in fear lest he approach me, for I was exceedingly ashamed.

"The first three months will pass," Mrs. Gottlieb said, "and you will be well again." My husband's misfortune shocked me and gave me no rest. Was he not born to be a bachelor? Why then have I robbed him of his peace? I longed to die, for I was a snare unto Akaviah. Night and day I prayed to God to deliver unto me an infant girl who would tend to all his needs after my death.

My father returned from Wiesbaden. He had retired from his business, though in order not to remain idle he spent two or three hours of the day with the man who had bought his business. And he would come to visit us at night, excepting those nights when it rained, for on such nights the doctor forbad him from venturing out of the house. He would arrive bearing apples, or a bottle of wine, or a book from his bookshelf —a gift for my husband. Then, being fond of reading the papers, he would relate to us the news of the day. Sometimes he would ask my husband about his work and he would grow embarrassed when he spoke to him. Other times my father spoke of the large cities he had seen while traveling on business. Akaviah listened like a village boy. Is this the student who came from Vienna and spoke to my mother and her parents of the wonders of the capital? How happy I was in seeing them talking together. When they spoke so I remembered the exchange between Job and his friends, for they spoke in a similar fashion. One speaks and the other answers. Such was their way every night. And I would stand vigilant, lest my father and my husband quarrel. The child within me grows from day to day. All day I think of nothing but him. I knit my child a shirt and buy him a cradle. Also the midwife comes now and then to see how I am faring. I am almost a mother.

A night chill invades the fields far and wide. We sit in our rooms and in our rooms there is heat and light. Akaviah put his notebooks aside and he approached and embraced me. He sang a cradle song. Suddenly his face clouded over and he fell silent. I did not ask what had made him grow sullen, and I was glad that my father came home. My father took out a pair of slippers and a red cap—presents for the child. "Thank you, grandfather," I said in a child's piping voice. We sat at the table and ate supper. Even my father agreed to eat from the dishes which I prepared today. We spoke of the child about to be born. Now I glanced at my father's face and now at my husband's. I beheld the two men and I longed to cry, to cry in my mother's bosom. Has my husband's sullenness brought this about, or does a spirit dwell within the woman? My father's and my husband's faces lit up, by the force of their love and compassion each resembled the other. Evil has seventy faces and love has but one.

I then remembered the son of Gottlieb's brother on the day Gottlieb had come to his brother's home and his brother's wife had been sitting with her son; Gottlieb had hoisted the boy up in the air and he had danced about with him, but lo, his brother had entered and the boy had glanced now at Gottlieb and now at his brother, and he had turned his face away from them both, and in a fit of tears he had flung his limbs out toward his mother.

So ended the chronicles of Tirtza.

In my room at night whilst my husband would bend over his lore and I feared lest I disturb him in his work, I would sit and write my memories. Sometimes I would ask myself, to what purpose have I written my memories, what new things have I seen and what do I wish to leave behind? Then I would say, it is to find rest in my writing, so did I write all that is written in this book.

FACING
THE SEA

BY DAVID FOGEL

translated by Daniel Silverstone*

*   I would like to thank Zvia Walden without whose help this translation would not have been possible. This translation is dedicated to Esther Silverstone. *D.S.*

M ADAM BREMON SAID: —Make yourselves at home. There's no one here all day. —Her wrinkled face seemed smaller beneath a wide-brimmed straw hat. She stopped washing the linen by the garden wall. In the room she showed them, an opaque, hot, viscid darkness had jelled, because the shutters had been closed so long. Adolph Barth kept wiping his forehead. —Anyway, you are facing the sea. Twenty yards. Go! Out with you, Bijou—She scolded the bleary-eyed black-and-white spotted puppy that was entangled between her feet.

—Yes, we are facing the sea.—Adolph Barth and his companion exchanged whispers. —Good enough. We'll stay.

Toward evening, when the heat had passed, they brought their suitcases from the train station. The sea was spread out in its richest blue. Fisherman drifted from the shore, spreading their nets from boats scattered here and there across the horizon. In the garden nearby, the tables were set for supper.

Gina lay back languorously on a colorful beach towel. She wore a light green cotton bathing suit that accentuated her shapeliness. A flowered Chinese parasol planted in the ground behind her blossomed above her head. Next to her, Barth, in sunglasses, fingered the searing gravel and flicked pebbles into the water.

Dull brown nets, from which wafted the acrid odor of fish and brine, were spread out to dry behind them. The air just above the ground trembled with the heat.

Cici came out of the water and sat beside them, folding his legs Oriental-style. Droplets clung to his matted chest. —The water is warm,—he said with an accent, obviously Italian.

—You're shaking.

—I've been in the water for over an hour.

Gina rolled onto her side facing the two men, Cici and Barth. Flies hovered over a forgotten little fish left beside a nearby boat which had been drawn out of the water.

—In three days you have managed to tan a bit, madam.—Cici's eyes wandered over the roundness of her pale thighs. He moved himself closer and compared his skin, the color of copper coins, to hers, as pale as ivory.

—No, not yet like yours.—And to Barth: —Put your hat on, or lie next to me under the umbrella.

—So what is your real name?—asked Barth.

—Francesco Adasso. But everyone here calls me Cici.—And after a moment: —My friend from Rome is here this morning. He is the translator from Cook's, you know. He should be here any moment now.

—Wonderful,—teased Gina.

He offered her a yellow pack of cigarettes. Gina refused. Cici and Barth smoked, lying on their bellies with the sun warming their backs. The sea sprawled motionlessly at their feet. Only on the horizon did a boat drift, dreamlike. But here, next to them, romped Stephano's brood, half a dozen dirty children aged two and up, giggling, screaming, and splashing water. And to the side, Latzi and Suzi were playing catch with Marcelle, the dark Lyonean who radiated charm and youthful vigor— the three of them looked as though they were cast of bronze.

—The girl from Lyon is very beautiful,—said Gina to no one in particular.

—She is,—Cici agreed. —But you, madam, are much more beautiful than she.

—Thank you!

Barth smiled with the corner of his mouth and flicked his cigarette butt in a graceful arc. —Suzi's lipstick seems much too pale. It doesn't blend with her tan.

—*Shiksa* taste.

—Aside from that, she is heavy about the middle.

—Latzi is also from Vienna,—interjected Cici.

—You mean Budapest . . .

The Japanese man, in his bathing suit, emerged from a row of houses opposite the beach, crossed the street that ran parallel to the shore, and approached. He seemed taller than most Orientals, and his face more clearly outlined. Following him was his companion, a European wearing a robe with huge saffron blossoms, and a light blue ribbon in her hair. She was shorter than he, and ten years older. She struck Gina as someone who was self-assured. The Japanese man dived into the water, while his companion remained with Latzi and Suzi, who had finished playing.

–Yesterday they drank until four again.–Cici knew everyone's whereabouts here.

–At Stephano's?

–No. At the Japanese house. A real bacchanal.

–And you?–Barth sat up. He dried his sweaty chest and thighs upon which the gravel had left a florid tattoo. His face was flushed, and locks of flaxen hair stuck to his forehead.

–I didn't feel like it,–replied Cici.

The translator from Cook's was dressed like a dandy in the season's fashion. His dark hair, glistening with grease, stuck to his scalp like a bandage. His face was smooth and bloated. He extended his left hand when Cici introduced him. His right hand, in a black glove, was false.

–Ah! So you live in Paris. I know it like the back of my hand.

That the translator knew everything like the back of his hand was immediately clear. He was especially familiar with foreign languages (the arts, if you please!). In Rome he had a friend, a Japanese poetess, evidence of which he brought with him: a book of Japanese poems with its vertical lines—"a gift from her." He didn't know how to read it yet, but this Japanese fellow would teach him. It's all arranged. And the lady? Would she be willing to teach German in exchange for an Italian "lesson"?

The "Arab," so named for his ability to imitate an Arabic accent, lived and worked with Cici, and clung to the translator like his right-hand man. He would punctuate the translator's words with nodded agreement, prepared to pounce on anyone daring to doubt them.

–Gina rose to swim.

–Please. Wait while I undress–The translator slid behind the beached boat, the "Arab" behind him. After a few minutes he reappeared, naked. The whiteness of his skin contrasted with the tans of the others, making him look immodest. His false hand was left behind among his clothes; the stump of his arm was wrapped in a towel. He dropped the towel, dived into the water, and began to swim. The "Arab" followed close behind.

—Teach me the backstroke,—Gina said to Barth. And then: —I was swimming behind you, but I didn't have the strength and returned. You tend to go out too far. Don't let anything happen!

Cici swam in a circle around Gina. Breathlessly and heavily he pumped his arms and legs, making waves. —Look here! Move your arms and legs like this. One-two! One—now you try.

—Gina let herself go, falling back onto Barth's outstretched arms, which supported her under the water. Close by, Marcelle stood and watched. —You don't know how to swim on your back, madam? It's simple. Here!—She dived in and showed her, laughing through shining mouselike teeth.

—And when shall we race, Mademoiselle Marcelle?—asked Barth.

—Any time you like.

—This afternoon, All right?

—If I don't go to Nice.

—You like the little one, huh?—Gina said to Barth when Marcelle turned away. And to Cici: —Mr. Cici, you must learn the backstroke by tomorrow, understand?—she teased.

The translator and the "Arab" approached. The translator crouched down, lowering himself chin-deep in the chest-high water. He remained in this position while he was near them. Even so, his maimed arm twinkled beneath the clear water. Gina and Cici were splashing each other now, while Barth, arms outstretched like smokestacks, sailed through the crystalline blue water. When he returned, he reminded Gina about lunch. The sun shone now directly overhead. On the main street, facing the sea, was a single row of houses cracked by waves of glowing molten orange. Passersby trampled their shadows underfoot.

Stephano's grocery three houses down the street from Madam Bremon's pension was run by his wife—a thin Neapolitan woman of about forty whose body was ravaged by childbearing and hard work. Madam Stephano was never seen outside her territory. She always wore the same dress, which, once white, was now grayed by dirt. Her blue-black hair, always uncombed, hung in tangled clumps which fell over her wrinkled face. Her bare legs, in tattered cloth shoes as always, were pale white, laced with blue veins. The southern sun had no effect on Madam Stephano's skin.

Stephano himself was in charge of selling wine and liquor. A robust and burly despot, Stephano, unlike his wife, did not deprive himself of earthly pleasures. He loved to eat well, drink a lot, and love women. He was a bully and a troublemaker with whom people avoided conflict. Between him and the other Neapolitans (most of the town's inhabitants were Neapolitan and only a few were French), most of whom were related to him and were also named Stephano, existed an everlasting animosity. He kept away from them, as if he were excommunicated.

Besides the flock of little children, the Stephanos had an older son, Joseph, a naval recruit in the nearby port, and a daughter, Jejette. An attractive peasant of sixteen with flushed gums and red eyelashes whose body was buxom and solid, she was good for any sort of work. She helped her parents in the store, worked in the kitchen and did all the housework, ran the café on the rooftop veranda, got drunk with her customers, danced the fox trot and waltz with them to the sounds of the hoarse Gramophone, let loose her fleshy parts to stealthy pinches, and laughed loud and often.

–Nice swimming, huh?–Stephano greeted them.

Gina wore only a skimpy bathrobe. The freshness of the water still clung to her face. Stephano set his eyes upon her feverishly. –Hurry, Madam Stephano! I'm famished! Hey, you bastards! Look out for the wine!–Stephano roared across the street at the children who were crawling under a table set for lunch with a large bottle of wine, beneath a shading plane tree.

Madam Stephano and Jejette weighed the butter, cheese, fruits, and vegetables for Gina. Barth studied the tins of preserves stacked on the shelves.

–A child, madam?–Madam Stephano asked, her teeth shining.

–Not yet,–replied Gina.

–Hey! You haven't fulfilled your obligation, you!–Madam Stephano reproached Barth. –A healthy woman like this, and pretty, too! You know you're pretty, madam!

–And my husband?–asked Gina.

–Him too, of course! I like him, ha, ha, ha!

–You hear that?–said Barth to Stephano.

Stephano, who was bent over wine crates in the corner, rose to his formidable height. –I agree, ha, ha, ha! My wife and Barth, and me and you, madam. A fair trade, isn't it?

Jejette spread her lips in a conspirator's smile.

–I'll think about it,–Barth said with forced humor.

Stephano raised a full bottle of pink wine and waved it in the air. –You see this? I advise you to take it! Try it and then come and tell me! I've never had rosé like this before.

–Nice. We'll try it.

–And some evening, why don't you stop by my café,–said Stephano as they were leaving. –It's the world's meeting place! Come on over and we'll have a drink together!

In the garden, Madam Bremon, beneath her wide straw hat, was scrubbing her laundry as usual in the trough by the well. Didi, her three-year-old grandson, tumbled on the ground with Bijou. Didi's head was large and round, set with bulging eyes. The torpid afternoon was embroidered by the droning hum of flies, Didi's muffled squealing, and the wet slapping of Madam Bremon's laundry. As Barth and Gina passed her, Madam Bremon told them that Cici, "that Italian," she added in a tone of dismissal (the French here, masters of the land, didn't like the Italians), had stopped by a few minutes ago to return a book that Gina had left on the beach.

Diligently Gina prepared dinner, Barth helping at her side. After a short while, they sat down in the dining room which was wrapped in semidarkness—Didi and Bijou gaping at them, their eyes eagerly following each movement, one with his thumb in his mouth, the other wagging his tail and blinking his bleary eyes.

–Here!–Gina offered them some bread with butter and cheese. Didi swallowed a sardine also, but Bijou turned it down.

The food and rosé left a pleasant weariness in their limbs. Soon after they finished, they retired to their room upstairs. There they remained, naked, two exquisite young bodies, saturated with sun and sea. An evil thought entered Gina's mind: how good it would be if gorgeous Marcelle were with them now, and maybe another beautiful woman, here, all together, in the rarefied dusk scented with perfume and cologne, and overflowing with the stunning vapors of lust . . .

Who could have imagined the heart of man?

–Did you finish your soup, Didi?–Mr. Larouette, Madam Bremon's son-in-law, would ask his son the same question every evening at exactly seven o'clock when he returned from Nice, where he worked as a book-keeper for a wholesale oil and wine firm. Mr. Larouette was short and broad-shouldered, his legs bowed in the shape of an urn. A straw cap was perched on the tip of his enormous skull. With a habitual motion, he tilted the cap back to his neck and wiped his face down from his forehead.

Madam Bremon poured him a glass of wine and offered him her usual answer regarding Didi: –He ate well, and behaved as he should.

Sitting on his father's lap, Didi nuzzled into him. Lifting his dumb face, encrusted with sweat and dust, he nagged for a boat ride.

–Wait a while, Didi,–was the reply.

Mr. Larouette's wife was staying a few weeks in the mountains because of a contaminated lung. But his mother, a fat and bilious matron, could be seen now, as every evening at this time, spread out in an armchair by the door of her house, ten houses down the street. Her wicked face was pointed seaward, casting a pall of dread on Mr. Larouette and Madam Bremon, her son's mother-in-law. She fabricated all kinds of ailments and considered herself dangerously ill. She had an extreme fear of walking, and was convinced that if she dared cross the street—just twenty steps from her house to the beach—she would surely collapse and die. Therefore she wouldn't leave her doorstep, and sat overflowing the edges of her chair, absorbing everything within earshot and acknowledging all the passersby with responses based on merit. She knew the gossip and slander of the town in all its detail, though no one knew where from, as she was never seen talking to anyone.

She controlled her house like a tyrant. No one would dare defy her word, nor disrupt in any way the routine which she dictated. Her son, Mr. Larouette, the single heir to her worldly possessions, was forced to submit his monthly earnings in full to her. She would issue him, as she would to a schoolboy, a few francs a week for his personal needs.

–Swimming in the sea is tiring, isn't it, madam!–Mr. Larouette called through the open window to Gina, who was sunk in a hammock on the small veranda. She swatted lazily at the hum of an invisible mosquito.

–The heat is oppressive. One must get used to it,–she replied.

–The heat doesn't bother me much.

–Probably because you were born here.

–True.–He emptied his glass of wine and stood up. –Excuse me, but we must begin dinner. Come with me, Didi. Then the "godmother" will come for you.–Didi called Madam Bremon the godmother; he only called Madam Larouette grandma. As he was leaving, Mr. Larouette said: –If you'd like to come for a short sail—after dinner.

–Thanks. We'll see.

–Better yet, on Sunday,–he added, –then I'm free all afternoon.–He left with Didi and Bijou, walking pigeon-toed.

When the day's heat had begun to diminish, they stepped out of the house and, hesitating for a moment, looked back and forth along the street. Fishing boats were scattered across the sea as evening settled quietly upon them. The aroma of roasted fish arose from somewhere, and something at once strange and familiar saturated the air. Stephano sat outside with his family around the table, surrendering himself to a huge bowl of pasta and tomato sauce. He beckoned to Barth and Gina, but they declined his invitation and retreated to the opposite side of the street, passing the pension where guests were now sitting down in the garden for dinner. Among them were Latzi and Suzi, in high spirits as always, talking and laughing loudly. Slowly, they continued down the empty street, walking on dust which muffled their footsteps. They came to a villa hidden in a garden at the end of the street, from which burst the thick and slightly hoarse barks of an invisible dog. On their right, the sea had mingled with the evening, swallowing the fisherman and their boats. A light and soothing spray is underfoot, and all at once you find yourself plucked from a place, not specific, though its shape is permanently imprinted in the soul, and you are reattached to something else limitless that is both within you and without. They stood for a short while in silence, filling their lungs with the freshness of the evening, before returning.

The spacious café near Madam Larouette's house was empty. A lonely light bulb shared its meager light with a covered veranda.

—Hey, Patron!—Barth shouted into the empty room.

A dark young girl brought them cold lemonade.

Cici appeared immediately after, squat and square in his dark dress shirt, its collar thrown open. His palms were hard and flat as boards, his muscular arms round and thick like iron bars. His broad, protuberant jaw testified to his athletic bearing. He sat opposite Gina.

—Aren't you working now?—Barth asked.

—My boss is in Normandy for a few weeks, so we have nothing to do until he returns.

Cici had been living here for three years, engaging himself in all sorts of temporary work, as he had no specific skill. During the fishing season, when the schools of sardines are sighted, he takes to the sea with the fishermen in the evenings, remaining with them through the night, spreading and hauling their nets. Lately, he worked with the "Arab" as a builder. They were working on a three-story building behind Stephano's house which was about to be finished. They had done everything by themselves: framing, flooring, installing doors and windows. They had fixed a small ground-floor room into a bedroom, with two old metal cots, and lived there as they worked, in the midst of the pungent odors of cement, plaster, paint, and sawdust.

Gina's blue cotton dress suited her. A red woolen shawl was loosely draped over her shoulders. Her flushed face, on which the sun's rays had cooled by now, resembled a ripe, velvety fruit, and was wrapped in a relaxed expression. Cici sat across from her, unable to take his eyes off her. A full glass of beer stood on the table before him, its head of foam diminishing and disappearing while he studied her. Cici rose and went to switch on the Gramophone. After wiping his hands with a handkerchief, he bowed with exaggerated politeness and asked Gina to dance to the sound of a sweet and rusty waltz. He danced tastefully, pliant and graceful, despite his low stature, leading well. But his heavy hand scorched her back like red-hot iron, and Gina was relieved when the waltz was over. Cici wiped the sweat from his face.

–No,–Gina said, –it's not easy dancing tonight. The heat gets trapped in your limbs.

Barth sat and smoked, battling without respite the mosquitos which bit through the cloth sandals on his feet. He stood up and danced a Charleston with Cici, the two of them shaking their bodies toward one another and swaying from side to side like ships tossed on a stormy sea.

–So where is the boat you once mentioned?–Gina turned to Cici.

–It's Stephano's brother's boat. It has a leak.

–Pity! On a night like this I would have loved to sail.

–I'll try and find another. Maybe tomorrow if Marco doesn't go fishing.

Bored, Barth said: –After the sun sets, the charm of a place like this changes. I can imagine the winter, and the rainy days.–He suggested going to Stephano's. –It's not as confining, at least,–he said. At first Cici declined to join them. Several days before, he had had words with Stephano. But he reconsidered and accompanied them nevertheless.

Stephano's rooftop veranda was reached by a staircase built on to the outer wall of his house. The Gramophone was already hoarse from blaring wild jazz. Latzi was dancing with Suzi. The Japanese fellow and his girl were drinking black coffee and cognac. Also, several villagers, young fishermen and their wives, were drinking red wine with Stephano. Jejette was serving the guests and tending to the Gramophone, exposing her flushed gums and lips in constant laughter.

No sooner had they sat than the Japanese fellow asked Gina to dance. Cici followed their swirling with darkening eyes. In a single gulp, he emptied the glass of cognac that Jejette had brought. Gina returned, exhausted. She had had enough for one night. She couldn't dance anymore. Yet when Stephano approached, she gave in so as not to embarrass him, despite the disgust his closeness aroused in her. Cici sat as though on glowing coals. As if to take revenge on somebody, he rose to dance, alternating partners: first Jejette, then the Englishwoman, the Japanese fellow's friend, then Suzi, who was a full head taller than he, and back again. But his mood remained foul.

Barth, who was smoking endlessly, his long legs crossed, chuckled to himself. The reason for Cici's sudden change of mood hadn't escaped his notice, and he saw it as slightly ridiculous. How could that Cici ever imagine this? Couldn't he understand that it could go nowhere? The vast gap between Gina and Cici, these two beings so distant and different from each other, could never be bridged! Barth could rest assured! Cici was not the man to take Gina from him!

Marcelle appeared with a friend, a young Parisienne, unattractive, who was staying awhile with her parents in their private villa. The two girls joined Gina and Barth at their table. Immediately Barth's bored expression disappeared from his face: −The sea suits you, Mademoiselle Marcelle.

−I love the sea, it's true.−And she added: −I could bathe night and day.

−Yet you don't bathe that often,−Gina remarked.

−The doctor forbad it. He even suggested I go to the mountains. But my aunt lives here.

The moon had risen. A shimmering carpet of silver spread across the sea, toward the horizon. The waves glittered like sequins. From nowhere, a rich baritone voice swelled into a touching Italian folk song. Gina half shut her eyes and leaned back against the railing of the veranda. The cigarette in her hand went out. But Stephano's coarse laugh, which burst from the neighboring roof at that moment, tore something just beginning to form inside her. She threw an angry glance up at him. As though reading her thoughts, Marcelle said: −How crude he is!

A dark tranquillity was spilling over the village onto the sea. On this evening, in this place, one feels oneself secure from all despair. For no particular reason, Barth thought of the director of the office in which he worked as head engineer. An aging bachelor sporting a pointed beard scattered with gray, he was a man free of all lusts and passions. His weekly day of rest was always one of mortification, since he did not know what to do with it. And if sometimes it happened that Barth would stop in at the office on a weekend afternoon to finish a sketch, the fellow would consider it a special grace, for it would ease his tedium. Barth felt sorry for the old man, whose pointed beard now seemed quite pathetic to him, as if it itself expressed the banality and cheerlessness of the man's life. He looked at Marcelle: her narrow face, delicately outlined, her dark gray eyes shaded by long lashes, her full mouth thirsting for life, and he could not understand how any man could feel miserable as long as such beautiful creatures were still to be found. And Gina herself! Wouldn't just a single glance from her suffice to dull the bitter stings that pierce you? Indeed, he thought, fate had been good to him. It had afforded him a precious woman with whom to arrange his life as a summer scene in which even the thunderclouds offer a blessing. He picked up her hand to stroke it. Gina sent him a loving smile.

–You are staying here until autumn, I presume?–Barth turned to Marcelle.

–Until the end of August. What do you expect? One has to work.

–To work? Your face belies it.

–Even so, I am in nursing school.

Stephano was dancing with Jejette now. Cici could not resist remarking that such a relationship between father and daughter wasn't normal, a fact known to all. Yet nobody reports him.

–They are afraid of him. No one wants to put his life on the line.

Afterward, the interpreter arrived, accompanied by the "Arab." They joined the other group, the Japanese fellow, Latzi, and their women. The interpreter immediately took off his jacket and began to dance with each woman in turn, his false hand resting limply on the shoulder of his partner. His laugh was hollow and hoarse, without feeling. Marcelle said that she could not bear him, this interpreter, there was something false in his nature. Cici came feebly to his defense, then stopped. After all, he only met him here and had known him just a short time.

Barth looked out along the sleepy road, anointed in moonlight. Along the carpet of pebbles which sloped to the sea, several fishing dories were scattered. Opposite some of them, drowsy fishermen gathered with their wives and children. They lived in the houses across the street and slept here in the coolness of the night. Small waves wandered from the horizon to stroke the shore with light, muffled slaps. The scene, rendered in the moon's gossamer light, seemed unreal.

—If only we could bathe now!

Barth immediately caught on to the Parisienne's idea: —Why not? It's not cold at all! And you, Gina?

—Don't be silly! It's not worth catching pneumonia.

Marcelle was ready to join in. And Cici, whose good spirits had suddenly returned, felt as if he could stay in the water a half hour or more, if they would.

Barth went with Marcelle first. Behind them were Cici, Gina and the Parisienne. Barth put his arm through Marcelle's. —Do you realize that you're beautiful?

—So I've been told,—she said, turning with a smile.

Ah, how well did this Marcelle know how to smile enchantingly. A slight sadness touched Barth's heart at the sight of her delicate and seductive smile. He was suddenly filled with a torrent of extra strength. Now it would be the right time to run until breathless, to jump, to climb a tree, to be embroiled in combat. The warmth of her bare arm flowed through his shirt sleeve like a current of electricity. Yes, now he must plunge in, it was no longer caprice. The heat was overbearing on this cool and dewy night. As if to himself, he muttered: —It's true. I haven't seen many women as beautiful as you, and I've had the occasion to see women, after all!

—Your wife.

—I could say this to her face. She is too beautiful to be jealous of a friend of hers.—Unintentionally he squeezed her arm. The pebbles crunched underfoot. —Here we are!—He let go of her arm and turned around: —Well, children!

In vain Gina tried to dissuade them. Hidden behind a nearby boat, Cici and Barth stripped off their clothes, and in one leap threw themselves stark naked into the water. The girls followed. Barth caught a fleeting glimpse of Marcelle's nude body as she ran the few steps to the water.

—Not cold at all!—He called to Gina, who sat close to the shore. He moved closer to Marcelle, and swam beside her. Unintentionally he touched her while swimming, and he caught his breath. —This swim. I'll never forget it,—he whispered so Cici wouldn't hear.

Marcelle burst into laughter for no reason.

—Come out,—Gina urged, —you'll all catch cold and die!

He could have swum all night, but in spite of that, he hurried out. He wiped the droplets of water from his body, rubbed his skin vigorously, and began some strange calisthenics to increase his circulation, for it turned out that the air was cooler than the water. His movements seemed stranger still in the glow of moonlight.

–What's this for? Why?–Gina snapped as he, now dressed, approached her.

–We have to run!–Barth said as the others appeared. –Let's go. To the pension! We'll see who's first!

Everyone ran, except Gina. Afterward he stopped to wait for her.

The pension was already dark. Empty tables and chairs could be seen through the fence in a patchwork of moonlight. A dog came running down the street, his paws sinking mutely in little clouds of dust. As he approached, it became clear that the dog was none other than Bijou, spotted black and white. He recognized Barth and lingered, turning his head toward the rest of the group opposite the pension. Then he approached, wagging his tail and affectionately licking Barth's hand. Hoarse melodies continued to shower down from Stephano's roof across the street. Couples whirled, and a large pool of electric light washed from his roof almost to the edge of the sea.

–I'll go with you to Nice.

–No, I'll go alone.

Cici's expression was imperious. His jaws tightened. –Could you stop me from coming?

–Of course not. But I do want to go alone.

–If you only knew, madam.–He looked down and continued: –I'm prepared, if you command, to cross the sea, to swim to Algiers, or to starve for two weeks.–He put the palm of his hand to his shirt, over his heart. Gina stifled her laugh. Cici looked up. –I'd rather you wouldn't laugh.

–Aha! You forbid me?

–I'm from Naples, madam!–Cici tossed a pebble into the air. –In Naples we cut off the head.

–Ah!

–We cut off the head,–repeated Cici.

–Great, so what?

Cici was silent. Gina spread a towel over her thigh, which the sun had begun to redden. –If you are a friend of Barth's, then why don't you talk like this when he's with us? Try and speak like this to his face.

–I could say it to his face, I have nothing to hide.–Pausing, he continued: –You'd better not torture me.

–You're talking nonsense, Mr. Cici.

–You are the only woman, the first. I haven't loved a woman like this yet.

–How does this affect me? I can't imprison myself in a box. I have never encouraged you.

–They say you aren't married to him at all.

–So what! It's no one's concern!

Cici lowered his head and bent down, mechanically sifting gravel through his fingers. Gina's face was flushed to the roots of her hair. She said: –You're going too far, sir! If you want me to continue talking to you, you will have to stop speaking such nonsense.

Cici didn't answer. He had gone too far. But what difference did it make? He was filled with a wretched sadness. Why had she come here, of all places, to spend her vacation? Aren't there enough beaches in the world? –And so, you don't want me to join you?

–No.–She turned her other side under the umbrella. –When my husband gets well, you can join us sometime.

–Since the day you came, I haven't been able to sleep. I lost my appetite. When I see you, I feel like I'm going to burst.–And after a moment: –An Italian doesn't talk like this for nothing. You'd better get out of this place while there is still time.

–If you don't stop immediately, I'll ask you to leave.

–Excuse me, madam.

Nearby, Latzi and Suzi were romping on the beach with the interpreter and the "Arab." The interpreter was somewhat tanned by now, though the difference between him and his friends was still immediately obvious. The remnant of his arm was wrapped in a towel as usual. Gina could overhear fragments of their conversation—about Italy and about Nice. She felt slightly intimidated by the man beside her, who belonged to another species, another social stratum, whose character was not clear enough to her. It was impossible to know what he was capable of. Nevertheless, she was unconsciously aroused by his unbridled passion. Gina was not without coquettishness. In a hidden corner of her soul, it was somehow pleasurable to be the cause of a man's insomnia, a man who two weeks ago was not aware of her existence.

Gina glanced at Cici. He sat dark and motionless. His collar was thrown open over his shoulders, revealing the broad convexity of his bare chest. This strong man, resembling a cast bronze statue in his stance, seemed so pitiful seated next to her in his misery.

The water quietly washed the shore. Nearby crawled a boat filled with naked bodies, noise, and laughter. Stephano's brood, accompanied by Marcelle and her Parisienne friend, were in it. Stray arms and legs, outstretched over the gunwales, splashed the water. The sounds of their voices were interspersed with a heavy, intense silence. A tall Englishman glided sidestroke along the shore, followed faithfully by his slender Great Dane. Twice a day, in the morning and early evening, the Englishman would swim the same distance with his dog, behind Stephano's house and along the length of the entire village—always in the same straight line, as if swimming in an invisible lane. For a while Gina followed them with her eyes.

The ice cream peddler appeared on the street with his pushcart, announcing his wares in a molten voice. Gina rescued Cici from his ruminations by giving him some change to buy ice cream. When he returned, he sat beside her again, folding his legs beneath him. He studied her avidly as she licked her capuccino-colored ice cream.

–Why didn't you buy one for yourself? Didn't I ask you?

Cici dismissed the question with a wave of his hand. –You've a hard heart, madam.

–You think so?

After a minute, as he dug in his pack of cigarettes: –Is it because I'm a worker . . .

–You're talking nonsense! I love my husband.

–I'm no more a fool than anyone. I haven't read books, but I've thought about what's on my mind.–He tapped his finger to his forehead.

–I don't doubt it. Give me a cigarette.

Cici continued: –I may go to Paris, I'll find a living there too. I could sell fish. I have connections.

Gina blew smoke rings, neatly formed in the sun. For a while she studied the nails on her outstretched toes, then turned her head back toward the nearby group that by now included Marcelle. Marcelle waved to her, smiling warmly. In front of Stephano's store a truck was being unloaded of a barrel and several crates with black inscriptions. Stephano's awesome roar was heard. Madam Stephano appeared at the door in her bare white feet and uncombed hair.

–You're quiet, madam. You have nothing to say to me.

–Nothing.

–Tonight I'll get a boat—

–Not tonight. When my husband gets better.

–How you torture me.–He rose suddenly, as if he had reached an important decision, and walked to the water.

–I'm so glad you came.–Barth lay in bed, wearing gray silk pajamas, the sheet pulled up to his chin. The room was washed with a warm semidarkness.

–One should visit the sick,–said Marcelle.

–I'm not seriously ill,–laughed Barth. –If you hadn't come today— I'll surely get up tomorrow.

–You've been here five days. What did you have then?

–A fever. Slight congestion. Now it's all over.

–It must mean that swimming at night is dangerous. It's a wonder I too didn't fall ill, since I'm very sensitive.

–You see, sometimes it's the nonsensitive who are struck. Don't you want to move your chair a little closer, so I can see your face?

–And where is Gina?

–She has some errand in Nice.

Marcelle leaned back in her chair. A necklace of blue glass clung to her. The richness of her tan was enhanced by her white cotton dress. Her thighs, dusted with a light down, were shapely and muscular, like a dancer's.

Barth gazed at her quietly for a moment. Then he ran his fingers through his thick blond hair to the back of his neck. –Your hat, don't you want to take it off?

Marcelle did as he asked. She placed her broad white panama on a chair. With a graceful shake of her head, she fluffed her curly black hair, cut like a boy's. For some reason she smiled an absent smile to herself. –It's so warm in here, warmer than outside.

Barth sat up and took Marcelle's hand, long and slender, and touched it to his lips. He held it close, stroking it tenderly many times.

The house was imbued with a deep stillness. The buzz of a hidden fly, just awakened, enriched the yearning silence and became part of it. Soon it was torn by the cry of a child that burst outside. The voice seemed like Didi's, and Barth imagined his plump face, contorted by tears and ugly, as he had seen it many times.

Her head tilted slightly, Marcelle was sitting slumped, close to the bed, her magnificent eyes gazing straight ahead. She was listening to an enchanted world which once was, and wasn't at all, one hand absently stroking the sculpted arm of the chair, the other surrendered to Barth. After a moment, she pulled her hands back and crossed her legs. –So tomorrow you'll be getting up already.

–Tomorrow I'll be getting up already.–After a moment, he grumbled, as if to himself: —It was clear to me all along that you would come. I've been waiting all along. Whenever footsteps scratched in the garden, my whole self sprang up toward you. And I—He stopped in mid-sentence and set his eyes on her.

Marcelle remained seated, leaning back, her head turned slightly from him, a warm smile cast upon it. Her eyes were half-closed, hidden through long lashes. Between her lips, slightly parted, smooth and even teeth shone white, seeming whiter still against the bronze of her skin and the hint of down at the corners of her mouth that lent an indescribable beauty to her features.

There she was, sitting in front of you, Marcelle. The nymph as distant from your life as the limits of the earth, yet within the reach of a hand. And at that moment it became clear that a man is able to extract in a single instant the essence of all the joy allotted him for a lifetime and to feed on it for the rest of his days, from that moment alone. All the fatigue left in Barth by the fever melted from him.

Outside, the rusty voice of the ice cream peddler could be heard as if from another world. He called out in single announcements. A molten silence stretched between the announcements. Barth turned his body toward Marcelle, until his head almost touched hers. He peered deeply into her delicate eyes for a few minutes, his heart exploding with each pulse. All of a sudden, he wrapped his arms around her neck and pulled her toward him. Darkness settled upon the world, past, present, future. Their lips mingled with one another's.

Then she freed herself from his arms. On either side of her nose a slight pallor rose. With disobedient hands Barth peeled off her dress, and the slip beneath it. She let loose a muffled laugh, slightly hoarse, and jumped onto Barth's bed, sinking her teeth into his neck, his shoulders and chest, like a wildly stampeding animal.

Gina planned to return on the six o'clock train. She had remained two hours to stroll at her leisure and look at the lovely things in the shop windows. She stood erect, her lightly tanned face revealing an inner fire despite her tranquil expression. Her silk dress was the color of wild strawberries, and large rings were in her ears. She exuded the fragrance of exotic countries, from lands across the ocean where people run naked, their impulses wild and noble, rooted in prehistoric times and God. Men stopped in their paths, wondering about the proud arrogance of her stance, or the splendor of her movements. Some turned and followed her and tried with jumbled half-sentences to coax her into a café or casino. The heat bore the choking scents of the city. The horses' heads were dressed in tattered straw hats, dusty with age. Their ears poked through two special holes and twitched incessantly against the biting flies.

As she turned onto the main boulevard, Cici appeared before her, dressed in his best Sunday dark suit.

—Ah?—Gina was taken aback.

—I don't mean to trouble you, madam. I'll go away, if that's what you want.—Squat, square, and muscular as a lumberjack, he stood before her. His bare head rested on shoulders without the grace of a neck.

It slipped from Gina's mouth, in spite of herself: —You can walk with me for a while.—And within a minute she corrected herself: —A half hour at most, then you must leave me.

Cici's face lit up. He made a motion to kiss her hand, but she pulled back, a gesture of disgust unnoticed by him.

Amid the bustle of the boulevard he strode beside her, so small and pathetic in comparison to her. For a while he was silent. Yet a great exhilaration pounded within him, his pulse exulting for the magnificent woman beside him. He cast his gaze directly ahead, without seeing anything. —Lately I've been working from the inside scaffolding. I also had work to do outside, in the shade. Nevertheless, I worked all day long in the sun, because from there I could see you walking to Stephano's store and to the beach.

Gina pretended not to hear. The heat was wrapped around her like a hot bandage. The wide boulevard seemed too narrow for her. And the squat Italian who clung to her, with his face red as brick, couldn't ease the heat; on the contrary. —I thought you were going to visit my husband.

—I couldn't stay back there. I just wanted to hear you say that you didn't hold it against me.

—No, why should I?

—I think I didn't behave politely this morning.

Gina stopped from time to time at the shop windows. She entered a cosmetic store to buy something. Cici waited outside for her. They continued along the boulevard which led to the beach, the casino, the big hotels, and the mansions which stood facing the sun and the sea. The shore here was very colorful with the beach umbrellas, the tents, and the bathing suits of the many bathers. Along the sparkling asphalt of the beach road, cars flew back and forth, honking noisily. The casino's

veranda was filled to capacity, and the band was tuned for the afternoon's dance.

No, Gina did not accept Cici's invitation to the casino. She reminded
him that his time was up and that he had to leave her. Cici obeyed, and
walked in the opposite direction. Yet a few minutes later, she saw him,
not far away, leaning against the pier facing her. Furious, she stopped a
taxi and jumped in. She let herself out in the center of the city, where
she sat down at a sidewalk café, and breathed deeply, as if redeemed.

When she finished her iced coffee, she glossed her lips and lit a cigarette. What an annoyance! Let him find me now! But she was suddenly
struck by a wave of pity for this man, and had he appeared now and sat
beside her, she certainly would not have protested.

She leaned back, enjoying her respite from the bustle of the street. As
she studied the passersby, examining the faces and dresses of the
women, it got hotter and hotter. The life-pulse was pounding forcefully,
as strong within her as without. Aware of her physical sensations, she
was aroused with love for her mysterious and agitated body, as if, somehow, it were a creation apart from her.

A man seated at the next table, who hadn't taken his eyes off Gina all
this time, slid his chair over. As if continuing a conversation interrupted
just a minute ago, he said: —This city must be seen in the spring. Then
it is lovely.

He was a man of about thirty, his face open, and his gaze straight,
inspiring trust.

Gina smiled. —Who would you have said that to if I had not entered
this place?

—I wouldn't have said it.

—But now you feel like praising the city.

—Hmmm . . . not exactly.—He called the waiter to bring him a pack
of cigarettes. —Actually, I'd like to offer you my sincerest thanks.

Gina raised her eyes to him, surprised.

—Because you came here and you are so beautiful.

—I have to admit, I hadn't thought of coming here to give you pleasure,—smiled Gina.

—It's all the same.—He opened the pack of cigarettes and pushed a
finger inside. He wiped his broad, handsome forehead. —You see,
madam, sometimes a person wakes up in the morning, and everything
is as it should be. The summer presents itself to him. The sun has
painted a bit of a window at the top of the blue wall. The bustle of the

street has the same smell and color as the day before. Apparently, nothing has changed, not even a bit, isn't it so? And yet he immediately feels that this is not it. Something is missing today. Suddenly he can't understand the meaning of the simplest things, neither their relationship to himself nor their relationship to each other—as if it became clear that the ultimate purpose that gives value to every thing and deed is not there at all . . . Then he continues, out of habit, with his daily trivial actions —everything is fine. Except from that point on there is no meaning to it all.–He lit the cigarette, which had gone out. –And suddenly, quite by chance, there appears a strange woman, and all at once he is reconnected to the world.–After a short silence: –If I'm not mistaken, madam is from Germany.

–Let's say from Vienna.

–Well then, we can rid ourselves of the constraints of a foreign language.

But Gina was preparing to leave, lest she miss her tain.

–Hey, why? You'd do me an honor by letting me drive you. In ten minutes you'll be home.–He introduced himself as Irwin Kraft from Munich, a prosecuting attorney who retired because to make a profession of revealing other people's crimes was against his nature.

At that moment, Cici passed hastily in front of the café, on his way to the nearby station. Gina smiled gleefully to herself as she imagined his disappointment at not finding her there.

–And so you float around at leisure in your car?

–Something like that.

–Not a bad life.

–Not always.

He suggested a drive through the city before taking Gina to her destination. Gina sat beside him, next to the wheel in the large gray sedan. They meandered through the network of streets, some of which were steeply inclined up the hills on which the city rested. They passed through the quarter of villas hidden in tranquil gardens and continued along the cobalt bay, which looked like a picture postcard. A refreshing wind blew toward them. And when he let her off by Bremon's house, it was agreed between them that he would come one day soon to take them for a trip in the surroundings.

The translator was trilling Italian folk songs in a loud, shrill voice, while the "Arab" sat beside him, smoking. In spite of the door being opened to the balcony, the room was filled with an asphyxiating heat.

The table, usually extended, was pushed by the sofa in order to make room for guests. Many bottles had already been emptied, and limbs were already leaden. Latzi wanted to dance, just to dance, and the Japanese fellow, who was giving the party, took care of that as well. The Gramophone and a stack of records stood ready on a stool in the corner.

Suzi chatted with Gina, then seated herself beside Barth. —You're not drinking, Mr. Barth. Apparently you prefer to be the only sober one among drunkards, to see them in their foolishness.

—Not so. I've drunk more than anyone. What can I do if the drink has no effect on me! Anyway, the night is young.

The Japanese fellow's companion sat close to them on the sofa. She fanned her hot and leathery face with a colorful paper fan. She refilled Barth's glass and handed it to him. —Then may you drink to the health of all the beautiful women here!

Barth did as she asked, saying: —Cheers to the mistress of the house especially, and all beautiful women in general!

The flesh along this small woman's neck was wilted, scattered with many fine pendulous wrinkles, hanging limp, like an empty sack. The burden of all her years was borne by this neck. Yet Suzi was brimming with rustic health and joyous vitality, though somehow dull. —Will you be coming to Vienna soon?—she asked Barth.

—Maybe in the winter. For Christmas.

—Then you must visit us! Call first, or just pop in to the Café Museum. We're there every evening.

—Great. I'll remember that.

Latzi had switched on the Gramophone and was dancing with Marcelle. Cici invited Gina and, in the middle of the dance, blurted in her ear: —That strange man interests you more than I do.

—Which strange man?

—The one that brought you from Nice in his car three days ago—Cici was already a little drunk, his tongue was looser.

—Listen, mister,—exclaimed Gina, —by whose permission do you spy on me?

—I wasn't spying. I just happened to see.

—I forbid you to follow me! Do you hear?

—I won't tell anyone. Don't worry. I also saw you sitting with him in the Café Monaco.

—Don't speak to me anymore!—Her voice quivered with rage.

At that moment the waltz finished, and she went to sit beside Marcelle. Cici gulped down a glass of wine. His jaws were loosening even more. Now that the Gramophone was silent, the translator started singing again. And Cici was humming along, his untrained voice deep and turbid. The waves of the warm melody spilled over the balcony into the darkness of the night, which was furrowed with light breezes, like a man's breath, and into the breadth of the sleepy sea. A hidden tremor stirred in the hearts of the listeners, and a burning and strange day shimmered before them, spread over fields of yellow grain on the plains of a nostalgic land. Then Latzi, accompanied by his wife, sang a Viennese folk song:

> *Ja, ja, der Wein is' gu—et,*
> *I' brauch' kei' neuen Hu—et.*
> *I' setz' mei' alten auf,*
> *Bevor i' a Wasser sauf'.*

Gina leaned against the balcony railing. She looked at the deserted midnight street and beyond, toward the sea that heaved silently, interwoven with night into one great heaviness. There arose in her a slight sadness, not without a touch of pleasantness. For some reason, she recalled a night, a few years ago, when she had first come to know Barth. After a long walk in the Prater parks, she had stood in her room before an open window, also facing the summer night, and the gentleness of her feelings toward Barth, as if swelling from that night into her soul, filled it to overflowing and compelled her to cry and sing. Through dense silence, she seemed to sense the strike of a match, an unreal scratch in the next room, where her father might have lit a cigarette while studying his textbooks. Her father, Professor Karl Funken, his eyes filled with supreme wisdom and understanding which could probe the depths of her soul so painlessly, those eyes that she loved. He was a rare person, whose presence alone could soothe the heart with comfort and strength. Actually, she had been born under a good sign, Gina thought. Her life had flowed with pleasure, full and clear, without the superfluous turbulence which may disrupt internal balance. Her love for Barth, deep, consistent, never knowing fatigue or boredom, contributed a lot to it.

Latzi drew closer, quietly, and uprooted her from her thoughts. —Excuse me, madam, if I'm interrupting, for some time I have wanted —I mean your face is very interesting. One could make an excellent portrait. I would love very much to paint your portrait.

This man bothered her. A real barber, she would think of him as she dismissed him with a yes and no answer and hurried inside. She sat in an empty chair beside Barth, who was talking to Marcelle and didn't notice her coming. A line that slipped out of his mouth that very minute made her somehow shiver. —The way something appears is sometimes different from the way it is, it could even be its opposite— . . . Gina wondered about the nagging feeling that this line, which apparently did not refer to her, inspired in her. Moreover, there arose in her an inexplicable fear of the continuation of their conversation, as if something which would truly sadden her might be said along the way. She felt compelled to end their conversation immediately. She moved her chair nearer to Barth and put her hand on his arm. He turned to her and smiled softly.

—What is it, Gin?—he whispered enticingly, and added: —Maybe you're bored?

Gina looked up and gazed at him, her dark eyes now tinged with a light sadness, so familiar to him. He gently stroked the skin of her cool arm, smooth like the skin of a peach, until her face lightened into a scant smile. —People aren't happy here,—she said, —or maybe it just seems that way to me.

Facing them with his back to the wall, Cici looked at her, his heavy, insistent gaze not leaving her for a moment, and she was uncomfortable. —Maybe it would be best if we went to sleep.

—Soon,—replied Barth without moving.

The Gramophone began to play again. Gina rose, pulling Marcelle with her to dance. In a corner of the room, the Japanese fellow, tipsy by now, kept kissing Jacqueline, the little Parisienne, Marcelle's friend, who from time to time uttered a sharp, grating laugh. Not far away sat the Englishwoman, a foolish smile jelling on her flushed face. Through the mists of fox-trot and alcohol, she gestured to them with her fan. The translator pulled her from her stupor and began to dance with her.

They went out onto the drowsy road. Gina, Barth, and Marcelle. They walked quietly in the middle of the dewy street, and the tepid night slowly lifted the alcoholic haze from them. The mixture of drunken voices and the sounds of the Gramophone receded into the background, becoming more and more attenuated, and finally lost its reality. A remnant of the evening's vapid feeling remained inside Gina. She felt empty and bored. A warm fatigue was spreading through her limbs. She sat on one of the rocks that were scattered along the length of the beach.

–Eating and drinking, that's an intimate matter. There is something immodest in it with strange people to whom you have no tie . . .

–Sometimes a tie is created by sharing a meal,–commented Barth.

Sitting with their backs to the sea, they looked at the row of darkened houses and were filled with the night's loneliness. Far away, a few short barks punctured the night as if with nails. Then nothing else. Just behind them, the ocean heaved ceaselessly with muffled breath.

After a moment, they rose and continued their walk to the edge of the village, to the point where the shore outlines a semicircle, as if embracing the water. They then retraced their steps, and turned into the side street where Marcelle lived. When Gina and Barth returned to the main road, Cici caught up with them. He was running toward them, extremely upset, almost crying. It was a bizarre sight. He began to talk immediately, in fragments, and in a choked voice quite unlike him.

–You understand, and madam will excuse me . . . Such a disgrace! . . . Don't think I'm drunk . . . I'm not drunk, not a bit, you hear! . . . I'm not trying to defend myself—it's not my nature . . . you know me a little! . . . I don't want to embellish anything . . . Imagine, a man drunk as Lot, as a skunk, who can't tell a cow from a chicken! So what did he do to me, would you ask? Nothing . . . absolutely nothing. I asked forgiveness from him . . . I cried in front of him . . . I kissed him . . . I am a man of justice, you can tell! That's my nature! . . . and he forgave me . . . in front of everyone he forgave me . . . and cried too . . . But I'm not sure if he did it for show and because he was drunk. He was the only one who was really drunk, much more than the translator or Latzi. But how can I be sure? I don't want him to hold a grudge . . . because I admit my mistake soberly and I regret it, you're my witnesses. Everyone cried with us and everyone kissed everyone else . . . but . . .

–But what happened there?–Barth interrupted. Tell things the way they were!

–Tell . . . there's nothing to tell . . . It's not even interesting . . . Do you find a smack interesting? This work, I don't like it . . . better call it an accident, an idiotic incident, than a premeditated act. It just happened, and only then did I realize it. But drunk I am not . . . He was drunk, not me.

They were passing by the Japanese man's house, from which burst a thunderous hail of wild laughter. Cici stopped, and stretched his arm out toward the orange squares of light of the door and the two open windows: –Here, can you hear? They're laughing! . . . Laughing! Un-

less they're hiding their grudge under the laughter . . . the Japanese
guy especially . . . him more than anyone else . . .

–My God! What happened already!–Gina cried, excited.

–This is it, madam! Nothing happened . . . almost nothing . . . It's
just that Jacqueline threw off her dress and danced naked. Suzi also
stripped and danced. Then the Englishwoman joined them. Three of
them naked. Because the three of them were drunk, and all danced.
There is nothing so say against that. They were drinking and dancing,
off and on. Afterward, Jacqueline found herself in my lap, didn't she?
Because the lights were back on . . . she was crying because she was
drunk. I felt sorry for her. And so she sat on my lap and cried. And then
the Japanese guy, naked also except for his bathing trunks, told me to
get her off my lap, didn't he? Nothing wrong with that. Didn't he buy
her with his own money? But the girl didn't feel like it. Because she said,
"Watch out for Cici! He knows how to box!" And the Japanese guy said
to me, because he was drunk: "Really? You know how to fight? Let's
see!" And he grabbed me by the nose and pulled me here and there like
this–Cici imitated the Japanese guy's action with his own hand. –You
understand that it was not the pain but the humiliation. No one has ever
dared pull me around by my nose. Everyone laughed at me. And then I
jumped and planted a punch right under his eye. One of my best! . . .
His eye swelled totally. And immediately I felt badly and asked forgiveness. With tears and kisses. Because maybe he had no bad intention—
drunk as he was. And yet I was not drunk.

Gina suddenly burst out laughing. By now they had reached their
apartment and the garden gate, and Bijou pushed himself under the
latch and threw himself on them with grunts of contentment. Barth
shook him off with a slight rebuke.

–You're laughing, madam! There's no place for laughter here. Cici,
his head is still in its place. You'd better not laugh! What do you say,
Mr. Barth? Did I act improperly? I'm neither a doctor nor an engineer,
it's true, but I'm not a boor! And certainly not a villain, that's for sure!
It's not my way to hurt anyone by word or by gesture, you'll admit that
yourselves, the Japanese guy is a decent fellow, a drunk though. I regret
the incident. I don't want him to hold a grudge. That's it. But there's no
place for laughing here.

–And you haven't drunk a thing all evening?–teased Gina.

–What do you mean, haven't drunk? I did drink. But not much.
Anyway, here, we're used to drinking. Have I ever acted like a drunk-

ard? Here . . . would you like to go for a sail now? I can take Marco's boat. No? Not because I insulted you, God forbid. If I insulted you unintentionally with anything I said, let me apologize—He put his hand on his breast. —Well, I should go back to the Japanese fellow right now.

—Why don't you go to sleep?—said Barth. —It's already three in the morning.

—No, I wouldn't be able to sleep, not until I knew for sure that he has nothing against me.—Cici ran back to the Japanese man.

They were still in the middle of breakfast. Kraft, self-assured, greeted them simply. Although he had already eaten at his hotel, he agreed to drink a cup of coffee with them, for the "sake of hominess." A simple and modest good feeling prevailed in Madam Bremon's dining room. The thin semidarkness was sweetened by a spray of sunlight streaming diagonally through the door, in which joyous flies bathed.

Gina placed in front of him a saucer of jam, and buttered him a roll. All her being radiated a virginal freshness, yet something in her graceful movements, soft and animated, was endowed with a motherly calm. Irwin Kraft, enchanted by her at first sight in a way not diminished by habit, felt a moment's secret sadness when he recalled another young woman whose essence had been quite different. The other would evoke feelings of confusion around her. Her movements, incoherent because of an inner disorder, always caused anxiety in objects and in people, to a point where their special identities were canceled. In his imagination flashed the image of a grotesque illustration of this idea, an upside-down table, its legs in the air, a change making it so ridiculous that now you don't know for what use it was intended.

He leaned back in his chair and wiped his sweet mouth with a napkin. —And now, I think—a pity to waste anything of such a beautiful day.

Gina asked him to wait a moment for Marcelle. He will excuse her for inviting her on her own to join them. She is a lovely girl, charming, and "won't spoil the view." She herself would run upstairs in the meantime to get ready.

Marcelle brought with her the radiance of the morning, burnished orange and blue. She sat diagonally across from Kraft, wearing a tight, steel-colored dress and a similarly colored beret. Light conversation flowed slowly, brightened by the lightning of her clear laughter. Barth mused, with no bearing on the conversation, that this Kraft was actually endowed with something straightforward and captivating. How sharp were Gina's perceptions, how right and to the point her judgments of people! For this, one could rely on her, without a doubt or hesitation.

Gina returned and everyone rose. Within a few minutes, the car was rolling along the smooth road, glossy black, that ran like a spine through all the coastal villages, inlaid with the lush greenery of southern flora. Their first stop after a short drive was in a small bathing town which had only recently become popular. This town rose in the sun's heat with its new hotels colored chocolate, lemon, and light coffee, the casino adorned with miniature palms, the huge garages, and the magnificent restaurants and their verandas shaded from the sun by huge color-ful umbrellas—an international meeting place for celebrities—various sports heroes, beauty queens, film stars, polished salon writers, various adventure seekers, and just crazy American women and the like. All of them wandering on the clean streets, spread out to the shore, half-naked in their bathing suits and also in their pajamas. Someone dressed in regular clothing here would certainly seem of a different species.

Kraft parked the car by a pine grove set on top of a small hill next to the casino. They left their clothes in the car and walked through the small grove where some bathers were sprawled on benches scattered among the trees or on the dark ground, which was covered with dry and trampled needles in a patchwork of glowing sunlight. Here and there a joyous laugh would sparkle in the viscous heat and reverberate through the silence of the tall trees. Freeing themselves of clothes renewed an inborn sense of freedom. The touch of sunlight made their laughter clearer, somehow more wild and free. Although strangers to one an-other, they saw themselves as a single family: their nakedness canceled the distance between them, making them fundamentally equal to each other, as at the time of birth and death.

–I'm surprised you didn't decide to settle here,–said Gina, turning to Kraft. –In the summer it's as if Nice were a hall decked for a party to which the guests didn't show up.

–I prefer it to this pandemonium. Would you like to live here?

–My drowsy fishing village, I wouldn't exchange it for anything.

On the other side of the grove, which came suddenly to a steep slope, a swirling mélange of colors shone before them, sparkling in the sun: bathing paraphernalia and hundreds of boats gliding back and forth not far from the shore—a mixture of all the tones of the spectrum set against the sea's vivid blue, which softened as it approached the horizon, blend-ing into the lighter pastel of the sky and fusing with the lush green groves and gardens to the right.

–Hey, boys! Who's ready to jump in?–Marcelle's good spirits imparted a beautiful luster to her dark, half-laughing eyes, and animated her well-carved, shapely limbs. She hopped from one foot to the other.

–I'm with you!–cried Barth.

–And you, Gina?

–No,–she smiled. They are people who are settled, she and Kraft. Isn't it so?

They walked down the broad stairs that led from the grove to the water. Down, Marcelle and Barth departed to a narrow, damp, wooden, pier that ran from the shore to a point where the sea was deeper than a man's height and ended in a high, square platform with a board on one of its sides inclined into the water for sliding. They swam far out to a necklace of red buoys that enclosed an area reserved for swimming. Side by side on their backs, they gazed up into the depths of the sky, spilling still and pure upon them. The noise around them, pierced by shrieks, was slightly muffled, as though filtered through a curtain. At times they encountered an icy current, as if they entered a root cellar. The violent change in temperature sent a shudder through their flesh, a shudder of panic. Immediately, a thought forced itself on him, the frightful possibility of a heart attack, although the heart was completely healthy. The newspaper would later report a terse and typical announcement, the sort that the eye glances over inadvertently while one sips the morning coffee. At times like these, Barth would decide that if he ever made it out of the water, he would never swim again. Yet the next time, as soon as he touched the water, he was compelled to outdistance himself, as if driven by a youthful recklessness whose pointlessness was not unknown to him.

–We're going back!–announced Barth, frightened, although he wasn't particularly tired.

In the midst of the stunning clamor, Gina and Kraft sat on the warm sand and waited for them, their feet outstretched to the little waves that broke on them. They walked into the water to rinse the sand from themselves as everyone returned to dress, for it was already noon.

Soon after lunch, they found themselves rolling down the lustrous road. The sea to their left, now seen, now hidden, and whose sight alone somehow sweetened the insufferable heat. The car sliced through the sleepy yellow air, drawing forth little tongues of wind that licked their faces and hair. How pleasant to cut through the flesh of the day, to wrest from it even the faintest comfort.

Sunk in the luxurious softness of the seat, Gina closed her eyes and imagined flying backward, but then forced herself to gather her senses and realign her sense of direction. But as she opened her eyes, she was seized for a moment with a slight dizziness. It became evident that despite her effort to direct her inner sense in the direction she was going, she nevertheless experienced slight confusion; and in that sudden transition to reality, it was as if something in her were jolted out of place. She repeated this game a few times. Then she fixed her gaze on Marcelle, who sat beside her. She focused on her profile, an outline of pure and open lines. A moment passed as the lines blurred and quivered before her eyes. From the imbroglio of vague sensations that stirred within her, one clear thought slowly detached itself and floated to consciousness. It was of prophetic certainty that needed no evidence, that from her, Marcelle, no great evil shall come to her, not now or ever. For this, Gina stirred with sympathy for Marcelle, perhaps because for a moment she saw Marcelle as weaker than herself and unlikely to harm her in any way. She took her hand. Marcelle turned, looking at Gina strangely, as if jolted from a dream.

–Do you like him?–She gestured with her chin toward Kraft's back.

Marcelle considered the broad and straight back in the tight robe that revealed the agility and strength of an athletic man. –He's not unpleasant.

Without pause, Gina whispered: –If you love him, jealousy is not my nature . . .

–Him?

–Of course not.–She started speaking about Barth, who was sitting with Kraft in the front seat, analyzing his qualities and revealing his strengths before this Marcelle, as if driven by an impulse to heighten any danger. –He's worthy of love,–she concluded. –A woman who isn't carried away by him doesn't have her senses in the right place. That's my frank opinion.

–Not bad advertising,–joked Marcelle. And then: –Don't you think that all this would awaken suspicions about him? Or are you prepared for it?

–You've had the chance to get to know him a bit by now. The car was now crossing a bridge which spanned a broad and shallow river. Through its crystalline waters the rocks could be seen scattered along the bottom. Kraft turned to the back seat to announce that they were going to the mountains, not to visit tourist attractions, but to go wherever the road led them.

At about four o'clock, Kraft stopped in front of an inn in a quiet mountain village whose streets were empty. Dogs dozed in the shade cast by the low houses, their trembling tongues wagging from side to side. They drank some bad coffee and had a light snack. The innkeeper, sleeves rolled up, was armed with a sharply pointed moustache and a curl on his chin on which remained a single long strand of beard, for coquetry perhaps. A spotted cat, basking in the peaceful day, sprawled across one of the solid brown tables.

–It seems as if the world is purged of all annoyance and noise. Suddenly a man can hear the sound of his own voice, without a filter,–Barth said as he put a roll filled with butter, tomato, and cheese into his mouth.

–Not every man wants to hear himself,–Kraft pointed out. –Most run to the clamor.

After a while they returned to the car and rolled up and down, stopping on one village and then in another, and when evening fell, they turned home, filled with the lowing of strange animals and intoxicated by the smells of a simple, innocent existence, old as the earth and ceaselessly regenerating until infinity.

The jukebox spilled muffled jazz into the darkened hall. A few couples swirled casually. A red gas pump stood tall in front of the café which opened on to the national road. Cars flew past intermittently, their headlights blinding. From the nearby railroad station, behind the gardens which spread from the street, there rolled from time to time the clear and rhythmic sound of signal whistles, soon after which a train, heaving and huffing, would send a shriek into the hush of night.

They sat in the back garden, which bordered the long hall used for dancing. Moths and mosquitos hovered around the bare light bulbs which hung between the eucalyptus branches. Red-and-white checked tablecloths covered the big round liquor tables.

Cici rose and entered the hall to feed the jukebox a fifty-centime piece. He returned to his place to the accompaniment of a hoarse and lazy waltz. He wanted to dance again. Gina declined on the pretext of fatigue. She drank the remainder of her liquor and continued to suck her cigarette with short and frequent puffs.

–Is Mr. Barth coming here to meet you?

–We didn't plan it.

–And you didn't visit her?

–Yes. This evening.

–Her sickness isn't critical, I hope.

–It's hard to say. Spitting blood. But she is better. Her fever is down.

—Too bad. Such a charming girl. She doesn't look after herself. Swimming in the sea certainly doesn't help her.

—It seems so. She must avoid a few things. Her lungs can't bear abuse.

—But then . . . on your trip with the German. She was all right then.

—She didn't fall ill until six days ago.

—The beach is lonely without her. She brought a carefree and playful spirit.—After a moment, he continued in a voice trembling with a touch of sadness not befitting his athletic bearing: —The summer, you know, I look forward to it eagerly. Sometimes a visitor you may like happens to drop in.

A female visitor, you mean?

—No, even a male. Simple enough. Winter is terribly boring here. As soon as I finish work I change my clothes and go to Nice. Almost every evening. To play cards and drink Pernod, I don't care.—He smiled toward the third table and a group of two men and three women, beside which an enormously heavy dog, spotted white and orange, panted. —Sunday,—Cici lowered his voice, —I was with them at Bouche-de-Loup. They needed a third, for the governess. After all, they have to keep her busy while they fuss with their guys. The tall one, see, the fat one, she's the mother. A widow. Worse than the daughter. The young one's husband works in Nice. He doesn't come but once every few days, appears in the evening, and is gone by morning. And here the merry-making continues. After all, they're not ugly, neither the first nor the second. And the guys are brothers, partners to a mother and daughter. Sometimes their father joins them.

—They can be seen often at the beach, with a boy of about four.

—The boy sleeps, as children do. And they make love.

—And you took the nanny yourself.

—She's no less than they, is she? Neither less pretty nor less young. Anyway, it was only during that trip. What do you want? A man gets bored, and feels sorry for someone, too.—He continued: —Do you think I couldn't have them, too? Anyone I want! But this one is more appealing to me. Her position doesn't affect me either way. By the way, I was invited to their house for dinner, but I didn't go.

Gina eyed the third table from time to time, her wondering but disinterested glance going from one face to another in the group, portions of whose loud conversation reached her. She was extremely bored. Several times this evening she had asked herself what demon forced her to agree to join him at the café. She ordered another drink and emptied the glass in a single gulp.

–Are you planning to leave already?–cried Cici when he saw her reach for her handbag.

–One call still walk for a while,–slipped from Gina's lips. She regretted it as she spoke.

Cici wouldn't let her pay. She would offend him by doing so. It was customary for the cavaliers to pay, not the ladies. Furthermore, it was he who had invited her. She had to relinquish her will to his, as it seemed of special importance to him. His face was already flushed with the feelings of injustice.

He suggested a different route, partly on the national road but mostly through garden paths. The evening percolated through one as a light and aromatic beverage. The lungs expanded. The half-moon appeared and disappeared periodically behind the bank of trees to their right, sometimes hanging motionlessly for a moment from an upper branch, casting its cool and peaceful light on the empty street glowing subdued, and on the gardens and vineyards which spread out to their left. There were no houses here, or they were hidden in deep gardens, invisible and far removed from the street. And from there, from the depths of the garden, an angry bark would burst occasionally, in response to their muffled footsteps. Treading casually, silently, sometimes together, sometimes apart, each was given to his own thoughts. The spaces between passing cars lengthened. There were no passersby.

They turned onto the path, dark and narrow, the hedges on each side scratching their legs. Cici put his arm through hers. A slight tremor passed through her at the touch of his arm, but she let him do it. They continued in silence. Only Cici's breath could be heard, heavy and urgent. Gina was uncomfortable. His visible excitement, transmitted to her, started little by little to conquer her being. What happened to her suddenly? A strange languor came over her limbs, paralysis. Walking became difficult for her. An animal stupor coated her insides and cast a fog upon her mind like the numbness following a strong drink. The pressure of a muscular arm was vaguely felt, as though distant from the limits of her existence. She saw, and didn't see, the winding path strewn with rocks. She was walking like a sleepwalker.

They reached a small clearing. The narrow stream nearby sent its timid rush into the stillness. In a remote corner of Gina's soul, a feeling that she had always walked this path, and would continue along it until the end of her days, came upon her, mingled with the fragile rush of the stream, the fragrant night, and even the strange man. As if all her past life and the possibility for future life had been pumped out of her.

Unknowingly, she sank to the slope of the riverbank, with Cici outstretched at her feet, whispering with boiling breath, incoherent words. No, Gina didn't understand a thing. She only sensed her body burning, as if touched by fever. And Cici's scalding, biting kisses on her hands, on her bare arms, on her neck, on her face. In these kisses was the stomping of a mad, murderous animal. Had she wanted to protest, she would not have been able. And had he wanted to kill her, she would not have protested. She had no control of herself whatsoever. Indistinctly, she felt something happening in her body, which was terrible and caused killing pleasure—but all as if in a nightmare, a decree which cannot be changed and against which one cannot rebel.

Later, they found themselves walking again between the hedge and bramble along the narrow path. Gina hung on Cici's arm, one hand cupped between his broad, calloused palms. From time to time he bent and touched his ardent lips to the back of this hand, slender and smooth as velvet, with piety, as if it were a holy object. He would give his life for her, for the precious creature who was walking beside him. He had never wished for such joy, nor could he even have imagined it in a dream. How could he prove to her that his life was given to her, and that it was hers to do with as she pleased? A fleeting thought flashed through his mind, whether he should not throw himself into the water in front of her.

But Gina walked silently beside him, lurching as if sick with wine. Something strange and terrible had pierced her life, something irreversible which would now remain in her forever. Everything else from this point on would lose significance relative to it. But could anyone be responsible for it but herself? It was nothing but a hidden side of her being, hidden even to herself, that all of a sudden was revealed by external circumstances. It wasn't merely the event that was important here, for it would be possible to erase it or cancel it by forgetting. But the fact that she was capable of this for no reason, simply because the evening was beautiful, the path quiet, and by chance a man beside her. It was enough to drive one mad. And she didn't even have the right to be upset with the man next to her, and vent her anger. Why? Why should he let this opportunity pass? He does love her! No, there is no one to blame but herself! What foolishness on her part, what stupidity, and how purposeless! She could spit into her own face!

She freed herself with such suddenness from his arm that he stopped in his path and turned his wondering face to her. They were approaching the shore now, and the first houses of the village, with the darkness thinning. They weren't far away from the pension. In a tone that would not accept objection, she ordered: –Now leave me! I am going alone.

Hurriedly, she pulled her hand away as he bent to kiss her. She left him stunned, and disappeared with rapid footsteps, as if running away, without turning her head back.

Barth was already home, preparing for sleep. It was apparent that he had come in only a few minutes before her. It was about half-past twelve. The hoarse strains of the Gramophone still burst from Stephano's roof, and occasionally a loud, licentious laugh which Gina recognized as Latzi's. She was surprised, though, since only a moment ago, as she was passing Stephano's house, she had no sense of the music or the clamor of his guests. But it really didn't matter to her. She took off her dress and slip and stood over the basin by the door to wash herself with cold water. She rubbed her sun-browned body with a large rust-colored sponge. The outline of her bathing suit marked her body like a pale white tattoo. She rubbed with a certain anger, as though to scour some unseen stain. She didn't say a word. Barth undressed while smoking a cigarette. Then, cautiously, he climbed on the bed, stood to his full height, and slapped the wall where it joined the ceiling. "Damn!" he said to himself. "Got away." Lean, erect, he stood on the bed and combed the emptiness of the room. No, the mosquito had slipped away! After the lights were turned out, on the verge of sleep, then the shrill, vengeful whine would be heard very near to the ear, the bite jarring him abruptly into angry wakefulness. There was no choice but resignation. He climbed down from the bed and approached Gina as she was drying herself. He put his arm around her waist.

–Why so quiet, little Gin?

Gina didn't answer. After a moment: –How is she?

–Her fever went up again. I stopped by the café,–he added. –I thought I'd find you there.

–I went earlier, but got bored and went for a walk. Were you there all along?

–Of course not. I left at ten and wandered around the streets.

–And why didn't you come earlier to the café?–she added with concealed anger.

–Earlier? I didn't want to interrupt,–he joked, –as you were in the company of a cavalier.

Gina slid her blue nightgown over her head. Not without a hint of contempt, she thought bitterly to herself: "Yes, yes, my friend, in the company of a cavalier." As she neared the bed she said: –It would have been better if you had disturbed us.

And she lay down.

Her unusual tone of voice escaped Barth. He poured himself a glass of water and emptied it in a single gulp. He asked if she wanted to read a bit. No, she didn't want to read. He turned out the light and opened the door to the balcony. The sound of voices and laughter rushed into the room at once, louder, clearer, as if from the balcony itself. Through the sounds could be heard the tail end of Jejette's shrill laugh. Truncated, grating, in which there was an annoyingly immature impudence. In front of Gina an image of her, full-bosomed, flashed suddenly, and an unpleasant feeling came up in her. She lay on her back, close to the wall, her two hands away from her body, this body which seemed strange to her, and to which her intimate attachment was cut. This body of hers was different now, incomprehensible, not the same as yesterday. It aroused fear and nausea in her. An alien element was newly revealed, and despicable. Always unknown to her, it lay latent and ready to subjugate her at any time. She lay motionless, afraid to move lest she touch this body, silent and heavy. If only she could vomit. Simply. Maybe then she could relieve her disgust. She was grateful to Barth for lingering on the balcony. He stood leaning against the railing, his head turned toward Stephano's roof. She could distinguish his dark silhouette. If only he would remain standing thus forever! She could not bear his closeness now, his touch, as she could not bear her own. "Ah! You son of a bitch! Ha, ha, ha!" Stephano's drunken roar could be heard, exultant. It was followed by a moment of silence during which a straining ear could distinguish the delicate lapping of the sea as it rhythmically slapped the shore. Gina's body burned feverishly. She pushed away the sheet that covered her. If only it were possible to sleep, and forget everything for a few hours! But there was no hope that she would soon fall asleep.

Barth entered the room and lay down beside her. Quietly she rolled to the wall so as not to arouse his notice. But he moved his body close to her, pressing against her full-length, his lips seeking hers in the darkness. –You're not sleeping, Gin my dear.

Gina recoiled, then sat up. –Oh, it's unbearably warm . . . why don't we go for a breath of fresh air, or up to Stephano's?

–Now? At this hour?

–So what! I must . . . if not I'll toss awake until morning. I feel it. If you're too tired, I'll go alone.

—Perhaps not . . . try washing with cold water again.

Gina jumped out of bed.

—Of course I won't let you go alone at this hour.

On Stephano's roof, it wasn't yet late at all. Jubilant spirits prevailed. The Japanese fellow and the interpreter stood entangled in each other's arms between two rows of tables that ran along the length of the roof. Marionettelike, they offered each other loud and ringing kisses while Jejette stood by with her two clenched fists planted on her hips, resembling an hourglass. She laughed and followed them with her eyes as a referee on a playing field. Latzi bowed to the Japanese fellow's girl and struck his fist to his chest, exclaiming in a rusty voice: "Me! . . . Believe me, madam, no on else but me!" then sank back exhausted onto a chair, covering his face with both hands. Suzi sat in a chair like a shapeless bundle, laughing silently to herself, not looking at anyone.

—Here they are! You son of a bitch! Ha, ha, ha!—Stephano greeted them. —Jejette!

The two wrestlers separated and set their stupid eyes on the two guests.

Gina drank cognac, one glass, then another. That beastly event still lurked in a corner of her soul, ready to pounce and ambush her. She ordered another drink. —No, I can't right now,—she answered the interpreter curtly when he asked her to dance. He turned around, bumping into Jejette, and planted a loud, sucking kiss on her mouth, to everyone's amusement.

—What? My girl! Son of a . . . my daughter! An immature girl?! I'll show you!—Stephano cried.

Latzi jumped between them: —Stop! Don't you understand a joke?! Here, we are your guests!

—Ah, you're right, ha, ha, ha! Guests! Jejette, shame! Two bottles of rosé! Two! It's on me!

Gina declined the invitation to join the group. She remained seated. The cognac had eased the gnawing in her heart, but a feeling of sadness had settled in her, and a yearning for another place, undefined, different, and far from here. Mechanically she pulled her lipstick and mirror from her handbag and glossed her lips. The moon was hung overhead, from nothing, it seemed. A dull breeze, saturated with the vapors of drunkenness, enveloped this roof, though it seemed incompatible with the purity overhead and the moon's fragile smile.

Barth sat sullenly, legs crossed, waiting for Gina to rise. He didn't drink much. He didn't like to drink on command, without any inner need. What foul spirit had possessed her suddenly? What woman rises at midnight, dresses, and dashes to drink cognac at Stephano's? And among such drunk and despicable people whom he knows she cannot bear! Who can fathom a woman's heart? This behavior—one should add it to a list of woman's deeds which apparently are not defined by the laws of cause and effect and which no logic could analyze . . . Barth turned and watched Gina sitting motionlessly, staring toward the boisterous group nearby. She didn't look at them, but rather gazed through them, tight-lipped as though holding back some bit of speech so that it wouldn't escape. His heart soured. Despite the arrogance of her profile, there was something afflicted in her sitting as she was. It called to mind another night, on a bench, by a street light in the city park. They had met only recently, and their relationship had not yet developed the stability born of mutual compatibility, nor had they undergone the necessary pruning and trimming of irregularities of character. It was a tremor straining gingerly inside them, a timid, uncertain joy which flickered like a flame in the wind. Beyond a trellis, the click-clack of the late, empty tram could be heard as it rattled back and forth—an external detail engraved in his memory. After a concert and a stop in a café, they had sat there, in the clear night, on the way to her house. Why was she suddenly given to dark thoughts, strange thoughts, as now, which cast a pall between himself and her? She had remained in this self-imposed imprisonment for several days, without noticeably changing her behavior toward him. He had felt suddenly cast aside, into an empty world, without value.

–Aren't you ready to come back, Gin?

She recoiled from the touch of his hand and looked at him strangely. She mumbled through an absent and excruciating half-smile, more to herself than to him: –Yes. I suppose so.

He parked his car not far from the pension and came out in his bathing suit, ready to swim. The morning was still young, though already anointed with molten sunlight. The calm sea, and the dewy homes and gardens facing it, were covered with a dreamlike chiffon. The fishermen's wives, under broad straw hats, were already busy mending their nets on the shore clear of bathers. Near them, dark and dirty, half-naked children romped in the gravel. Simplicity, naturalness, as it has been for generations, since the ascent of humanity, just so, unaffected by the passage of time. For a moment, Kraft felt very near the quintessence of existence. An unmuddied joy of life washed him all at once. Polite and friendly, he greeted the fishermen's wives and went to lie on the gravel. Diagonally opposite him, Madam Stephano was already at the front of her store. She was hidden beneath his wispy hair, and her feet shone white in tattered cloth shoes. Shading her eyes with one hand, she looked along the shore as though searching.

–Mar-ti-no!–she called in a dry and broken voice which echoed all the way up. –Mar-ti-no! Come-to-wash!

Kraft turned his gaze toward Barth and Gina's house. If only a man could express himself over a distance, without language, as though through some wireless soul-to-soul telegram! Here you are, for example, you want to see her at this moment, yearning with every bone in your body—and she, it seems, not even one nerve of her is moved because of it. She will come, for sure, but in another hour or two, as she will. She'll be surprised to find you here. You rushed here like a released arrow in vain.

The scratch of approaching footsteps startled him. With faint hopes, he turned his head. –You're up early!

Barth smiled broadly and extended his hand: –It's been several days since you were last here.

–What about you? How is Gina?

–Gina?–Barth sat beside him on the gravel. –She's been in a terrible mood. Two days already. Maybe you could cheer her up a little.

–Me? Why don't you undress?

–I have to go and visit Marcelle first.

–She's not up yet?

–Still weak. She has to stay in bed another few days,–and added: –Charming girl, don't you think?

–Hmm. Yes.

They smoked in silence. A light northerly wind sent a shiver across the surface of the sea. Barth rose. –I must go. Will you be here all day?

–I don't know. We'll see.

Kraft walked out to his car to get a book, then returned and stretched out close to the water. He hadn't read more than a few pages before Gina appeared. He jumped up and greeted her with unconcealed delight. Gina spread her towel on the gravel and sat down. She reached for the book. –May I see?–She glanced at the lemon cover, flipped briefly through the pages, and returned the book to its place. Kraft watched her studiously. Her face seemed to him slightly downcast.

Latzi emerged from the pension equipped with his paints and a stretched canvas. He greeted them from afar and walked toward

Bouche-de-Loup. Yet after a few steps, he stopped by Stephano's house and set up his easel.

–I'll probably return to Munich soon.

–What's the hurry?–Gina, on her back, played with the handle of her umbrella. Her expression was completely relaxed.

–Urgent business.

–I was sure you didn't have any business. It seems you told me so once.

–I have a wife.

–And she can't come here?

–No, she can't.–He smiled bitterly to himself, and added: –We are about to divorce.–He reached for a leather cigarette case. After a slight pause: –Will we see each other again, madam?

–I don't know. I think not.

–Pity.–After a moment he repeated as if to himself: –Great pity.

Gina suddenly felt sorry for him, for no apparent reason other than that to her he seemed so miserable. She gazed at him warmly, soothingly. Then she looked out to the smooth sea at her feet and to a tiny boat that receded to a point on the horizon. Kraft grabbed a handful of gravel and with absentminded application scattered it. A ship with black sails appeared as though sketched on the azure horizon. –Here, look!– pointed Gina.–It looks as if it rose from the depths of eternal night. The ship stood motionless and was disappearing in front of them, motionlessly. The smaller boat also could not be seen now. The sea still lolled silently, smooth and bare.

–This summer,–he whispered, –I'll think of it for a long time.–He kept his eyes on her and added: –Will you let me write you sometime?

–What's the point?

With resignation he said: –You're right, actually.

Kraft was quiet. From the side, he watched her as if to engrave her image deep in his memory. His heart shriveled at the thought that he would no more see her charming face, her youthful lips exultant with an unsatiated thirst for living, her omniscient chin, sharply rounded, her eyes, dark as wine, whose gaze pierced without damaging, the clear feminine forehead crowned with thick hair, dark chestnut, and wavy. –Would you like to join me on another trip before I leave?

–When are you leaving?

–In about three days.

–I don't think I'll be able to.

She sat up. She was hot. They entered and swam shoulder to shoulder in the blue water, cool and rejuvenating. It momentarily washed away any bitterness and poured a simple animal exuberance into them. Nowhere was any soul to be seen. Just the two of them in the breadth of an infinite ocean. They shared an unspoken feeling of mingling with the innocence of nature and its lofty wisdom.

After returning to the shore, Gina smiled at Kraft, friendly. Through her tanned face, a fresh paleness filtered, her eyes shone, pure and lustrous. They were back lying on the coarse gravel, smoking silently as the sun dried their skin.

Suzi came and stretched out nearby. But Latzi continued to stand and paint by Stephano's store while Stephano and his brood stood around him in a semicircular array. And this summer morning was slowly and silently poured back into the ocean of time, as thousands of mornings before it, a morning embroidered with strands of orange sun, blue sea, green gardens, and transparent silence, and secret threads which united, yet didn't unite, this couple.

–The Japanese fellow hasn't been here today yet?–Suzi called.

Gina shook her head.

Kraft rose to say he was returning to Nice. With a slightly bashful smile, he added: –Sometimes, a man may take his own life, for the fear of dying.–He bent and kissed her hand. –Say good-bye to Barth.

–Won't you stop by another time before you leave?

–Probably not.

He went to the car. He honked, two, three times, and without turning his head, was off in the blast of his engine. The cloud of white dust that gathered along the road sank slowly back to the ground.

Toward evening the fishermen were still drifting on the surface of the darkening sea; the aromas of dinner had begun to leave the streets of the village. The broken sound of a trumpet could be heard along the main street. In front of Stephano's, there stood a small, slender man dressed in a threadbare tuxedo, a black tie, and tattered shoes white with dust. He held a short trumpet to his lips. Shuffling on her toes, Madam Bremon walked to the garden gate: –The Italian, and his two daughters,–she exclaimed mockingly.

Gina finished eating a slice of watermelon, cleared the table, and went out to relax on the balcony armchair. Barth sat beside her on a chair. She lay back deep in reverie. Lately, she hadn't said more to Barth than what was required by day-to-day necessity. To Barth, she seemed changed somehow. In vain he sought the reason. Time and again he received answers to his questions which revealed nothing to him, until he gave up asking. Yet, he consoled himself, in time her sullen mood would leave her and all would be restored to normal.

Madam Bremon took a chair from the room and sat with them, arms crossed: –Oh! I'm so tired. All day in the boiling sun!–Her hair, scattered with gray, was still thick and curly. It was gathered at the back of her neck in a bun the size of a fist. Bright eyes and a pleasant smile animated her wrinkled face.

She was free for a leisurely chat: –Next week my daughter will return from the mountains. She'll look after Didi herself.

Her sons were already married, save one, who had joined the army and remembered her with an occasional picture postcard from Indochina. The rest of her children settled in Saint-Laurent-sur-Var, six kilometers from here. And herself? As long as she still had strength, she would never make herself a burden to anyone! Above all, she liked to stand on her own two feet. She had always earned a living with her own hands. Years ago, when she was still living with her husband, she had sold flowers. Early every morning she would deliver flowers to Nice, Monaco, Monte Carlo, because her husband, you should know, never lifted a finger. He was always lazy. He would wake up in the morning, pick up his rifle, and go hunting. Hunting was his passion. He would wander around all day, devil knows where, and return for his soup in the evening. Once in a while, he brought a jackrabbit or hare, though usually he brought nothing at all. When he finished his meal, he would light up his pipe and while away the evening in a bar. All the worries were hers alone. When the babies had grown, she said to him: That's it, my friend! Either you go to work, or we separate! And then she moved here.

And her husband? He went hunting, as before, and was a burden to her eldest son, the one who visited her Sunday with his children. Maybe you think he was a weak man? If only you had seen him! Big and strong! You'd put him at thirty-five, no more! Unlike her, whose drudgery had prematurely aged her body. What do you expect, with five children! Feed them, raise them, marry them off, all by a widow . . . it was as though she were a widow.

–And you daughter married Mr. Larouette after you moved here?– Barth inquired.

No, she had married before. Ten years ago. She was nineteen at the time. Madam Bremon had objected at first, even though he was wealthy. The old hag owns everything, you should know. The house they live in and its huge garden. The house next door, rented to the Japanese man on the first floor. All hers, along with huge tracts of land and the vineyard. And apart from that, plenty of cash in the banks. And being an only child, it is all his to inherit. And he has a good position, too, in the wine and oil firm. So why did she object to the match? Because of that stingy and shifty old hag. It's well known in this area, certainly within a hundred-kilometer radius. They, members of the Bremon family, are poor, but they know how to behave. They know what is decent and proper. There is even a limit to miserliness, after all! But her daughter insisted. She wanted only him. The children loved each other. Finally, she gave her permission. And she's not sorry. Her daughter is happy with him. He adores her like the apple of his eye. He even treats her, Madam Bremon, with great respect. And friendly relations prevail between them. You can plainly see! He provides her with wine and oil the year around, though she doesn't need any, thank God! For years she has done the washing for the pension, and she has all that she needs, but it is a sign of dedication on his part. As she always says: a man who loves his wife, loves his mother-in-law.

And his mother? She's better off not seeing her! She's very careful not to run across her, but she always sends to call for her, for one errand or another. Have you ever seen such a stinking creature?! She weighs over a hundred kilo and never budges!

–But must you go when she calls for you?

–Must! Of course not! No one can force me! Yet I don't want to get on her bad side! It's hell! She might make up the worst lies and make your name dirt, you have no idea what that woman is capable of, the old hag! I want peace. There was a time when we didn't even exchange greetings, two uninterrupted years. Then once she sent for me and I went. What do you expect? My own daughter lives in her house, after all. I can't lock myself out forever! But I'll avoid her door if I can help it.

The balcony was already full of darkness. Gina rose.

–We're going out for a bit?!

As they passed Stephano's, the storekeeper called from the door: –Aren't you coming up? We have a show today.

There was no way out.

There were about two dozen townsmen at the tables, some of them with their wives. Stephano, his sleeves rolled up, was having a drink with one group, laughing and roaring in his coarse voice. Jejette was serving.

The Italian in the tuxedo was trying hard to tune his violin, letting out stray and solitary notes. Two undeveloped girls, ages eight and ten, sat motionlessly at a nearby table, wearing pink dresses, short and bell-shaped. Pink ribbons, tied like huge butterflies, were knotted in their wispy hair. Their scrawny legs were clad in knee socks, white once, and sandals coated with yesterday's mud and dust. Sunk in blatant poverty, they sat courteously, with forced seriousness, waiting their turn, looking blankly ahead. Overhead, musty stars were beginning to flicker.

Gina and Barth chose the outermost table, close to the door. Cici appeared immediately. He shook the Italian's hand and approached them. —I saw you coming up.

Gina's face darkened momentarily.

—You know him?—inquired Barth.

Cici sat down. —He has a tubercular wife and nine children each smaller than the other. They came from Italy eight months ago. He looked long, but couldn't find a job. Now he goes from door to door with his daughters and brings home a few sous. If you could only see the shack they live in! Not fit for a dog.

The Italian began to play the violin, his young girls standing close by, stiff as rods, singing an Italian children's song in thin, timorous voices. The song and accompaniment were so pathetically ridiculous, so annoyingly incompetent, that Gina and Barth averted their eyes in embarrassment. It was a caricature which aroused disgust and nausea. Never before had they heard anything like it. Afterward, they passed around a small bowl. After the collection, the father began a solo from *Carmen*, his face cast like a wax mask, motionless and lacking any life expression. No, Barth would never again go to the opera to hear *Carmen*! Afterward, the two girls sang a duet, their father conducting them with his outstretched finger.

The Japanese fellow arrived with his girlfriend. Stephano called to them, waving his hand. One of the young girls passed around the collection dish once again. She then stripped off her pink dress, remaining in flesh-colored underwear. She lifted a small box from under a table. It was open at both ends. She placed it on a faded red carpet that her father had unrolled on the floor. Bending and twisting her head through her legs, she wriggled back and forth through the open box. Stephano clapped his hands, roaring with laughter. She squeezed herself into the box again, this time with her sister rolling her to and fro across the carpet, their father supervising the job. At the end of this number, there was an intermission. The Italian ordered coffee for his daughters. They drank it reluctantly, tired, pale, and sleepy.

When Barth turned to the next table and got involved in a conversation with the Japanese fellow and his friend, Cici found the moment to whisper: —It's been a few days. I haven't been able to speak with you. You're avoiding me.

—You are mistaken. I have nothing to talk with you about.

—But, that night . . . —Cici whispered passionately.

—What?! Don't you dare, do you hear!!!—Her face turned red. She trembled with restrained fury.

—But this is not a game, lady,—and then he added, conciliatory: —If only you knew my heart!

—Enough! I don't want to hear anything! Not even another word!

Cici turned pale. Through his teeth he hissed: —I'm not a toy, madam! I don't let anyone use me as they need me and throw me away afterward! Watch yourself!

—Ha, ha, ha!—She laughed in his face. And then she said: —You have spoken to me for the last time!—She turned her face away from him.

Mechanically he began to fidget with his empty glass. Pale, thin-lipped, his broad mouth sealed as though with nails. He parted his lips slightly, and through the crack, his even teeth sparkled white.

At that moment, Stephano's drunken roar could be heard above the clamor of the guests: —That's enough! I won't allow any more! You son of a bitch!

All heads turned at once toward him. He stood opposite the startled Italian, whose violin already rested on his shoulder, ready to play, and thundered: —The concert is over! I won't permit it! *Finito!*

Cici rose and marched heavily, pale and square, and stood before Stephano. Suddenly there was silence. The starry night was cool on the roof tonight, and breathless. Cici said quietly, ominously: —Let the people finish! Let the people earn their living!

—What? A beggar? A bum? Are you giving me orders in my house?!—And a dull, heavy blow landed on his head.

In an instant, a knife flashed. Stephano clutched his left side with both hands. A dark spot was spreading across his light shirt. As he fell to the floor, he screamed: —He killed me! He murdered me! Son of a—

Cici bolted through the cluster of tables and disappeared. The voice of a woman broke into a whimper. Jejette screamed.

Barth and Gina took advantage of the confusion and slipped downstairs. When they turned into their house's garden after an hour's walk, a figure, veiled in shadow, emerged from a wall and came toward them.

Cici put a finger to his lips, signifying silence, and whispered: −I just wanted to say good-bye. I'm escaping tonight.

Gina extended her hand, and he kissed it. Then, silently, he pressed Barth's hand, and slipped away.

−Why, for God's sake? Isn't there any other way?−He sat on the edge of the bed, his feet dangling above the floor. He held his head in his two hands and remained frozen for a while. The evening twilight filtered quietly through the door open onto the balcony, mingled with vague, distant, and isolated cries. A gentle breeze blew from time to time. Beyond the few treetops in front of the balcony, the sea could be seen, a shudder racing across its surface.

Gina took a bundle of dresses from the closet and placed them over a chair. Two leather suitcases lay open on the floor.

Barth lifted his head again and followed her deliberate movements. He had a feeling he would never see her again. In one fell swoop, everything was suddenly unimportant and superfluous. For him now, there was no reason to go back to Paris if only to get up early each morning to get to work on time at the engineering office—no reason to work, or to rest.

−Emotional crisis . . . is there no other way to overcome it?−He felt his words were in vain, and that no earthly power could prevent her from enacting her decision. Nevertheless, he continued to speak, if only from the intensity of his desperation.

−If you must be alone for a time, it could be arranged so that no one would suffer . . . We could rent a room in Paris. Or maybe it is because of Marcelle? . . .

She stopped packing for a moment, and set her eyes on him. −Marcelle?

−Nonsense, of course!

−I know.−And after a second: −All this is not directed against you, Barth. My feelings for you haven't changed.

−Then why this? Why? What happened suddenly? Don't you have any faith in me?

−Do you want me to lie to you? I have never lied to you. Do you think that I know why? I can't even explain this to myself, except that it is directed against me . . . just me. I feel that we must stop. There is no other choice. All week, I have struggled in vain with this feeling.

She continued folding her dresses, packing them meticulously in the suitcases, one after the other. The room's void was filled with strangeness. The attraction that had developed over the past weeks, to these four walls, to the furniture, to every detail of this room, vanished at once, as if it had never been. Gina herself, who stood packing her bags with clothes and things, even she was now a stranger. There was no longer any bridge to her.

As if thinking aloud, Barth spoke, in a warm voice, seething with an ocean of sadness: –Didn't I sense these last days that something was about to happen? Every minute was filled with that certainty. And you? You were silent. As though I didn't deserve being spoken to? The two of us together, maybe we could have found a solution. I knew you were suffering. If we had examined together the reason, openly, maybe it could have been erased.

Outside it was darkening. Shadows had begun gathering in the corners of the room. Not far away, someone's loud and intermittent laughter could be heard. "It's not Latzi," Barth said trivially. He sat frozen in the same position, a sickly fever infiltrating his bowels. He could feel his rapid, agitated heartbeat.

She closed the balcony door and switched on the light. As she passed him, she slipped her hand through his tousled hair, toward the nape of his neck. Then she continued packing. Something heavy spread through the room, making the air dense and unfit to breathe.

–And why necessarily tomorrow, Gina? Couldn't you wait a few more days?

–You're tearing my heart.

–And you yourself? Look, Gin, think it over again. You love the sea. We'll finish our time here, then you can see. Maybe you're afraid your resolve will weaken meanwhile? If it does—then your decision is unnecessary! It just isn't possible to destroy the lives of two people like this! Just in caprice!

Gina stood erect, not doing anything, her arms hanging limply at her sides. Her eyes shone feverishly, seeming larger, and encircled by dark rings. Her lips looked somehow used now. –I didn't say I wouldn't come back.

–I might come back–she repeated more for herself to hear than for him. She stooped over her suitcases again.

–If only I knew it would last a month, three months, half a year!–He rose and walked to the balcony door. Standing there, he faced the room. Silently, he followed her movements. From outside, the muffled sounds of a piano could be heard, probably from a nearby pension. And this music, it also was no more familiar, a part of the necklace of luminous days and nights colored by sun and moon. On the contrary: it was alienating, annoying, like a strange element which did not belong here. Certainly now was not the time for an evening's light and pleasant melancholy to spill into the soul unconsciously, and to spread as the distant and diffuse scent of violets. Now, in this void, lay the scattered fragments of something irreversibly shattered, neither his nor Gina's fault, rather by the cruelty of fate—orphaned, gnawing, and piercing to tears. The six weeks thay had spent here was time to mold bright and refreshing memories. It had become clear to them both that the time hadn't all been entirely pleasant, on the contrary, had been filthy, in the stupefying heat, plagued with mosquitos, even boredom, yes, simple boredom, and that it will leave bitterness because of its ending, which may cast its shadow backward. This place had robbed him of Gina without his knowing why. And now, there was no recourse.

He stood leaning against the door, his eyes set on Gina with a hollow and unseeing gaze. After she shut one of the suitcases, she stretched and sat herself in a chair. She would do the rest early tomorrow. She was tired.

He sat beside her. He took her hand and stroked it. Not a sound entered from outside now. Silence enveloped them. Had it not been for the two suitcases in the center of the room declaring the certain ruin of a stable and regular life, one might think that nothing had changed, that this evening's tranquillity mingling with two silent people was not different at all from similar evenings which had preceded it in this room or in another.

As he wrapped his arm around her waist to draw her closer, he sensed her slight resistance. He let her go.

–Let's go out for a bit.

He rose without a word.

In the café near the Japanese house, they sat alone on the covered veranda, dark and mosquito-ridden, whose screen walls were covered with climbing tendrils which bore bunches of green, unripe berries. Barth was drinking a mixture of wine and cognac, his face increasingly flushed. He didn't speak. From time to time he glanced opposite him, to Gina, and opened his mouth as if to speak, though he didn't say a word.

–Shall we ruin this evening with drunkenness?

He set glassy eyes on her, his face a strangely tragic mask. After a

moment, he replied hoarsely: —I had no idea you could be so cruel.—
Suddenly, as if to himself, he added: —Maybe there is another man
here . . .

—Why the probing? If that were so, would I have kept it from you? In
spite of everything, I regard you as a true friend. Maybe someday I'll be
able to talk about it. When I understand myself better . . . If I could
say anything now it would certainly come out coarse, and false. One's
deeds—they aren't always self-explanatory . . . Let me first try and
resolve this on my own, for clarity. One thing I can tell you: my feeling
of respect for my own body has been shaken. The reason? It might be
small or insignificant . . . but as long as I cannot live with it, I cannot
live with you . . .

—Words! Sophistry!—a caustic outburst, unlike him. And in a different voice, pleading: —Tell me, Gin, do you want me to uproot you from
my heart? Yes?

—I would be very miserable.

They both remained silent. His eyes cast down on the table, Barth
drank with mute obstinacy.

Marcelle appeared, wearing a woolen sweater, her face sunken and
pale through her tan. She smiled slightly, as if ashamed of her apparent
weariness. Silently, Barth extended his hand to her, and returned his
gaze to the table.

—I'm happy to see you out and around,—Gina said courteously to her.

—I've been out since yesterday.—And with another slight smile: —I
have no intention of succumbing.

—No. Don't do it. But it might be better to take precautions in the
evenings. The night is cool.

—The worst of it is that the doctor explicitly forbad me to bathe in the
sea.

—You've bathed enough, I would think. Next summer I'm sure you'll
be allowed to again.

—Next summer . . .

To Gina, it seemed that Marcelle had matured, had become more of
a woman than she had been before her illness. It was as if she had caught
a glimpse of the mystery of life and death. All at once she felt closer to
her, deeply close, unconditionally. —I'm leaving here tomorrow,—
slipped out of her mouth.

—By yourself?

—By myself,—and added immediately: —I must travel to my parents
in Vienna.

Barth, like an echo, repeated: –Yes. Must travel to Vienna. What will you have, Marcelle? Hey, you?–he thrust his voice into the void of the hall. –A hot glass of milk for Mademoiselle Marcelle!

–And now it is up to you to amuse him in his widowhood,–Gina joked.

–I'll do what I can, madam, as long as he will agree to be consoled by me.

They chatted for a while, idle chat, without Barth's participation. The surrounding silence mingled with the dull murmur of the sea. When Marcelle rose to leave, they accompanied her out.

The train would arrive at any moment. They stood silently on the platform. They had nothing to say to each other because they had too much to say to each other. Barth's knees and thighs throbbed with tremendous fatigue as though all strength had been sapped from them. A painful void filled his chest. The train had not yet arrived, but it would not be late, not late. There was no hope for some unexpected mishap, a broken track, for example, which might cause delay. Maybe then she would abandon her journey entirely . . . Yet on the other hand, Barth hoped it would hurry, if only to hasten the end of the ending. Such waiting was difficult to bear. He poked a cigarette between his lips, forgetting to light it. Passengers, carrying woolen blankets on their arms, were standing next to fancy suitcases and trunks, or pacing back and forth along the platform. The glass foyer was filled with a quiet and stubborn heat. Porters were pushing their metal dollies laden with piles of luggage. On the third track, a single engine passed with a shriek and a column of thick and opaque smoke. Barth began to pace unconsciously and without direction, then changed his mind and returned to Gina. She leaned against his body and touched her lips to his cheek. She took his hand between her two burning palms and stroked it slowly, silently. Why is life such that a single stone could land and cause such desolation, without one ever knowing from whose hand it had been cast? Who was to blame? Soon the train would come, and she would journey from here, never to return. Soon something would be torn irreparably in her heart. And after a time, even if she did return and renew her life, she would still be unable to mend this tear, the tear of the separation which was about to begin in a few minutes. She would never to able to pick up where she stopped, at that exact place.

The train approached, like a giant beast with heaving breath. A blast of heat was felt as the engine passed. It lurched to a stop and passengers clamored to their places. Barth carried the hand luggage. "It will stop for fifteen minutes. I'll go buy some more fruit." He disappeared, and returned immediately with a paper bag filled with large peaches.

Again they stood on the platform, by the car stairs now, not knowing what to say to each other. Barth remembered the cigarette dangling coldly from his lips, and struck a match. Indistinctly, an official announced the garbled names of stops and destinations no one could understand. Gina would pass through all of these jumbled stations during the night, and the train would distance her further and further. It would not be difficult to climb on a train such as this one afternoon, and pass through days and nights and garbled stops to reach her—but nevertheless you will never board and never arrive. From now on you have no emotional possibility of doing so. He set his eyes on her and saw that she was quite pale, and veiled in sadness. Her eyes were sunk in their sockets. He would have screamed to her: "Why, Gin, why and for what?!" But the words died on his lips. Then he clasped her like a wild animal and pressed her to his chest, almost crushing her. He saw tears welling in her eyes, though they never fell. "En voiture!" cried the conductor. A whistle shrieked. She pulled herself from his arms and jumped onto the train. "Don't think badly of me, 'Dolph, and forgive me!" The train lurched forward. Gina leaned out the open window and waved her handkerchief. For a long while, she could distinguish his figure, standing still, like a lifeless post, head tilted slightly, holding his hat high and motionless.—

Paris, 1932

THE
HILL OF EVIL
COUNSEL

BY AMOS OZ

translated by Nicholas de Lange

1

IT WAS DARK. In the dark a woman said: I'm not afraid. A man replied: Oh, yes, you are. Another man said: Quiet.

Then dim lights came on at either side of the stage, the curtains parted, and all was quiet.

In May 1946, one year after the Allied victory, the Jewish Agency mounted a great celebration in the Edison Cinema. The walls were draped with the flags of Great Britain and the Zionist Movement. Vases of gladioli stood on the front of the stage. And a banner carried a quotation from the Bible: PEACE BE WITHIN THY WALLS AND PROSPERITY WITHIN THY PALACES.

The British Governor of Jerusalem strode up to the stage with a military gait and delivered a short address, in the course of which he cracked a subtle joke and read some lines of Byron. He was followed by the Zionist leader Moshe Shertok, who expressed in English and Hebrew the feelings of the Jewish community. In the corners of the auditorium, on either side of the stage, and by all the doors stood British soldiers wearing red berets and carrying submachine guns, to guard against the Underground. In the dress circle could be discerned the stiffly seated figure of the High Commissioner, Sir Alan Cunningham, with a small party of ladies and army officers. The ladies were holding opera glasses. A choir of pioneers in blue shirts sang some work songs. The songs were Russian, and, like the audience, they were wistful, rather than happy.

After the singing there was a film of Montgomery's tanks advancing across the Western Desert. The tanks raised columns of dust, crushed trenches and barbed-wire fences under their tracks, and stabbed the gray desert sky with their antennas. The auditorium was filled with the thunder of guns and the noise of marching songs.

In the middle of the film, there was a slight disturbance in the dress circle.

The film stopped suddenly. The lights came on. A voice was raised in a reproach or a curt command: Is there a doctor in the house?

In row 29, Father immediately got to his feet. He fastened the top button of his white shirt, whispered to Hillel to take care of Mother and keep her calm until things were sorted out, and, like a man plunging into a burning building at the risk of his life, turned and pushed his way to the staircase.

It transpired that Lady Bromley, the High Commissioner's sister-in-law, had been taken suddenly faint.

She was wearing a long white dress, and her face, too, was white. Father hurriedly introduced himself to the heads of the administration and proceeded to lay her limp arm across his shoulders. Like a gentle knight carrying a sleeping beauty, he helped Lady Bromley to the ladies' powder room. He seated her on an upholstered stool and handed her a glass of cold water. Three high-ranking British officials in evening dress hurried after him, stood in a semicircle around the patient, and supported her head as she took a single, painful sip. An elderly wing commander in uniform extracted her fan from her white evening bag, opened it carefully, and fanned her face.

Her Ladyship opened her eyes wearily. She stared almost ironically for a moment at all the men who were bustling around her. She was angular and wizened, and with her pursed lips, her pointed nose, and her permanent sardonic scowl, she looked like some thirsty bird.

"Well, doctor," the wing commander addressed Father in acid tones, "what do you think?"

Father hesitated, apologized twice, and suddenly made up his mind. He leaned over, and with his fine, sensitive fingers he undid the laces of the tight corset. Lady Bromley felt immediately better. Her shriveled hand, which resembled a chicken leg, straightened the hem of the dress. A crease appeared in the tightly closed mouth, a kind of cracked smile. She crossed her old legs, and her voice when she spoke was tinny and piercing.

"It's just the climate."

"Ma'am—" one of the officials began politely.

But Lady Bromley was no longer with him. She turned impatiently to Father:

"Young man, would you be kind enough to open the window. Yes, that one, too. I need air. What a charming boy."

She addressed him in this way because, in his white sports shirt worn outside his khaki trousers, and with his biblical sandals, he looked to her more like a young servant than like a doctor. She had passed her youth among gardens, apes, and fountains in Bombay.

Father silently obeyed and opened all the windows.

The evening air of Jerusalem came in, and with it smells of cabbage, pine trees, and garbage.

He produced from his pocket a Health Service pillbox, carefully opened it, and handed Lady Bromley an aspirin. He did not know the English for "migraine," and so he said it in German. Doubtless his eyes at that moment shone with a sympathetic optimism behind his round spectacles.

After a few minutes, Lady Bromley asked to be taken back to her seat. One of the high-ranking officials took down Father's name and address and dryly thanked him. They smiled. There was a moment's hesitation. Suddenly the official held out his hand. They shook hands.

Father went back to his seat in row 29, between his wife and his son. He said:

"It was nothing. It was just the climate."

The lights went out again. Once more General Montgomery pursued General Rommel mercilessly across the desert. Fire and dust clouds filled the screen. Rommel appeared in close-up, biting his lip, while in the background bagpipes skirled ecstatically.

Finally, the two anthems, British and Zionist, were played. The celebration was over. The people left the Edison Cinema and made for their homes. The evening twilight suddenly fell upon Jerusalem. In the distance, bald hills could be seen, with here and there a solitary tower. There was a sprinkling of stone huts on the faraway slopes. Shadows rustled in the side streets. The whole city was under the sway of a painful longing. Electric lights began to come on in the windows. There was a tense expectancy, as if at any moment a new sound might break out. But there were only the old sounds all around, a woman grumbling, a shutter squeaking, a lovesick cat screeching among the garbage cans in a backyard. And a very distant bell.

A handsome Bokharan barber in a white coat stood alone in the window of his empty shop and sang as he shaved himself. At that moment, a patrolling British jeep crossed the street, armed with a machine gun, brass bullets gleaming in its ammunition belt.

An old woman sat alone on a wooden stool beside the entrance of her basement shop. Her hands, wrinkled like a plasterer's, rested heavily on her knees. The last evening light caught her head, and her lips moved silently. From inside the basement, another woman spoke, in Yiddish:

"It's perfectly simple: it'll end badly."

The old woman made no reply. She did not move.

Outside Ernpreis the pants presser's, Father was accosted by a pious beggar, who demanded and received a two-mil piece, furiously thanked God, cursed the Jewish Agency twice, and swept an alley cat out of the way with the tip of his stick.

From the east, the bells rang out continuously, high bells and deep bells, Russian bells, Anglican bells, Greek bells, Abyssinian, Latin, Armenian bells, as if a plague or a fire were devastating the city. But all the bells were doing was to call the darkness dark. And a light breeze blew from the northwest, perhaps from the sea; it stirred the tops of the pale trees that the City Council had planted up Malachi Street and ruffled the boy's curly hair. It was evening. An unseen bird gave a strange, persistent cry. Moss sprouted in the cracks in the stone walls. Rust spread over the old iron shutters and veranda railings. Jerusalem stood very quiet in the last of the light.

During the night, the boy woke up again with an attack of asthma. Father came in barefoot and sang him a soothing song:

> *Night is reigning in the skies,*
> *Time for you to close your eyes.*
> *Lambs and kids have ceased from leaping,*
> *All the animals are sleeping.*
> *Every bird is in its nest,*
> *All Jerusalem's at rest.*

Toward dawn, the jackals howled in the wadi below Tel Arza. Mitya the lodger began to cry out in his sleep on the other side of the wall: "Leave him alone! He's still alive! *Y-a ny-e zna-yu.*" And he fell silent. Then cocks crew far away in the quarter of Sanhedriya and the Arab village of Shu'afat. At the first light, Father put on his khaki trousers, sandals, and a neatly pressed blue shirt with wide pockets, and set off for work. Mother went on sleeping until the women in the neighboring houses started beating their pillows and mattresses with all their might. Then she got up and in her silk dressing gown gave the boy a breakfast of a soft-boiled egg, Quaker Oats, and cocoa with the skin taken off; and she combed his curly hair.

Hillel said:

"I can do it by myself. Stop it."

An old glazier passed down the street, shouting, "Perfessional glazing! America! Anything repaired!" And the children called after him, "Loonie!"

A few days later, Father was surprised to receive a gold-embossed invitation for two to the May Ball at the High Commissioner's palace on the Hill of Evil Counsel. On the back of the invitation, the secretary had written in English that Lady Bromley wished to convey to Dr. Kipnis her gratitude and profound apology, and that Sir Alan himself had expressed his appreciation.

Father was not a real doctor. He was actually a vet.

2

He had been born and brought up in Silesia. Hans Walter Landauer the famous geographer was his mother's uncle. Father had studied at the Veterinary Institute in Leipzig, specializing in tropical and subtropical cattle diseases.

In 1932, he had emigrated to Palestine with the intention of establishing a cattle farm in the mountains. He was a polite young man, quiet, principled, and full of hopes. In his dreams he saw himself wandering with a stick and a haversack among the hills of Galilee, clearing a patch of forest, and building with his own hands a wooden house beside a stream, with a sloping roof, an attic, and a cellar. He meant to get together some herdsmen and a herd of cattle, roaming by day to new pastures and by night sitting surrounded by books in a room full of hunting trophies, composing a monograph or a great poem.

For three months he stayed in a guesthouse in the small town of Yesud-Hama'alah, and he spent whole days wandering alone from morning to night in eastern Galilee looking for water buffalo in the Huleh Swamps. His body grew lean and bronzed, and his blue eyes, behind his round spectacles, looked like lakes in a snowy northern land. He learned to love the desolation of the distant mountains and the smell of summer: scorched thistles, goat dung, wood ash, the dusty east wind.

In the Arab village of Halsa, he met a wandering Bavarian ornithologist, a lonely and fervently evangelical man who believed that the return of the Jews to their land heralded the salvation of the world, and was collecting material for a great work on the birds of the Holy Land. Together they roamed to the Marj-'Ayun Valley, into the Mountains of Naphtali and the Huleh Swamps. Occasionally, in their wanderings, they reached the remote sources of the Jordan. Here they would sit all day in the shade of the lush vegetation, reciting together from memory their favorite Schiller poems and calling every bird and beast by its proper name.

When Father began to worry what would happen when he came to the end of the money that his mother's uncle the famous geographer had given him, he decided to go to Jerusalem to look into certain practical possibilities. Accordingly, he took his leave of the wandering Bavarian ornithologist, gathered his few possessions, and appeared one fine autumn morning in the office of Dr. Arthur Ruppin at the Jewish Agency in Jerusalem.

Dr. Ruppin took at once to the quiet, bronzed boy who had come to him from Galilee. He also recalled that in his youth he had studied the tropical countries in Landauer's great *Atlas*. When Father began to describe the project of a cattle farm in the hills of Galilee, he took down some hasty notes. Father concluded with these words:

"It is a difficult plan to put into practice, but I believe it is not impossible.

Dr. Ruppin smiled sadly:

"Not impossible, but difficult to put into practice. Very difficult!"

And he proceeded to point out one or two awkward facts.

He persuaded Father to postpone the realization of his plan for the time being, and meanwhile to invest his money in the acquisition of a young orange grove near the settlement of Nes Tsiyona, and also to buy without delay a small house in the new suburb of Tel Arza, which was being built to the north of Jerusalem.

Father did not argue.

Within a few days, Dr. Ruppin had had Father appointed as a traveling government veterinary officer and had even invited him for coffee in his house in Rehavia.

For several years, Father would get up before sunrise and travel on sooty buses up to Bethlehem and Ramallah, down to Jericho, out to Lydda, to supervise the villagers' cattle on behalf of the government.

The orange grove near the settlement of Nes Tsiyona began to yield a modest income, which he deposited, along with the part of his government salary, in the Anglo-Palestine Bank. He furnished his small house in Tel Arza with a bed, a desk, a wardrobe, and bookshelves. Above his desk he hung a large picture of his mother's uncle the famous geographer. Hans Walter Landauer looked down on Father with an expression of skepticism and mild surprise, particularly in the evenings.

As he traveled around the villages, Father collected rare thistles. He also gathered some fossils and pieces of ancient pottery. He arranged them all with great care. And he waited.

Meanwhile, silence cut him off from his mother and sisters in Silesia.

As the years went by, Father learned to speak a little Arabic. He also learned loneliness. He put off composing his great poem. Every day he learned something new about the land and its inhabitants, and occasionally even about himself. He still saw in his dreams the cattle farm in Galilee, although the cellar and attic now seemed to him unnecessary, perhaps even childish. One evening, he even said aloud to his great-uncle's picture:

"We'll see. All in good time. I'm just as determined as you are. You may laugh, but I don't care. Laugh as much as you like."

At night, by the light of his desk lamp, Father kept a journal in which he recorded his fears for his mother and sisters, the oppressiveness of the dry desert wind, certain peculiarities of some of his acquaintances, and the flavor of his travels among godforsaken villages. He set down in carefully chosen words various professional lessons he had learned in the course of his work. He committed to writing some optimistic reflections about the progress of the Jewish community in various spheres. He even formulated, after several revisions, a few arguments for and against loneliness, and an embarrassed hope for a love that might come to him, too, one day. Then he carefully tore out the page and ripped it into tiny pieces. He also published, in the weekly *The Young Worker*, an article in favor of drinking goats' milk.

Sometimes, in the evening, he would go to Dr. Ruppin's home in Rehavia, where he was received with coffee and cream cakes. Or else he would visit his fellow townsman the elderly Professor Julius Werthei-mer, who also lived in Rehavia, not far from Dr. Ruppin. Occasionally there was a distant sound of faint, persistent piano music, like the supplications of a desperate pride. Every summer the rocks on the hillside roasted, and every winter Jerusalem was ringed with fog. Refugees and pioneers continued to arrive from various foreign parts, filling the city with sadness and bewilderment. Father bought books from the refugees, some of them musty books with leather bindings and gold tooling, and from time to time he exchanged books with Dr. Ruppin or with elderly Professor Julius Wertheimer, who was in the habit of greeting him with a hurried, embarrassed hug.

The Arabs in the villages sometimes gave him cold pomegranate juice to drink. Occasionally they would kiss his hand. He learned to drink water from an upraised pitcher without letting the pitcher touch his lips. Once a woman directed a dark, smoldering glance at him from some way off, and he trembled all over and hurriedly looked away.

He wrote in his journal:

"I have been living in Jerusalem for three years, and I continue to yearn for it as though I were still a student in Leipzig. Surely there is paradox here. And in general," Father continued thoughtfully and rather vaguely, "in general there are all sorts of contradictions. Yesterday morning, in Lifta, I was obliged to put down a fine, healthy horse because some youngsters had blinded it in the night with a nail. Cruelty for its own sake seems to me to be something sordid and thoroughly unnecessary. The same evening, in Kibbutz Kiryat 'Anavim, the pioneers played a Bach suite on the phonograph, which aroused in me profound feelings of pity for the pioneers, for the horse, for Bach, for myself. I almost cried. Tomorrow is the King's birthday, and all the workers in the department are to receive a special bonus. There are all sorts of contradictions. And the climate is not kind, either."

3

Mother said:

"I shall wear my blue dress with the V-shaped neckline, and I shall be the belle of the ball. We'll order a taxi, too."

Father said:

"Yes, and don't forget to lose a glass slipper."

Hillel said:

"Me, too."

But children are not taken to May Balls at the High Commissioner's palace. Even good children, even children who are cleverer than is usual for their age. And the ball would certainly not end before midnight. So Hillel would spend the evening next door with Madame Yabrova the pianist and her niece, Lyubov, who called herself Binyamina Even-Hen. They would play the phonograph for him, give him his supper, let him play a little with their collection of dolls of all nations, and put him to bed.

Hillel tried to protest:

"But I still have to tell the High Commissioner who's right and who's wrong."

Father replied patiently:

"We are right, and I'm sure the High Commissioner knows it in his heart of hearts, but he has to carry out the wishes of the King."

"I don't envy that king because God is going to punish him and Uncle Mitya calls him King Chedorlaomer of Albion and he says the Underground will capture him and execute him because of what he's done to the Remnant of Israel," the boy said excitedly and all in one breath.

Father replied mildly, choosing his words with care:

"Uncle Mitya sometimes exaggerates a little. The King of England is not Chedorlaomer, but George the Sixth. He will probably be succeeded on the throne by one of his daughters, because he has no son. To kill a man except in self-defense is murder. And now, Your Majesty King Hillel the First, finish up your cocoa. And then go and brush your teeth."

Mother, with a hairpin between her teeth and holding a pair of amber earrings, remarked:

"King George is very thin and pale. And he always looks so sad."

When he reached the end of the third form, Hillel wrote a letter and typed it in triplicate on his father's typewriter. He sent two of the copies to the King in London and to the High Commissioner: "Our land belongs to us, both according to the Bible and according to justice. Please get out of the Land of Israel at once and go back to England before it is too late."

The third copy passed from hand to hand among the excited neighbors. Madame Yabrova the pianist said, "A child poet!" Her niece, Lyubov Binyamina, added: "And look at his curly hair! We ought to send a copy to Dr. Weizmann, to give him a little joy." Brzezinski the engineer said that it was no good exaggerating, you couldn't build a wall out of fine words. And from Gerald Lindley, Secretary, there came a brief reply on official government notepaper: "Thank you for your letter, the contents of which have been duly noted. We are always receptive to the opinions of the public. Yours faithfully."

And how the geraniums blazed in the garden in the blue summer light. How the pure light was caught by the fingers of the fig tree in the yard and shattered into nervous fragments. How the sun burst up early in the morning behind Mount Scopus to torment the whole city and suddenly turn the gold and silver domes to dazzling flames. How joyfully or desperately the throngs of birds shrilled.

The metal drainpipe absorbed the heat and was sweet to the touch in the morning. The clean gravel that Father had spread along the path that wound down from the veranda steps to the fence and to the fig tree to the bottom of the garden was white and pleasant under bare feet.

The garden was small, logically planned, uncompromisingly well kept: Father's dreams had laid out square and rectangular flower beds among the rocky gulleys, a lonely island of clear, sober sanity in the midst of a savage, rugged wasteland, of winding valleys, of desert winds.

And surrounding us was the estate of Tel Arza, a handful of new houses scattered haphazardly on a hilltop. The mountains might move in one night and silently enfold everything, the houses, the hesitant saplings, the hopes, the unpaved road. A herd of Arab goats would arrive to munch and trample chrysanthemums, narcissuses, snapdragons, sparse beginnings of lawn here and there. And the shepherd would stand silent and motionless, watching the ravaging goats and looking perhaps like a scorched cypress tree.

All day Hillel could see the ranges of bare mountains all around. At times he could sense in the bright-blue flood the autumn piling up in unseen valleys.

Autumn would come. The light would fade to gray. Low clouds would seize the mountains. He would climb to the top of the fig tree, and from there in the autumn light he might be able to see the sea and the desert, the islands in the tattered clouds, the mysterious continents that Father had told him about dryly and Mother with tears of longing.

Father used to say that the beautiful lands had vomited us up here in blind hatred, and that therefore we would build ourselves a land a thousand times as beautiful here. But Mother would call the land a backyard, and say that there would never be a river, a cathedral, or a forest here. Uncle Mitya the lodger used to chuckle through his rotten teeth and utter broken phrases about birth pangs, death throes, Jerusalem killing its prophets, God's curse on ruined Babylon. He was also a vegetarian.

Hillel could not make out from these words whether Mitya agreed with Father or with Mother. What Mother said seemed to him incongruous, and he would go down to the bottom of the garden to hide among the branches of the fig tree and sniff for the autumn. Autumn would come. Autumn sadness would accompany him to school, to his music lessons with Madame Yabrova, to the "Zion's Ransom" lending library, to his bed at night, into his dreams. While a rainstorm raged outside, he would compose an article for the class newspaper. The word "forest," which Mother had used when she wanted to denigrate the land, cast a strange, melancholy spell over him.

4

Hillel was a pudgy, awkward little boy. He had a hiding place at the end of the garden, behind the fig tree or up among its branches, which he called his "hideaway." He would hide himself away there and secretly eat sticky sweets that the women gave him, and dream of Africa, the sources of the Nile, the lions in the jungle.

At night he would wake up with attacks of asthma. Especially in the early summer. Feverish, suffocated, he would see the horrific smile of the terrifying white thing through the slats of the shutters and burst into tears. Until Father appeared holding a small flashlight, to sit on his bed and sing him a soothing song. Aunts, neighbors, and nursery-school teachers adored Hillel, with Russian kisses and Polish displays of affection. They called him "Little Cherry." Sometimes they would leave heavy lip marks on his cheeks or his mouth. These women were plump and excitable. Their faces wore an expression of bitter complaint: life has not been as kind to me as I deserve.

Madame Yabrova the pianist and her niece, Lyubov, who called herself Binyamina Even-Hen, in the determined way they played the piano, seemed to be nobly refraining from repaying life for what it had done to them. Mrs. Vishniak the pharmacist would grumble to Hillel and say that little children were the only hope of the Jewish people, and particularly of herself. At times Hillel wrapped himself in introspection or sadness, and then he would delight them with a sweet phrase, such as:

"Life is a circle. Everyone goes around and around."

And stir ripples of emotion.

But the children of Tel Arza called him by the unpleasant nickname "Jelly." Unkind, skinny girls, vicious Oriental girls, enjoyed knocking him down on a heap of gravel and pulling his blond hair. Keys and amulets hung around their necks. They emitted a pungent smell of peanuts, sweat, soap, and halvah.

Hillel would always wait until they had had enough of him and his curls. The he would get up and shake the dust off his gym shorts and his cotton undershirt; gasping for breath, his eyes full of tears, he would bite his lip and begin to forgive. How nobly forgiveness shone in his eyes: those girls did not know what they were doing; they probably had unhappy fathers and brothers who were high up in the underworld or in football; their mothers and sisters probably went out with British soldiers. It was a terrible thing to be born an Oriental girl. And one of them had even started to grow breasts under her sweaty vest. Hillel reflected, forgave, and was filled with love of himself for his ability to understand and to forgive.

Then he would run to Mrs. Vishniak's pharmacy to cry a little, not because of the scratches but because of the cruel lot of the girls and his own magnanimity. Mrs. Vishniak would kiss him, console him with sticky candy, tell him about the mill on the banks of the blue river, which no longer existed. He would tell her, in carefully chosen words, about a dream he had had the previous night, interpret the dream himself, and leave behind a delicate mood of poetry as he went off to practice the piano in the dark, airless house of Madame Yabrova and Binyamina. He returned the caresses he had received from Mrs. Vishniak to the haughty bronze Beethoven on top of the sideboard. After all, Herzl, in his youth, was called a madman in the street. And Bialik was always being beaten.

In the evening, before he went to bed, Hillel would be summoned to his father's room in his pajamas. This room was called the study. It contained bookshelves, a desk, and a glass-fronted showcase of fossils and ancient pots; the whole was skeptically surveyed from a sepia photograph by the famous geographer Hans Walter Landauer.

He had to utter an intelligent sentence or two for the benefit of the guests. Then he was kissed and sent off to bed. From across the corridor came the sounds of the grownups talking passionately, and Hillel in his bed caught their passion and began to pamper his tiny organ with his fingers through the opening of his pajama trousers.

Later, the forlorn sound of Lyubov Binyamina's cello came to him through the darkness, and he suddenly despised himself. He called himself "Jelly." He was filled with sorrow for all men and women. And fell asleep compassionately.

"He's a real *mensh*," Mrs. Vishniak would say in Yiddish. "Clever. Witty. A little devil. Just like the whole family."

Beyond the low fence, which Father had made from iron posts and old netting and painted in bright colors, began the wasteland. Plots of scrap iron, dust, smelling of thistles, of goat dung; and farther on, the wadi and the lairs of foxes and jackals; and still farther down, the empty wood where the children once discovered the remains of a half-eaten Turkish soldier in the stinking tatters of a janissary's uniform. There were desolate slopes teeming with darting lizards and snakes and perhaps hyenas at night, and beyond this wadi, empty, stony hills and more wadis, in which Arabs in desert robes roamed with their flocks all day long. In the distance were more and more strange mountains and strange villages stretching to the end of the world, minarets of mosques, Shu'afat, Nabi Samwil, the outskirts of Ramallah, the wail of a muezzin borne on the wind in the evening twilight, dark women, deadly-sly, guttural youths. And a slight hint of brooding evil: distant, infinitely patient, forever observing you unobserved.

Mother said:

"While you, Hans, are dancing like a teddy bear with that old lady you treated, I shall sit all alone in my blue dress on a wickerwork chair at the end of the veranda, sipping a martini and smiling to myself. But later on I, too, shall suddenly get up and dance, with the Governor of Jerusalem, or even with Sir Alan himself. Then it will be your turn to sit it out by yourself, and you won't feel at all like smiling."

Father said:

"The boy can hear you. He understands exactly what you're saying."

And Hillel said:

"So what?"

For the occasion, Father borrowed from his neighbor Engineer Brzezinski an English evening suit made by the Szczupak textile factory in Lodz. Mother sat on the shady balcony all morning altering it to fit him.

At lunchtime, Father tried the suit on at the mirror, shrugged his shoulders, and remarked:

"It's ridiculous."

Mother, laughing, said:

"The boy can hear you. He understands everything."

Hillel said:

"So what? 'Ridiculous' isn't a dirty word."

Father said:

"No word is dirty in itself. In general, dirt lies either behind words or between them."

And Mother:

"There's dirt everywhere here. Even in the grand ideas you're always putting into Hillel's head. Even in your stray remarks. And that's also ridiculous."

Father said nothing.

That morning the newspaper *Davar* said that the politics of the White Paper were leading up a blind alley. Hillel, with an effort of the imagination, could almost visualize the "blind alley."

Mitya the vegetarian lodger padded barefoot from his room to the kitchen to make himself a glass of tea. He was a tall, etiolated young man with thinning hair. His shoulders always drooped, and he walked with short, nervous steps. He had an odd habit of suddenly chewing the tip of his shirt collar, and also of angrily stroking every object he came across, table, banister, bookshelf, Mother's apron hanging on a hook in the kitchen. And he would whisper to himself. Engineer Brzezinski declared hotly that one day it would emerge that this Mitya was really a dangerous Communist in disguise. But Mother good-naturedly offered to launder his few clothes with the family wash.

As Mitya shuffled to the kitchen, he waved his hand in every direction in greeting, as though confronting a large crowd. Suddenly his glance fell on the words "blind alley" in the headline on the center page of *Davar*, lying open on the oilcloth on the kitchen table. He bared his bad teeth and snarled furiously:

"What rubbish."

Then, clasping the hot glass in his large white hands, he strode stormily back to his room, locking his door behind him.

Mother said softly:

"He's just like a stray dog."

After a short pause, she added:

"He washes five times a day, and after each time he puts on scent, and even so he always smells. We ought to find him a girlfriend. Perhaps a new immigrant from the Women's Labor Bureau, poor but charming. Now, Hans, you go and shave. And Hillel—go on with your homework. What am I doing in this madhouse?"

5

She had come from Warsaw as a young woman to study ancient history at the university on Mount Scopus. Before a year was up, she was in despair at the country and the language. Nyuta, her elder sister in New York, had sent her a ticket to go from Haifa to America aboard the *Aurora*. A few days before the date of her departure, Dr. Ruppin had introduced her to Father, shown him her beautiful watercolors, and expressed in German his sadness that the young lady was also leaving us, that she, too, found the country unbearable and was sailing to America in disappointment.

Hans Kipnis looked at the watercolors for a while and suddenly thought of the wandering German ornithologist with whom he had traveled to the remote sources of the Jordan. He traced the lines of one of the pictures delicately with his finger, hurriedly withdrew his hand, and uttered some remarks about loneliness and dreams in general and in Jerusalem in particular.

Mother smiled at him, as though he had accidentally broken a precious vase.

Father apologized and lapsed into an embarrassed silence.

Dr. Ruppin had a pair of tickets for a concert that night by a recently formed refugee chamber orchestra. He was glad to present the tickets to the young couple: he could not go anyway, because Menahem Ussishkin the Zionist leader had unexpectedly arrived from abroad a day or two earlier, and as usual had convened a frantic meeting for that evening.

After the concert, they strolled together along Princess Mary's Way. The shopwindows were brightly lit and decorated, and in one of them a small mechanical doll bobbed up and down. For a moment, Jerusalem looked like a real city. Ladies and gentlemen walked arm in arm, and some of the gentlemen were smoking cigarettes in short cigarette holders.

A bus stopped beside them, and the driver, who was wearing shorts, smiled at them invitingly, but they did not get on. An army jeep with a machine gun mounted on it rolled down the street. And in the distance a bell rang. They both agreed that Jerusalem was under some cruel spell. Then they agreed to meet again the next day to eat a strawberry ice cream together at Zichel's Café.

At a nearby table sat the philosopher Martin Buber and the writer S. Y. Agnon. In the course of a disagreement, Agnon jokingly suggested that they consult the younger generation. Father made some remark; it must have been perceptive and acute, because Buber and Agnon both smiled; they also addressed his companion gallantly. At that moment Father's blue eyes may perhaps have lit up behind his round spectacles, and his sadness may have shown around his mouth.

Nineteen days later, the Nazis publicly declared their intention of building up their armed forces. There was tension in Europe. The *Aurora* never reached Haifa; she changed her course and sailed instead to the West Indies.

Father arranged to see his fellow townsman Professor Julius Wertheimer, who had been his patron ever since he had arrived in Palestine. He said he wanted to consult him on a personal matter. He was confused, furtive, obstinate, and tongue-tied. Professor Wertheimer listened in an anxious silence. Then he drove his cats out of the room and closed the door behind them. When they were alone, he warned Father obliquely not to complicate his private life unnecessarily. And it was precisely these words that brought Father to the certainty that he was finally in love.

Ruth and Hans were married in Jerusalem on the day that Hitler declared in Nuremberg that he was bent on peace and understanding and that he detested war. The guests consisted of the officials of the veterinary department, including two Christian Arabs from Bethlehem, the Ruppin family, some refugees and pioneers, a few neighbors from Tel Arza, and an emaciated revolutionary student from the university who could not take his blazing eyes off the beautiful bride. He it was who toasted the happy couple on behalf of all their friends and vowed that right would triumph and that we would see as much with our own eyes. But he spoiled the effect of his words by getting thoroughly drunk on one bottle of Nesher beer and calling the bridegroom and bride respectively *"burzhui"* and *"artistka."* The guests departed, and Father hired a taxi to convey Mother's few belongings from her simple room in

Neve Sha'anan to the house he had been making ready for several years in the suburb of Tel Arza.

There, in Tel Arza, in the little stone-built house facing the rocky wadis, there was born to them a year later a fair-haired son.

When Mother and the baby came home from the hospital, Father indicated his diminutive estate with a sweep of his hand, gazed raptly at it, and pronounced these words:

"For the moment this is a remote suburb. There are only young saplings growing in our garden. The sun beats down all day on the shutters. But as the years pass, the trees will grow, and we shall have plenty of shade. Their boughs will shelter the house. Creepers will climb over the roof and all over the fence. And the flowers will bloom. This will be our pleasure garden when Hillel grows up and we grow old together. We shall make an arbor of vines where you can sit all day through the summer, painting beautiful watercolors. We can even have a piano. They'll build a civic center, they'll pave the road, our suburb will be joined to a Jerusalem ruled by a Hebrew government with a Hebrew army. Dr. Ruppin will be a minister and Professor Buber will be president or perhaps even king. When the time comes, I may become director of the veterinary service. And immigrants will arrive from every country under the sun."

Suddenly he felt ashamed of his speech, and particularly regretted his choice of some of the words. A momentary sadness trembled around his mouth, and he added hastily, in a matter-of-fact tone:

"Poetry. Philosophizing. A pleasure garden with overhanging vines, all of sudden. Now I'll go and fetch a block of ice, and you must lie down and rest, so that you won't have a migraine again tonight. It's so hot."

Mother turned to go indoors. By the veranda steps she stopped and looked at the miserable, rusty pots of geraniums. She said:

"There won't be any flowers. There'll be a flood. Or a war. They'll all die."

Father did not answer, because he sensed that these words were not directed at him and that they should never have been spoken.

His khaki shorts came down almost to his knees. Between his knees and his sandals his legs showed brown, thin, and smooth. Behind his round spectacles his face bore an expression of permanent gratitude, or of slight, pleased surprise. And in moments of embarrassment he was in the habit of saying:

"I don't know. It's just as well not to know everything. There are all sorts of things in the world that are better left alone."

6

Here is how Mother appeared as a girl in her old photograph album: a blond schoolgirl with a kind of inner, autumnal beauty. Her fingers clasping a broad-brimmed white hat. Three doves on a fence behind her, and a mustached Polish student sitting on the same fence, smiling broadly.

She had been considered the best reader in her class at the high school. At the age of twelve, she had already attracted the enthusiastic attention of the elderly Polish literature teacher. The aging humanist, Mother would recall, was deeply moved by her charming recitations of gems of Polish poetry. "Ruth's voice," the pedagogue would exclaim with hoarse enthusiasm, "echoes the spirit of poetry, eternally playing among streams in a meadow." And because he secretly considered himself a poet, he would add, overcome by the force of his emotions, "If gazelles could sing, they would surely sing like little Ruth."

When Mother repeated this sentence she would laugh, because the comparison seemed to her absurd. Not because of the idea of gazelles singing, but because she simply couldn't sing. Her affections at that time were directed toward small pets, celebrated philosophers and artists, dancing, dresses trimmed with lace, and silk scarves, and also her poor friends who had neither lace-trimmed dresses nor silk scarves. She was fond of the unfortunates she came across, the milkman, the beggar, Grandma Gittel, the maids, and her nanny, even the local idiot. Provided that suffering had not disfigured their outward appearance, and provided that they carried themselves woefully, as if acknowledging their guilt and attempting to atone for it.

She translated from Polish a story she had written on her fifteenth birthday. She copied it out neatly and told Hillel to read it aloud:

"The blue sea allows the sun's rays to draw up its water, to make clouds that look like dirty cotton wool, to pour down rain on mountains, plains, and meadows—but not on the ugly desert—and eventually all the water collects and has to flow back once more into the sea. To return to it with a caress."

Suddenly she fell into a rage, snatched the paper out of the boy's hands, and tore it into shreds.

"All gone!" she cried with desperate pathos. "Dead and done for! Lost!"

Outside, a wintry Jerusalem Sabbath, windswept, lashed by dead leaves. Inside the little house in Tel Arza, the kerosene heater burned with a blue flame. On the table there was tea and oranges, and a vase of chrysanthemums. Two of the walls were lined with Father's books. Shadows fell on them. The wind howled from the wadi. Mists touched the outside of the window, and the panes rattled. With a kind of bitter mockery, Mother spoke of her childhood in Warsaw, rowing on the Wisla, playing tennis in white clothes, the Seventh Cavalry Regiment parading down the Avenue of the Republic every Sunday. Occasionally she turned abruptly to Father and called him Dr. Zichel instead of Dr. Kipnis, Hans, Hanan. Father would rest his fingers on his high brow, unperturbed, unsurprised, silently smiling at the recollection of the acute remark he had made in Zichel's Café to the writer Agnon and the philosopher Buber. They had both been delighted; they had consulted him about the strawberry ice cream, and even complimented his companion.

When Mother was sixteen, she allowed the handsome Tadeusz to kiss her at the bridge: first on the forehead, later on the lips, but she let him go no further. He was a year and a half younger than she, an elegant, handsome youth, without a trace of acne, who excelled at tennis and sprinting. Once he had promised her that he would love her forever. But forever at that time seemed to her like a small circle bathed in pleasant light, and love like a game of tennis on a clear blue Sunday morning.

Handsome Tadeusz's father had been killed in the Polish war of independence. Tadeusz also had a cute dimple when he smiled, and wore sports shirts all through the summer. Mother loved to kiss Hillel suddenly on his own dimple and say:

"Just like this one."

Every year, on the national holiday, Ruth and Tadeusz would both stand on a decorated stage in the school playground. Old chestnut trees spread their branches overhead like a rustling bridal canopy. Tadeusz's task was to light the Torch of Liberty—the same liberty for which his father had given his life. Pupils and teachers stood in serried ranks, frozen in a strained silence, while the wind toyed with the flags of the Republic—no, don't touch the photograph—and Ruth recited the immortal lines by the national poet. Bells rang out joyously from atop every church in Warsaw. And in the evening, at the ball at the home of the director of the opera house, her parents permitted her to dance one waltz with General Godzinski himself.

Then Zionism broke out. The handsome Tadeusz joined the National Youth Corps, and because she refused to spend a weekend with him at his aunt's in the country, he sent her a disgusting note: "*Zidowka*. Dirty Jewess." The old teacher who was fond of the phrase "singing gazelles" died suddenly of a liver disease. And both her parents, too, in a single month. The only memento she had left was the sepia photographs, printed on thick card stock with ornamental borders.

Nyuta, her elder sister, quickly found herself a widowed gynecologist named Adrian Staub. She married him and went with him to New York. Meanwhile, Mother came to Palestine to study ancient history on Mount Scopus. She took a small room at the end of the world, in the suburb of Neve Sha'anan. Nyuta Staub sent her a modest allowance every month. In that room she was loved by several wonderful men, including, one Hannuka festival, the furious poet Alexander Pan.

After a year, she felt defeated by the country and the language, and decided to join her sister and brother-in-law in New York. Then Dr. Ruppin introduced her to Father, and he told her shyly about his dream of setting up a cattle farm in the hills of Galilee with his own hands. He had a fine Galilean smell. She was desperately tired. And the *Aurora* changed course, sailed to the West Indies, and never reached Haifa.

To the northeast, in the white summer light, one could see Mount Scopus from the window of the house in Tel Arza, crowned by a marble dome, a wood, and two towers. These lonely towers seemed from a distance to be shrouded in a kind of veil of solitude. At the end of the Sabbath the light faded slowly, hesitantly, poignantly:

As though forever. And as though there were no going back.

Father and Mother used to sit facing each other in the room that Father called his study. The celebrated geographer Hans Walter Landauer gazed down skeptically on them from his large portrait. And their pudgy son built complicated brick castles on the mat, demolishing each suddenly with a wave of his hand because he always wanted to build a new one. At times he would ask an intelligent question of his father, and he always received a considered reply. At other times he buried his face in his mother's dress, demanded to be cuddled, and then, embarrassed at seeing her eyes fill with tears, returned silently to his game.

Sometimes Mother asked:

"What's going to happen, Hans?"

And Father would answer:

"I confidently hope that things will take a turn for the better."

As Father uttered these words, Hillel recalled how last Pentecost he had gone out with his friends to hunt lions or discover the source of the Nile in the woods of Tel Arza. He recalled how a faded golden button had suddenly flashed at him, and blue cloth, how he had knelt down and dug with both hands, tearing away the pine needles, to uncover the treasure, and found a rotting military tunic, a terrible, sweet smell coming from the tarnished gold, and how as he went on digging he had discovered white ivory among disintegrating buckles, large and small white tusks, and all of a sudden the ivory was attached to an empty skull that smiled at him with a kind of chilling affection, and then the dead teeth and the eye sockets. Never, never again would he search for the source of the Nile anywhere. Never.

On weekdays Father traveled around the villages wearing khaki trousers, sandals, a neatly pressed blue shirt with wide pockets stuffed full of notebooks and writing pads. In winter he wore brown corduroy trousers, a jacket, a cap, and over his shoes he wore galoshes that looked like twin black warships.

But on Sabbath Eve, after his bath, he would appear in a white shirt and gray trousers, his damp hair combed and neatly parted, smelling of shaving lotion and almond-scented soap. Then Mother would kiss him on the nose and call him her great big child. And Hillel would laugh.

Every morning, a bib with a picture of a smiling rabbit was tied around Hillel's neck. He ate Quaker Oats, a soft-boiled egg, and yogurt. On the Quaker Oats package was a wonderful picture of an admiral with a bold and resolute look on his face, a three-cornered Napoleon hat on his head, and a telescope in his only hand.

In Europe at that time, there was a world war going on. But in the streets of Jerusalem, there were only singing bands of friendly soldiers, Australians, New Zealanders, Senegalese looking like chocolate-cream soldiers, lean Scots wallowing in beer and homesickness. The newspapers carried maps with arrows. Sometimes, at night, a long military convoy crossed Jerusalem from north to south with dimmed headlights, and a smothered roar seemed to sound in the darkness. The city was very still. The hills were hushed. The towers and domes looked thoughtful. The inhabitants followed the distant war with anxiety but without any passion. They exchanged conjectures and interpretations. They expected a change for the better that would surely come about soon and might even perhaps make itself felt in Jerusalem.

7

In Tel Arza no civic center was built, and the road was not paved. A stone quarry was started on one of the farther slopes. Mr. Cohen opened a small workshop producing modish furniture for the notables of Jericho and Bethlehem, the Governor of Jerusalem, and even for the palace of Emir Abdullah in Transjordan. Engineer Brzezinski climbed onto the roof of his house and rigged up an enormous radio antenna so as to be able to catch the signals of the farthest stations each night. He also built a telescope with his own hands, and installed it, too, on his roof, because he had promised himself that he would be the first to see them when they arrived.

At night the valleys all around were alive with sounds. The wildness of the rocks and mountains reached out to touch the house. Jackals howled nearby, and the blood froze at the thought of them padding softly, tensely, among the saplings, up to the shuttered windows, perhaps even onto the veranda. A single Mandatory street lamp, encased in small, square panes and topped with a green dome, cast a solitary light on the unpaved road. The fingers of the fig tree at the bottom of the garden were empty. There was nobody outside in the dark. The square-paned lamp cast its light in vain. All the residents were in the habit of shutting themselves up in their houses as soon as darkness fell. Every evening Madame Yabrova played the piano, and her niece, Lyubov Binyamina, the cello, with desolating sadness. Father's fellow townsman the elderly Professor Julius Wertheimer collected clippings from foreign newspapers that mentioned anything to do with supernatural phenomena. He considered the laws of nature to be a practical joke, and he longed to find a loophole in them, perhaps some revealing formula that would enable him and the whole persecuted Jewish people to escape from the pull of gravity and to float up into spheres where the contagion had not yet spread.

Every night, far into the small hours, Engineer Brzezinski twiddled the tuning knob of his ratio, seeking and finding and then abandoning different stations, Berlin, London, Milan, Vichy, Cairo, and Cyrenaica. Some of the neighbors said that he often brought bottles of arak back with him from his work on the northern shores of the Dead Sea, and that at night he got drunk on this frightful Oriental drink.

He would tell them how as a young man he had been the director of a gigantic engineering project in Russia, how he had set up the hydroelectric power station in Taganrog, "like writing an epic poem." Then he had fallen foul of Stalin; he was captured, imprisoned, tortured; he escaped by the skin of his teeth and finally reached Jerusalem via Afghanistan, Teheran, and Baghdad. But here, at the Dead Sea Works, he was given trifling little jobs to do: mending pumps, keeping an eye on the generator, repairing miserable fuse boxes, supervising some provincial transformer.

One night he suddenly shouted "Fire! Fire!" at the top of his voice. He had come across a broadcast of Beethoven's *Eroica* Symphony from some Nazi station in the Balkans.

Father immediately got out of bed, dressed, and bravely crossed the dirt road; he knocked on the door and called out politely, "Mr. Brzezinski, please, Mr. Brzezinski."

The door did not open. There was no fire, either. Only the smell of dying campfires borne on the wind from the depths of the wadi. And the wail of a distant muezzin, or perhaps it was a hungry jackal crying in the woods. On nights like these, Hillel would wake up with an attack of panic and asthma. He could see through the slats of the shutters the skull of the Turkish janissary hovering in the dark air, grinning at him with its dead teeth. He would pull the sheet up over his head and burst into tears. Then his father would get up and come into his bedroom with bare feet, to straighten the bedclothes and sing him a soothing song:

> *Night is reigning in the skies,*
> *Time for you to close your eyes.*
> *Lambs and kids have ceased from leaping,*
> *All the animals are sleeping.*
> *Every bird is in its nest,*
> *All Jerusalem's at rest.*

Then, toward dawn, Mitya the lodger might suddenly cry out in his sleep on the other side of the wall: "Ruthless! Don't touch him! He's still alive! *Y-a ny-e zna-yu! Y-a ny-e po-ni-ma-yu!* Nothing!"

Then silence.

Outside in the fields, there was nothing but jackals and mist until morning.

8

Mitya addressed Father:

"In that evening suit, Dr. Kipnis, you look like the spit and image of the martyred Haim Arlosoroff. There is no peace for the wicked. So I shall ask you a small diplomatic favor. Could you pass along a short message from me to the foreign High Commissioner? Just one or two urgent sentences? It is a message the High Commissioner has been secretly waiting for for some time, and he probably cannot understand why it has not yet come."

Father said:

"If I do actually manage to have a private conversation with the High Commissioner, which I very much doubt."

Mitya suddenly grinned, baring his rotten teeth. He chewed his shirt collar, with an expression of pain and disgust on his bony face and a fire in his eyes.

"Give him this message, word for word: our true Messiah will surely come, he will not tarry. He will come whirling a flaming sword in his hand. He will come from the east and lay all the mountains low. He will not leave any that pisseth against the wall. Do you think, Dr. Kipnis, that you can repeat this message word for word without making a mistake?"

Father said:

"I don't think I can undertake to convey that message. And certainly not in English."

And Mitya, frantically stroking the oilcloth on the kitchen table, replied in a hoarse voice:

"Jerusalem, which slayeth its prophets, shall burn the new Hellenizers in hellfire."

At once he added politely:

"Good evening, Mrs. Kipnis. *Pozhal'sta*, why are your staring at me so cruelly, I was simply making a small joke with your husband. I shall never forgive myself if, heaven forbid, I have accidentally frightened you. *Nikogda*. I must beg your pardon right away; there, I've done it. How magnificent you look, Mrs. Kipnis, in your blue evening dress, if I may make so bold. How magnificent, too, is the springtime in our Jerusalem on the eve of the great destruction. And the hot tap in the bathroom is dripping and dripping and knows no rest. Surely we ought to do something without further delay. How much time do we have left? There, I've apologized and I've gone. *Da*. Good night. May the name of the wicked rot, and the innocent shall see it and be glad. Now good night once again to you all. Happy is he who waits His coming."

He nearly knocked the child over as he dashed back to his room, panting, his arms hanging limply at his sides, his fists clenched. But he did not slam his door; he closed it gently behind him as if taking great care not to hurt the door or the doorpost or the sudden silence he had left behind him.

Mother said:

"The High Commissioner could never understand how a boy like Mitya suffers. Even the King couldn't help. Or the Messiah himself, not that I believe in him."

She closed her eyes and continued in a different tone of voice:

"But *I* could. I could easily rescue him from the madness and death that are building up inside him. Yes, me. That's loneliness, Hans, that's real exile, despair, depression, persecution. I could come to him in the middle of the night in my nightgown, sweetly perfumed, and touch him; or at least I could bring him another woman in the night and happily stand by and watch. I could put out the rising fires and give him peace and quiet. So what if he smells. To the forests and the sea, every man and woman in the world stinks. Even you, Hans. And then to hear him moaning between my hands, shouting in disjointed Russian, singing, grunting like a felled ox. Then resting peacefully. I'd close his eyes with my fingers and lull him to sleep. Even the stars and mountains would love me for it. Now, stop looking at me like that. I want you to know once and for all how much I loathe, yes, loathe, your Wertheimers and Bubers and Shertoks. I wish your terrorists would blow them all sky-high. And stop looking at me like that."

Father said:

"That will do, Ruth. The boy can hear you; he understands almost everything."

She drew the child violently toward her, pressed his head against her, and covered his face with rough kisses. Then she said quietly:

"Yes, you're quite right. You've already forgiven me, Hans. The red taxi will be here soon, and we'll go to the ball. Stand still, Hans, while I tie your silly bow tie for you. I've really got no complaint against Buber and the rest of them. There, now you've remembered how to smile. At last. Why are you smiling?"

Father said nothing.

9

Mitya had left his kibbutz in the Jezreel Valley because of an ideological argument at the end of the week in which Hitler had captured Warsaw. At the same time, he had also suddenly inherited some jewelry from his only relation, a forgotten aunt who had died in Johannesburg.

He had hastily sold the jewelry to a crafty Armenian goldsmith in the Old City and decided to settle in Jerusalem to study, with the aim of proving once and for all that the natives of Palestine were descended from the ancient Hebrews. He tried to produce conclusive proof that all the Arabs, nomads and peasants alike, were simply Israelites who had been forcibly converted to Islam and whom it was our duty now to rescue. Their clothes, the shape of their skulls, the names of their villages, their eating habits, and their forms of worship all bore abundant witness, he claimed, to the truth that the Jewish Agency was trying to hush up. But they could not pull the wool over *his* eyes.

For a pioneer, he was a skinny lad, with drooping shoulders and abrupt gestures. He was an uncompromising vegetarian, who called meat eating "the source of all impurity." His hair was thin, fair, almost white. When Mitya stood by himself in the kitchen making tea in his glass with its ring of worn gold paint, Hillel would sometimes observe a lonely, fanatical glint in his eye. His birdlike profile looked as though he were forever suppressing a sneeze. And he would chew the points of his shirt collar with his rotten teeth.

On his arrival, he had paid Father two years' rent in advance, and was given permission to look over the headlines in the daily newspaper and to use the typewriter occasionally. Once he typed out with two fingers an "Epistle to Those Who Are at Ease in Zion," in which he voiced various complaints and sounded a prophecy of doom. But the newspapers all either rejected his letter or simply ignored it. And once he hinted to Father that since the Babylonian Beasts had murdered the heroic Abraham Stern, code-named "Yair," he himself had become the secret commander of the Fighters for the Freedom of Israel. Father did not believe this any more than he believed Engineer Brzezinski, who said that Mitya was a dangerous Communist agent in disguise.

Mitya was ruthlessly clean and tidy.

Whenever he had finished in the lavatory, he would produce a small can inscribed in English, "Baby's Delight," and sprinkle the seat with perfumed talcum powder. When he had read the newspaper he would fold it neatly in four and place it carefully on the end of the bookshelf. If ever he met anyone as he came out of the bathroom or the lavatory (which he called "the throne room"), he would turn pale and mutter an embarrassed apology. He cleaned and scrubbed his own room twice a day.

Despite all this, a faint yet repulsive smell, like that of old cooking fat, always accompanied him in the corridor and escaped from under his door; it even clung to his glass with the worn gold ring.

No one was allowed into his room.

He had fitted a double Yale lock onto his door, and he always locked it even when he only went to wash. Sometimes he would cry out in his sleep in the early hours of the morning. In Russian.

During the summer months, Mitya would set off on foot in the direction of Mount Scopus, crossing hills and valleys with his disjointed gait, spurning roads and paths, advancing in a line straight as an arrow in flight. He would traverse the suburb of Sanhedriya like a hurricane, skirting the police training school, with his birdlike head thrust forward, a distant look in his eye, and finally, panting but undeterred, he would emerge into the district of Sheikh Jarrah, where he would always break his journey to drink his morning coffee among mustached, kaffiyeh-wrapped Arabs, with whom he attempted persistently to enter into conversation, but without success, since he could speak only classical Arabic, and that with a heavy Russian accent. The Arab coffee-drinkers nicknamed him al-Hudhud, "the hoopoe," perhaps because of his crest of thinning hair.

He would spend whole days on end in the basement of the national library on Mount Scopus, endlessly covering little cards with feverish notes. When he came home in the evening, he would sometimes bare his rotting teeth in a grin and pronounce some cryptic prophecy:

"I promise you that tonight a mighty explosion shall resound. The mountains shall drop sweet wine, and all the hills shall melt."

Because those were eventful days, his prophecies sometimes came true in a way. Then Mitya would smile modestly, like a humble artist who has won a prize with one of his works.

During the last year of the World War, Hillel peeped through the keyhole and discovered that Mitya had huge maps hanging on all the walls of his room, from the ceiling almost to the floor. He had other maps spread out on his desk, on his bed, and on the straw matting. These maps were covered with thick black and red arrows, flags, buttons, and matchsticks.

"Daddy, is Uncle Mitya a spy?"

"That sort of foolishness is beneath your dignity, Hillel."

"Then why is he like that? Why has he got maps in his room, and arrows?"

"You're the spy, Hillel. You spied on Uncle Mitya. That's not a nice thing to do, and you'll promise me right now that you won't do it again."

"I promise, but . . ."

"You've promised. Now that's the end of it. It's wrong to talk about people behind their backs."

One day in 1944, Mitya proposed to Father that the British fleet should storm up the Bosporus and through the Dardanelles "like a rod of anger," gain mastery over the Black Sea, ravage half of the Crimea with fire, land "myriads of armies" all along the Slavic coasts, knock the heads of the two tyrants together, "and grind to dust the dragon and the crocodile of Egypt." Father considered this utterance in silence, proffered a mild, sympathetic smile, and remarked that the Russians were now on the side of the Allies.

"You are the generation of the wilderness. You are the seed of slaves," Mitya replied vehemently. "You have all been stricken with blindness. Chamberlains. Arlosoroffs. Gandhis. Plebeians. Eunuchs. I don't mean you personally, Dr. Kipnis, heaven forbid! I was speaking in the plural; you in general. I can see from your wife's eyes that she agrees with me deep in her heart, but because she is wise and sensitive she prefers to remain silent, and of course she is quite right. Surely no remnant shall remain of all the eunuchs. When they cry with upraised voice and outstretched throat 'eternal people,' 'forever and ever,' 'Jerusalem, the eternal city,' surely every stone of Jerusalem bursts out laughing. Now I must beg your pardon and bid you good night. I'm sorry; good night."

Once, when Father was out working in the villages and Mother was at the hairdresser's, Mitya trapped Hillel at the dark end of the corridor and addressed his fevered utterances to him:

"We who have returned to Zion, and especially your generation, whose souls have not been perverted by exile, have an obligation to make children by force by the women of the fellahin. We must give them children who look like you. Masses of fair-haired children. Strong and fair and fearless. It's a matter of life and death. A new breed, thoroughbred, lusty steppe-wolves instead of namby-pamby scholars. The old eunuchs will die off. Blessed are you, for you shall inherit the earth. Then a flame shall issue forth from Judah and consume Perfidious Albion. What could be easier. We know how they go out alone at night to gather firewood. They wear long dark dresses down to their ankles, but underneath their dresses they have nothing on at all. They must be conquered and mounted by main force. With holy zeal. They have women who are dark and hairy as goats, and we have rods of fire. We must spill fresh blood, dark, warm blood. Your parents may call you Hillel, but I shall call you Ithamar. Listen to me, young Ithamar. You are a new recruit: I order you to learn to ride a horse, to use a dagger, to toughen yourself up. Here, take a biscuit: you can't refuse, I'm your commanding officer. This'll all be a closely guarded secret between the two of us: the Underground has no pity on traitors and informers. Who is this that cometh from Seir, with dyed garments from Edom? It is you and the rest of your generation. Nimrods, Gideons, Jephthahs, all of them skilled men of war. You shall see and behold with your own eyes, O new recruit Ithamar, the whole British Empire brought down into the dust like a rag doll. The Inheritor shall come marching from the east. He shall ascend the mountain and discomfit the plain with an iron hand until those lascivious, black hairy she-goats of the fellahin scream at us in terror and delight. Lascivious she-goats! Now, take this shilling and run and buy yourself a mountain of chewing gum. It's yours. Yes. From me. Never disobey orders, Now, scram!"

Suddenly his blazing eyes fell on Mother's apron hanging on a peg beside the mirror in the corridor. He bared his teeth and hissed:

"Painted Jezebel, mother of whoredoms!"

And he shuffled furiously back to his room.

Hillel ran out into the garden. He climbed up into his hideaway among the boughs of the fig tree, the sweaty shilling tightly clasped in his hand. He was tormented by ugly yet persistent images. Jezebel. Fellahin women. Lascivious she-goats. Long dresses with nothing on underneath. Thoroughbreds. And the sweaty word "mounted." His free hand felt for the fly of his trousers, but there were tears in his eyes. He knew that the asthma would start mercilessly as soon as he dared to touch his taut organ. Iron hand. Ithamar. Rag doll. Marching from the east.

If the old days of the Bible suddenly came back, I could be a judge in Israel. Or a king. Mitya could be a prophet in a hair mantle, and the bears would eat him like the wicked Turkish soldier. Daddy would pasture the royal flocks in the fields of Bethlehem. And Mommy wouldn't be a Jezebel.

Among the flower beds, Dr. Kipnis appeared. His hair was still wet from the shower, his khaki shorts came down almost to his knees, and between his shorts and his sandals his legs showed brown, thin, and smooth. He was wearing nothing over his vest. His eyes, behind his glasses, looked like blue lakes in a snowy landscape.

Father carefully connected the rubber hose to the garden tap. He made sure it was well attached, and he regulated the flow of water precisely. He stood alone, quietly watering his garden in the early-afternoon sunshine, humming to himself the song "Between the Euphrates and the Tigris."

The water carved out branching and interlacing furrows. From time to time, Father bent down to block its path and direct it where it was needed.

Hillel suddenly felt an ecstatic, overwhelming love for his father. He scrambled out of his hideaway in the fig tree, ran up the path through the summer bird song through the breeze laden with the scent of the distant sea through the streaming afternoon sunlight, flung his arms around his father's waist, and hugged him with all his might.

Hans Kipnis passed the hose from his right to his left hand, stroked his son's head tenderly, and said, "Hillel."

The boy did not reply.

"Here, Hillel. Take it. If you want to water the garden for a bit, take the hose, and I'll go and clip the hedge. You can. Only be very careful not to aim the water at the plants themselves."

"Daddy, what does 'Perfidious Albion' mean?"

"It's what the fanatics call England when they want to be rude about it."

"What does 'fanatics' mean?"

"They're people who are always sure that they know best what's right and what's wrong and what ought to be done, and try their hardest to make everybody else think and act the same way."

"Is Uncle Mitya a fanatic?"

"Uncle Mitya is a sensitive man who reads a lot of books and spends a lot of time studying the Bible. Because he worries a great deal about our plight, and also perhaps because of his personal sufferings, he sometimes uses words that are not quite the words I myself would choose to use."

"What about Mommy?"

"She's having a rest."

"No, I mean, is she also a fanatic?"

"Mommy grew up surrounded by wealth and luxury. Sometimes it's hard for her to get used to conditions here; you were born here, and perhaps you are sometimes surprised by her moods. But you're a clever boy, and I'm sure you're not angry with Mommy when she's sad or when she longs to be somewhere completely different."

"Daddy, I've got something to tell you."

"What is it, son?"

"I've got a shilling that I don't want at all. And I don't want you to start asking me who gave it to me, 'cause I won't say. I just want you to take it."

"All right. I'll look after your shilling for you, and I won't ask any questions. Only mind you don't get your new sandals wet when you're watering the grapes. Now I'm going to fetch the shears. Bye-bye. You ought to be wearing a hat in this heat."

10

Toward sunset, when the mountains were shrouded and the wind swept knowingly through the woods and the valleys and the bell of the Schneller Barracks resounded forlornly, the preparations were complete.

All that remained was to wait for the taxi, say good-bye, and go. Nothing had been overlooked. Hans Kipnis, in his borrowed dress suit and impeccably polished black shoes, with his hair neatly parted and smoothed down with water, with his round glasses, looked like a mild, good-natured Evangelical minister setting out with a pounding heart for his wedding.

"My own Dr. Zichel," Mother said with a laugh, and bent over to straighten the white handkerchief in his top pocket.

She was a little taller than he, and her scent was the scent of autumn. She was wearing her blue evening dress with its daring neckline. The light shone in her drop earrings. Ruth was erect and sensuous as she walked with a slow, rounded motion, like a large cat, to wait outside on the veranda. She turned her bare back on the house and looked out into the desolate twilight. Her blond plait had settled on the arch of her left shoulder. Her hip rubbed slowly, with a dreamy rhythm, against the cool stone parapet.

And how the bells had rung throughout Warsaw at the national festival. How all the marble horsemen had reared up in every square. How her warm voice had carried over the playground of the school as she had read the searing lines of the Polish national poet:

> *Slain cavalrymen never die,*
> *They fly high through the air like the wind,*
> *Their horses' hoofs no longer touching the ground.*
> *At night in the storm in the snow you can hear them flying past,*
> *Foam-flecked winged steeds and valiant horsemen,*
> *Forever flying over forests and meadows and plains,*
> *Ghost warriors eternally riding into battle.*
> *At night in the storm in the snow they wing their way high over Poland.*
> *Cavalrymen never die, they become transparent and powerful as tears. . . .*

Ruth's voice conveyed a melancholy echo of violins, the tempestuous thunder of war drums, the roar and sigh of the organ. How they had all loved her. The handsome Tadeusz had stood stiffly at attention half a pace behind her on the platform, holding aloft the blazing Torch of Liberty. Elderly teachers who had themselves fought as cavalry officers in the great war for the liberation of Poland, and who still relived it in their dreams on happy nights, wept to hear her reciting. They stood with their eyes closed and strained toward her with all the force of their longing. She received their love and desire in her heart, and her heart was ready to bestow love on all good men.

She had never throughout her school days encountered bad men until both her parents died within a month of each other, and her sister, Nyuta, suddenly married the widowed gynecologist and left with him for New York. She believed that if bad men really existed outside fairy stories, they must lurk in dark corners. They could never come near her, with her gleaming white tennis dress and her expensive racket. Hence she was inclined to feel a certain sympathy even for them, if they existed. Their lot must be a sad one. What a terrible thing it must be, to be a bad man.

By seven o'clock, the mountains were growing dark. The lights of Jerusalem came on. In every house the iron shutters were pulled closed and the curtains were drawn. The inhabitants sank into worry and longing. For an instant the hills of Jerusalem seemed to be heaving and swelling like a sea in the dark.

Hillel was left with Madame Yabrova the pianist and her niece, Binyamina. They would play the phonograph for him, give him supper, let him play for a little with their collection of dolls of all nations, and then put him to bed. Meanwhile the taxi arrived, with its yellow headlights, and gave a long horn blast that sounded like the cry of an animal.

The whole street came out to see Dr. and Mrs. Kipnis off to the May Ball at the High Commissioner's palace on the Hill of Evil Counsel.

Mitya the lodger stood grinning darkly on the doorstep of the house, his silhouette hunched with suffering, clasping a half-drunk glass of tea between his hands. He was chewing the point of his shirt collar, and his lips were mouthing something in the darkness, a curse or a premonition of disaster. The elderly Professor Julius Wertheimer, keeping his place with his finger in a German edition of the New Testament, raised his hat slightly and said sadly, as if they were leaving on a long journey to another continent:

"Don't forget us."

Mrs. Vishniak the pharmacist waved them good-bye and good luck from where she sat on a wickerwork chair under the single Mandatory street lamp. Two tears hung from her painted eyelashes, because not long beforehand the announcer on "The Voice of Jerusalem" had said that times were changing and that things would never be the same again.

At the last minute. Engineer Brzezinski emerged on the other side of the road, slightly drunk and holding a huge electric lamp. He was a big-boned man with thick red hair and freckles. He was panting like a woodcutter and trembling with emotion. He thundered to them at the top of his voice:

"Just you tell them, doctor, tell them to their faces! Tell them to leave us alone! Tell them to go away! Tell them the White Paper is rotten! Tell them the whole country is getting more and more rotten every day! Tell them once and for all! And tell them that life as a whole is a rotten trick! Cheap! Miserable! Provincial! You let them know! And tell them that we, *sam chort znayet*, will never stop suffering and hoping until our last breath! Tell them!"

Suddenly he fell silent and pointed his great lamp furiously up at the dark sky, as if he were trying to dazzle the stars themselves.

Then the taxi choked, roared, and moved off in a cloud of dust.

The street was left to itself. Everyone had gone indoors. Only the square-paned street lamp continued to shed its forlorn light in vain. The wind blew. The fig tree ruffled its leaves and settled down. Its fingers were still empty. Dogs barked in the distance. It was night.

11

Lyubov Binyamina was a short, heavy girl with a swarthy complexion and a pointed chin. She looked like a plump, slow-moving, melancholy partridge. Only her lips were painted a bright scarlet. Her heavy bust forced out the front of her dress almost violently. There was always something slovenly about her appearance: a dangling button, a bad cough, a yellow oil stain on her Viennese-style dress. She wore clumsy brown orthopedic shoes, even around the house. She had thick down on her arms, and she wore a man's wristwatch. Hillel suddenly recalled the terrible things Mitya had said about the fellahin women going out alone at night to gather firewood, looking like hairy black she-goats. He bit his lip and tried hard to think of something else, but Binyamina kissed his earlobe and called him "child poet," and he buried his face in the carpet and blushed to the roots of his curly hair.

Madame Yabrova, by contrast, displayed the somewhat threadbare remnants of a former grandeur. She spoke with a heavy emphasis, in long, emotional sentences, in a strong voice coarsened by the Simon Arzdt cigarettes she chain-smoked. She would rush around the room, furiously wiping her mouth, picking things up and putting them down again, and turning on her heel with a kind of clumsy agility, like an aging prima donna. She had a slight gray mustache and bushy black eyebrows. Hillel could not take his eyes off her double chin; it reminded him of the pelican in the zoo on Prophet Samuel Street.

Madame Yabrova had changed, as she did every evening, into a theatrical mauve velvet evening gown. She filled the room with a mingled smell of mothballs, baked fish, and eau de cologne.

After a few affectionate words, she suddenly released Hillel, silenced her niece with a hoarse reprimand, and exclaimed:

"Be quiet. We must both be quiet. The child has an inspiration."

They earned their living by giving private music lessons, one on the piano and the other on the cello. They sometimes traveled by bus to remote settlements to favor the pioneers with Friday-night recitals. Their playing was always precise and free from frills and graces, if a trifle academic.

Every available surface in their home was scattered with mementos: tiny ornaments, elaborately carved candlesticks, lumps of rock, hand-made objects of wire and raffia, on the piano, the dining table, the coffee table, bronze busts including a glowering Beethoven, Oriental pots, plaster-of-Paris figurines, a china replica of Big Ben, dolls in motley national costumes, a copper Eiffel Tower, water-filled glass globes in which, when they were shaken or turned over, fake snow slowly fell on a rustic cottage or a village church.

One whole shelf was alive with woolly animals: polar bears, leopards, deer, centaurs, zebras, monkeys, elephants, all wandering hopelessly through a forest of green baize or dyed cotton wool. Every quarter of an hour a headless cuckoo popped out of the wall clock and emitted a sound resembling a hoarse bark.

Hillel was seated in a deep armchair surrounded by large philodendrons. Here he huddled in his gym shorts and cotton undershirt, with his legs tucked beneath him.

He thought about the fanatics, of whom Daddy had said that they thought they always knew best what was right and what was wrong and what ought to be done, and wondered in a panic whether Daddy and Mommy might not be secret fanatics, because they, too, always seemed to think they knew best.

Madame Yabrova said:

"If you promise me never to pick your nose, you may have a piece of marzipan after your supper. Lyubov, *krasavitsa*, put down that filthy novel of yours for a moment and pop into the kitchen to get some bread and butter and jam for our guest. *Spassibo.*"

Lyubov said:

"It's not a filthy novel, Auntie. It's nothing of the sort. It's true it's not exactly suitable for children, it's got all sorts of disasters and erotic scenes in it, but there's nothing dirty about it. And anyway, Hillel's almost a grown man. Just look at him."

Madame Yabrova snickered:

"*Bozhe moi*, Lyubov! Nothing dirty, indeed! Smut! Filth! That's all she has in her head. The body, Lyubov, is the purest thing there is in the whole world. Writers should write about love and suchlike with proper reticence. Not with all sorts of filth. Hillel is old enough, I can see, to know what is love and what is simply disgusting."

Hillel said:

"I don't like jam. I want some marzipan, please."

The room smelled dank and brown. In six vases of assorted shapes and sizes, last weekend's gladioli drooped and wilted. The windows were all closed to keep out the wind or the sounds of the night. Mommy and Daddy were far away. The shutters were closed, too. The curtains were drawn. Madame Yabrova was chain-smoking her Simon Arzdt cigarettes. The air was turning gray. She reached out to touch the child, who had glumly eaten half a buttered roll; she felt the muscles of his arm and exclaimed dramatically:

"*Molodyetz! Soldatchik!*"

Madame Yabrova put a record on the phonograph. Two suites for flute were followed without an interruption by an infectious dance tune. She kicked off her shoes and moved heavily around the room in her bare feet in time to the music.

Meanwhile, Hillel had consumed a soft-boiled egg from a chipped enamel mug, and rounded off his meal with a piece of marzipan. He played for a while with the glass globes with fake snowflakes. He was tired, drowsy, and miserable. He was suddenly seized with a vague apprehension.

Lyubov Binyamina Even-Hen came back into the room in a pink dressing gown. Her heavy, restless breasts were straining at the top button. Madame Yabrova switched on the lamp on the piano, which was carved in the form of a blue nymph, and turned off the overhead light. The elaborate glass chandelier went dark, and so did the room. Drowsily Hillel let himself be fed a spoonful of plum preserve that tasted like sticky-sweet glue. Shadows came and went, whispering, exchanging secret giggles in Russian. Through his drooping eyelids, through the haze of cigarette smoke, Hillel seemed to see Binyamina slowly, painstakingly unfastening all the hooks and catches of her aunt's velvet dress. The two women seemed to be floating on the smoke and mingling with the blocks of shadow. They were seemingly dancing on the carpet, dancing and smoking in time to the music of the phonograph among the ornaments and figurines, one in a pink dressing gown and the other in a black petticoat.

Then, in the dark, they leaned over him from either side of the deep armchair, stroked his curly hair and his cheeks with honeyed fingers, felt his chest through his cotton shirt, and carried him off to bed in their arms. His nostrils suddenly caught a strange smell. His eyes were shut tight with tiredness, but some sudden stimulus, a throb of sly curiosity, made him open them just a crack. The light was poor. The air in the room was full of smoke and sweat and eau de cologne. He caught a strange, heart-pinching glimpse of the waistband of Binyamina's knickers through the opening in the front of her dressing gown. And a faint sucking sound behind the bed. A moist whisper. Russian. A vague, unfamiliar feeling thrust its way up and down his spine. Not knowing what it was, he lay motionless on his back and glimpsed a shoulder, a hip, unknown curves, and his heart pounded and pounded like a frightened rabbit's.

He went on breathing deeply, calmly, as if he were fast asleep. Now even he was shocked at his slyness. Sleep had deserted him completely. He could feel the blood throbbing in his ankles. He smelled a blend of strong smells, and he knew that a large woman was blowing on his cheek to see if he was asleep. The sheet rustled. Fear and excitement clashed in his breast, and he decided to go on pretending to be a little boy fast asleep. He suddenly remembered the gleam in Uncle Mitya's eye as he spoke about she-goats. He also remembered the words "Perfidious Albion," but he could not remember what they meant. Hands were pulling at his gym shorts. His organ, which was taut like a thin pencil, was being touched with something like warm, sticky jam. He gritted his teeth, and forced himself with all his might not to recoil, not to stop his rhythmic breathing. Asleep. Feeling nothing. Not here. Far away. Only don't let it stop now the feel of velvet she-goats silk jam pink transparent more more. And the naughty Oriental girls who knocked him down on piles of gravel and pulled and pulled his hair and one of them was beginning to grow breasts under her vest. Mommy. A wet, licking feeling up his spine. And pinching. Then the slender pencil began to sneeze convulsively between the fingers of the musical women. The boy stifled a moan. Madame Yabrova let out a low, fleshy laugh. And Lyubov Binyamina suddenly panted like a thirsty dog.

The lamp on the piano went out. The room was dark and still. He opened his eyes and saw nothing but darkness. There was not a sound to be heard. Nothing stirred. In that moment Hillel knew that Daddy and Mommy would never come back and girls would never fight with him again on the gravel heap and there would be no more Mitya or anyone, they had all gone away and would never return. He was alone in the house alone in the neighborhood there was no one in Tel Arza no one in Jerusalem no one in the whole country he was left all alone with the jackals and the woods and the nibbled skeleton of the Turkish janissary.

12

The guest of honor at the ball was the Hero of Malta, Admiral Sir Kenneth Horace Sutherland, V.C., K.B.E., Deputy First Sea Lord.

He was standing, tall, pink-faced, and broad-shouldered, on the edge of the illuminated fountain, resplendent in his spotless white uniform and gleaming medals. He was holding a cocktail in his right hand, while in his left he twirled a single magnificent rose. He was surrounded by officers and gentlemen, by red-fezzed Arab dignitaries with gold watch chains strung across their bellies, and by wistful, sparkling-eyed English ladies, while tall, pitch-black Sudanese servants moved everywhere brandishing silver salvers, with snow-white napkins draped over their hooked arms.

Admiral Sutherland was telling a slightly risqué story, in a dry delivery spiced with naval slang, about the American general George Patton, a performing monkey, and a hot-blooded Italian actress by the name of Silvana Lungo. When he got to the punch line, the men guffawed and the ladies let out shocked shrieks.

Colored lights shone under the water in the marble pool, more lights hung suspended in the air, paper lanterns glowed among the trees, and the light breeze ruffled the pines. The gently sloping lawns were dotted with rose beds and divided by impeccably kept gravel paths. The palace itself floated on the beams of concealed floodlights. Its arches of Jerusalem stone were delicately, almost tenderly, carved.

At the foot of the veranda clustered some prominent figures of the Jewish community, including many of the leading lights of the Jewish Agency, the two elderly bankers Shealtiel and Toledano, Mr. Rokeah, the mayor of Tel Aviv, and Mr. Agronski of the *Palestine Post*. They were gathered in an excited semicircle around Captain Archibald Chichester-Browne, the British government spokesman, with whom they were engaged in a good-natured altercation. But for once the captain was disinclined to be serious. He pronounced one or two uncharitable remarks about the Arab League, which the prominent Jews interpreted as a favorable sign. Moshe Shertok dropped a hint to the others that they should be satisfied with this achievement and change the subject immediately, so as not to overstep the mark.

And so the conversation turned to the potash works that were rapidly being developed beside the Dead Sea. Captain Chichester-Browne took the opportunity to compare the Jewish kibbutzim to the early Christian communities that had once existed in the same region, and while on the subject, he even saw fit to praise Professor Klausner's work on the origins of Christianity. His audience drew further encouragement from these remarks, and mentally noted with glee that he had voiced two favorable sentiments in rapid succession. The captain then took his leave of the Zionist gentlemen with a charming, carefully modulated smile; he gestured ironically with his chin toward a group of Arab dignitaries from Bethlehem, winked at Moshe Shertok, and remarked confidentially that the other gentlemen were also demanding their pound of flesh. With that, he turned on his heel and walked over to join them.

After advancing slowly in a procession with other guests, Dr. and Mrs. Kipnis were eventually presented to the Military Governor of Jerusalem, to Lady Cunningham, and finally to Sir Alan himself.

Old Lady Bromley was nowhere to be seen. Perhaps she had fainted again. Sir Alan and Lady Cunningham greeted Father: "Pleased to meet you," "So glad you could come." Sir Alan allowed his grave blue glance to rest searchingly for a moment on Mother's black eyes as he said, "If I may say so, dear lady, your beauty and that of Jerusalem were molded by the same divine inspiration. I dare to hope that you will not be bored by our modest entertainment."

Mother responded to the compliment with one of her beautiful autumnal smiles. It hovered on her lips, as fine and transparent as the tears of the slain cavalrymen in the Polish poem.

Then a steward showed them to the bar and handed them over to an Armenian barman. Father immediately opted for a tomato juice, while Mother, after a moment's hesitation, the smile still playing faintly around her lips, asked for a glass of cherry brandy. They were conducted to a pretty wicker table and seated between Mr. Tsipkin, the Citrus King, and Madame Josette al-Bishari, the headmistress of the Arab National High School for Girls. They exchanged polite remarks.

Presently, the Military Governor of Jerusalem delivered a short, witty address from the veranda of the palace. He began with a reference to the crushing defeat inflicted on the enemies of humanity by Great Britain and her allies in May of the previous year. He paid a tribute to the guest of honor, Admiral Sir Kenneth Horace Sutherland, the Hero of Malta, and declared that the world had not yet seen the German, Italian, or lady who could resist him. He also paid tribute to the holy character of Jerusalem. He delivered an impassioned plea for fellowship and understanding among the adherents of the various religions. He added jokingly that if love did suddenly spring up among the different religious groups, the first thing the lovers would do would be to kick out the British. It was well known, he said, that in a love affair there was no place for a third party. But we British had always believed in miracles, and the idea of a Trinity was not entirely unfamiliar to Jerusalem; so whatever happened we would continue to haunt Palestine in the role of Holy Spirit, for which, of course, we were uniquely suited. A toast to the Crown. A toast to the Hero of Malta. Another toast to Sir Alan and his charming lady. And, if they would kindly refill their glasses, a final toast to the spring and to amity among all the inhabitants of the Holy Land, Moslems, Christians, Jews, and Socialists.

Then the dancing began.

From among the trees, which were hung with colored lights, the musicians of the police and military bands advanced in threes, their buckles gleaming. The whole hill resounded with the sound of percussion and brass. From behind the palace, fireworks lit up the sky over the city and the desert. The admiral, flushed and tipsy, roared, "Heave ho, me hearties! Splice the main brace! All guns fire!"

How colorfully the ladies' ball gowns blossomed by the light of the lanterns and fireworks. How riotously the music flowed into the heart of the night. How joyfully, how frenziedly, the couples whirled, the ladies twined like young vines, the men whispering sweet words into their ears. The Sudanese servants, coal-black faces atop white tunics, stared in amazement.

The last days of Rome must have been like this, Father thought to himself. As the idea flashed through his mind, his optimistic blue eyes may have reflected a momentary sadness behind his round glasses.

Mother was immediately snatched up by Mr. Tsipkin, the Citrus King. Then she could be seen, blond and radiant, in the arms of the Swedish consul. Then again resting lightly against the shoulder of a dark giant sporting a pair of Latin mustachios. With hardly a pause to draw breath, she was swept up by a one-eyed, battle-scarred colonel with predatory yellow teeth.

Father looked away. He struck up a desultory conversation with his neighbor, Madame Josette al-Bishari. No doubt he was telling her all about the cattle he inspected, or perhaps preaching with ill-suppressed zeal about the benefits of drinking goats' milk.

The High Commissioner himself was wandering, lost in thought, among the guests. He paused for a moment at the table where Madame al-Bishari and Dr. Kipnis sat; abstractedly he picked up a cocktail biscuit, eyed it cautiously, and returned it to the dish. He smiled faintly at Madame Josette or Dr. Kipnis or perhaps toward the lights of Jerusalem behind their shoulders, and eventually he spoke:

"Well, well. I see you are both sitting it out. Why aren't you dancing? I expect you're secretly hatching some sort of intrigue; but I've caught you red-handed, in the name of the Crown. Just my little joke. Good evening to you both."

He turned and moved away, a slim, erect figure, to continue his tour of the tables.

Father said, in English with a heavy German accent:

"I know a man who superficially resembles Sir Alan but hates him bitterly."

Madame Josette answered at once, in fluent German, with a kind of strangled fervor:

"Anyway, there's no hope."

"I am unable to agree with you on that point, madame," Father said.

Madame Josette smiled patiently. "I shall try to explain myself by means of a small illustration. Take yourselves, for example. You have been leaving Europe for Palestine for forty years now. You will never arrive. At the same time, we are moving away from the desert toward Europe, and we shall never arrive, either. There is not even the ghost of a chance that we shall meet one another halfway. I suppose, sir, that you consider yourself a social democrat?"

Father expressed surprise. "Surely we are meeting at this very moment?"

To these words he received no reply.

The headmistress of the National High School for Girls slowly gathered up her belongings from the table, her silk handkerchief, her Virginia cigarettes, her fan with its picture of Notre Dame; she apologized in French, which Father could not understand, and a feminine slyness glimmered for an instant in her eyes. She moved slowly away from the table, an elegant yet unremarkable woman, thickening slightly around the hips, in a long Marlene Dietrich dress. Then she was gone.

He followed her with his eyes until she had vanished in the throng. Then he caught sight of his wife, thrown high above the lawn, with her mouth gaping open in a soundless exclamation of pleasure, than landing gently in the broad hands of the Hero of Malta. She was disheveled and excited, her lips parted, her blue dress lifted above her knees.

Admiral Sutherland laughed hoarsely and gave an exaggerated bow. He seized her hand and raised the palm to his lips, kissing, blowing, nuzzling. She touched his cheek quickly. Then the music changed, and they started dancing again, pressed tightly together, with her head on his shoulder and his arm around her waist.

The fireworks had finished. The music was dying away. Guests were already leaving, and still she whirled with the Hero of Malta on the dance floor on the lawn toward the wood, until the darkness and the trees hid them from Father's sight.

Meanwhile the High Commissioner had withdrawn. The Military Governor had left, in a convoy of armored cars and armed jeeps, for the King David Hotel. The last guests had taken their leave and disappeared toward the parking lot. Captain Chichester-Browne and even the Sudanese servants had deserted the lawns and vanished into the inner recesses of the palace.

Darkness fell on the Hill of Evil Counsel. The paper lanterns went out one by one. Only the searchlights continued to claw the gentle slope and the bushes that were gradually sinking into ever-deeper shadows. A dry coldness rose from the Judean Desert, which bounded the palace on the east. And groups of palace guards armed with Bren guns began to patrol the grounds.

Father stood alone beside the deserted fountain, which was still pouring out jets of light and water. Now he spotted a single goldfish in the marble pool. He was cold, and desperately tired. His mother and sisters had probably been murdered in Silesia or somewhere else. The cattle farm in Galilee would never exist, the monograph or poem would never be written. Hillel would have to be sent to a boarding school in one of the kibbutzim. He will hate me for it all his life. Dr. Ruppin is dead. Buber and Agnon will also die. If a Hebrew state is ever established, I shall not be running its veterinary service. If only the Underground would come this very minute and blow the whole place sky-high. But that's not a nice thought. And I—

In his borrowed dress suit, with a white handkerchief peeping out of his top pocket, with the strange bow tie and his comical glasses, Hans Kipnis looked like a pathetic suitor in a silent film.

He closed his eyes. He suddenly remembered the wandering Bavarian ornithologist with whom he had cut a virgin path many years before to the remote sources of the Jordan in the farthest corner of the country. He recalled the coldness of the water and the snowy peaks of Mount Hermon. When he opened his eyes again, he saw Lady Bromley. She appeared like a wizened ghost from among the bushy oleanders, old, spoiled, seething with venomous zeal, in a dark shawl, doubled up with malicious glee.

"What you have lost tonight, sir, you will never find again. If you like, you can leave a message with me for the head gardener. But even he cannot save you, because he is a drunken Greek and a pathetic queer. Go home, my dear doctor. The party's over. Life nowadays is just like a stupid party. A little light, a little music, a little dancing, and then darkness. Look. The lights have been turned out. The leftovers have been thrown to the dogs. Go home, my dear doctor. Or must I wake up poor Lieutenant Grady and tell him to drive you?"

"I am waiting for my wife," said Father.

Lady Bromley let out a loud, ribald guffaw. "I have had four husbands, and none of them, I repeat, none of them ever said anything as fantastic as that. In all my life I've never heard a man talk like that, except perhaps in vulgar farces."

"I should be deeply grateful, madam, if you could give me some assistance, or direct me to someone who can help me. My wife has been dancing all evening, and she may have had a drop too much to drink. She must be around somewhere. Perhaps she has dozed off."

Lady Bromley's eyes suddenly flashed, and she growled wickedly:

"You are the native doctor who poked his fingers into my corset ten days ago. How rotten and charming. Come here and let me give you a big kiss. Come. Don't be afraid of me."

Father rallied his last resources. "Please, madam, please help me. I can't go home without her."

"That's rich," gloated Lady Bromley. "Listen to that. That's wonderful. He can't go home without his wife. He needs to have his wife next to him every night. And these, ladies and gentlemen, are the Jews. The People of the Book. The spiritual people. Huh! How much?"

"How much what?" Father asked, stunned.

"Really! How much will that rotten drunkard Kenneth have to pay you to calm down and keep your mouth shut? Huh! You may not believe it, but in the twelve months since the end of the war, that stupid young hothead has already sold three woods, two farms, and an autograph manuscript of Dickens, all for cash to silence the poor husbands. What a life. How rotten and charming. And to think that his poor father was once a gentleman in waiting to Queen Victoria!"

"I don't understand," said Father.

Lady Bromley gave a piercing, high-pitched laugh like a rusty saw and said, "Good night, my sweet doctor. I am really and truly grateful to you for your devoted attention. Jewish fingers inside my corset. That's rich! And how enchanting the nights are here in Palestine in springtime. Look around you: what nights! By the way, our beloved Alan also used to have a thriving sideline in other men's wives when he was a cadet. But that leech Trish soon sucked him dry. Poor Trish. Poor Alan. Poor Palestine. Poor doctor. Good night to you, my poor dear Othello. Good night to me, too. By the way, who was the raving lunatic who had the nerve to call this stinking hole Jerusalem? It's a travesty. *Au revoir*, doctor."

At three o'clock in the morning, Father left the palace on foot and headed in the direction of the German Colony. Outside the railway station, he was given a lift by two pale-faced rabbis in a hearse. They were on their way, they explained, from a big wedding in the suburb of Mekor Hayim to their work at the burial society in Sanhedriya. Hans Kipnis arrived home shortly before four, in the misty morning twilight. At the same time, the admiral, his lady friend, his driver, and his body-guard crossed a sleeping Jericho with blazing headlights and with an armed jeep for escort, and turned off toward the Kaliah Hotel on the shore of the Dead Sea. A day or two later, the black-and-silver Rolls Royce set out eastward, racing deep into the desert, across mountains and valleys, and onward, to Baghdad, Bombay, Calcutta. All along the way, Mother soulfully recited poems by Mickiewicz in Polish. The admiral, belching high-spiritedly like a big, good-natured sheepdog, ripped open her blue dress and inserted a red, affectionate hand. She felt nothing, and never for an instant interrupted her gazelle song. Only her black eyes shone with joy and tears. And when the admiral forced his fingers between her knees, she turned to him and told him that slain cavalrymen never die, they become transparent and powerful as tears.

13

The following day, a heat wave hit Jerusalem. Dust rose from the desert and hung over the mountains. The sky turned deep gray, a grotesque autumnal disguise. Jerusalem barred its shutters and closed in on itself. And the white boulders blazed spitefully on every hillside.

All the neighborhood was gathered excitedly in the garden. Father stood, in khaki shorts and a vest, staring tiredly and blankly up into the fig tree. His face looked innocent and helpless without his round glasses.

Mrs. Vishniak clapped her hands together and muttered in Yiddish, *"Gott in Himmel."* Madame Yabrova and her niece tried angry words and gentle ones. They held out the threat of the British police, the promise of marzipan, the final threat of the kibbutz.

Engineer Brzezinski, red-faced and panting, tried unsuccessfully to join two ladders together. And Mitya the lodger took advantage of the general confusion to trample the flower beds, one after another, uprooting saplings and tearing out plants and throwing them over his shoulder, chewing his shirt collar and hissing continuously through his rotting teeth, "Lies, falsehood, untruth, it's all lies."

Father attempted one last plea. "Come down, Hillel. Please, son, get down. Mommy will come back and it'll all be like before. Those branches aren't very strong. Get down, there's a good boy. We won't punish you. Just come down now and everything will be exactly the same as before."

But the boy would not hear. His eyes groped at the murky gray sky, and he went on climbing up, up to the top of the tree, as the scaly fingers of the leaves caressed him from all sides, up to where the branches became twigs and buds, and still on, up to the very summit, up into the gentle trembling, to the fine delicate heights where the branches became a high-pitched melody into the depths of the sky. Night is reigning in the skies, time for you to close your eyes. Every bird is in its nest, all Jerusalem's at rest. He saw nothing, no frantic people in the garden, no Daddy, no house and no mountains, no distant towers, no stone huts scattered among the boulders, no sun, no moon, no stars. Nothing at all. All Jerusalem's at rest. Only a dull-gray blaze. Overcome with pleasure and astonishment, the child said to himself, "There's nothing." Then he gathered himself and leaped on up to the last leaf, to the shore of the sky.

At that point the firemen arrived. But Engineer Brzezinski drove them away, roaring: "Go away! There's no fire here! Lunatics! Go to Taganrog! Go to Kherson, degenerates! That's where the fire is! In the Crimea! At Sebastopol! There's a great fire raging there! Get out of here! And in Odessa, too! Get out of here, the lot of you!"

And Mitya put his arms carefully arund Father's shaking shoulders and led him slowly indoors, whispering gently and with great compassion, "Jerusalem, which slayeth its prophets, shall burn the new Hellenizers in hellfire."

In due course, the elderly Professor Julius Wertheimer, together with his cats, also moved into the little stone house in Tel Arza. An international commission of inquiry arrived in Jerusalem. There were predictions and hopes. One evening Mitya suddenly opened up his room and invited his friends in. The room was spotlessly clean, except for the slight persistent smell. The three scholars would spend hours on end here, drinking tea and contemplating an enormous military map, guessing wildly at the future borders of the emerging Hebrew state, marking with arrows ambitious campaigns of conquest all over the Middle East. Mitya began to address Father by his first name, Hanan. Only the famous geographer Hans Walter Landauer looked down on them with a look of skepticism and mild surprise from his picture.

Then the British left. A picture of the High Commissioner, Sir Alan Cunningham, appeared in the newspaper *Davar*; a slim, erect figure in a full general's uniform, saluting the last British flag to be run down, in the port of Haifa.

A Hebrew government was finally set up in Jerusalem. The road in Tel Arza was paved, and the suburb was joined to the city. The saplings grew. The trees looked very old. The creepers climbed over the roof of the house and all over the fence. Masses of flowers made a blaze of blue. Madame Yabrova was killed by a stray shell fired on Tel Arza from the battery of the Transjordanian Legion near Nabi Samwil. Lyubov Binyamina Even-Hen, disillusioned with the Hebrew state, sailed from Haifa aboard the *Moledet* to join her sister in New York. There she was run over by a train, or she may have thrown herself underneath it. Professor Buber also died, at a ripe old age. In due course Father and Mitya were appointed to teaching posts at the Hebrew University, each in his own subject. Every morning they packed rolls and hard-boiled eggs and a Thermos of tea and set off together by bus for the Ratisbone and Terra Sancta buildings, where some of the departments of the university were housed temporarily until the road to Mount Scopus could be reopened. The elderly Professor Julius Wertheimer, however, finally retired and devoted himself single-mindedly to keeping house for them. The whole house gleamed. He even discovered the secret of perfect ironing. Once a month Hanan and Mitya went to see the child at school in the kibbutz. He had grown lean and bronzed. They took him chocolate and chewing gum from Jerusalem. On the hills all around Jerusalem, the enemy set up concrete pillboxes, bunkers, gun sites.

And waited.

1974

MUSICAL MOMENT

BY JOSHUA KNAZ

translated by Betsy Rosenberg

THE BIRD ON the tray was gorgeous. With green and purple feathers, pampered and plump it sprawled heavily on the cold copper that sent it in broken reflection. The lanky neck drooped over the metal rim of the tray, looping through languor or self-love, head tucked, beak grazing the base of the bloody throat, the eyes glazed, stunned, despairing, pining over the catastrophe.

I never wearied of looking at that picture. Each Sabbath afternoon when we used to visit my father's Aunt Frieda, I would stare at it for a long while in a deliberate effort to learn the secret: why did the picture evoke in me a feeling of dangerous pleasure? Slightly to the right of the picture in the corner of the room sat my father's grandmother in her customary chair, a clean, wide, well-starched kerchief tied around her head in a triangle, the point touching her collar, the broad base overhanging her blind eyes, shading them. She sat in her armchair, there in the corner, like a stranger, an emissary from a world as yet unknown to me. Her face was doughy and her toothless mouth would gape from time to time as if to speak, then close abruptly with a compression of the lips and a look of resignation as though it would be too bothersome to say anything. Sometimes the glimmer of a smile would spread over her countenance only to fade among her countless wrinkles and finally vanish into the look of resignation.

We used to visit her each Sabbath afternoon. My father's Aunt Frieda opened the door for us, handsomely dressed as always, a chestnut wig curling down to her neck and two exquisitely dainty amber earrings hanging from her lobes. She was an elderly woman, but pretty nonetheless, elegant, tall and slender, and I will always recall her face reflecting goodness. Her husband, my father's uncle, stood by his old mother, shouting into her ear whenever someone arrived. Sometimes deafness impaired her wits or else memory failed her, and then my father's uncle would speak to her in their language, identifying the relative who had just walked in, and she would nod to show she understood. Sometimes she would mutter something in her husky crone's voice and then her son would laugh uproariously, sporting with his old mother to entertain the company. A light green cloth with shining gold fringe was laid on the round table, and next to it sat my two German "aunties," my father's cousins, Frieda's daughters. We could hear my father's uncle in hilarious conversation with his old mother about the coming of the Messiah or some such thing, until Frieda begged him to stop. Then she sliced and served the pale cake and we drank it down with a glass of thick, sweet wine.

My two German aunties were talking cheerfully in their language. Having settled their business, they gave me an appraising look and entered into conversation with my parents on the subject of my blinking. My parents hinted that they should drop the subject since I would be sure to understand what they were talking about, and my father pressed my shoulder to show me that he didn't care about my blinking. And my mother told them in their language not to mention it in front of me again because it would only upset me and aggravate the blinking. And when I heard her say that, I was surprised, because I didn't feel upset in the least, and I told myself that even my own mother didn't know my real feelings. And maybe no one ever would.

Orna, my father's cousin, was forceful, enterprising and stubborn, whereas her sister was reticent, a pacifier, inclined to mild depression. They were almost inseparable, though each sister had a family of her own. My parents' hints and appeals were of no avail. Orna ignored them. She believed with all her might in self-control and willpower. She rose from the table took me by the hand, and told me to come along. My father grinned encouragingly to offer me support; no doubt, in anticipation of what I was in for with my cousin. She led me to the far side of the room, sank me down on the big, dark old leather couch, and sat beside me. She leaned over me, her face so close to mine I could see her pores and the faint quivering of her wrinkles. Behind Orna's shoulder I saw the old woman sitting in the corner, and above her, a little to the left, the picture of the expiring bird. First of all, Auntie Orna let me know, in her opinion the blinking business was due to pampering, like thumb-sucking among little children. And just as we fight thumb-sucking, we can fight this blinking too. The way to fight thumb-sucking, as we all know, is to sprinkle mustard or hot pepper on the offending finger, so that when next the child puts it in his mouth, the result is so disastrous that he will think twice about doing it again, unless, that is, he wants another taste of hell. And there are likewise devious strategies against blinking which for the moment she would not divulge. And lest I forget, the fight against blinking, like the fight against thumb-sucking, is waged for the sake of the child, the child and his family. Auntie Orna, pronouncing "family" in her special German accent, beamed with a look of surpassing responsibility and earnestness. We know of course, she said, that thumb-sucking is dangerous. There are juices in the mouth that decompose matter, so that the sucked thumb is gradually eaten away until nothing but a stub is left, which is so spindly that it falls off before you know it, and the child has a handicap for the rest of his life. As for blinking, we know that the lids are connected to the eyes with tiny muscles whose job it is to protect that most dear to us of all, our eyes, from dust and foreign matter. But if the muscles are abused, they deteriorate like a worn-out hinge that lets the door bang every time the wind blows, leaving the house open to havoc. Children who abuse their eye muscles lose control over them, so that sometimes while they're sleeping in the middle of the night they open their eyes without even noticing it, like certain kinds of animals. When this happens they have the most *horrid* nightmares.

"This must be stopped!" said my Auntie Orna. "It upsets your parents and embarrasses the entire 'family.' People ask questions, they don't understand. And if not for the sake of your own well-being and further development, then at least for the sake of the 'family' you must make every effort to stop this ugly, ugly blinking."

Pronouncing "ugly, ugly," Auntie Orna made a face, jerking, twisting it vehemently this way and that, squeezing her eyes shut, contorting her body, compressing her lips, then opening her eyes and goggling, then suddenly squeezing them shut again to show me just how terrible it looked. I knew she was overdoing it and I burst out laughing. Orna couldn't help laughing herself, but she kept saying, "That's how it looks! I want you to know that's exactly how it looks!"

My auntie, Orna's sister, approached the leather couch and asked her sister to leave me alone and come back to the table. She couldn't sit there without Orna. But Orna rattled away in their language and her sister smiled sadly, apologetically, and made a small gesture of dismissal and resignation. She remained standing near us for a little while longer and then went back to the table.

My Auntie Orna arrived at a new step-by-step procedure to stop my blinking. I was to count to twenty between blinks. After getting used to that, I was to count to thirty, and then forty. By the time I reached a hundred, she assured me, the habit would be broken. She asked me to begin, there and then, with the first exercise, from the simple to the difficult, to count to twenty without blinking. I did as she asked. Watching her, I began counting in a low voice. When I got to seven, I already had a strong impulse to close my eyes, if only for an instant, but I controlled myself.

Little by little the room grew dim around me, when all at once I noticed my father's old grandmother, facing me, sequestered in her chair. And through the dimness I thought I saw her clasping her hands over her head in a signal of distress. She was probably only adjusting her kerchief, but I perceived it otherwise, and I heard my Auntie Orna as though from far away counting with me in a loud, measured voice, nine, ten, eleven, a voice that chastened and commanded like a fateful clock, unrelenting, twelve, thirteen, fourteen . . . and my eyes were brimming over with the strain and I could no longer see my father's old grandmother because now my lashes were jammed together, tenaciously.

My parents rushed to deliver me from Orna who was sounding her disappointment and ridiculing me. My failure implied her own, the failure of her system and maybe even of the "family," and she raged at my parents for being too lenient and for spoiling me to my detriment. "He'll never stop," said my Auntie Orna. "He'll never stop. He won't even try, not for his own sake, not for his parents' sake, and not for the sake of the 'family.' "

My father wiped my eyes with his handkerchief and I kept trying to explain that I wasn't really crying, that the tears were falling because of the strain. But they wouldn't listen to what I said, either because they didn't believe me or because they didn't think it was important. But it was important to me. Because I had to vindicate myself so Orna wouldn't think I was a spoiled and inconsiderate crybaby. When I opened my eyes next I was back at the table facing my auntie, Orna's sister, who smiled her crushed and sorry smile. Orna herself was holding forth, and I knew they were talking about me. My father's Aunt Frieda returned to the table with an iridescent glass dish full of sweets. She set it down before me and stroked my neck. I wiped the last tears away with the back of my hand, and I hated my Auntie Orna for putting me to shame.

On our way home I asked my parents to please let me take up my violin lessons again. The lessons had been discontinued some years before against my will. I have never forgotten the aroma of colophony. It reminded me of separation and of the initial high hopes, a sour sort of bitter, heady smell. My imagination soared on it, and my heart thrilled with adventure. It seemed to pass from the rosined bow to the strings, from the strings into the sound, into the very enigma of the violin. On our way home I had a violent longing for it and for my violin, which had been taken from me for medical reasons.

Long consultations had been called for at the time. In those days, toward the end of the war, when we were living in a small neighborhood on Mount Carmel, I went downtown with my mother, and there, on one of those quiet streets, in a two-story house not far from the Israel Institute of Technology, I met my first violin teacher, Mrs. Chanina. She was tall and ample, with chestnut hair in a thick Russian-looking plait that rolled down her neck. My first violin teacher Mrs. Chanina tested my musical ability and consented to give me lessons. As my mother left the teacher's room she announced that my father would buy me a "quarter" violin and we would come for lessons twice a week.

This was around the time I first associated the alluring aroma of colophony with my teacher Mrs. Chanina. I saw in her a hitherto un-dreamed-of beauty and majesty. If today I saw her or a picture of her from those days, perhaps she wouldn't look so beautiful and majestic anymore. But I do understand what made her so exciting. It was the Slavic grace of her manner when she spoke. She had a deep, soft voice and eyes the color of her hair, the color of her drapes and furniture, brown with an auburn luster, a velvety brown with subtle, warm high-lights. Her stature, her thoughtful, unhurried movements, her bearing, and her way of tilting her head a little to the right, all this raised her high in my esteem. And when she lifted her violin to play, her eyes flashed fire. As if the sleeping gypsy were stirring in her, as if the violin were stirring her gypsy blood to frenzied provocation, that's how I picture her today when I close my eyes and try to imagine her, the way she moved.

She was so friendly too, she spoke so gently, and she held dominion over her surroundings like a queen. Around this time I had my first whiff of colophony, and I rubbed it assiduously on my bow. My father found "colophony" for me in the encyclopedia: so named after a small village in Asia Minor, whence this substance was exported. A clear yellow or light brown solid, it is derived from the residue of distilled turpentine. Nonsoluble in water, it will dissolve in ether or alcohol. Used in the manufacture of lacquer, to caulk boats, to rub on the bows of stringed instruments, and as a reducing agent in metal smelting; used predominantly in the manufacture of soap and pharmaceuticals and as an emollient in the preparation of various salves and ointments.

Some time later, Mrs. Chanina observed that I had made excellent progress, and she suggested that my parents enroll me at the Haifa Conservatory to study theory. One winter afternoon my parents took me to the conservatory. They settled whatever they had to settle in the office, and led me to one of the classrooms. They were going to wait for me in the corridor. As I struggle to recapture these hazy, incoherent scenes, an abysmal feeling pours out of my heart to vent itself on the world. But I can't think why.

When I walked into the classroom with the secretary, the other pupils, who were older than I, were already seated and waiting for the lesson to begin, and they probably turned to look at me. I was to occupy a double desk next to a boy who had the beginnings of a mustache. He was leafing through his notebook, and I don't know what went through my mind just then, but I was probably nervous. I must have wondered what would happen now and what I was doing here among these older children who had nothing to do with me. And I imagined I heard wisecracks and giggling from some quarter, though it may not have been directed at me. A hush fell over the room as our teacher, a white-haired gentleman with silver spectacles, walked through the classroom. He spoke to the class, and played something on the piano. Then he asked questions, and the pupils answered. We were on the top floor of the old building, and through the narrow window I could see the street below, the people, the traffic, the cyclists, the Arab vendors with their carts. Gradually the pallid winter sky gave way to dusk, and lights went on in the street and in the houses. Then the classroom lights went on and the faces of the older children were visible again, and the boy beside me was writing in his notebook. My notebook lay before me, blank and new. I couldn't think of anything to write. I thought about my parents waiting for me in the corridor, and I was impatient for the lesson to be over so we could go home.

Afterward my parents asked me eagerly about the lesson, and I said it was fine. Had I understood what they were learning? Yes, yes, I lied, I understood. They were very pleased with me and I couldn't look in their eyes. I knew I mustn't disillusion them. Their loving enthusiasm made this clear enough. I remember this as my first humiliating encounter with failure, and with the shame of having to lie to disguise it.

How comforting it was to be back with my teacher Mrs. Chanina, in the house I knew so well. I hoped I would never return to the conservatory, but a week later my mother took me again. I walked into the classroom and sat down. This time the chair next to mine was empty, the boy with the beginning of a mustache having moved elsewhere, to sit with one of the older children. I slid over to be near the window, where I could watch the traffic in the street and the people hurrying like swarming locusts. I don't know why, but suddenly I was seized with anguish. The whirling and swirling eddy of traffic made me so dizzy I might have fallen out the window and lost everything I had. I tried to turn my eyes away, but I couldn't. In the street one familiar figure stood out prominently against the crowd. She was looking directly at me, beckoning for me to jump down. I could see her clearly, her features, her gestures, and there was no mistake about it, she was addressing me. She opened her arms to embrace me. Then she vanished, and I finally managed to turn away from the window. The eerie scene had worn me out, and I was drowsy. I saw the older children writing in their notebook as the teacher played various scales on the piano and commented in a weary, monotonous voice. I hid my face in my hands, wishing it would be over soon. I tried to visualize the corridor behind the door, to penetrate the wall, to make sure she was waiting for me. I tried to imagine myself pacing up and down the empty corridor with nowhere to go. I was getting as far as the office at the head of the stairs when a peal of laughter startled me, and as I dropped my hands I saw the entire class in an uproar and the old teacher leaning over to pat my shoulder. He smiled a little doubtfully, and another peal of laughter rang through the room.

Then he continued with the lesson. On my right was the dangerous window, and on the left, at the far side of the room, was the door that led to the corridor. I glanced around. I picked up my blank new notebook and tiptoed to the door. Slowly I turned the handle, opened the door, closed it stealthily behind me. Just as I had thought, my mother wasn't there. I walked down the empty corridor the way I had in my imagination, feeling abandoned and betrayed; I bit my lip, so I wouldn't scream. I stopped at every doorway and listened for my mother. Gradually my sense of propriety gave way to angry despair, and in furious pursuit, I opened door after door and peeked into each of the rooms, where I found lessons in progress, people quietly sitting about, or no one there at all. But my mother wasn't anywhere to be found. From the end of the corridor I heard a violin playing with piano accompaniment. I hadn't paid attention to it earlier because of my desperation. But as I approached the doorway, I heard the music clearly now, and it was sad and beautiful and mysterious. The door wasn't closed all the way and I peeped into the room, but I couldn't see anything. I opened the door a little wider and I saw the violinist, a tall boy wearing shorts and knee socks. His hair was black, combed neatly, and he was playing a large violin. He was so absorbed in the music that he closed his eyes; when his left wrist quivered over the bridge during the vibration, he bent over in his great emotion, and then he braced upright while playing the string passage. I could only see his profile, but the pianist was facing me, and she was a nice-looking girl with curly hair and glasses. They were alone in the room, absorbed in the music. Suddenly, the boy stopped playing and they talked, and I was afraid they would discover me behind the door, so I stepped back. Then they started from the beginning, and I resumed my post by the door and listened.

The music, sometimes lyrical and sometimes passionate, was touching me. My fear and pain and loneliness of a few minutes before were thrust aside before the sadness and the dignity, the surrender and the rebellion, the order and the flow of this beautiful music in three-quarter time. Sometimes the violin would draw out the theme, almost weeping, while the piano challenged and provoked, trying to break its line of thought, and sometimes the piano accompanied in conciliation, in joy or contrition, indulging the violin, cherishing, clinging. One variation gave way to another, and the piano sang the theme, true in its fashion to the sad, ennobling beauty of the melody, while the violin opposed it with a counterrhythm, meeting the piano at the cadences, then leaving it again, until they finally merged.

When they had played through the final variation, the pianist stood up, and I stepped back and leaned ever so innocently against the wall. They left the room, she with her music tucked under her arm, he lovingly holding his violin case. They stood in the corridor talking together, and I longed to be him instead of me. I watched him from afar, my fear and self-pity giving way to a new emotion, that took me out of myself. The pianist said good-bye and walked into one of the rooms. He wandered down the corridor, aimlessly it seemed, lost in his reflections. Just then the pupils from my class began to pour out the door, and the boy with the beginning of a mustache called out "Uri!" and the violinist turned around, happy to greet him. The teacher came out of the room and looked at me as if he didn't know who I was, and then I saw my mother hurrying up the stairs.

"Were you waiting long?" she asked breathlessly.

"The class just got out," I said.

"How was it?"

"Fine."

"Did you participate?"

"Uh-no."

"Why not? Didn't you understand it?"

"I don't ever want to come back here again," I said, purse-lipped.

I refused to look at her, so I shall never know the expression on her face. She was silent. She held my hand and we walked down the stairs. I felt guilty with my hand in hers.

"I saw you down in the street, so I knew you weren't waiting for me." Now I could look at her. She bit her upper lip. "Is that why you don't ever want to come back?"

"No," I said, "that's not why."

Later, on the bus as we were winding up the hill, I told her about the boy and the wonderful music. She asked me to sing it for her and I sang what I thought sounded like the melody into her ear. It sounded pitiful to me compared with Uri's playing, but my mother was very impressed, and that evening when my father came home from work, she asked me to sing it for him. But however much I tried, it was lost, every note of it; all that was left was the memory of impression.

"Why don't you want to go to the conservatory anymore?" asked my father.

I didn't know what to say.

"Was it because I didn't stay and you were afraid of being alone?" asked my mother, with a trace of severity in her voice.

"No." I said. "Because it's not good there. They don't teach well."

"Why don't we give it some more time?" my father suggested, and I relented. My mother promised never to leave the corridor again when she was supposed to be waiting for me. I told my parents nothing at all about those lessons. Today, they seem like a strange dream that has neither beginning nor end. For years I have been trying to forget them.

Whenever I practiced the violin, Uri haunted me. My own playing seemed contemptible to me, no matter what my teacher Mrs. Chanina or my parents said. I despaired of attaining those magnificent heights, the domain of my betters.

One evening my mother asked me what was bothering me. I didn't know why she looked so worried. Did I sleep well, she wanted to know. When my father came home from work he too seemed worried. Strange, unaccountable things were going on, but they were outside, beyond my control, and there was nothing I could do about it. It concerned me, yet did not concern me. I was charged with a dark secret even I was not allowed to know, but which I had to keep until it could be told.

That winter and the following spring were unexceptional to all outward appearances, and yet, there was something in the atmosphere, something dark lurking around me, something that sneaked up on me and tried to sap my last reserves.

Twice a week my mother took me to the conservatory, and I would sit in the class like an outsider. No one ever paid any attention to me, and I must have gotten used to it. I never heard a word they said. I only hoped to meet that boy Uri some day and ask him what the piece he played was called. But I never did meet him, and whenever I walked down the corridor with my mother I would pull her to the doorway where I'd heard him play, and beg her to wait and listen: maybe it would happen, maybe I would relive the fabulous moment. But usually no one was inside, or else someone else was playing in the room. It was the same with every other room along the dingy corridor. He had vanished.

One day before the lesson, the boy with the beginning of a mustache walked up to me and asked me why I blinked all the time. I was confused, but I realized he was a bully and trying to hurt my feelings. I didn't answer him. After the lesson I told my mother about the boy and what he said. She looked so pained I was ashamed of myself. I felt as if I had the plague, or as if I were witnessing some terrible disaster, and I couldn't stop it, and no one could save me, and all they could do was confirm it or reassure me a little.

"If anyone asks you," said my mother, "just tell them you're tired. Say your eyes need rest. And after you rest it goes away. Just say you need rest. Rest is the best thing." The strain of telling a lie showed on her face. I wasn't tired. I didn't need to rest, and my eyes didn't either. And no one could give me what I needed. I looked at my face in the mirror. Nothing unusual there. It seemed like a conspiracy of silence.

"Are you feeling better?" asked the doctor. He was standing next to my father and mother as if they were all in league.

"Yes," I said, "I'm fine."

"Has anything unpleasant happened lately?"

I tried to think, but I couldn't remember anything of the kind.

He peered into my face but avoided looking at my eyes.

"How old are you?"

"Seven."

"Do you bite your nails?" He looked at my hands.

"What?! That's crazy!" I told him.

My mother shuddered, but I didn't know why. I searched her eyes, trembling at the prospect of disgrace. The doctor noticed my discomfiture and advised my parents to leave the room so he and I could have a little talk. When they were out of the room, he smiled at me and asked: "How are your parents, okay?"

"They're fine," I said.

He chuckled skeptically and asked, "Do they give you a hard time?"

"What do you mean?" I wondered. "What do you mean, they give me a hard time?" I loved them so much. What could he be thinking of?

"Do you think they're pleased with you?"

"I do whatever they tell me," I said.

His eyes lit up at this. He must have heard the undertone of anger in my voice.

"Are my questions making you angry?" asked the doctor.

"No," I protested. "No."

He smiled a dubious smile.

"Hay, you haven't checked my eyes yet," I said.

But he went on with his questions. He wanted to hear about school, about my friends and the games we played, and about the violin. I couldn't figure out why he was so interested in everything. Then he showed me to the waiting room, and asked me if I minded sitting there alone for a while so he could talk to my parents some more. They closed the door behind them, and I sat alone in the waiting room. Time passed. Daylight flooded the room through the open window. The furniture was bright, the curtains were bright. I was worried that I would be afraid, as I was at the conservatory when my mother left me and I was alone. But it was all right in the doctor's waiting room, I was getting used to the bright furniture, and I strained to hear what they were talking about in the other room behind the heavy door. But all I heard was the rumble of the traffic outside. Ages passed, and I wished it would be over so we could go back to normal life. But normal life was spoiled beyond repair, and it wouldn't do to pretend otherwise.

At long last they opened the door and the doctor patted my shoulder and said good-bye. I asked, "When are you going to check my eyes?" and he smiled blandly. I walked outside with my parents. As soon as we were on our way, my mother scolded me for being rude to the doctor and embarrassing her very much. I didn't understand what she meant.

"When the doctor asked if you bite your nails, you said, 'You're crazy.' "

"No I didn't. I said 'THAT'S crazy!' "

"No," said my mother, "You did not. You said 'YOU'RE crazy!' "

My protestations were all in vain. My father rested his hand on the back of my neck, and we walked the streets of Haifa in the afternoon light. But even my father's hand wasn't much comfort in the face of such a howling injustice.

My father said, "Why is it so important?"

But my mother was firm. I hated her. I knew that she was wrong and I was right. The injustice of it. Her pain weighed against mine, her failure against mine. Here we were, two people, antagonizing each other, mistrusting each other, thinking only of ourselves. She accused me of forgetting my manners, and worse, of allowing this sinister defect to mar my features unimpeded, and surely weakness of character is what brought it on, and where it would end was anybody's guess. But I knew I was right, and I would never surrender. I held on for dear life and looked to my father in desperation, and he smiled back at me with sympathy and confidence. It was a most important smile. We had formed an alliance against her. Now she had to face us both. She had made up her mind though, and, alas, no one could change it. She was unhappy and I thought it was because of her mistaken idea that I had been rude to the doctor. We walked into a German café downtown and they ordered hot chocolate for me and coffee for themselves.

My mother forgot my bad manners and smiled at me, though her pleasure was not untinged. "I'm afraid we'll have to stop your violin lessons for a while," she said. I thought this was a punishment for my so-called rudeness, and I raised my eyes in appeal to my father; I knew he wouldn't lead me astray. But he confirmed it.

What bothered me was not so much the discontinuation of my lessons, but the injustice of it, and all because of a mistake, and because we didn't trust each other.

"The doctor said you should stop for a while, because it has a harmful effect on your eyes," my father explained.

"I didn't say YOU'RE crazy! I said 'THAT'S crazy!' "

"It isn't important," said my mother, much to my surprise.

And if this was no longer important, the order of importance of everything was open to question. I gazed at this man and woman I loved most dearly, and I wondered if they were really mine. Twilight permeated the café and a pleasant breeze drifted through. In the street, workers hurried home, carrying their briefcases. An elderly lady at a nearby table buried her face in a German-language paper bound in a wooden frame with reading handles. An atmosphere of suspicion settled in the quiet spaces of the café.

"For how long?" I inquired.

"Until the blinking goes away," replied my father. "Let's hope it won't be long."

"You can stop after the recital," my mother said.

The recital for the end of the year of the Haifa Conservatory was two weeks away.

They were especially nice to me, emphatically nice, but the disappointment they were trying so hard to conceal was contagious, and I felt the futility of it all. Still, it was heartwarming to be bound together by a common destiny. I said no more, I remember; I wasn't going to beg for a reprieve.

My teacher Mrs. Chanina cheered me throughout the final lesson, and wished me luck in the upcoming recital. According to her, it wouldn't do me any harm to have some time off; as a matter of fact, I would probably take up my lessons with redoubled enthusiasm and even more splendid results. I stood before her with downcast eyes, and she caressed my neck. I didn't look at her as we were saying good-bye, and I didn't even turn around for a last look at the house as we were leaving. It just didn't feel like a separation. It was all so meaningless, a trifling matter, a silly technicality. But I never returned to the house, and I was destined to see my teacher Mrs. Chanina only one more time, the night of the recital.

She was in the front row with the other teachers, and we were somewhere in the middle. I remember sitting between my parents, bursting with the anticipation of Uri's performance, as though I was finally about to cancel a debt to myself, a debt of incomprehensible longing. As the outstanding pupil at the conservatory, he was due to appear last, to crown the evening. I watched him sitting there with his family, wearing a white shirt and long blue trousers, his hair combed neatly and parted at the side. He didn't show signs of being nervous. He was probably twelve or thirteen at the time, but I considered him very grown-up. I remembered how I'd listened from my hiding place to the music flowing out into the dingy corridor, and how I'd come to idolize him. How handsome he looked when he played the violin, how masterful and sure, and everything about him was gracious, sublime, unattainable, ideal. The way he sat, for instance, between his elderly parents, flanked by an older brother and sister in their distinguished row, their earnest faces, the clothes they wore, the way they nodded to the music, and applauded at the end of each piece, how perfectly beautiful it was. Sometimes between performances, one of them would lean over and address a question or comment to Uri, but it was impossible to guess what they were saying.

Toward the end of the recital, Uri stood up, and accompanied by the well-wishing of his family, he left the Hall. Mrs. Duniah-Weizman, principal of the Haifa Conservatory, introduced each of the players with a personal anecdote that was sure to please the guests and relations in the audience. Now it was Uri's turn, and the atmosphere grew festive and formal. The accompanist with the curly hair and glasses entered first, followed by Uri, holding his violin. Mrs. Duniah-Weizman raised her head and waited for absolute silence. At last, without further ado, she pronounced Uri's name, the name of his accompanist, and the piece they were going to play, the "La Follia" variations by Corelli.

Uri folded a handkerchief on his chin rest, and his violin sparkled beneath the platform lights. He tucked his instrument under his chin and raised his bow. He closed his eyes, he seemed to concentrate, opened his eyes, and with a nod from his accompanist began to play.

The sadness of the music swelled through the hall and was heightened by the trills at the end of each phrase. Something mysterious transformed the feverish and apparently happy dance into a sort of a desperate yet majestic dirge. Uri's hand was full of controlled emotion and inner strength. Never in my life had I heard such beautiful playing, almost terrifying in its purity, provocative, utterly dispassionate, both cool and ecstatic. And as the rhythm accelerated, the tall boy in the white shirt, blue trousers and grown-up shoes appeared to be wrestling mysterious forces. Sometimes he looked troubled, but it was only the exertion of a flawless performance, sounding the quickening sequence of chords with his nimble fingers. His concentration was so deep that it took him away from the platform and from the many eyes that were watching him, away from the piece itself, from its darkness, wildness, menace. He stood there, the paragon of an ordered world.

I felt how something happened within me, how I was enthralled. I could not immerse myself in the music, not completely, the beauty was unbearable. I watched the attentive audience, I looked at their eyes, I scanned the recital hall, and apprehensively, I peeped at the two closed doors. I knew that any minute now somebody was likely to run in screaming: Stop it! Stop the music! And I knew who that would be. I'd seen him many times on Kings Street, that crazy old beggar, and I couldn't get him out of my mind. I knew he was crouching behind the doors. The audience will be in an uproar, Uri's violin will shake in his hands, the pianist will faint, Uri will raise his head, stop playing, his face pale with guilt and indignity. I saw his parents and his brother and sister as they listened, somewhat numb and unconcerned. But how they will recoil when the wild man rushes through the doors and pounces on the platform screaming: Stop it! Stop it now! Mrs. Duniah-Weizman sat in the front row with the teachers, nodding her head to the rhythm of "La Follia." Little did she know what lurked out there. But I could see him, I saw his fists strike the air, as he waited for the crucial moment. He an old man, dressed in rags, with murderous red eyes and a violent face.

One variation followed another, and I sat there feeling puny and exposed. I felt my father's eyes resting on me briefly, and I searched them for signs of rebuke, in case he had seen the dread on my face, or something queer in my behavior. I listened to the terrible silence all around. The piano and violin hewed away in that terrible silence, and the audience was resting like the dead, in row upon row of family and friends, waiting for a verdict of some sort, waiting with the calmness of despair. I look around. Now my mother takes a handkerchief and wipes a tear from the corner of her eye. She is prone to displays of emotion, especially while listening to music, but this time I believe she's crying over me. I look down at my clothes, at my best short trousers, nicely ironed, at my shining laced-up shoes, and I hate them, I hate them, I hate their intimacy, their affinity, their solemnity, I hate their ridiculous, petty pretentiousness. I raise my eyes to the burnished doors, where someone calculates the perfect entrance. I am sweetly, wildly, breathless with anxiety, and I try to turn my attention to the marvelous music and forget all the rest, to capture these moments as they flit by forever. But the circle of brightness is impenetrable, for everything rebounds to the hall, to the danger behind the doors. And the danger does not materialize. Any minute now he'll make his entrance. He's rehearsing his part now, practicing the bitter shout at the audience who are unwitting accomplices to a terrible injustice: Stop the music! Stop it at once! I demand justice! Start the concert again. Start all over again!

But this is not what he intended to say. There's something else, and while he ponders, biding his time behind closed doors, the music nears conclusion, and my heart is pounding with apprehension that he still might break in, and I pray the piece will soon be over before he commits the crime. Yet another variation, and his fist freezes in midair instead of battering the panels of wood. His eyes are red like a killer's eyes, the enormity of his task is paralyzing him, he gasps and groans, and the filthy cloak around his shoulders ripples with the heaving of his chest, and tufts of grizzly hair jut through the slashes in his shirt. I knew the man, I knew him well. How often had I noticed him at his downtown station, drawn to suffer the sight of him as we passed him by, but I never dreamed that someday he would be linked to the recital. Can he create such a terrible infamy? Will he dare? And here it is happening.

There was a deafening noise that threatened to bring the building down. The last strains of the music died and the audience rose and applauded. It was almost cataclysmic. My parents were applauding too, with radiant faces. The pianist with the curly hair and glasses took a bow, and Uri at her side with violin and bow in his left hand stared directly at the audience. The trace of the smile was perceptible on his face, exhausted though he was after so much concentration and detachment, and he squinted at the blinding platform lights like someone who has just woken up and doesn't quite know where he is yet, and a certain gesture of his free right hand seemed to say, "What am I doing here with all these people?"

The doors were opened, and no one was there. The audience applauded on and on. Mrs. Duniah-Weizman helped Uri off the platform, and she hugged him. My mother smiled at me in great satisfaction, and my father took my hand and led me to the door. My mother said Corelli was probably one of the greatest composers. Pupils, teachers, and families clustered throughout the hall, chattering, laughing and shaking hands. By the doors, we ran into Mrs. Chanina. She patted my head affectionately and drew me aside. Her touch was pleasing, and I thought she seemed a little flustered though I couldn't tell why. She leaned down and whispered in my ear, "Music will always be your consolation." Maybe she said that to all her former pupils, or maybe she divined something. Suddenly I knew that here it was, the moment of separation I had avoided the day of our last lesson, in all its pathos. And I knew that I would never again set eyes on this warmhearted, majestic woman, who was so dear to me. I wanted to cry, but I had lost my bearings, so I closed my eyes and made believe that everything would come to a standstill until it was safe to open them again. When I did open my eyes, my teacher Mrs. Chanina was gone, and my parents led me out into the night. We made our way to the bus stop.

It was a warm summer night, and a pleasant sea breeze caressed our faces. We strolled in silence, still thinking about the recital, lost in our private musings. I was glad we weren't talking. The night air was like a soothing balm. I felt it in my limbs, it was almost as if someone else had cried my tears for me and I was purified. I looked at my parents and imagined that the three of us had lately escaped from a dangerous, seduction dream. My hand felt secure in my father's hand. And then I realized that deep inside me I was happy my lessons had been stopped. Did I not know that the happiness was—for the first time in my life—a sigh of relief, of letting go, of accepting. It was a happiness of matters being taken out of my hands, willy-nilly, I was free. But then I experienced it differently: I felt that I was reunited with my parents as we walked to the bus stop, that we were bound together by a new destiny, and our recent trials could no longer stand in our way.

Some months later we left Haifa and moved back to our moshava. And that Sabbath afternoon in autumn as we set forth from my Great-Aunt Frieda's house, I recalled the aroma of colophony and all the hope and longing it had stirred in me. I asked my parents if I could take up my violin lessons again, and the memory of colophony revived me like a mysterious potion. Even as I write these words I feel an upsurge of hope and expectancy, almost as if I were waiting for the return of someone I loved, who was all but lost and yet nearer and dearer than ever before, or as if I were waiting for some new, redeeming turn of events, however unlikely, with the promise of romance and adventure.

Some time later, the first rains fell. I stood in my room, watching the rain outside my window. I opened my eyes as widely as I could, and stared at the gray light. I tried to count to twenty without blinking. The ordeal seemed to take on a heavy significance, and as I counted nine, ten, I trembled, my eyes brimmed over, and everything was blurry. I was dizzy, the room was spinning round and round to the rhythm of my heartbeat.

Just then, my mother walked into the room and stood behind me.

"What are you doing?"

"Nothing."

"Aren't you doing your homework?"

I didn't turn around to face her. "I'm thinking," I said.

"And just what are you thinking about so hard?" she asked, not unkindly. She approached the window, and looked at my face.

"I was just trying to see if I remember anything about the violin. But I don't. Zero. Nothing. I was trying to remember Schubert's "Musical Moment," that was the last thing I played in Haifa, but I don't remember any of the notes, or what the left hand does, or the fingering, or anything. I'll have to start from the beginning."

She didn't answer. She looked rather doubtful and also baffled. Tears were flowing over my cheeks, and I said, "If I start playing again, the blinking will probably go away. I really think it might."

"It will go away in a few years anyhow," said my mother.

"How do you know?"

"The doctor said so then."

And then I remembered the doctor, and our quarrel over my rudeness, and I felt injured again.

"Then why did my lessons have to stop?"

She made inquiries and found that Mr. Alfredi was the best violin teacher on our moshava. That evening when my father came home from work, it was decided that my mother would take me to Mr. Alfredi's the following day and sign me up for lessons. The rains continued all night long, but when I came home from school the next day, it wasn't raining anymore and I was very excited. But it started raining again in the afternoon, and my mother, who wanted to postpone our excursion for better weather, understood my sorrows. I put on my poncho and she fastened my hood, tied a kerchief around her head, and took my umbrella. Thus we ventured out into the mud and the pouring rain.

"If anyone knew where we were going in this flood, they'd think we were crazy!" said my mother. But she didn't sound reproachful in the least, she was mischievous, my partner in a silly escapade. Hardly anyone else was abroad in the flood. Mr. Alfredi's house was all the way over on the western border of the moshava, and our house was in the east. East to west, we trudged against the wind that splattered our faces with rain and our clothes were soaked. We held hands in our joint struggle against the forces of nature and my mother laughed and shouted so that I would hear her behind the curtain of wind and rain and the barrier of my hood, "We're crazy! You know that, we're crazy!"

When we arrived at the first-floor apartment that was Mr. Alfredi's music school, no one was there. We went through the porch that led to his door, and found it locked. There was a note tacked on it: "No lessons today on account of my aunt's funeral. Alfredi." My mother smiled and said, "We're out of luck." She may have been referring to our futile walk through the pouring rain, or she may have felt that the aunt's funeral falling this very day was inauspicious. We waited a while longer on the porch, sheltered from the wind and rain, and I tried to peep through the shutters and see what the room was like inside, but it was too dark. Suddenly we heard peculiar noises coming from the hallway near the porch, sounds of thrashing and thumping and groaning. We hurried to the hallway, and in the semidarkness at the foot of the stairs, we stumbled over violin cases and music books in disarray, and buffeting bodies that wriggled and tangled in a heap. My mother switched the light on, and we watched as three children stopped abruptly on the floor like some animal with multiple limbs holding its breath. We saw that they were three boys piled on top of each other, wearing blue ponchos. My mother yanked the uppermost by the arm, and as he scrambled to his feet, the boy who was under him also rose, and they gasped and panted and slapped the dust off their ponchos. The third boy trembled as he continued to lie on the floor, and tucked his head between his knees in fear or pain. My mother tried to help him up, but he obstinately refused assistance, shifted his shoulders, and trembled all the more. My mother bent over him and tried to find his face. She coaxed him until he finally stood up. He was a small, skinny boy, much younger than the other two.

"Who are your parents?" my mother charged the older two, who were grunting vindictively in the corner. "Who are your parents? I want to have a word with them."

The older one, a dark-haired boy with shifty eyes, giggled insolently and didn't answer her. The other, who was fat and rosy-cheeked, said, "That'll show him he's not so hot."

My mother glanced anxiously at the skinny little boy, to see if he was hurt.

"They broke my fingers!" he bawled in a rage of self-pity. "They did! They broke my fingers so I wouldn't be able to play." He cried and fretted primly over his hands. "They were trying to break my fingers!" He held them out for my mother to see, and she examined them with some concern, but there were no signs of injury. "Now I'll never be able to play, and Mr. Alfredi is going to have something to say about that!" he added.

The two older boys stood in the corner looking chastened, and the dark one with the shifty eyes took one cautious step in the direction of the door, while the fat one with the rosy cheeks tugged nervously at his poncho with a sideways glance at the skinny boy to see how he was faring.

The dark one said, "He started it. He always does." My mother looked at the pale skinny boy and said to the older two, "You should be ashamed of yourselves, big strong boys knocking him down like that in the dark."

They gathered their music and violin cases, and we all stepped out on the porch to wait for the end of the storm.

"There's nothing wrong with your fingers, Yoram, and stop bawling," said the dark one. "Let me see."

Yoram held his hands out gingerly and winced with pain. His eyes were pale, too pale, and his hair was blond and cropped. The dark one looked at the fingers and announced, "There's nothing wrong with him, he's a liar!"

"We were just messing around," said the fat one, trying to placate my mother. "We always do and nothing ever happens."

"And does Mr. Alfredi permit this sort of thing?" asked my mother.

The two boys grinned sheepishly and Yoram leaned against the railing hugging his violin case and contemplating the interminable rain. "When Mr. Alfredi finds out," said Yoram deep in contemplation, "he'll kick you out like dogs." They laughed.

After a while the older two, who were tired of waiting for the rain to stop, tied their hoods, hid their violin cases under their ponchos, and walked out to the road. Yoram followed suit and tried to catch up with them, and finally we saw the three of them disappearing around the bend.

Next day the rain had stopped, and my mother and I set off once more for Mr. Alfredi's music school. As we entered the room, Mr. Alfredi was demonstrating a difficult passage for the dark boy with the shifty eyes. Then the dark boy lifted his bow and repeated the passage. Mr. Alfredi noticed our presence and motioned us to be seated and wait. It seemed that the boy was a new pupil, but he played remarkably well. My mother looked at the teacher. He was very tall, with reddish-gray hair, a long sharp face, and a big nose the tip of which seemed to have worn away. I thought him very ugly and I saw by the look on my mother's face that she was no more favorably impressed with the man. When the boy had finished playing the passage, he looked up and smiled at us disarmingly as though he feared we would tell on him. Mr. Alfredi assigned him an exercise, and the lesson ended abruptly.

I tried to think about my teacher Mrs. Chanina's house in Haifa, but my memories of a few years before were as vague as a distant dream. All I could recall was the color of the plait that rolled down her neck and the furniture that stood out against the background of white walls. And one thing more: the sensual quivering of her nostrils, the faint quivering probably only I could discern, when she narrowed her eyes in ecstasy. I also remembered what she had said at the recital and I wondered if I would understand someday. Mr. Alfredi's studio was small and shabby, and the delapidated wooden shutters outside creaked in the wind. We were sitting on a most peculiar sofa with an even more peculiar rug covering it, surrounded by an odd assortment of chairs, some of them folding chairs. My mother gave Mr. Alfredi an account of my musical accomplishments, but he didn't seem to be very impressed.

Looking at him more closely, I could see the great freckles that covered his face and the pockmarks on his long, corroded nose. His small, watery eyes had no definite color. He put a training violin in my hands, flipped the pages of a music book, and asked me to play whatever I could remember.

I stared at the music and at the violin in my hands, and I didn't remember anything. Nothing flashed out of the not-so-distant past in my moment of trial. All was lost, my work had gone for nothing. I stood numbly, looking from Mr. Alfredi's countenance which expressed doubt and derision to the little violin I was holding in my hands. Mr. Alfredi asked me to play a note, any note. I drew the bow over one of the strings, and a sound came out that was so hideous I dropped the bow at once and looked at the floor.

"What did you play then?" asked Mr. Alfredi. "What pieces did you play in Haifa, what exercises?" I opened my mouth, but I was speechless. I racked my brains for the name of one of those pieces, but I couldn't remember. After a long silence, Mr. Alfredi turned to my mother and said, "We seem to have forgotten everything." My eyes implored her to come to my assistance. My mother said, "He did play Schubert's 'Musical Moment' at the recital, and Mrs. Duniah-Weizman said . . ."

Mr. Alfredi interrupted, "We'll have to start all over again. He doesn't remember anything." He looked incredulous. A little girl pupil had walked into the studio, and I was overcome with embarrassment as the conversation proceeded.

"And why do you blink like that all the time?" asked Mr. Alfredi. "Is that nice, huh? How do you suppose you'll ever become a violinist and play in a concert when you go blink, blink, blink all the time?"

The girl giggled quietly and hid her face behind her hand. There was a golden heart-shaped ring on that cupped little hand.

"Never mind," said my mother on our way home, "he's an excellent teacher, that's all that counts."

And Mr. Alfredi did in fact prove to be an excellent teacher, and a pleasant man at that. When I got used to him, I even found him charming. How incongruous was that gangly body of his when he stood to play the violin. Suddenly limp and helpless, wheezing and moaning so noisily he all but drowned out the pianissimos, he seemed to be on the point of expiration. And his left wrist wobbled to produce a vibrato, and a frightful pathos sealed his eyes and took his breath away till he seemed about to collapse on the floor. Then just in time, he would breathe his fill, and moan with every sweep of the bow. I didn't particularly care for the cloying emotions Mr. Alfredi displayed at the most inappropriate passages and even the dullest of etudes. I began to dislike those displays of emotion in music and displays of emotion of any kind. When I first heard Yoram play, I was amazed. So young, and already Mr. Alfredi's best pupil. But I didn't like his playing either. He gave a perfect imitation of his teacher. In fact he surpassed Mr. Alfredi's technique and even outdid his emotionalism. He ran through complicated chords and difficult transitions with astonishing ease, and the charm of a real child prodigy. And when he played the slow, expansive movements, he echoed Mr. Alfredi's histrionic style and even transcended it.

Yoram's whiny vibrato and the tragic accents of his bow were sickening somehow. It was indecent, the way he bared himself with charms so stale and calculated. I began to suspect that inside this pale, skinny little boy lurked an old buffoon who would stoop to any trick in the book to hook his audience. Still, I couldn't help admiring his courage. Dauntless, he defied the world and its conventions. There was something of the trained monkey about him when he played—freakish, gaudy, suspect, but heroic, too, in his audacity.

I myself never learned to play with vibrato. No matter how we tried, Mr. Alfredi and I, my wrist would always turn to stone at the critical moment. He loosened my left elbow, checked my grip, but nothing worked. I knew it wasn't the real thing without a vibrato, though I supposed it might be achieved with a little more reserve. Mr. Alfredi said it would come in time, but one, two, three years went by and no vibrato. Was it perhaps my aversion to displays of emotion that inhibited the movement of my wrist? But why then was I no more successful when I practiced alone at home? Maybe I already knew that I would never be a great violinist, not even Mr. Alfredi's prize pupil. I soon found out that pupils come and pupils go, but I will always be among the second-best. I was convinced that "disability" with the vibrato was the chief stumbling block to my progress, and it was convenient to lay the blame on a mere technical failure. Still, Mr. Alfredi did decide that I would play second violin with Yoram in the Bach double concerto for the recital at the end of the year.

Though Yoram lived on my block, we hadn't met till the day of the flood, the day my mother and I found him in a scrimmage with the other two boys, hollering "They were going to break my fingers so I wouldn't be able to play!" Yoram and I went to different schools, and he was several years younger. He asked if we could have some rehearsals at his house, and I agreed. Yoram and his parents lived in a one-room apartment on the first floor of a two-story house with a yard. A clump of bushes growing wild in the yard and a grove of tall caesaurina trees planted by the road obscured the house from view.

Now as I approach the house in my imagination, I stop under the tall old trees and see the house behind the bushes. I am rooted to the spot. The sight distresses me. I can't breath.

An oppressive week has gone by, and a baffling anxiety prevents me from continuing this story. I feel restless. I can't concentrate. I sit for hours by my typewriter, but my fingers are as sluggish as my mind. I counsel myself, skip this section, go on to the next, but I can't shake off this sense of oppression, and there is no getting round it, I shall have to face the memory and discover what underlies my anxiety, and only then will I be free. The old caesaurina trees in front of Yoram's house figure in three incidents in this story: the rehearsal at Yoram's house, the Eitan episode, and the great scene which always reminds me of a folk play. But which of these three incidents transmits these waves of anxiety? Again and again, I come up against a brick wall, and I have trouble breathing.

I can remember many similar attacks of anxiety, and on each occasion, I knew the cause lay in something I had ignored, either in thought or deed. I also knew that I must struggle to penetrate the moment that gave rise to the feeling, to untie the knot, to restore the moment to its true proportions which are usually not so large as they appear later. I was not always successful, but when I was, the wheel turned back, I faced the moment and settled my accounts with it, and as a result, I experienced a marvelous sense of well-being, as if a lost possession had found its way back to me or as if a bitter, long-standing quarrel had finally been settled. But this moment, where shall I find it, where did it go, and what has it to do with the story I'm trying to tell? It taps me on the

shoulder, and demands satisfaction, and holds me under the shade of
old caesaurina trees in front of Yoram's house.

It's late, my house is locked, and I put a record on to drown out the
noise of the air conditioner. It's very hot outside. At times, the stubborn
hum of the air conditioner can be like a dreary lullaby to the silence. But
at this painful moment it sounds more like a ferocious beast, mocking
my unhappiness. Funny how this phantom pain will emanate from
inanimate objects that have not yet been contaminated. And now, the
page in my typewriter is rising line by line.

A week has gone by, and I feel better. I try to visualize the path that
leads to the bushes, the overgrown bushes that hide the first floor of the
house from the road. The tiles on the floor were cracked and broken. I
knocked on the door. Yoram's mother answered. She was pale and
skinny like her son, and her movements were unnecessarily brusque.
Yoram wasn't home, much to my surprise, although we'd made a date
to rehearse. His mother said he would be home soon and asked me to sit
down and wait for him, despite his bad manners. She showed me where
to put my violin, and interrogated me about my family, and I suppose
she was satisfied, because she left me alone in the room. I don't remember what the room looked like, but I do remember that it was dark there
in the early afternoon, perhaps because the bushes in front of the house
kept out the light.

Yoram's mother walked in a little while later and I saw that she was
much older than my mother. Her hair was gray, her face was wrinkled,
and her back was bowed. She looked nothing like Yoram. She sat down
beside me, and faced me.

"What do you think?" she opened abruptly. "He won't get him home
in time, and he knows he has a rehearsal, if you don't mind."

I began to feel uncomfortable.

"What a sense of timing. You think all that equipment he buys him
will do any good? Now, just before the recital? It won't do any good at
all, if you don't mind. What does he want from him? Tell me? Let him
practice in peace. But not him, no, not him, he buys him all those rifles
and pistols and all those complicated boxes, the main thing is he
shouldn't have his mind on the violin. Is that how they raised Yehudi
Menuhin? Is that how they raised Yasha Heifetz? Never! And he wants
him to go out for sports at the Junior Maccabee Club, if you don't
mind. Who needs it? You think it does his hands any good? A violinist
has to have the most sensitive hands in the world, if you don't mind. But
he's afraid he'll grow up like a girl. Who ever heard such nonsense, grow

up like a girl. Playing the violin makes you a girl? Are Yehudi Menuhin and Yasha Heifetz girls?" She hooted in triumph.

She didn't wait for my reply, but said, "If you want you can wait for Yoram outside," as if she'd noticed something about me. "You have to practice for hours and hours. You have to be dedicated. Otherwise it's no good. If you're not dedicated, you're wasting your time, right? Because later the hands get hard and rough and crooked, and then it's too late. Even Mr. Alfredi doesn't understand. God!" She clasped her hands. "God in heaven! Nobody understands. They see but they keep quiet. They don't care. They see it under their very noses, but they turn away. You have to throw it in their faces. You have to pry their hearts open, you have to break in like a thief to make them understand, right? You can go outside and wait," she said, and opened the door for me.

I sat on the front stairs and finally Yoram and his father showed up, empty-handed. I stood to greet them. Yoram's father was short and skinny, and he wore a visor cap. When he looked at me I saw his eyes were cold and pale like his son's, and also very proud. We went into the house and Yoram's father left us in the room. Yoram was quiet. He took out his violin and rubbed his bow with colophony, and mumbled something to himself. We tuned our violins and began to play Bach's double concerto. A few minutes later Yoram's father stood in the doorway yelling, "Horrible! Disgusting!" He stared at me in revulsion, in accusation, and slammed the door shut. Yoram stood still for a moment concentrating, and then asked me to start again from the beginning, because, he said, my entrance was a little off. We began it again. We had practiced so often with Mr. Alfredi that we rarely needed to interrupt our playing with corrections. In the slow, pensive second movement, where the second violin answers the first, as if echoing it, Yoram was playing with his usual emotional vibrato when suddenly we heard a prolonged scream behind the door. Yoram stopped playing and hurried to the door carrying his violin to see what his mother's screaming was about. I stood alone in the room and I was frightened. I heard doors opening and closing and the sound of muffled voices, and another piercing scream that rang in my ears like the cry of a wounded animal. Yoram's father stalked in, looking as unruffled and proud as he had before. He said, "You'd better go home now, Yoram is busy. Come back another time."

He waited while I packed my violin, and walked me to the door. In the hallway I heard her scream again, and this time I heard what she was screaming—"Murderer! Murderer!" And then the door closed behind me.

When I got home I was too ashamed to tell my parents what I'd seen and heard at Yoram's house. I was old enough to keep my secrets. But I remember that I watched them out of the corner of my eye. They were busy at whatever they were doing, and I answered them in silence, made them swear on oath to always let me have my way. But they weren't paying any attention to me. How easy it was to watch them like this, to watch their every move. But as I did so I became aware that my power over them was strictly limited. I dreaded the unknown, the equivocal, unforeseeable times to come. I went to my bedroom and stared out the window. The light was fading. For some reason, my father's old grandmother who had died long ago suddenly entered my mind. I remembered the way she used to sit in her armchair, far away from everything and everyone around her. My father's uncle, her own son, claimed that all she ever thought about was the Messiah, and maybe he was guessing, or maybe she had revealed something to him. But she had always looked to me like a phantom sitting there, an optical illusion. She was no longer a part of her surroundings. She had felt the coup de grâce and was preparing for the fabulous journey that lay ahead. As I stood in my room watching twilight fall, I recognized for the first time in my life that the painting hanging over my great-grandmother's armchair, the painting of a pampered bird languishing in its own blood, was a painting of Death. Now I understood why I had always associated it with the old woman in the chair. It was a secret treaty, a covenant of redemption. Till now, death had only meant the disaster that would take away the man and woman I loved so much, as it had taken my grandfather away from me. Sometimes I would wake up in the middle of the night terrified by a vision that disappeared almost immediately and strain to hear them breathing in their room, afraid they might be taken from me in their sleep. But this evening after the rehearsal with Yoram I was stunned by a new discovery—I knew no more about them than they knew about me. I could watch them and threaten them silently as much as I cared to but I could never turn back the clock to the days when their lives were centered around me. They had their secrets, and their secrets would follow them from now on like shadows, beyond my control. This made me feel a little helpless and nostalgic, but also excited, for anything could happen now that I was on my own, and everything was waiting for me, I only had to mature and be all on my own. I sat there thinking in the darkness of my room when all of a sudden my mother opened the door.

"What are you up to, sitting there in the dark doing nothing?"

I turned around anxiously to face her, as if she'd caught me out, and I didn't know what to answer. She switched on the light looking puzzled and angry, and I was furious with her for calling me to account like that. I tried to look upon her as some vaguely familiar stranger.

"I feel like it," I said.

"Who ever heard of such a thing, sitting in the dark, staring out the window, doing nothing?" said my mother. "That's absolutely unheard of. Idleness is the mother of evil. Idleness leads to decadence."

"I want a little decadence," I said.

After my initial anger had worn off, I decided that I should adopt the art-of-living-together policy, to pay less attention to her. I felt an urgent need to do something, I knew not what. She stood in my room for a while, looking amazed. Was she perhaps confused to learn that the old rules no longer applied? Was she disconcerted?

"You don't practice nearly enough," said my mother. "A week from now you're playing with Yoram in the recital. You have a responsibility, have you not? Do you want him to show you up in front of everyone?"

"It'll be okay, don't worry."

"Well, someone has to worry. And it will not be okay, because you couldn't care less."

Was my declining interest in the violin already so apparent? She had interrupted my thoughts when she entered the room, and those thoughts seemed infinitely precious to me now. This new impetus to attend to my own thought processes, to question my status vis-à-vis the others, held the promise of a vast field of discovery, for me alone, and I was eager to get on with it. I had to do something now, immediately, and I needed absolute privacy. But what did I want to do? And then something incredible happened, something that led me to believe in the invisible mover, the hand that guides my footsteps in a meaningful progression.

Next door where my uncle lived there was a big Hebrew library. I had often browsed through his books and had even borrowed some of them. Having nothing better to do just then, I wandered over to my uncle's house and looked through the books in his library. I picked a book off the shelf and opened it at random. The author was G. Shoffman, and I had never noticed the book before. My eyes fell on the heading: *The Violin*.

"I do not care for this instrument and I hereby challenge its sovereignty. It is enough to consider the way it is played, by rubbing two surfaces against each other, to send shivers of revulsion up the spine. Certain low notes and transitional tones are especially unpleasant to the ear. The strings, incidentally, are made from animal tissue! This is also somewhat repulsive.

"I suppose one ought to consider the excellence of such famous instruments as the Ira Stradivarius played by virtuosi (though I suggest we might be critical even here!), but as for the cheap variety in the hands of pupils—a harmonica would be preferable! In the latter case of violin we have to bear with a mournful scream, a sniveling plea for mercy that is enough to induce a severe case of melancholia.

"Yes, melancholia. The nightmare of the Jewish Ghetto screams out of these fiddles. The Diaspora Jew practically venerated the violin. It was his sine qua non, Yidel mit'n fidel. In every Jewish household, the beloved son, whether he was gifted musically or a complete imbecile, had to 'saw away' on his violin, for the pleasure of his mother, who found her greatest fulfillment in the violin. Come what may, the violin prevailed. Trials and tribulations, every kind of care and woe, debts, installments, bill collectors—and the violin!"

I read these words by Shoffman, and my heart began to pound. Was it just a coincidence? I thought about the disgraceful rubbing of surfaces against each other, and the Diaspora Jew in his ghetto, sniveling and begging for mercy, and I smoldered. I read the paragraph over and over and over again. At last I made up my mind what to do. I had found myself a worthy enterprise: to stop my violin lessons.

For the time being I kept this decision to myself. I didn't want to inform my parents. Not yet. I was afraid it would make them very sad. What sacrifices they had made for my violin lessons in those times of austerity, and what happiness my progress had given them. But it had to be done. I didn't know when yet. First I had to get through the recital.

A few days before the recital we rehearsed at Mr. Alfredi's together with our accompanist. My heart wasn't in it. Since reading Shoffman's article I could barely suppress my loathing for the instrument. But to my great amazement, I found that I was playing more fluently and accurately than I ever had before, as if the music was playing itself without any guidance from me. It was better than ever. I wondered whether anyone else noticed, and after I finished playing the slow, pensive, second movement, Mr. Alfredi clapped his hands and called out to me, "Bravo! Bravo!" He praised me warmly and said that I had evidently been practicing a lot at home. When we went on to the third movement, I was surprised to note what great pleasure the compliment gave me, I had so naively believed that I was indifferent.

After the rehearsal, Mr. Alfredi said he hoped I would play as well at the recital. And I knew the recital would be the grand finale of my musical career.

On our way out of Mr. Alfredi's studio, Eitan, the dark-haired boy with the shifty eyes, followed me. He had waited to hear us play the double concerto after his own rehearsal had ended. Eitan was younger than I, but taller, and he looked as if he knew the secrets of life. We seldom met at Mr. Alfredi's, and when we did, we hardly ever exchanged words. I suspected that he felt unfriendly, if not hostile, toward me, and I usually avoided him.

But as I left Mr. Alfredi's studio, Eitan caught up with me. We walked along in silence. Then Eitan said, "I can't stand the way Yoram plays. He thinks he's the greatest violinist in the world. In my opinion, you played the Bach double better than he did."

I thought he was trying to flatter me, and I couldn't decide what he was driving at.

"Oh, he's got technique," said Eitan, "I'll give him that much. But he plays like a fake. And Mr. Alfredi thinks he's the world's greatest. But what does Mr. Alfredi know? He didn't even get into the orchestra."

I found myself wanting to tell Eitan about my decision to stop taking lessons, but I was afraid. If Mr. Alfredi found out about it, it might not be very pleasant; I didn't want him to know until the last possible moment. I didn't want to estrange him yet.

"Ugh," I said, "the violin. You call that an instrument? Surfaces rubbing against each other, and a horrible, sniveling sound coming out."

Eitan gaped as if he hadn't understood me properly, as if he ascribed some obscure meaning to what I'd said, but he seemed to accept my statement as confirmation of his.

We had walked almost as far as my house when Eitan stopped and said, "I walked you to your house, now you walk me to my house." Eitan lived in the neighborhood by the railway, on the other side of the moshava. I didn't understand what he wanted. I thought he was joking. I looked at him. He was perfectly serious, and the shifty twinkle was gone from his eyes.

"But I have to go home now. They're waiting for me, they'll worry," I lied.

"Come on," said Eitan, "it'll only take fifteen minutes, come on, it'll be all right."

"I can't," I said.

We stood there doggedly, holding our violin cases, and neither of us would budge. It wasn't late, and I didn't really mind walking him home, but a strong perversity took hold of me, maybe because he sounded so eager and peremptory, and because I had always been suspicious of him. Eitan peered around. He bent over suddenly and dropped his violin case in the middle of the road. Then he looked directly at me with an inscrutable expression. It took me years to figure out what that expression meant. He took a few steps back and said, "I don't care. I'm leaving it here, and if anything happens, it's your responsibility, because you're supposed to walk me home, and you won't, so just remember, if anything happens to my violin, it's your responsibility!"

This was totally unexpected. He actually left his violin case in the middle of the road, turned his back, and walked away. I didn't know what to do. It was my responsibility, he said so. If I didn't move it over to the curb where it wouldn't get run over, terrible things might happen. This was so disturbing that I crouched to pick it up, but Eitan veered around with amazing alacrity and rushed to move his violin back to the middle of the road.

"Don't you dare touch it, you hear? It isn't yours, you have no right to touch it. It isn't yours! If anything happens, it's your responsibility, because you don't keep your promises!"

"I never promised you anything," I objected.

His face was twisting in anger or pain. I was afraid he would hit me. But all he said was, "Come on, walk me home, what do you care? Please. I'll tell you all kinds of things."

With brilliant insight I realized my only chance to escape this predicament was to run for it, and leave him standing in the middle of the road with his violin, and then it would be his responsibility. And as I ran home, I could hear him shout, "Remember, it'll be here all night, and if anything happens to it it'll be your responsibility, damn you!"

I got home winded and I hoped he wasn't following me to prolong this inane argument. A few minutes later, however, I began to worry that he really had left his violin in the middle of the road. His behavior had certainly been odd. Nobody else behaved like that. I sneaked out to look for him. It wasn't dark yet, but I couldn't see him or his violin. I thought maybe he was lying in ambush in somebody's yard, and I edged along our fence, waiting for him to spring at me. But time passed and nothing happened. I took courage and advanced out into the open, but there was no sign of him. I stopped in front of Yoram's house, under the caesaurina trees, and I squinted at the horizon. People were walking to and fro, but Eitan wasn't among them. I figured that as soon as I had left, he'd picked up his violin and gone home. But I wasn't relieved, no, I was old enough to understand what I had done and I was shocked. I was miserable and penitent, and I didn't know what to do. Why was I so bad? I turned my face away from the road so no one would see if I started crying. I was afraid, something had to be done, urgently, but what? I had never given Eitan a second thought, I had only seen him a few times in my life, and yet now he loomed so fatefully over me that I was paralyzed. "Remember, it's your responsibility!" his voice rang in my ears. I had never felt so responsible before. With my back to the road, I could see the bushes in front of Yoram's house.

I considered various excuses to justify myself and prove his irrationality—lame excuses that paled and faltered beside my shame and misery. Whatever I might say in self-defense was countered by the inscrutable expression he wore as he put his violin in the middle of the road. It haunted me for years. In my selfishness I hadn't realized that he was asking for friendship. If only I had been more sensitive he wouldn't have gone to such extremes. I hated myself then as I always hate myself when I realize, too late, too late, that someone is asking for help and friendship. Maybe I lack the faculty to recognize the allusive secrets of another's heart, to understand the whispered implications.

During those painful, shameful moments, while I leaned against the trunk of one of the tall old trees, not knowing where to turn or what to do, I could only wonder how in the world I was going to make amends. I wanted nothing better than to stand before him with downcast eyes and say I was sorry, so sorry for the wrong I'd done. And the more I begged him, the more I groveled, the more I would suffer and the less ashamed I would be. But at the time it would have been impossible for me to display emotions of this sort. They were too private, they couldn't be shared. He had to forgive me, it was the only way. Even if he forgot the whole incident, I would be miserable until he pardoned me. I had to see him. I had to see him now. I had to see what he was doing.

This growing need to see him was my only hope to escape from under the trees where I'd been standing heaven knows how long in a state of unprecedented anguish. I finally tore myself away and set off for Eitan's neighborhood.

I thought I would reconnoiter the neighborhood till I spotted him in the window or maybe outside in the yard. I would see what he was up to, but he wouldn't see me. It was getting dark as I carried my burden of guilt up to the road, and I remember the fresh smell of dust on that miserable summer evening. When I reached the neighborhood by the railway I was frightened. It was an unpaved road, on either side of which were cottages in a row and black wooden sheds and giant eucalyptus trees. I hoped I might hear a violin somewhere. Maybe he was drowning his sorrows in music, and that way, I would be able to locate his house. Looking up at the glimmering windows, I walked through the neighborhood, but I couldn't find him. Hadn't he gone home? Where was he? My guilt was overpowering me and I wandered up and down. Finally I gave up, feeling very sorry for myself.

I walked home slowly, The more I pitied myself, the less I suffered the agonies of remorse. I pictured myself as a tortured penitent in order to escape the all-pervading memory of Eitan. It was a contest, and the advantage shifted back and forth. I knew that I would never be one of those children of "The Heart," those marvelous children I had cried over in bygone days.

I was apprehensive about meeting Eitan at the recital. In a small room that usually served as the office of the Histadrut Cultural Building, we unpacked our cases. Mr. Alfredi was nervously giving out last-minute instructions. A few pale pupils tuned their instruments and rosined their bows. Leaning against a desk in the corner was Eitan, looking much the same as he always did. The shifty sparkle in his eyes was back. I wasn't sure I ought to speak to him. Would he look my way? What would he say to me? It was surprising to see that he hadn't changed in any way. I didn't know whether to laugh or cry. And perhaps he was only testing me. Maybe this was just another one of his old tricks. Maybe he'd forgotten everything. Or was he seething inside and merely saving face? I stood in the doorway and he smiled his usual noncommittal smile. I didn't have the nerve to approach him. I put my violin down and hurried out to sit with my parents in the auditorium.

"You aren't even nervous," said my mother. "That isn't a good sign. You don't care. You don't care about anything."

Yoram's mother walked into the auditorium and my mother followed her with her eyes. When the gray-haired lady had seated herself, my mother whispered something I couldn't hear to my father. I knew it was about Yoram's mother. My father nodded a reply and stared at the woman's back. What did they know that I didn't know? But I could only scratch the surface of things. The rest remained unfathomable.

After the recital, as we were leaving the auditorium on our way home, I cautiously mentioned to my parents that maybe I ought to drop my violin lessons, temporarily, of course, so that I could devote more time to my studies at the Gymnasia. I thought I noticed my father smiling to himself in the dark as if he'd foreseen this. My mother pretended to be shocked but I could tell their disapproval was not serious.

"I've noticed lately," said my mother, "that you're losing interest in everything. Nothing interests you anymore."

I protested and mentioned my studies again.

My father said, "Do what you think is best."

I told them about G. Shoffman's article which I had found in my uncle's library. My mother was horrified at what I had discovered in her beloved brother's library. "Nonsense!" she said. "I don't believe anyone would print such utter nonsense." And of course she was right, but at the time the article had seemed to me the height of reason. My father said, "It doesn't matter. If you want to stop, there's no point in arguing about it."

I had a vague perception of leaving them again, of coming into my own. I wasn't worried anymore about hurting them or breaking faith.

"Remember how I ran with you in the pouring rain like a madwoman?" said my mother. "You were so determined. I thought we'd wait a day or two, but not you, you couldn't wait."

I remembered that rainy day, and it seemed irrelevant just then. I loved my father's calm, his moderation, his sense of proportion, and especially his irony when he said, "You'll go to Mr. Alfredi yourself and tell him about your decision."

"Of course," I said reluctantly. "Yes."

I hadn't thought about that. Once again I understood the growing significance of the word *responsibility*. "Yes," I added as an afterthought, "I'll tell him myself after vacation."

At home I put my violin where I always kept it, and I knew that I would never touch it again.

Mr. Alfredi's summer vacation, which lasted a month or two, began after the yearly recital. One day my mother looked at my face and asked me a question that seemed to come from somewhere far away. "Have you noticed anything about your face?"

I hadn't. But I learned from her expression that my blinking was going away. I found indications of this gradual change in my milieu, but it had nothing to do with what was going on inside me. It was just something external, a meaningless mechanism. When the vacation was over I decided to go to Mr. Alfredi and take my leave of him properly. Once again I set off on the long walk, by the same route with never a detour or shortcut. I felt timid, worried that it would be unpleasant. How could I look in Mr. Alfredi's eyes when I told him the news? He might feel hurt, he might feel deceived after all these years, he might even yell at me. But I knew this was the test of my responsibility, and I would have to face the consequences of living my life as I saw fit. Just as I walked up the path to Mr. Alfredi's music school, another of those mysterious coincidences took place which highlight the symbolism and symmetry of my life.

I heard the old familiar melody. It issued out of eternity, this music I had loved so dearly once, returning to me like an errant lover, strange and discovered anew. I was transfixed. It took me several minutes to identify the piece by name, the "La Follia" variations by Corelli. I hadn't heard it in all the years since the recital at the Haifa Conservatory.

I stood and listened to the muffled sounds emerging from the house. My heart was pounding. I had reached the crossroads. How well I remembered the boy in Haifa who had played the "La Follia" variations, but how difficult it was to recall the boy in the audience who listened to him with so much envy and longing. The music was swelling as I climbed the stairs. Mr. Alfredi was playing all by himself in the studio. He nodded for me to wait. Did he notice I had come without my violin? I listened to him, moaning and wheezing as he always did, and I tried to remember the enigma of the music which had so enthralled me once. But "La Follia" was now a tattered beggar, throwing herself at my mercy, asking me to remember the pride of her youth. But I had other things to think about. Where was the enigma? The more I listened the more I hardened myself against the insipidity of the music and the excessive ardor Mr. Alfredi lent it as he played. Here was another sign that I had made the right decision. The crossroads were behind me, the worst was over.

Mr. Alfredi said, "What a pity. And soon we'll be starting chamber music, and I thought you might switch to the viola." He smiled sweetly. I saw he wasn't angry at all. He wasn't shocked. Maybe I hadn't deceived him. Maybe he was used to it. Maybe that was just the way of things. I told him how difficult school was, that I wanted to devote more time to my studies. Only for a couple of years, of course. And he smiled, and nodded.

We parted amicably, and as I was leaving the house I heard him playing "La Follia" again, though it was hard to imagine why. He didn't even get into the orchestra!

I made my way home, filled with vague new hopes. I was free and happy, optimistic. It was autumn, the time of fresh beginnings, the time I love the best. The High Holidays were drawing near, and with them a poignant expectancy, a flurry in the air. On our street I saw a crowd of people standing under the caesaurina trees in front of Yoram's house. As I approached the crowd, I saw Yoram's mother weeping bitterly and someone supporting her arms so she wouldn't collapse. Nearby stood Yoram's father, the invariable visor cap shading his pale, proud eyes. In the center stood Yoram, glancing fitfully from one to the other. Neighbors and passersby were shaking their heads sadly or whispering together. Some of them had taken it upon themselves to brief the newcomers. The scene must have been in progress for some time.

Yoram's mother was clasping her hands and screaming, "Murderer! Murderer! He wants to take my boy away so he won't be a violinist. He wants to ruin him! He wants to turn him into what he is. Save him! Save him from that murderer!"

Yoram's father didn't react. He didn't seem inclined to fight with her. Finally he lost his patience and played his last card. "Yoram," he called, "come with me and you'll get the badge of the Palmach."

I stood on the sidelines hoping Yoram wouldn't notice me. Between the heads of the crowd I saw him look at his father, imploring him not to set such awful temptation in his way. But his father repeated, "Remember, Yoram, the badge of the Palmach!"

Yoram's mother had nothing comparable to offer, and she appealed to the crowd, with only justice and mercy left to rival the badge of the Palmach. "He wants you to think I'm crazy so they'll take my boy away. But I'm not crazy! I'm normal! I won't give that murderer my child! He won't turn him into another murderer!"

The crowd followed these proceedings, inclining first one way, then the other. Some took sides and pleaded for the claimants, others vacillated because it was so difficult to judge.

For a moment I believed Yoram was looking at me. I fidgeted. It was degrading. How could they take their problems out in public, out in the street, I wondered. This scene, skinny little Yoram standing between his parents, pale and torn with indecision, surrounded by the pitying crowd, this scene was unforgettable. A few months before, we had played the Bach double together at the recital, and now he was a stranger. I didn't recognize him, I didn't pity him, and I didn't feel his pain. I was simply disgusted by this shameful display in the street. I refused to have anything to do with it.

"He has the hands of a great violinist!" Yoram's mother screamed.

She grabbed his hand and raised it sky-high to prove her point. And Yoram's father said, "If you come with me you'll be a man. If you stay with her you'll go crazy like her."

Yoram lost his head. I saw him wrench away from his mother and stop his ears with both hands. It was a hard choice, between a murderer and a crazy woman. His strength was failing. I couldn't bear to watch any more. I walked away and then turned around for a last look. This time the scene appeared in a new light: it was a theatrical performance. The actors were stuck in their roles, loving every minute of the old drama, the theme of the father and the mother and the child prodigy. I never forgot this scene. Little by little I lost my youthful, haughty contempt and I learned to love the play and the three players who wandered far and wide searching for a sympathetic audience to fight their battles and see justice done. But many years went by before I could understand how much love and compassion were revealed in this play.

When I got home that autumn afternoon I was still disgusted with what I had beheld. My erstwhile hopes had fled.

"I've been noticing lately that your eyes are getting better," said my father, "Sometimes you don't blink at all. Have you noticed?"

I hadn't. I went to look at myself in the little bathroom mirror. What was there to see? I had never been able to see myself blinking. How could I tell that I'd stopped? My face was sealed as usual.

One fine day I stopped scowling and the mysterious malady disappeared. I never understood what brought it on, and I could no more understand why it vanished.

My mother said, "That's what the doctor said. He said it would go away in adolescence."

The word *adolescence* coming from her sounded insulting for some reason.

Then the stigma was gone, and quietude descended on my face forevermore.

A POET'S CONTINUING SILENCE

BY A. B. YEHOSHUA

translated by Miriam Arad

HE WAS LATE again last night, and when he did come in he made no effort to enter quietly. As though my own sleep did not matter. His steps echoed through the empty apartment for a long time. He kept the lights in the hall turned on and fussed about endlessly with papers. At last he fell silent. I groped my way back toward the light vague sleep of old age. And then, the rain. For three weeks now this persistent rain, sheets of water grinding down the panes.

Where does he go at night? I do not know. I once managed to follow him through several streets, but an old acquaintance, an incorrigible prose writer, buttonholed me at one street corner and meanwhile the boy disappeared.

The rains are turning this plain into a morass of asphalt, sand and water. Tel Aviv in winter—town without drainage, no outlets, spawning lakes. And the sea beyond, murky and unclean, rumbling as though in retreat from the sprawling town, sea become background.

Not five yet but the windows are turning gray. What was it? He appeared in my dream, stood there in full view before me, not far from the seashore, I think, dark birds were in his lap, and he quelled their fluttering. His smile amazed me. He stood and faced me, looked hard at me and gave a feeble smile.

Now the faint sound of snoring reaches me from his room and I know I shall sleep no more. Another boat sails tomorrow or the day after and I expect I shall board it at last. This anguish will dissolve, I know, I have only to preserve my dignity till the moment of parting. Another twenty hours or so, only.

Though I do not see him now, I know he is asleep, hands over heart, eyes shut, mouth open, his breathing clear.

I must describe him first. What he looks like. I can do that for, though not seventeen yet, his features appear to have settled. I have long regarded him as unchanging, as one who will never change.

His slightly stooping figure, fierce frame craned forward in submission. His flat skull. His face—coarse, thick, obtuse. The pimples sprouting on his cheeks and forehead. The black beginnings of a beard. His close-cropped hair. His spectacles.

I know very well—will even proclaim in advance—that people think he is feebleminded; it is the general opinion, and my daughters share it. As for myself, I am ready to concede the fact, for it contains nothing to betray *me*, after all, nor to reflect upon the soundness of my senses. I have read scientific literature on the subject and I assure you: it is a mere accident. Moreover, he does not resemble me in the least, and barring a certain ferocity, we two have nothing in common. I am completely unafraid therefore, and yet for all that I insist he is a borderline case. He hovers on the border. The proof? His eyes. I am the only person to have frequent occasion for looking into his eyes and I say at times (though rarely, I admit), something lights up in them, a dark penetrating vitality.

And not his eyes alone—

And yet—

He was born late in my life. Born accidentally, by mistake, by some accursed miracle, for we were both, his mother and I, on the threshold of old age by then.

I have a vivid recollection of that time, the time before he was born. A gentle spring, very long, very wonderful. And I, a poet with five published volumes of verse behind me, resolved to stop writing, resolved with absolute, irrevocable conviction, out of utter despair. For it was only during that spring that I had come to admit to myself that I ought to keep silent.

I had lost the melody—

My closest friends had already started to daunt and to discourage me, dismissing everything I wrote. The young poets and their new poetry bewildered, maddened me. I tried to imitate them secretly and managed to produce the worst I ever wrote. "Well then," I said, "I shall keep silent from now on . . . and what of it?" As a result of this silence, however, our daily routine was disrupted. Sometimes we would go to bed in the early hours of the evening, at others spend half the night at crowded cafés, useless lectures or gatherings of aged artists gasping for honors at death's door.

That long, wonderful spring, filled with gentle breezes, bursting with blossoms. And I, roaming the streets, up and down, swept by excitement and despair, feeling doomed. Vainly I tried to get drunk, proclaim my vow of silence to all, repudiating poetry, jesting about poems computed by machines, scornful, defiant, laughing a great deal, chattering, making confessions. And at night writing letters to the papers about trivial matters (public transportation, etc.), polishing my phrases, taking infinite pains with them.

Then, suddenly, this unexpected pregnancy—

This disgrace—

We found out about it in early summer. At first we walked a great deal, then shut ourselves up at home, finally became apologetic. First we apologized to the girls, who watched the swelling figure of their elderly mother with horror, then to the relatives come to cast silent looks at the newborn infant.

(The birth occurred one freezing day in midwinter. The tufts of grass in our garden were white with frost.)

We were imprisoned with the baby now. (The girls would not lift a finger for him and deliberately went out more than ever.) We two wanted to speak, tell each other: what a wonderful thing, this birth. But our hearts were not in it, quite clearly. Those sleep-drunken night trips once more, the shadow of the tree streaking the walls, damp, heavy diapers hanging up through all the rooms, all of it depressing. We dragged our feet.

Slowly, sluggishly it grew, the child, late in everything, sunk in a kind of stupor. Looking back now I see him as a gray fledgling, twitching his weak limbs in the cot by my bed.

The first suspicion arose as late as the third year of his life. It was the girls who broached it, not I. He was retarded in his movements, he was stuttering badly, unprepossessing, a heavy growth—hence the girls declared him feebleminded. And friends would come and scan his face, looking for signs to confirm what we dared not utter.

I do not remember that period in his life very well. His mother's illness took up most of my time. She was fading fast. Nothing had remained of her after that late birth but her shell. We had to look on while she withdrew from us into the desert, forced to wander alone among barren, arid hills and vanish in the twilight.

Each day marked its change in her.

The child was six when his mother died. Heavy, awkward, not attached to anyone in the household, withdrawn into himself but never lost in dreams—anything but a dreamy child. Tense, always, and rest-less. He trembled if I ran my fingers through his hair.

If I could say with pity: an orphan. But the word sticks in my throat. His mother's dying left no impression, even though, due to my own distraction, he trailed behind us to her funeral. He never asked about her, as though he understood that her going was final. Some months after her death, moreover, every one of her photographs disappeared, and when we discovered the loss a few days later it did not occur to us to question him. When we did, finally, it was too late. The light was fading when he led us to the burial place; in a far corner of the garden, beneath the poplar, among the traces of an old abandoned lime pit, wrapped in an old rag—the slashed pictures.

He stood there in front of us a long time, stuttering fiercely, his small eyes scurrying.

Yet nothing was explained—

For the first time our eyes opened and we saw before us a little human being.

I could not restrain myself and I beat him, for the first time since he was born. I seized his wrist and slapped him hard in the face. Then the girls beat him. (Why did they beat him?)

He did not understand—

He was startled by the beating. Afterward he flung himself down and wept. We pulled him to his feet and dragged him home.

I had never realized before how well he knew the house, how thor-oughly he had possessed himself of every corner. He had collected his mother's pictures out of obsolete albums, had invaded old envelopes. He had even found a secret spot in the garden that I did not know of. We have lived in this house for many years and I had spent many troubled nights pacing up and down this small garden, but I had never noticed the old extinguished lime—pale, tufted with gray lichen.

Were these the first signs? I do not know yet. None of us, neither I nor the girls, were prepared to understand at the time. All we feared was the shame or scandal he might bring down on us. Hiding him was impossible, but we wanted at least to protect him.

You see—the girls were single still—

At the beginning of the year I entered him in the first grade of a school in the suburbs; and during his first week at school I left work early in order to wait for him at the school gate. I was afraid the children would bait him.

Noon, and he would be trudging by my side under the searing September sky, his hand in mine. The new satchel lashed to his back, cap low over his forehead, lips slightly parted, the faint mutter of his breathing, his eyes looking at the world nakedly, without detachment, never shifting the angle of his inner vision.

Acquaintances wave their hats at me, come over, shake my hand, bend over him, take his little hand, press it. They try to smile. His dull upward glance freezes them. Imbecile, utter imbecile.

After a week I let him come home by himself. My fears had been uncalled for. The children did not need to take the trouble to isolate him —he was isolated to begin with.

The girls were married that year. On the same day, hastily, as though urged on to it, as though they wished to flee the house. And they were so young still.

A year of turmoil. Not a week went by without some sort of revelry in the house. With tears in their eyes the girls would demand that I hide him, and weakness made me comply. I would take him out and we would wander through streets, fields, along the beach.

We did not talk. We watched sunsets, the first stars; rather, I watched and he would stand by my side, motionless, his eyes on the ground. But then the rains came and turned the fields into mud and we were forced to stay indoors. The two suitors had appeared on our horizon, followed by their friends and by their friends' friends, and the whole house went up in smoke and laughter. We tried hiding him in the maids' room, but when he could not sleep we would sneak him into the kitchen. There he would sit in his pajamas and watch people coming and going, then get up and wipe the cutlery; just the spoons at first, then they let him do the knives as well.

Gradually he gained access to the drawing room, the center of commotion. Serving sweets or biscuits to begin with, then filling glasses and offering lighted matches. First, people would draw back at the sight of him. A brief hush would fall upon the room, a kind of sweet horror. One of the suitors would start up angrily from his seat to go and stand by the dark window, seeking refuge in the gloom. Nothing would be audible in the silent room but the child's excited breathing as he moved from one to another with a hard, painful solemnity, his tray held out before him. No one ever refused to take a sweet or a biscuit.

People became used to him in time. The girls softened toward him and tolerated his presence. His small services became indispensable. And when, late in the evening, everybody would be overcome with lassitude, his own face would assume a new light. One of the guests, flushed with drink, might show a sudden interest in him, pull him close and talk to him at length. The child would go rigid in his grip, his eyes dumb. Then he would go to empty ashtrays.

By the end of that summer we two were alone in the house.

The girls were married one day in mid-August. A large canopy was put up in our garden one afternoon beneath a deep blue sky. Desiccated thorns rustled beneath the feet of dozens of friends who had gathered there. For some reason I myself was suffocating with emotion. Something had snapped within. I was tearful, hugging, kissing everybody. The child was not present at the wedding. Someone, one of the bridegrooms perhaps, had seen to it that he be absent, and he was brought back only late in the evening. The last of my friends were tearing themselves from my embrace when my eye suddenly caught sight of him. He was sitting by one of the long tables, dressed in his everyday clothes except for a red tie that someone had put around his neck. A huge slice of cake had been thrust into his hand, the soiled tablecloth had slipped down over his knees. He was chewing listlessly, his eyes on the yellow moon tangled in the branches of our tree.

I went over and gently touched his head.

Flustered, he dropped the cake.

I said: That moon . . . To be sure, a beautiful moon . . .

He looked back at the moon as though he had not seen it before.

Thus our life together began, side by side in the quiet house with flasks of perfume and torn handkerchiefs still strewn about. I—a poet fallen silent, he—a feebleminded, lonely child.

Because it was that, his loneliness, that he faced me with.

I understand that now.

For that he was lonely at school goes without saying. During his very first week at school he had retreated to the last bench, huddling in a corner of the room, a place where he would stay for good, cut off from the rest of his class, the teachers already having considered him hopeless.

All his report cards were inscribed "no evaluation possible," with the hesitant scrawl of a teacher's signature trailing at the bottom of the sheet. I still wonder how they let him graduate from one class to the next. For though occasionally he would be kept back in a class for a second or even a third year, he still crawled forward at the slow pace they set him. Perhaps they were indulging me. Perhaps there were some teachers there who liked my old poems.

Mostly I tried to avoid them—

They did their best to avoid me too—

I do not blame them.

If we were nevertheless forced to meet, on parents' day, I always preferred to come late, to come last, with the school building wrapped in darkness and the weary teachers collapsing on their chairs in front of empty classrooms strewn like battlefields and illuminated by naked bulbs.

Then I would appear stealthily at the door, my felt hat crumpled in my hand. My long white mane (for I had kept my mane) would cause any parent still there—a young father or mother—to rise from their seat and leave. The teachers would glance up at me, hold out a limp hand and a feeble smile.

I would sit down and face them.

What could they tell me that I did not know?

Sometimes they forgot who I was.

"Yes sir, whose father please?"

And I would say the name, a sudden throb contracting my chest.

They would leaf through their papers, pull out his blank card and, closing their eyes, head on hand, would demand severely:

"How long?"

Meaning, how long could they keep him since it was a hopeless case.

I say nothing.

They would grow angry. Perhaps the darkness outside would increase their impatience. They insist I take him off their hands. Where to? They do not know. Somewhere else. An institution perhaps . . .

But gradually their indignation subsides. They admit he is not dangerous. Not disturbing in the least. No, on the contrary, he is always rapt, always listens with a singularly grave attention, his gaze fixed on the teacher's eyes. Apparently he even tries to do his homework.

I crumple my hat to a pulp. I steal a look at the classroom, floor littered with peel, torn pages, pencil shavings. On the blackboard—madmen's drawings. Minute tears prick my eyes. In plain words I promise to help the child, to work with him every evening. Because we must not give up hope. Because the child is a borderline case, after all.

But evenings at home I yield to despair. I spend hours with him in front of the open book and get nowhere. He sits rigidly by my side, never stirring, but my words float like oil on the waves. When I let him go at last he returns to his room and spends about half an hour doing his homework by himself. Then he shuts his exercise books, places them in his schoolbag and locks it.

Sometimes of a morning when he is still asleep I open the bag and pry into his exercise books. I look aghast at the answers he supplies—remote fantasies, am startled by his sums—outlandish marks traced with zeal and beyond all logic.

But I say nothing. I do not complain about him. As long as he gets up each morning to go mutely to school, to sit on the back bench.

He would tell me nothing about his day at school. Nor would I ask. He comes and goes, unspeaking. There was a brief period, during his fifth or sixth year at school, I think, when the children bullied him. It was as though they had suddenly discovered him and promptly they began to torment him. All the children of his class, the girls not excepted, would gather around him during recess and pinch his limbs as though wishing to satisfy themselves that he really existed, flesh and blood, no specter. He continued going to school all the same, as indeed I insisted that he do.

After a few weeks they gave it up and left him alone once more.

One day he came home from school excited. His hands were dusted with chalk. I assumed he had been called to the blackboard but he said no. That evening he came to me on his own and told me he had been appointed class monitor.

A few days went by. I inquired whether he was still monitor and he said yes. A fortnight later he was still holding the post. I asked whether he enjoyed his duties or whether he found them troublesome. He was perfectly content. His eyes had lit up, his expression became more intent. In my morning searches of his bag I would discover, next to bizarre homework, bits of chalk and a rag or two.

I have an idea that from then on he remained monitor till his last day at school, and a close relationship developed between him and the school's janitor. In later years they even struck up some sort of friendship. From time to time the janitor would call him into his cubicle and favor him with a cup of tea left by one of the teachers. It is unlikely that they ever held a real conversation, but a contact of sorts was established.

One summer evening I happened to find myself in the neighborhood of his school and I felt an impulse to go and get acquainted with this janitor. The gate was shut and I wormed my way through a gap in the fence. I wandered along the dark empty corridors till I came at last upon the janitor's cubicle, tucked away beneath the stairwell. I went down the few steps and saw him.

He was sitting on a bunk, his legs gathered under him, darkness around. A very short, swarthy person deftly polishing the copper tray on his knees.

I took off my hat, edged my way into the cubicle, mumbled the child's name. He did not move, did not appear surprised, as though he had taken it for granted that I would come one night. He looked up at me and then, suddenly, without a word he began to smile. A quiet smile, spreading all over his face.

I said: "You know my son."

He nodded, the smile still flickering over his face. His hands continued their work on the tray.

I asked: "How is he? A good boy . . ."

His smile froze, his hands drooped. He muttered something and pointed at his head.

"Poor kid . . . crazy . . ."

And resumed his calm scrutiny of my face.

I stood before him in silence, my heart gone cold. Never before had I been so disappointed, never lost hope so. He returned to his polishing. I backed out without a word.

None of this means to imply that I was already obsessed by the child as far back as that, already entangled with him. Rather the opposite, perhaps. I would be distant with him, absentminded, thinking of other things.

Thinking of myself—

Never had I been so wrapped up in myself—

In the first place, my silence. This, my ultimate silence. Well, I had maintained it. And it had been so easy. Not a line had I written. True, an obscure yearning might well up in me sometimes. A desire. I whisper to myself, for instance: autumn. And again, autumn.

But that is all.

Friends tackled me. Impossible, they said. . . . You are hatching something in secret. . . . You have a surprise up your sleeve.

And, strangely excited, I would smile and insist: "No, nothing of the kind. I have written all I want to."

First they doubted, at last they believed me. And my silence was accepted—in silence. It was mentioned only once. Somebody (a young person) published some sort of resumé in the paper. He mentioned me *en passant*, disparagingly, calling my silence sterility. Twice in the same paragraph he called me that—sterile—

Then let me off—

But I did not care. I felt placid.

This wasteland around me—

Dry desert—

Rocks and refuse—

In the second place, old age was overtaking me. I never imagined that it would come to this. As long as I move about town I feel at ease. But evenings after supper I slump into my armchair, a book or paper clutched in my lap, and in a while I feel myself lying there as though paralyzed, half dead. I rise, torture myself out of my clothes, receive the recurring shock of my aging legs, drag myself to bed and bundle up my body in the clothes, scattering the detective novels that I have begun to read avidly of late.

The house breathes silence. A lost, exhausted tune drifts up from the radio. I read. Slowly, unwittingly, I turn into a large moss-covered rock. Midnight, the radio falls silent, and after midnight the books slip off my knees. I must switch the silent radio off and rid myself of the light burning in the room. It is then that my hour comes, my fearful hour. I drop off the bed like a lifeless body; bent over, racked by pain, staggering, I reach for the switches with my last strength.

One night, at midnight, I heard his steps in the hall. I must mention here that he was a restless sleeper. He used to be haunted by bad dreams that he was never able to relate. He had a night light by his bed, therefore, and when he woke he would go straight for the kitchen tap and gulp enormous quantities of water, which would calm his fears.

That night, after he had finished drinking and was making his way back to bed, I called him to my room and told him to turn off the light and the radio. I still remember his shadow outlined at the darkened doorway. All of a sudden it seemed to me that he had grown much, gained flesh. The light behind him silhouetted his mouth, slightly agape.

I thanked him—

The following night he started prowling through the house again about midnight. I lay in wait for his steps and called him to put out the light once more.

And every night thereafter—

Thus his services began to surround me. I became dependent upon them. It started with the light and sound that he would rid me of at midnight and was followed by other things. How old was he? Thirteen, I think . . .

Yes, I remember now. His thirteenth birthday occurred about that time and I made up my mind to celebrate it, for up till then I had passed over all his birthdays in silence. I had planned it to be a real party, generous, gay. I called up his class teacher myself and contacted the other teachers as well. I invited everybody. I sent invitations in his name to all his classmates.

True, all the children in his class were younger than he. Hardly eleven yet.

On the appointed Saturday, in the late morning hours, after a long and mortifying wait, a small band of altogether ten sniggering boys showed up at our place waving small parcels wrapped in white paper. Not a single teacher had troubled himself to come. None of the girls had dared.

They all shook hands with me, very much embarrassed, very much amazed at the sight of my white hair (one of them asked in a whisper: "That his grandfather?"), and entered timidly into the house which none of them had ever visited before. They scrutinized me with great thoroughness and were relieved when they found me apparently sane.

The presents were unwrapped—

It emerged that everyone had brought the same: a cheap pencil case worth a few pennies at most. All except one curly-headed, rather pale boy, a poetic type, who came up brazenly with an old, rusted pocket-knife—albeit a big one with many blades—which for some reason excited general admiration.

All the presents were accompanied by more or less uniform, conventional notes of congratulation. The little poet of the pocketknife had added a few pleasing rhymes.

He accepted his presents silently, terribly tense.

It surprised me that no one had brought a book.

As though they had feared he might not be able to read it—

I waited on them myself, taking great pains with each. I served sandwiches, cake, sweets and lemonade, then ice cream. They sat scattered over the drawing room, embedded in armchairs and couches, munching sweets, not speaking. Their eyes roved around the room incessantly, examining the place as though suspicious of it. Occasionally tittering among themselves for no good reason.

My boy was sitting forlornly in a corner of the room, more like a visitor than the guest of honor at his own party. He was munching too, but his eyes were lowered.

I thought my presence might be hampering the children and left them. And indeed, soon after I had gone, the tension relaxed. Laughter began to bubble up in the room. When I returned after a while I found them all with their shoes off, romping on the carpet, jumping up and down on the couch in their stockinged feet. He was not among them. I went to look for him and found him on the kitchen balcony, cleaning their shoes.

He said: I am the monitor—

Thus ended his birthday party. Their clothes in wild disarray, stifling their laughter, they put on their shoes, then rose to face me, shook my hand once more and were off, leaving nine pencil cases behind them. As for the old pocketknife that had aroused so much admiration, the little poet who had brought it asked there and then to borrow it for a week and apparently never returned it.

It is in self-defense that I offer these details, since before a fortnight had passed he was polishing my shoes as well. I simply left them on the balcony and found them polished. He did it willingly, without demur. And it became a custom—his and mine. Other customs followed.

Taking my shoes off, for instance. I come back from work late in the afternoon, sink down on the bench in the hall to open my mail. He appears from one of the rooms, squats at my feet, unties the laces, pulls off my shoes and replaces them with slippers.

And that relieves me to some extent—

I suddenly discover there is strength in his arms, compared with the ebbing strength in mine. Whenever I fumble with the lid of a jar, fail to extricate a nail from the wall, I call upon him. I tell him: "You are young and strong and I am growing weaker. Soon I'll die."

But I must not joke with him. He does not digest banter. He stands aghast, his face blank.

He is used to emptying the garbage can, has done it since he was eight. He runs my errands readily, fetches cigarettes, buys a paper. He has time at his disposal. He spends no more than half an hour on his homework. He has no friends, reads no books, slouches for hours on a chair gazing at the wall or at me. We live in a solid, quiet neighborhood. All one sees through the window are trees and a fence. A peaceful street. What is there for him to do? Animals repel him. I brought him a puppy once and a week later he had lost it. Just lost it and showed no regret. What is there for him to do? I teach him to tidy up the house, show him where everything belongs. He catches on slowly but eventually he learns to arrange my clothes in the cupboard, gather up the papers and books strewn over the floor. Mornings I would leave my bedclothes rumpled and when I returned at night everything would be in order, severely in order.

Sometimes I fancy that everything is in readiness for a journey. That there is nothing to be done but open a suitcase, place the curiously folded clothes inside, and go forth. One day I had to go on a short trip up north, and within half an hour of informing him he had a packed suitcase standing by the door with my walking stick on top.

Yes, I have got myself a stick lately. And I take it along with me wherever I go, even though I have no need of it yet. When I stop to talk with people in the street I insert it in the nearest available crack and put my whole weight on its handle. He sharpens the point from time to time to facilitate the process.

To such lengths does he go in his care of me—

At about that time he also learned to cook. The elderly cleaning woman who used to come in now and then taught him. At first he would cook for himself and eat alone before I came back from work, but in time he would prepare me a meal too. A limited, monotonous menu, somewhat lacking in flavor, but properly served. He had unearthed a china service in the attic. It had been a wedding present, an elaborate set containing an assortment of golden-edged plates decorated with flowers, cherubs and butterflies. He put it into use. He would place five different-sized plates one on top of the other in front of me, add a quantity of knives and forks, and wait upon me with an air of blunt insistence.

Where had he learned all that?

It transpired that a story about a king's banquet had been read in class. I am roused.

"What king?"

He does not remember the name.

"Other heroes?"

He doesn't remember.

I ask him to tell the story, at least.

He starts, and stops again at once. It has become muddled in his head. His eyes cloud over. The first pimples have sprouted on his cheeks.

A thought strikes me: viewed from a different angle he might fill one with terror.

At night he assists me in my bath. I call him in to soap my back and he enters on tiptoe, awed by my nakedness in the water, picks up the sponge and passes it warily over my neck.

When I wish to reciprocate and wait upon him in turn, nothing comes of it. Arriving home I announce: tonight I am going to prepare supper! It appears supper is served already. I wish to help him in his bath, and it appears he has bathed already.

I therefore take him with me at night to meetings with friends, to artists' conventions, for I still belong to all the societies and unions. I have accustomed people to his presence and they notice him no more, much as I do not notice their shadow.

He always sits in the last row, opening doors for latecomers, helping them out of their coats, hanging them up. People take him for one of the attendants, and indeed, he is inclined to attach himself to these. I find him standing near a group of ushers, listening grim-eyed to their talk. At times I find him exchanging words with the charwoman who stands leaning on her broom.

What does he say to her? I am never able to guess.

Does he love me? How can one tell. Something in my behavior seems to frighten him. Perhaps it is my age, perhaps my silence. Whatever it is, he carries himself in my presence as one expecting a blow.

Strange, for there is peace between us. The days pass tranquilly, and I imagined this tranquility would last our life together, till the day I would have to part from him, that is. I thought, how fortunate that in this silence of mine I am confronted by a boy of such feeble brains, on the border, and far from me.

True, I am sometimes overcome by restlessness, possessed by a desire to cling to somebody. Then I rush off to Jerusalem and surprise my daughters with a visit of an hour or two.

They receive me affectionately, hang onto my neck and hug me hard. And while we stand there in a clinging embrace their husbands look on, a faint expression of contempt in their eyes. Afterward we sit down and chat, bandying about the kind of word play and witticisms that irritate the husbands. Still, they utter no word of complaint, knowing full well that I won't stay, that if I come like a whirlwind—so I go. After an hour or two I rouse myself for a speedy departure, still harboring the dregs of my passion. They all urge me to prolong my visit, stay, spend the night, but I never do. I must go home to the boy, I argue, as though his entire existence depended upon me. More kissing and hugging follows; then the husbands take me to the station. We rarely speak during the short ride. We have nothing to say to each other. Besides, I am still suspect in their eyes. These white manes flowing down my neck, the stick jiggling in my hand. I am still some sort of a poet to them. The volumes of my poetry, I know, have a place of honor in their drawing-room bookcase. I cannot prevent that.

At such a time I prefer the child's dumb look.

Winter there are times when I draw the bolts at six. What do I do in the hours left till bedtime. I read the papers, listen to the radio, thumb the pages of books. Time passes and I make my bargain with boredom in private.

Summer I often walk back and forth along the beach or aimlessly through the streets. I am likely to stand in front of a building under construction for hours on end, lost in thought.

Trivial thoughts—

Years ago I would carry little notebooks with me wherever I went. Working myself up into a fever, fanning the flame of creation; rhyming, turning words over and over. Nowadays, not even a pang.

Where is he?

I look through the window and see him in the garden, under a bleak autumn sky. He is pruning the bushes and trees with a savage violence. Lopping off whole branches, tearing at leaves. He has it in particularly for the old poplar, cuts away with zeal the new shoots that have sprouted at its base, climbs up into the foliage and saws relentlessly. The tree bends and groans.

Sometimes my eyes stay riveted upon him for hours and I cannot bring myself to look away. His intent gravity, his rage. Shadows play over his face, his face which has taken on an absurdly studious quality owing to the thick spectacles he has begun to wear. He was found to be shortsighted.

I know he is trimming off more than necessary, that he pulls up plants, roots and all, in his vehemence. Still, I do not interfere and go on standing mutely by the window. I would tell myself: what survives will flower in the spring and make up for the damage.

When was the first time? That he found out about my being a poet, I mean. This madness that has taken a hold over us the past year, I mean.

Toward the end of last winter I fell ill and kept him home to nurse me. For several days we were together the whole day long, and he did not move from my side. This was something that had never happened before, for as a rule not a day would pass when I did not go out, wandering, sitting in cafés, visiting people.

I was feverish and confined to bed, dozing fitfully, eyes fluttering. He moved about the house or sat by the door of my room, his head turned in my direction. Occasionally I would ask for tea, and he would rouse himself, go to the kitchen and return with a steaming cup.

The light was dying slowly, gray sky flattening the windows. We did not turn on the lights for my illness had made my eyes sensitive.

The silence lay large between us. Could I hold a conversation with him?

I asked whether he had prepared his homework.

He nods his head from his corner of the room.

What could I talk to him about?

I asked about his monitorship. He replies with yes and no and shakes of his head.

At last I grew tired. I let my head drop back on the pillow and closed my eyes. The room grew darker. Outside it began to drizzle. During those days of illness my mind had started to wander with fantasies. Fantasies about the bed. I would imagine it to be a white, violent country of sweeping mountains and streaming rivers, and me exploring it.

Such utter calm. The warmth of the bed enveloping each cell in my body.

I started at the sound of his harsh voice, sudden in the trickling silence.

"What do you do?"

I opened my eyes. He was sitting by the door, his eyes on my face.

I raised myself a little, astonished.

"What? What do you mean? Now? Well, what? I'm dozing. . . ."

"No, in general . . ." and he turned away as though sorry he had asked.

In a while I understood. He was asking about my profession.

Had they been discussing "professions" in class?

He did not know—

I tell him what my profession is (I am employed by a newspaper-clipping bureau), but he finds it difficult to understand. I explain at length. Suddenly he has understood. There is no reaction. He seems a little disappointed. Hard to say why. He cannot have formed the idea in his feeble mind that I am a pilot or a sailor, can he?

Did he think I was a pilot or a sailor?

No.

What did he think?

He didn't think.

Silence again. He sits forlorn in the corner, a sad, somber figure. His spectacles gleam in the twilight. It rains harder now outside, the old poplar huddles in the garden, wet with tears. Suddenly I cannot bear his grief. I sit up in bed, eyes open in the dark, and tell him in a low voice that, as a matter of fact, I used to have another occupation. I wrote poetry. You see, father used to be a poet. They must have learned about poets in class. And I get out of bed in a fever of excitement, cross the dark room in my bare feet, light a small lamp, cross back to the bookcase, pluck my books one by one from the shelves.

He watches me in silence, his spectacles slightly askew, hands limp on the arms of his chair.

I grasp his wrist, pull him up and stand him before me.

Dry-handed I open my books in their hard covers. The small, untouched pages move with a faint crackle. Black lines of print on pale paper flit before my eyes. Words like: *autumn*, *rain*, *gourd*.

He remains unmoved, does not stir, his eyes are cast down, motionless. An absolute moron.

I sent him out of the room. I gathered my books and took them with me to bed. The light stayed on in my room till dawn. All night I lay groping for the sweet pain passionately poured into ancient poems. Words like: *bread*, *path*, *ignominy*.

Next day my fever had abated somewhat and I sent him off to school. My books I thrust back among the others. I was convinced he had understood nothing. A few days later, though, discovering all five volumes ranged neatly side by side, I realized something had penetrated. But it was little as yet.

That was his final school year, though the fact marked no change in his habits. He still spent about half an hour a day on his homework, wrote whatever it was he wrote, closed his exercise books, locked his bag and turned to his household chores. In class he kept to his remote corner, but his attendance at lessons had dwindled. The janitor would call upon him time and again. To help store away stoves in the attic or repair damaged furniture in the cellar.

When he was present in class he would sit there rapt as ever, his eyes unwavering on the teacher.

The final days of the year, their slack atmosphere—

Two or three weeks before the end of school a poem of mine was taught in class. The last pages of the textbook contained a collection of many different poems, some sort of anthology for every season, for a free period or such. An old poem of mine, written dozens of years ago, was among them. I had not aimed it at youth, but people mistook its intention.

The teacher read it out to the class. Then she explained the difficult words and finally let one of the pupils read it. And that was all there was to it. My son might have paid no attention to the occurrence from his back bench had the teacher not pointed him out to say:

"But yes, that is his father . . ."

The remark did nothing to improve the child's standing in class, let alone enhance the poem's distinction. In any case, by the end of the lesson both poem and poet were no doubt forgotten.

Apparently, however, the boy did not forget; he remained aglow. Possibly he wandered by himself through the empty classroom, picking up peel, wiping the blackboard, excited.

Coming back from work that evening I found the house in darkness. I opened the front door and saw him waiting in the unlit hall. He could not contain his passion. He threw himself at me, bursting into a kind of savage wail, nearly suffocating me. And without letting me take off my jacket, undo my tie, he dragged me by the hand into one of the rooms, switched on the light, opened the textbook and began reading my poem in a hoarse voice. Mispronouncing vowels, slurring words, bungling the stresses.

I was stunned in the face of this turbulent emotion. Compassion welled up in me. I pulled him close and stroked his hair. It was evident that he had still not grasped what the poem was about, even though it was not rich in meaning.

He held my sleeve in a hard grip and asked when had I written the poem.

I told him—

He asked to see other poems.

I pointed at my volumes—

He wanted to know whether that was all.

Smiling I showed him a drawer of my bureau stuffed with a jumble of poems and fragments, little notebooks I used to carry on my person and have with me always.

He asked whether I had written any new poems today. Now I burst out laughing. His blunt face raised up to me in adoration, this evening hour, and I still in my jacket and tie.

I told him that I had stopped writing before he was born and that the contents of that drawer should have been thrown out long ago.

I took off my jacket, loosened my tie, sat down to unlace my shoes.

He fetched my slippers.

His expression was despondent—

As though he had received fearful tidings.

I burst into laughter again.

I made a grab for his clipped hair and jerked his head with a harsh affection.

I, who would shrink from touching him—

A few days later I found the drawer wrenched open, empty. Not one scrap of paper left. I caught him in the garden weeding the patch beneath the tree. Why had he done it? He thought I did not need them. He was just cleaning out. And hadn't I said myself I wasn't writing anymore.

Where were all the papers.

He had thrown out the written ones, and the little notebooks he had sold to a hawker.

I beat him. For the second time in my life, and again in the garden, by the poplar. With all the force of my old hands I slapped his rough cheeks with their soft black down.

He trembled all over—

His fists closed white-knuckled and desperate over the hoe. He could have hit back. He was strong enough to knock me down.

But then, abruptly, my anger died. The entire affair ceased to be important. Relics of old poems, long ago lost. Why the trembling? Why, with my silence sealed?

Once more I believed the affair ended. I never imagined it was but the beginning.

Long summer days. Invariably blue. Once in a while a tiny cloud sails on its sleepy journey from one horizon to the other. All day flocks of birds flop down upon our poplar, screaming, beating the foliage.

Evenings—a dark devouring red.

The child's last day at school.

A day later: the graduation ceremony and presentation of diplomas.

He did not receive one, of course. He ascended the platform with the other pupils nonetheless, dressed in white shirt and khaki trousers (he was about seventeen years old). And sat in the full, heavy afternoon light listening gravely to the speeches. When the turn of the janitor came to be thanked he lifted his eyes and began a heavy, painstaking examination of the audience to search him out.

I kept myself concealed at the back of the hall behind a pile of chairs, my hat on my knees. The speeches ended and a short artistic program began.

Two plump girls mounted the stage and announced in voices shrill with emotion that they would play a sonata by an anonymous composer who lived hundreds of years ago. They then seated themselves behind a creaking piano and beat out some melancholy chords with four hands.

Stormy applause from enraptured parents.

A small boy with pretty curls dragged an enormous cello onto the stage and he, too, played a piece by an anonymous composer (a different one, apparently).

I closed my eyes—

I liked the idea of all this anonymity.

A storm of applause from enraptured parents.

Suddenly I became aware of someone's eyes upon me. Glancing around I saw, a few steps away, the janitor, sprawled on a chair, dark raisin against light window, dressed in his overalls. He made a gentle gesture with his head.

Two girls and two boys came on stage and began reciting. A story, a humorous sketch, two or three poems.

At the first sound of rhymes my boy rose suddenly from his place and began a frantic search for me. The audience did not understand what that spectacled, dumb-faced boy standing up at the back of the stage might possibly be looking for. His fellow pupils tried to pull him down, but in vain. He was seeking me, his eyes hunting through the hall. The rhymes rang in his ears, swaying him. He wanted to shout. But he could not find me. I had dug myself in too well behind the chairs, hunched low.

As soon as the ceremony was over I fled. He arrived home in the evening. It turned out he had been helping the janitor arrange the chairs in the hall.

The time had come to decide his fate. I reiterate: he verges on the border. A borderline child. Haven't I let the time slip by? Do I still possess my hold over him?

For the time being he stayed at home with me, took care of his father and began to occupy himself with poems.

Yes, he turned his hands to poetry.

It developed that those poetry remnants of mine, the little notebooks, thin little pages, were still in his possession. Neither thrown out nor sold. He had lied to me there by the poplar.

I did not find out all at once. At first he contrived to keep them hidden from me. But gradually I became aware of them. Scraps of paper began to flit about the house, edges sticking out of his trouser pockets, his bedclothes. He introduced a new habit. Whenever I send him on an errand he takes out a piece of paper and writes down the nature of the errand in his slow, elaborate, childish script full of spelling mistakes.

"Oblivion o'ercomes me," he suddenly informed me one day.

My walking stick had split and I had asked him to take it for repair. At once he extracted a little notebook, one of those old notebooks I used to cherish, used to carry in my pocket in order to scribble the first draft of a poem, a line, the scrap of an idea.

I felt my throat contract, sweat break out. My hand reached for the notebook as of itself. He surrendered it instantly. I leafed through with a feeble hand. White pages, the ragged remains of many others torn out. Then a single, disjointed line in my hurried scrawl: *"Oblivion o'ercomes me."* And then more empty pages, their edges crumpled.

Peace returned to me. He wished to leave the little notebook in my hands but I insisted that he take it back.

He went off.

Up in his room I rifled through his desk but found nothing. Then I took my mind off the whole thing. In the evening I found a yellowed piece of paper on my bureau and written on it in my indecipherable script:

This azure sky's the match of man.

And the words "azure sky" crossed out with a faint line.

I sweep up to his room and there he sits, huddled in a corner, waiting for me in dull anticipation. I fold the paper in front of his eyes, place it on his desk and leave the room. The following evening, after supper, I once again find two forgotten lines on my bureau.

Futile again before thee.

This long slow winter.

And this one I had already torn up.

And the day after, a slanting line in tortuous script:

My lunacy in my pale seed.

And harsh, violent erasures around the words.

And a small vase beside the torn-out page with a red carnation from the garden in it.

Here now, I must tell about the flowers.

For the house became filled with flowers. Old, forgotten vases came down from shelves and storeroom and were filled with flowers. He would gather buttercups on his way, pick crowfoot between the houses, steal into parks for carnations and pilfer roses from private gardens. The house filled with a hot, heavy scent. Yellow stamens scattered over tables, crumbled on carpets.

Sheets of paper are always lying on my bureau; sharpened pencils across.

In this way, with the obstinacy of his feeble mind he tried to tempt me back to writing poems.

At first I was amused. I would pick up the little pages, read, and tear them up; would smell the flowers. With the sharpened pencils I would draw dotted lines and sign my name a thousand times in the little note-books.

But soon this mania of his became overwhelming—

Those pages uprooted from my notebooks would pursue me all over the house. I never knew there had been so much I had wanted to write. He places them between the pages of books I read, in my briefcase, beneath my bedside lamp, beside the morning paper, between the cup and saucer, near the toothpaste. I draw my wallet and a scrap of paper flutters down.

I read and tear up and throw out.

As yet I make no protest. I am intrigued, curious to read what went through my mind in those far-off days. And there is bound to be an end to these little pages. For this much I know: there *was* an end to them.

Late at night, when I have long been buried under my bedclothes, I hear his bare feet paddling through the house. Planting pages filled with my personal untidy scrawl. Twisted, entangled letters, scattered words thickly underscored.

We maintain our wonted silence. And day after day he collects the torn-up scraps from ashtrays and wastepaper basket.

Except that the flow of notes is ebbing. One morning I find a page on my desk with a line written in his handwriting striving to imitate mine. Next morning it is his hand again, stumbling awkwardly over the clean page.

And the flowers filling every room—

And the sky filling with clouds—

My patience gave out. I rebelled. I burst into his room and found him sitting and copying the selfsame line. I swept up the remains of all the little notebooks and tore them up before his eyes. I plucked the flowers out of all the vases, piled them up on the doorstep and ordered him to take them away.

I told him: "These games are over."

He took the flowers, went to bury them in the nearby field and did not return. He stayed away three days. On the second I ransacked the town in a silent search. (The house filled with dust in the meantime. Dishes piled up in the sink.)

In the afternoon of the third day he came back, suntanned, an outdoor smell in his clothes.

I suppressed my anger, sat him down in front of me.

Where had he been? What done? Why had he run away?

He had slept in the nearby field, not far from home. Whenever I went out he would return and hide in his room. Once I had come in unexpectedly, but had not caught him. Why had he run away? He could not explain. He had thought I wished him out of the way. That I wished to write poetry in lonely seclusion. For that was what they had said at school about poets, about their loneliness. . . .

Those accursed teachers—

Or could it be some heavy, some new piece of cunning.

I must decide his fate. He is beginning to waver on the border.

I armed myself with patience, talked to him at length. Well, now what do you want, I said. For I, I have done with writing. I have written my fill. Then what do you want?

He covered his eyes with his palms. Blurted out some hot, stuttering words again. It was hard to follow him. At last I gathered from his confused jumble of words that he believed me unhappy.

You should have seen him—

This feeble-brained boy, boy on the border, his spectacles slipping slowly down his nose. Big. Nearly eighteen.

Late afternoon, an autumn sun roving leisurely about the rooms. Music is coming from the house next door. Someone is practicing scales on a violin. The same exercise, many times over, and out of tune. Only in one key the melody goes off every time into some sort of melancholy whine.

Suddenly I am certain of my death. I can conceive how the grass will go on rustling in this garden.

I looked at him and saw him as he is. An unfinished piece of sculpture.

Smiling I whispered: "See, I am tired. Perhaps you could write for me."

He was dumbfounded. He took off his spectacles, wiped them on his shirt, put them back.

"I can't," he in a whisper too.

Such despair. Of course he can't. I must cut loose. Ties, tangles.

Long years of mortification. One could cry. They left me alone with him. And again that dissonant whine.

"You'll help me," he whispers at me now, as though we were comrades.

"I will not help you."

A great weariness came over me. I stood up, took my hat and went out, walked twice around the scales player's house and went into town.

In the evening I came back and found him gone. I was obliged to prepare my own supper again and when I was slicing bread the knife slipped. It has been many years since I bled so.

I believed he had run off again, but he returned late at night, my room dark already. He began to prowl about the house, measure it with his steps, back and forth, much as I used to in former days when words would start to struggle up in me.

I fell asleep to the sound of his tread.

Next day he emptied out his room. All his schoolbooks, encyclopedias received as presents, copybooks, everything went out. The sheets of paper and sharpened pencils he transferred to his own desk.

The sky turned dim with autumn.

I began to play with the idea of retirement. Something in the romantic fashion. To give up work, sell the house, collect the money and escape, far away. Settle in some remote, decaying port. From there to an attic in a big city. In short, plans, follies. I went to travel agencies and was deluged with colorful pamphlets. I affixed a notice to the fence: For Sale.

A light rain fell.

One Friday I went to Jerusalem to see my daughters and spend the Sabbath there.

I received a great welcome. They even lighted candles in my honor and filled the house with flowers. My grandchildren played with the walking stick. I realized I had been neglecting everybody. At dinner they placed me at the head of the table.

I talked all evening about him, obsessively. I did not change the subject, refused to drop it. I demanded a solution for him, insisted he be found some occupation. I announced my plans for going abroad, wandering about the world for a bit. Someone must take charge of him. He can be made use of, too. He may serve someone else. As long as he is taken off my hands. I want my release, at last. He is approaching manhood.

I did not say a word about the poems.

For once the husbands gave me their full attention. The girls were puzzled. What has passed between you two? We rose from the table and transferred to armchairs for coffee. The grandchildren came to say good night in their pajamas. Gesturing with their little hands they recited two verses by a poetess who had died not long ago. Thereupon they put their lips to my face, licked me and went to bed. I went on talking about him. Impossible to divert me. They were all tired by now, their heads nodding as they listened. From time to time they exchanged glances, as though it were I who had gone mad.

Then they suddenly left me. Promising nothing, leading me gently to bed. They kissed me and went away.

Only then did I discover that a storm had been rising outside all evening. A young tree beat against the window with its many boughs. Thumping on the glass, prodding around the frame. All night it tried to force an entry, come into my bed. When I woke up in the morning all was calm. A sky of sun and clouds. The young tree stood still, facing the sun. Nothing but a few torn leaves, bright green leaves that trembled on my windowsill.

I went home in the afternoon. My sons-in-law had promised to find him employment. My daughters talked about a semiclosed institution.

Winter erupted from the soil. Puddles were forming between pavements and road. My reflection rippled and broke into a thousand fragments.

He was not at home. His room was locked. I went out into the yard and peered through the window. The window stood wide open and the room appeared tidy beyond it. The sheets of paper glimmered white on his desk. Something was written on them, surely. I went back into the house and tried to force the door but it would not yield. Back in the yard again I rolled a stone to the wall beneath his window and tried to climb on top of it but failed. My legs began to tremble. I am no longer young. Suddenly I thought: what is he to me. I went in, changed my tie, and went out in search of friends in cafés.

Saturday night. The streets loud. We are crowded in a corner of the café, old, embittered artists, burnt-out volcanoes wrapped in coats. Wheezing smoke, crumbling in our withered hands the world sprung up since Saturday last. Vapors rise from the ground and shroud the large glass front of the café. I sprawl inert on my chair, puffing at the cigarette butt, dancing my stick on the stone floor between my feet. I know. This town is built on sand, dumb and impervious. Under the flimsy layer of houses and pavements—a smothered desert of sand.

Suddenly a crowd of unkempt, hairy bohemians swarm by. A crowd of young fools. We scowl, squint at them. And there is my boy trailing after them, a few paces behind the crowd, his cheeks flushed.

They fling themselves on the chairs of a next-door café. Most of them are drunk. My boy stays on their fringes, huddled on a chair. Some sort of blustering conversation goes on. I do not take my eyes off him. Someone rises, takes a piece of paper out of his pocket and begins reading a poem. No one is listening to him except my boy. The reader stops in the middle, moves from one to the other, finally hovers intently over the clipped head of my son. A few of them laugh. Someone leans over the boy, pats his cheek. . . .

I am certain: nobody knows his name, nor that of his father.

Some minutes later I sit up, take my stick and go to the beach to look at the dark sea. Then home. I lie on the couch, take the paper and begin turning its pages. I linger over the literary supplement, read a line or two of a poem, a paragraph in a story—and stop. Literature bores me to tears. Abruptly I fall asleep, as I am, in my clothes. Dream I am taken away for an operation. Being anesthetized and operated on, painlessly. Wakened, anesthetized again, the still flesh dissected. At last I understand: it is the light shining in my face.

I wake, rise, shivering with cold, clothes rumpled. A soft rain outside. I go to the kitchen, put a kettle on and wait for the water to boil. Piles of dirty dishes tower over me.

A big dilapidated motorcar, its headlights off, crawls into our little street at a remarkably slow pace. It lurches somnambularly along the street. At last it brakes to a creaking stop in front of our house, beside the lamppost. Loud whooping and howling from inside. A long pause. A door opens and someone is discharged, pale, confused. It is my son. His features are petrified, no shadow of a smile. Another door opens. Someone else scrambles out, staggers into the middle of the road, dead-drunk. He goes over to the boy, grasps his hands and pumps them up and down affectionately. Then squeezes his way back into the car.

More yells and screams from the imprisoned human mass. A long pause. Then a jerk and a roar, and the blind battered wreck reverses and like some black turtle inches its way backward out of the street.

My son is standing by the lamppost, at the precise spot where he has been unloaded. For a long time he stands there unmoving, his body slightly bowed. Suddenly he doubles up and vomits. He wipes his mouth with the palm of his hand and strides toward the house. Passes by the kitchen without noticing me, enters his room and shuts the door. A faint cloud of alcohol floats through the hall.

Winter. With the first touch of rain these lowlands strive to revert to swamp.

An old half-blind poet, who publishes a steady stream of naïve, pitiful poems and woos young poets, meets me in the street, links his arm through mine and walks me round and round under a gray sky, through wet streets. Finally, he informs me with something like a wink that he has met my son in the company of young artists.

"A fine young man. Does he write?"

Rumors reach me from all sides. Some say they torment him. Others say that on the contrary, those degenerate creatures accept him gladly. It isn't every day that they get hold of such a tongue-tied moron. Meanwhile he has become one young poet's minion, and messenger boy to the editor of a literary magazine.

I reproach him with harsh words but he does not listen. Abstract-minded, his eyes flitting over the cloud-hung world, he does not even see me. His face has paled a little over the past few weeks, his blunt features taken on an ascetic, somehow spiritual look. I know: one incautious word on my part, and he will break loose, roam about the streets and disgrace me. Already he has neglected the house completely. He takes his meals outside. The garden is running to seed. And I had imagined that he felt some tenderness toward the plants.

When at home he shuts himself up in his room and throws himself into writing. We have not seen a single poem yet. But I know beyond question: he writes.

I come up against him in the hall, catch him by the sleeve and ask mockingly:

"Monsieur writes? Yes?"

He wriggles under my hand. My language startles him. He does not understand and looks at me in horror, as though I were beyond hope.

He is capable of staying locked up in his room for hours on end, wonderfully concentrated. Occasionally he enters the drawing room, goes to the bookcase, takes out a volume of poetry or some other book and stands a long time poring over it. As a rule he never turns over the page even once. Then he puts the book down quietly and goes out. Of late he has been referring frequently to the dictonary, digging into it, turning its leaves incessantly like a blind man. I doubt whether he knows how to use it.

I finally come over and ask him what he wants.

He wants to know how to write the sky.

"The sky?"

"The word 'sky' . . ."

"How? What do you mean, how? Just the way it sounds."

That does not help him much. He stands in front of me, fearfully grave.

"With an 'e' after the 'y' or without . . ." he whispers.

"With an 'e'?" I say thunderstruck. "What on earth for?"

He bites his lips.

"With an 'e'?" I repeat, my voice shrilling to a yell, "And, anyway, what do you want with the sky?"

This one remains unanswered. The dictionary closes softly between his hands. He returns to his room. A while later he steals back to the bookcase, takes the dictionary and starts hunting through it. I jump up.

"What now?"

"Independence . . ." he stammers.

"Independence? Well?"

". . . ance or . . . ence?"

Once again this inexplicable fury. The more so as all of a sudden I do not know myself how to spell independence. I pounce upon him, grab the dictionary out of his hands, search feverishly. . . .

Meanwhile my retirement plans are taking shape. From time to time people come to inspect the house put up for sale. I show them over the rooms, let them intrude into every corner, take them down to the cellar, around the yard, into the garden and back to the balcony. In a low voice I recite its merits, this house that I have lived in for thirty years. Then, coolly, I state the price. Before they depart I take down their name and spell out mine in exchange. They bend over the piece of paper and write my name with complete equanimity. Not the faintest ripple of recognition. Haven't they ever read poetry in their lives?

I shall apparently leave these regions in complete anonymity.

The garden, however, leaves a bad impression with the buyers. Weeds and mires. The boy refuses to touch a spade. I therefore take up the gardening tools myself and every day I weed out some of the boldest specimens and cover the puddles with them.

A farewell party at the office in my honor. All the office employees assembled an hour before closing time. Cakes were served, glasses raised. I was eulogized at great length. I even saw tears in some eyes.

No one mentioned my poetry, as though to avoid hurting my feelings. Finally, a parting gift: an oil painting, a murky sea.

I start packing my bags. Much vacillation in front of the bookcase. What shall I take, what leave? I send off urgent letters to my sons-in-law regarding the boy's fate. I engage them in telephone conversations, prevail upon them to act. Finally they make an appointment to meet me at a small café in town. Beside a small table they unfold their plans. They have looked around and made inquiries and finally found an old artisan in a Jerusalem suburb, a bookbinder who has consented to take on the boy as apprentice. He will be provided with his meals and sleeping quarters. The man used to have just a child himself, and it died of an illness. He has, however, laid down one condition: should the boy fall ill he will be returned at once. Like a seizure or some such case . . . On this point they were inexorable: they will not care for him in sickness.

The sons-in-law have therefore made further investigations and found a lone old woman, a few houses away from the bookbinder, who will be prepared to accept him when ill. Against a remuneration, of course . . . Well, and that is all. I must put my signature to both.

And they come out with papers.

I sign at once. Yet a rage flares up in me while I do.

"As far as seizures and sickness are concerned, your trouble was unnecessary. You know he isn't one of those . . . He is a borderline child. . . . I have said as much a thousand times. . . . But you won't begin to understand. . . . Oh well, let it go."

My sons-in-law collect the documents, barring one copy which they leave with me. They gulp the last of their coffee, give me a kindly smile.

"See, and you thought we weren't looking after you. . . ."

The day after I sign again, this time to transfer the house to a buyer found at last. When all is said and done, I have received a reasonable sum for it, and that just for the lot, since the house itself is going to be demolished.

The furniture has been sold in the lump. Three workmen appeared one day at dusk and began clearing the house of its furniture. Everything was taken except two mattresses. They even pulled the desk from under him while he sat writing at it. He was outraged. He prowled about the house, his papers fluttering white in his arms. A few slipped to the floor, and by the time he noticed, one of the workmen was already picking them up to wrap the lamp shades in. He threw himself at the man with all the strength of his heavy bulk. Tried to get his teeth into him.

It has struck me that dusk is a time when his senses are overcome by a heavy stupor.

Bank notes are filling my drawer. I obtain no more than a quarter of the things' value, but even so the money piles up. I wish to sell everything, and what I can't sell I give away. I have been forcing loads of books on my friends. Were the boy a little less occupied he would sell to his hawkers what I throw out.

We have even been making incursions into the cellar of late and dredged up old clothes, brooms, more books, manuscripts—my own and others'—trivia, simulacrums and crumbs and fables. A cloud of dust hovered on the cellar steps for three whole days.

I told my café friends: here, this is how a man cuts his bonds.

In addition I still pay regular visits to the tiny harbor of this big town in order to whip up a wanderlust. Wrapped in my overcoat, umbrella in hand, I wander among the cranes, sniffing salt and rust, trying to strike up a conversation with the sailors. I am still deliberating where to go. At first I had considered Europe as my destination, then thought of the Greek islands. I had already entered into negotiations with a Turkish ship captain regarding the Bosphorus when I went and bought, for a ridiculous price, a round-trip ticket on a freighter sailing the sea between this country and Cyprus. I went on board the ship myself and rapped my stick against the door of my prospective cabin.

This journey will be something of a prelude. Afterward we shall sail away again, farther away.

My son writes on throughout, writes standing as though in prayer. His papers are scattered on the windowsill, which serves him as a desk. Beside them lies a small dictionary which he has rescued from the debacle. When I look at his form the thought strikes me: why thus, just as he is, he may go and sleep with a woman. And who knows? Perhaps he already has—

He has not yet taken in the fact of my retirement, my impending departure. He is intent on his own. It was difficult enough to tear him away, one afternoon, and make him accompany me to Jerusalem to see the old bookbinder.

It was a gentle winter day, cloudy but no real rain. In Jerusalem we found the old bookbinder waiting for us at the bus station with a run-down commercial van, unbound books slithering about in the back. He took us to a suburb of the town, to the slope of a narrow, tree-tangled valley very close to the border. He motioned us into the house in silence, and in silence his wife received us. Tea and cakes were served and we were made to sit by the table forthwith.

I was very peased with them—

They scrutinized the boy carefully. Hard to say that he pleased them, but they were visibly relieved, having expected worse. Slowly, hesitantly, conversation began to flow between us. I learned to my surprise that the bookbinder had heard of my name and was, moreover, certain that he had read something by me (for some reason he thought I wrote prose). But that had been so long ago, nearly twenty years.

Truth to tell, I was gratified—

Wind rustled without. A samovar murmured on the table (such quaint habits). There is a large tree in the bookbinder's garden too, older even than ours, its trunk gnarled. Winter twilight was fading beyond the window, gray tinged by a flaming sunset. Intimations of borderland. He was sitting frozen by my side, an oversized adolescent, the cup of tea full in front of him, the cake beside it untouched. Sitting there haunched, his eyes on the darkening window. Not listening to our talk. Suddenly he pulls a sheet of paper, black with lines of lettering, out of his pocket, smooths it out in front of him, slowly writes a single word, and folds it up again.

Our conversation breaks off. The bookbinder and his wife look at him in amazement.

With a half-smile I said, "He writes . . ."

They did not understand.

"He is a poet."

"A poet . . ." they whispered.

Just then it began to rain and the sunset kindled the room. He was sitting near the window, his hair aflame.

They stared at me with growing disbelief. And he, pen dropping between his fingers, passes his eyes over us in a pensive glance.

I said to the bookbinder: "He'll publish a book of poetry. You can bind it for him."

The bookbinder is completely at a loss. Am I making fun of him? At last a doubtful smile appears on his face.

"Sure. He'll publish a book. We'll bind it here, together we will."

"For nothing?" I continue the joke.

"For nothing."

I stood up from my chair.

"All right, it's a bargain. D'you hear?"

But he hasn't.

(On our way out the bookbinder and his wife pulled me into a corner of the hall and reminded me in a whisper of that part about sickness, or seizures . . . reminded me of their nonresponsibility in such case. I put their minds at rest.)

We went out. The bookbinder could not take us back to the station because the headlights of his old car did not function. We therefore took our leave of him and of his wife and started walking along the road under a soundlessly dripping sky. He was in a state of complete torpor, almost insensible. Dragging his feet over the asphalt. We arrived at the bus stop, stood between the iron railings, the iron roof over us. Housing projects all about, bare rocks, russet soil. A hybrid of town and wasteland. Jerusalem at its saddest, forever destroyed. However much it is built, Jerusalem will always be marked by the memory of its destruction.

I turned to him and the words came out of my mouth pure and clear.

"The bookbinder and his wife are very good people. But you will have to behave yourself."

He kept silent. Someone rode past on a bicycle, caught sight of the boy's face and turned his head back at once.

Full darkness now. Lights went on in the building projects. We were standing under the awning, the two of us utterly alone. Suddenly I said:

"I had a glimpse of that page and saw—there's a poem there. See, you were able to write by yourself. You did not need me."

He raised his eyes to me, and remained silent.

I drew nearer to him, very near.

"Show me the poem."

"No."

"Why?"

"You'll tear it up . . ."

"No, no, of course I won't. . . ."

And I stretched out my hand to take the page. But he shrank back. I meant to use force but he raised his arms to defend himself. This time he would have hit me.

Again someone passed on a bicycle. From the distance came the rumble of the bus.

It had been the last word of his poem.

I did not know.

That was three days ago—

So terrible this season. The windows are covered with mist or frost. I cannot recall such a hard winter before. This lasting leaden gray, day and night, deepening yet toward dawn. Who's that in the mirror? Still I. A furrowed stone. Only the eyes stand out, glittering, amazingly alive.

I am about to leave. I have missed one boat, another is awaiting me. I have only to stuff the last things into the cases, fold the towels, pick up the money and be off. We have been living here on mattresses a full fortnight by now; and the new owner comes and looks at us every day. The man is reaching the end of his patience. He hovers about me in despair, waiting for me to be gone. Yesterday he even threatened me with a lawsuit. He has bought the house with his last pennies. He has his dreams.

Indeed, I must linger no more. I must send the boy to Jerusalem, to the old bookbinder waiting for him by the border. There must be no more lingering. For the boy is forever roaming about these nights. He has stopped writing. Yesterday I waited up for him till after midnight and still he had not come. He returned but shortly before the break of dawn. His steps woke me.

The balcony door creaks under my fingers. The floor is wet, strewn with broken leaves and branches, aftermath of the storm. A cold hopeless sky. A silent drizzle and the first light. This large and so familiar universe silently dripping here before me. The leaves in the tree rustling.

Was there no wish in me to write? Did I not long to write? But what is there left to write about? What more is there to say? I tell you: it is all a fraud. Look, even our poplar is crumbling. Its bark is coming off in strips. The colors of the garden have faded, the stones are gathering moss.

To be driven like a slow arrow to the sky. To sprawl on the cotton clouds, supine, back to earth, face turned to the unchanging blue.

Pensioned-off poet that I am—

It is pouring now. Drops splash over me. I dislodge myself and retrace my steps, A bleak silence over the house, the faint wheeze of a snore drifts through it. I go up to his room, night clothes trailing behind me. My shadow heavy on shut doors.

He is sleeping on a mattress too. His night light is on the floor by his head. He still cannot fall asleep without his eternal light. The slats of his shutter are slicing constant wafers of dawn light.

I look down silently upon the sleeper at my feet. When I turn to leave the room I suddenly notice some newspaper sheets strewn on the floor by his mattress. Terror grips me. I bend down at once, gather them up. The pages are still damp, the fresh ink smudges my fingers. I go over to the window, to the faint first light.

A supplement of one of the light, impudent tabloids. And the date—today's, this day about to break. I turn the pages with dead hands. Near the margin of one I discover the poem: crazy, without meter, twisted, lines needlessly cut off, baffling repetitions, arbitrary punctuation.

Suddenly the silence deepens. The sound of breathing has died. He opens his eyes, heavy and red with sleep. His hand fumbles for the spectacles by his mattress. He puts them on, looks at me—me by the window. And a soft, appealing smile, a little sad, lights up his face.

Only now I notice. It is my name plastered across the top of the poem, in battered print.

About the Authors

Gershon Shaked is Professor of Modern Hebrew Literature at the Hebrew University of Jerusalem and has taught at Harvard, the University of California, Hebrew Union College, Jewish Theological Seminary, and the University of Johannesburg. He was born in Vienna in 1929 and emigrated to Israel in 1939. A leading scholar and critic, Professor Shaked has written the standard *History of the Modern Hebrew Novel* (2 vols.) as well as numerous articles on Hebrew drama, poetry, and fiction. Among his dozen or more books are *The Narative Art of S. Y. Agnon* and *Dead End: Studies in Brenner, Berdichevsky, Shoffman and Gnessin*.

Alan Lelchuk was on the faculty of Brandeis University for fifteen years and, in 1982–83, Visiting Writer at Amherst College. Born in Brooklyn in 1938, he was educated at Brooklyn College, Stanford University, and the University of London, and received his Ph.D. in literature from Stanford in 1965. He is the author of three widely-translated novels, *American Mischief*, *Miriam at Thirty-Four*, and *Shrinking*. His short stories and literary criticism have appeared in leading magazines and periodicals (*e.g.*, *The Atlantic*, *New American Review*, *Sewanee Review*, *New York Review of Books*, and *The New York Times Book Review*). In 1971–72 he was associate editor of Philip Rahv's quarterly, *Modern Occasions*. In 1976–77 he received a Guggenheim Fellowship for fiction and, while a Guest Resident at Mishkenot Sha'Ananim in Jerusalem, met Gershon Shaked and began this anthology.